ONE
SHORT
SLEEP
PAST

A novel by

Daphne Low

Published in 2016 by OpusR LLC
P.O. Box 3715
Boulder, Colorado 80307-3715
USA

First Edition, November 2016

ISBN 978-0-9979742-0-1

Cover photograph, *Boulder Sunrise*, November 27, 2014
by Daphne Low
Cover design by Daphne Low

"One short sleep past, we wake eternally
And death shall be no more; Death, thou shalt die."

—John Donne, *Holy Sonnets: Death, be not proud*

For YK and BC

CONTENTS

Preface

This is an original historical fiction/mystery, a take-off from a long-standing myth told among the Chinese I had heard as a child in Macau—that a woman who died wearing red shall a vengeful ghost be. Many years later, I heard this same myth among the Chinese in Penang, Malaysia and in Singapore where I had spent some time. Death as empowerment, as a resource for unvanquished grievances speaks to me of irony, of defeat. Redemption, then, follows as the only deliverance to strive for.

Set in historical Leadville and in Denver, then and now, my story as couched in a transplanted myth is an amalgam of my sense of place and time put to a study of human affairs. A narrative of haunting passion, it has merits larger than a simple take on a folk superstition, for it delves into the individual's very personal search for fulfillment, be it a ghostly reach or a human endeavor.

Daphne Low, Ph.D. Psychology
Boulder, Colorado

Acknowledgements

This is a work of fiction set in Leadville and Denver circa 1890's and today's Denver. While some of the events in the heady days of Colorado's mining boom are based on records and some historical figures existed, the story and the happenings depicted therein are entirely fictional as are the characters portrayed. Any resemblance to actual persons or events, past and present, is completely coincidental and is used fictitiously. The views and opinions expressed by the individual characters in the novel do not represent the views and opinions of the author.

Many sources were helpful in providing for the setting of my novel in the 1890's. In particular: Terry Wm. Mangan, *Colorado on Glass*, 1975; Edward Blair, *Leadville: Colorado's Magic City*, 1980; Thomas J. Noel, *Rocky Mountain Gold*, 1980; Clark Secrest, *Hell's Belles, Denver's Brides of the Multitudes*, 1996; Phyllis Flanders Dorset, *The Story of Colorado's Gold and Silver Rushes*, 1970.

Materials for the Festival of Mountain and Plain were culled from *The Evening Post*, October 1895; *Rocky Mountain News*, October 1895; *The Daily News*, October,1895.

References for the train ride from Leadville to Denver include: Mark L. Evans, *The Ted Kierscey Photo Collection – The Denver South Park and Pacific Railroad*, 1995-2010; Chappell, Richardson & Hauck, *The South Park Line, A Concise History*,

Colorado Rail Annual No. 12, 1974; *Rocky Mountain Official Railway Guide*, 1960.

It is a pleasure to thank my friends, Arthur Hundhausen, an authority and an enthusiast in the history of railways for consultation about the South Park Line, and Katherine Harris for sharing her experience in her writing of *Long Vistas: Women and Families on Colorado Homesteads*, 1993.

Among the sources I had consulted for my education and appreciation of batik, one stands out: Pepin Van Roojen's *Batik Design*, 1993. For my learning about the art and craft of textiles: Susan Bosence's *Hand Block Printing & Resist Dyeing*, 1985. An exceptional reference for my introduction to photography is: S.F. Spira, Eaton S. Lothrop, Jr. and Jonathan B. Spira, *The History of Photography: As Seen Through the Spira Collection*, 2005.

ONE

SHORT

SLEEP

PAST

Ben

1

I wait up in the dark. Alley cats screeching, jarring nerves …

No siren in the dead of night. Only vibes agitating … thick and jumpy. The bristling squeals clam up all of a sudden. Ruffled shadows scuttling down the dumpster, scrambling off. A squad car turns in, spinning dizzying flashes of red and blue over the back of the houses, over the two pickups parked alongside. I walk up squinting. Two officers getting out.

"You called?"

"Got a stiff?"

"In here." My voice hoarse, my stomach in knots. I lead the way down the steps to the basement. A draft kicks in as we walk through the door left ajar. Bare bulb dangling on wire swings wildly, pulling shadows up the old brick wall, sliding them down the concrete floor. Inside my head, muffled cries strum like echoes from afar.

Watch out! There he lies, steps away, at the bottom of the stairs. His eyes wide open in a blank stare. The officers throw their flashlights over him. The beams shake, cones of light bobbing onto the floor. One officer kneels down, skims his light over those dead eyes, perfunctorily checks the neck for pulse. He gets back up.

"Holy shit!"

"Who's he?" the other officer asks.

"Hank Newt, my supervisor, Mile High Constructions."

"You?"

"I'm Ben. Ben Ballad."

He looks down, frowning.

I turn away, glance at the shaky gloom. A forbidding gloom.
I'm suddenly overcome with sadness.

A grim past in here?

The question flies darkly in my face, casting off, dredging up
that old thing within me—my other sight. Tha-at scourge. Long
buried, I had wanted it out of my life. But, on this night, in this
shadowy basement, it's giving me a kick-ass jolt.

What on earth has gotten it roused up after all these years?

I grit my teeth and hang tight ...

Before I take in another breath, I'm seized with a sense of loss
so grievous, so harrowing that I'm blindsided by it. Smack-bang,
I'm staring into pitch darkness!

I shut my eyes and hold still. Go away!

Inside my head, a pinhead light punches through the dark ...

End of a tunnel?

In a flash, my own sight returns. I break into a cold sweat.

Something unnatural is agitating in here, grim and unforgiving.
Whatever happened tonight that had brought about Hank's death,
brought it out of the dark.

Stay clear! Whatever it is, just stay clear!

"A-ahem." A dry cough puffs the air hazed with dust. Head
bowed, an officer coughs, covering his mouth. The ceiling bears
down like a groggy sky. Mustiness spikes sour with the dead
man's day-old sweat. A whiff of urine assaults. I hear my own
measured breathing.

Flashlights sweeping over Hank, arms clamped tight against a
rigid body, hands balled into tight fists.

What've you got in your hands, Hank?

One officer tosses his flashlight across the empty basement,
stirring gloom, stretching shadows. The beam falls over a pile of
studs and plywood boards stacked at one corner, folded ladder and
sawhorses lying on top. It hops down over Mile High's circular
saw on the floor, up the push broom leaning against the wall.

"What place is this?"

"It's getting fixed up to be an artist's studio."

"Hmm."

He walks about, scraping the concrete floor, grinding dirt, shifting sawdust. He pauses, bends down over a toppled work lamp not three feet from the body. Broken glass from the shattered lamp gleaming on the floor. Scattered nearby, a chisel, a hammer, a screwdriver.

There is no blood, not on the body, not on the floor.

Was there a scuffle?

"Don't move," the young officer says, gesturing me to stay put. His flashlight scours the floor for scuff marks. I see none. It goes over the worn-out soles of the dead man's work boots, runs up his stiff limbs held taut by an unseen rope.

"Touched anything?"

Flashlight scanning over my body.

"No, sir."

"Your hands. Let's see them."

I lay them out, palms up. My carpenter's rough chapped hands, big under his light.

"Over."

I turn them over. He scrutinizes my knuckles.

"Hmm."

He takes the light off me and walks over to the pint-sized door under the stairs. He taps at the padlock with it.

"What's inside?"

"Don't know. Been locked the whole time."

"What's upstairs?" He throws his light up the stairs by the old brick wall.

"Empty. Street level and second floor."

He steps over Hank, lighting his way up.

"Wha-at the hell!" his partner grunts. Older, stocky guy, thick guttural voice. He pushes his cap back and squats down. Big shadow covering the lifeless form which looks nothing more than a pile of tossed-out clothes. I make out the twill shirt, the same shirt I had seen on a warm body only hours earlier, the frayed jeans, worn at the knees. The small wasted figure on the floor, no longer the guy I had walked out with at quitting time.

"Gotta lock up. I'd let Joey off early today," Hank said,

reaching into his jeans pocket and pulled out a single key with a twisted wire looped through its hole. It is Joey's charge at Mile High, opening and locking up job sites. "Says he's gonna run down to Pueblo. His old lady's been hollering for him. She's been taken to the hospital this morning. Had a fall, broke a bone or something," he mumbled.

Then, he turned to me and beamed. "Hey, Phil and I are gonna go hunting tomorrow. Just got his license in the mail, yep!" he said in a peppy voice, more peppy than I'd heard in weeks. He put the key into the lock, broad shoulders hunched, his back humped up under the faded twill shirt. A slit of flesh peeked out a busted armhole seam. The tumbler clicked.

"Phil, you've met, eh? Nan's kid brother, at our July 4 cookout." He turned to me to confirm. A habit of his. His men got to understand what he wanted done.

I nodded.

Hey, TT, over here! Hank called out to the big guy coming into the backyard from the side of the house, two bouncy boys trailing behind.

I call him that, for short, cause he drives twenty-some tons. Know what that is, Ben?

I shook my head.

The RTD bus, fully loaded! Hank chuckled.

TT hung around Hank by the grill, munching bratwursts, swilling beer. They chatted about getting a hunting license come this Fall. Lotsa more cookouts, deer steaks, huh, Hank ole buddy? TT crowed.

He pulled the key out the tumbler, slipped it back into his pocket.

"You guys have fun tomorrow!"

"Looks like it's gonna be a nice day!" He blinked at the late afternoon sun that had canted down the alley. It put sheen over the dark asphalt, and cast a shine on the chrome of his pickup. In the orange light, his ruddy cheeks glowed, his crew cut a silvery gray. He grabbed his tool belt, picked up his beat-up lunch box and dented thermos. "See ya," he said, and walked to his pickup.

Goodbye, it was.

Hank had me over that July 4 on account of Jamie. I was sure of that. First and only time I was over at his house in the years we'd worked together.

My girl's home, he'd told me. Yep, she and Mike had split up. No kids. Should've left the bum a long time ago. Just turned thirty-one. Good thing she's got a teaching job at her old high school. Nan and I, we're glad to have her home, well, for a while.

You taught school once, didn't ya? He'd probably got that from Mary Lou at the office.

Yee-ah, I said. He heard my drawl and cut the conversation.

Jamie, the day of the cookout, was quick to tell me that she'd gotten a job teaching PE at Marshall High. Gonna coach a girl's volley ball team! She let out a nervous little laugh which she quickly bit back. Her lips were thin and hard, like her dad's, her fingernails bitten short.

His girl's home but he's gone for good.

I squat down next to the officer. "Step back." He motions me with his head. Back on my feet, I peer from behind, tracking the flashlight that burns into those blank eyes. Dead fish's eyes, sharp white rim, flat look quick-frozen. In a flash, a sudden thaw steals over them, sparking a bright red glint that zaps through the dull glaze. The glint dies without a hiss. Stark eyes return.

I shudder, a spasm tingling down my spine.

What was that? Something you saw, Hank?

Flashlight zeroing into those empty eyes still, blanching them. Two dead puddles, white and dark and opaque all at once.

Only the blood red afterimage stays pulsating in my head.

Something meant for me to see?

Me only?

As if in reply, a waft of a chill socks me in my face. I jerk back, clenching my jaw to keep my teeth from clattering.

Steady, steady now.

But I'm whetted.

The officer tilts Hank's stiff neck, side to side, looking for sign

of strangulation. He unbuttons his shirt hastily, exposing a chest
of matted gray-white hair. Not a scratch or bruise.

What about the darn cold?

Only I feel it!

The dead man's face. A weathered face. No longer Hank's,
his daylight snuffed out, ruddy color drained. Shriveled and gaunt,
it is more a mask than a face. A lead-blue skin stretched over
hollow cheeks. Like crackled earthenware, lines fish-tailed from
the corners of the sunken sockets, fissured around a squeezed
mouth. Ashen lips, crusted with dried up saliva, drooped at one
corner. Looks as if he was screaming his lungs out, got smacked
in the mouth. That blow must have knocked him right off his feet,
landed him flat on his back.

But where's the bruise?

Where's the impact?

What could have done that?

A nagging fear shoots up. It gnaws at me, compelling me to
see. To see a rage so blinding, so vicious, that when it lashed out,
it lashed out razor sharp and lightning quick.

What gave cause to this sudden rage?

What have you done, Hank?

"Could've gotten a skull fracture, the way he fell," says the
officer.

He goes on to look for bruises, defense wounds, rolling up the
sleeves to expose his forearms. None.

"Those fists, what the hell!" The officer picks up Hank's fists,
one, then the other. Heavy, unyielding, each a hammerhead
sticking out of a wooden handle. Big working hands tightly
clenched.

Clutching what?

He thrusts his hand into the dead man's pockets, pulls out a
wallet, a bunch of keys on a ring, key to his pickup, and this one
key looped with a twisted wire. He gets back on his feet.

"That's the key to the door." I point to that one key.

"You know why he came back?"

"No."

"Those his things?" The officer points to the tools lying on the floor.

"He might have brought them. They weren't here when we closed up for the day."

What for, Hank?

Footsteps coming down the stairs.

"Upstairs' clear. No sign of break in."

"Call in the wagon. CSU, too."

"Okey-doke."

Quick steps out. Static from the squad car radio grating the night.

The officer turns to me, "How'd you come to find him here, at this hour?"

Jamie called. One in the morning. She sounded like she got a lump in her throat. Ben, ahem, sorry to call at this hour. Won't I please go check on her dad at the Lodo jobsite? He'd gone there to pick up some tools he'd left behind. Said he needed them for his Saturday job. Left right after dinner, eight-thirty or so. Mom's worried sick that he's not back yet. No answer on his cell phone. They're worried something might've happened and, uh, he can't get help.

One yellow burst of highway lamp after another lit up the night. The Turnpike was an empty stretch at this hour. Unsettling questions floated through my mind: What're you up to, Hank? Hunting or moonlighting? Tools left behind?

I lowered the window. The cool air did nothing to hush the noise inside my head. There were the tidbits of idle talk ...

Good luck! Joey said to Hank one lunch hour.

Bent over his lunch box, the man was absorbed in marking his lucky numbers on a handful of lotto tickets. He had picked up a lotto fever just about the time we started work on this house. Just about when he got passed over for the Lodo Tower job.

Gonna win and quit? Joey chirped.

Lunch's over. Hank said, got up and walked off.

Then, there was that morning I overheard Joey telling him, hey, Hank, guys lookin for ya yesterday at da Tower site.

What guys?

Simm's guys, Joey hissed through the gap between his front teeth. Stan told em ya not on dis job. Ya shoulda see em big diggers dey bring in, Hank. And em dump trucks movin loads and loads of dirt. More dan I ever seen.

Hank was mum. The sight of Stan on that groundbreaking day might have crossed his mind. Stan, hard hat gleaming, plans in hand at the ready, standing a step behind the engineer, turning to talk to Simms' crew, grinning ear to ear at the hydraulic excavators. Any old hand would have given his all to be standing there amid the clawing, the rumbling, to see the earth opening up. Yep, opening her up for the LoDo Tower, a new construction, Mile High's big contract. And, Stan's the one picked for the superintendent job. Young guy, came over from Logan's a couple of years back, talking computer and yessirree.

O-oh, yeah, Teddy Simm himself come up to me end a day, Joey went on, leaning against his push broom. He wanna know if ya be on the hotel job out by da airport. I told him, ya wanna see Hank? Heck, he's jus down da street fixin up dat old house. Simm come by, Hank?

Driving on, listening to the hum of the engine, I tried to drown out Joey. Looking up at the harvest moon, open-faced and serene. Easy, now. The city came into view as I turned into I-25. An oasis of the night, dim lights sprawled out into drowsiness, tall buildings washed with floodlights stood palely against a sleepy skyline. A flame burning atop a refinery flare stack, keeping watch, keeping safe.

I took the 20th Street exit and headed to LoDo. Going along Market, I rounded the corner and turned into the back alley. There was Hank's Mile High pickup parked by the dumpster. The car door was not locked. His cell phone sat inside the cup holder, his roll of plans on the passenger seat. I rushed down the landing. The back door yielded as I turned the knob. Hank was cold on the floor.

I scampered out, picked up his cell and called 911. I then fumbled for the scrap of paper where I had jotted down Hank's home phone number.

"Jamie, I need to talk to your mother."

Nan came on. Voice faint and stifled, "Ye-es."

"Nan, I found Hank, at Lodo. He'd passed out on the basement floor."

Silence. Some rattling, then Jamie came back on, "You found dad? Is he alright?"

I took a deep breath and told her, "He's gone, Jamie. I'm so sorry." I paused. "I'd called 911. Officers are on their way."

Jamie seemed very far away at the other end. I waited. Alley cats screeching hell behind me. After a long silence, I heard her cry, "Oh, no, no." Another pause. "What h-happened?"

"I don't know, Jamie. Wait, the cops are here. I'll call you back."

I hung up before she could say that she was coming down right away with Nan. I wouldn't have wanted them to see Hank. Not the way he is now.

I could see her turn to huddle with Nan. Jamie's tears might have already told her. I could almost hear them sob.

I can't tell you how sorry I'm, Nan.

An officer hovers over Hank, taking pictures. *Flash, flash, flash.* I shut my eyes. Light flashing away in my head, snapping at Hank, his face, his fists. *Snap, snap, snap.* Chisel, hammer, screwdriver, work lamp. He picks up the chisel with his latex gloved hand, drops it into a paper bag, labels it, puts a numbered marker down on the floor. He does the same for the hammer, the screwdriver, the work lamp. Another officer dusting finger prints on the door knobs, inside and out, on the stair rail.

Someone in plainclothes shuffles in. He exchanges a few words with the older officer, turns to look at Hank.

"Hey, Gonz, have a look," he calls out to the guy in scrubs who has just shown up at the door.

"Yuk, what knocked ya off, man?" Gonz mutters as he puts on his latex gloves. He pulls a small flashlight out of his breast pocket, squats down by the body for a quick go over. "Like ya seen hell?" he says out loud.

"Coulda died of shock!"

"No physical trauma, as far as I can tell."

Not a word about the *cold!*

He pries open Hank's fist. "Aye, man, let go! Whatcha got there?"

The plainclothesman pitches in his flashlight. I edge a little closer.

"Yikes!" The grip cracks loose. Fingers like talons. Peeking through, a yellow glint! The shine of a gold coin punches right out the hollow of the dead palm, then fades away just as quickly. The hand is empty except for a shadowy stamp.

I crane to look. Where the gold has shone, the hollow holds the imprint of a coin. Bigger than a dollar coin. Under the glare of the flashlights, the engraving on the face stands out as if it has been charcoal rubbed. It looks like a triangle of a mountain peak with words on the rim. In the blink of an eye, the impression is gone. Only Hank's lifeless hand cups open, stays begging.

"Rigor mortis," Gonz mumbles. He gets back up on his feet, not bothering with the other fist. "Okay to take him, Lopez?" he turns to ask the plainclothesman.

Nothing about the *gold!*

Nothing about the *imprint!*

Nothing at all?

Lopez waves him off, then turns his dark marble eyes on me. "You the guy who found him?"

"I'm detective Lopez," he tells me, but he is busy looking down at Hank's driver's license pulled from the wallet. "Holy cow, *only* fifty-six, Hank Newt, that old guy?"

Grown old dying, he did. But I can't tell him that.

Those stealing hands. What hell have you raised, Hank? The gleam of gold, a mountain on the face of a coin, the engraved words—all that which had been branded onto Hank's palm now burns on my mind.

What unearthly fury is it that punishes a thief with such a vengeance?

Shadows, footsteps, muffled voices. A chokehold of unease grips the air. Somebody sneezes, wheezing away.

Lopez is eyeing me. He asks to see my driver's license. "Ben Ballad. You guys worked together?"

"Yes."

"Know him well?

"Sort of."

"Next of kin?"

He scribbles in his little spiral notebook—Nan, wife. Jamie, daughter. Hank's home phone number from the scrap of paper I show him. Toby, project manager for this job at Mile High. Ashley, tenant. Jed Roen, her husband, architect.

"Anything else?"

"Hank's cell phone here, may I use it to call Toby?" He nods, standing within earshot.

Toby's sleepy voice slurs in my ear—Who-o? U-uh, a-ahem, wha-at's up? Umm. I'm about to repeat myself when I hear a thud at his end, then a continuous beep over the line.

Did I mention where I'd found Hank?

"May I take that phone?" Lopez asks, putting out his hand.

I give it to him.

"We're outta here!" he calls out to the older officer.

"Okay, wrap it up."

My eyes follow Hank out on the stretcher.

Long night over, Hank.

Peace be with you.

At the door, I glance up the stairs. A sprinkling of dirt on the lower treads. Looks like crumbling grout. I turn to the chalk-lined figure on the floor. Hank, a chalk-lined figure.

I'm shaken up by what has come to pass on this night. I didn't know that here's a dark place, haunted by some horrific event that must have happened in the past. Someone must have died here. Snuffed out. Untimely. Broken-hearted. The grievance lives on, beyond healing, past amends. The old rancor flares up just now. Flares up because yet another wrong has been inflicted? In here, tonight?

For his intrusion, Hank has paid with his life. I shudder to think that once aroused this disturbance is not going to go away.

Shadows brush past, slip out into the alley bright with headlights and strobes. I see to it that the door is locked and return the key to Lopez. So the key with the twisted wire gets dropped into the paper bag along with Hank's other keys and wallet. An officer is ready with the yellow tape to cordon off the back door.

"Which pickup's his?" Lopez asks. We walk up to the Mile High vehicle. He jots down the license plate number, opens the door and shines his flashlight inside, locks it back up.

"Thanks, Ben." He turns to leave.

Vehicles powering up. I climb into my pickup to wait for my turn to pull out. Ignition on, I squint into my rearview mirror. I'm caught by the reflection of a red haze and a rushing motion. A slim figure is wobbling after the trailing fog of exhaust and taillights heading out the alley. I'm overcome by a quick compulsion to go after it.

I jump out of my pickup and step into a sudden whiteness, a sudden chill. Snow flakes inexplicably peeling down an ink black sky. No sign of exhaust or taillights. Just she, faltering on the snow-covered ground, her long coat flying about her, her hair dusted a shimmering white.

A distant rumble buckling the air … A big truck's barreling inside my head.

She's being swept into a snow shroud lit by a glare of approaching headlights out on the street. My legs are numb, but I sprint after her.

There, at the mouth of the alley, she turns back to look at me, her eyes glittering.

"A-Ashley!"

My cry breaks the spell. The mottling night dissipates just as abruptly as it has descended.

I stand rooted in the empty alley, heavy with loss.

Wagon gone, squad cars gone. My pickup stands on dry ground with its motor running, its door flung open. Hank's pickup stays put, mute as a derelict of the night.

Before daybreak, all is murky, all is silent. But for the thunder within me.
What premonition is this? I shudder.

It was just an accident. Nothing more. I've been telling myself that all along. But, deep down, I know better. I see it over and over again in my head how it had really happened.
Ellie!
I looked up as the screaming sky came crashing down. The ground beneath my feet gave way and I fell onto my knees.
Hadn't I seen it coming?
I did.
But, there! Sun and breeze were in my eyes as you were shinnying, giggling up the tree, reaching out for the snagged kite.
And *that*, what I saw, before it had even come to pass, when it was already too late …
A burst of ripped petals, torn leaves, broken twigs rained down where you lay. That gashed kite, too, with its trailing thread. The rock under your head oozing blood.
The tulip poplar lost a limb. I lost more.
I've not quite looked ma in the eye afterwards. On the run ever since, wanting it stubbed out—whatever it is in me that I see where others can't, and see it beforehand.
I shudder at its power to torment. For I'm helpless to forestall what is to happen.

2

A dreary murk hangs over the alley. I stare into the gloom, grip the steering wheel, turn around and pull out as fast as I can. Lowering the window, I take in a gulp of the cool air.

S-steady now. Don't look back. Just don't.

But amid drifting whiteness, her translucent gaze has left me breathless. I brood over her eyes brimming with tears.

What's real? What's not? This vision of Ashley—I can't fathom how she could have come into this frazzled September night and turned it into a wintry angst of her own. I was there, and she'd looked to me. Her angst, my foreboding?

You're not to fall, Ashley.

Now, why do I think that?

The day I met her, she'd come out of a haze of sun-shot plaster dust and held out her hand, "Hello, I'm Ashley." When I put my work glove back on, the feel of her hand lingered in mine. Behind goggles, I trailed her in spite of myself.

She stood on the gallery floor, surveying the old brick wall that rose double-height up the ceiling. She ran her hand gently over the worn brick surface.

When I turned around, she was gone. It was as if a crescent moon had glided through, and I had let go my heart to the silvery night.

A coyote howling at my heels …

It was Hank throwing down his crowbar.

Well, it's just that I don't get to see women coming to jobsites. I'd told myself.

Out on Market, a reflection of my pickup stealing past the newly installed glass front. Against the Victorian façade, the sheet glass looks starkly out of place. Out of sync, like me.
Pre-dawn now. The ashen-gray sky lightening. But it feels like twilight, as if I'm on the verge of riding into night all over again. My nerves are frayed.
Still, what's lurking in her basement?

A pale glow has risen over the Turnpike, raw like the underside of a fish's belly. To the east, a hint of salmon pink and gold flushes up the blanched sky to fringe the purple clouds. It's a different light this morning, a new day like no other. For I know that inside me, that stubborn old thing has sprung back to life. I shift in my seat and look to the sky.
The sun peeks, the gilded dawn ablush, lifting the sky over the front range, turning dark mountains blue. Light and shade, peaks and valleys stretch on forever. Above the range, the harvest moon hangs like a phantom, not letting go of the night.
But I let go. I let go the splendor of the moment. Taking the McCaslin exit at Louisville, I head for Marshall. From the day of the cookout, I remember the low ranch house under tall cottonwoods at the bend of a dirt road. I follow the roadside reflectors, telling myself that if I have gone past the trailer park I would have missed the turn. I slow down, tires grinding dirt, crunching along.
When I pull up the gravel driveway, it occurs to me that I hadn't called to say that I'm on my way. But there she is, her bob of straw hair stands out under the pallid porch lamp. How long has she been standing there? Jamie, her dad's girl, tall, big-boned, square-shouldered, now a shaggy specter leaning against the door. I step out into a startling breeze. The big cottonwoods rustling overhead, raining leaves.
I walk up to her, hoping that what had come to pass would come gentle to her, to her mom. I'm to make that happen. In the

early morning chill, her ruddy complexion looks blotchy, her thin lips quivering.

"I'm so sorry, Jamie," I sputter. I hug her, brushing against her cold cheeks. She lowers her puffy red eyes, murmuring something like "so-o sorry to ha-ave troubled you." She pauses, choked with tears.

No word comes to either of us.

"Shall we go in?"

"Oh, oh, yeah." She jolts, turns around to push open the door. Before entering, she looks up as if to make sure that it's me at her door and this is really happening. She sighs, lowers her head and lets me in.

The living room is dimly lit. A pale glow of the energy-saving fluorescent lamps washes the earth-tone room without warmth, without the golden feel of the season. A sallow gloom sags the place, except for one bright spot. Nan's corner of the room. A burst of red, orange and brown beats back the drab. The relief comes from a length of woven textile in brightly colored stripes stretched out on her loom. The small woman sits in her refuge under a lamp, her hands folded on her laps, her head bowed. Her short pepper gray hair is neatly combed.

"Mom, Ben's here," Jamie calls out in a loud voice.

She raises her head, looks our way. Then she turns quickly to search for something on top of the footlocker by her side. She looks past the colorful balls of yarn piled high in a basket. She bends down to pick something up, her pair of hearing aids, slips one on, then the other. Pushing back her chair, she stands, not taller than her floor loom. Her shawl slips off her shoulders, she stumbles on her step, nearly knocking over the floor lamp.

"Wait, mom! Don't walk." Jamie rushes over, puts one arm over her small shoulders, tucks a hand to support her from under her arm.

"My leg's asleep," she mutters as she bends down to hold onto her numb leg, letting go her eyes on me.

Nan must have sat on that wood chair all night. And she has on her street clothes and street shoes. She looks as if she is ready to leave the house any minute.

"Nan." I walk quickly up to her and give her my hand. She looks up, clasps mine in both of hers. Small, trembling hands. Her eyes are red but clear and dry. She gives me a wistful look. In that look, I see a sheet of steady shine, like a reflecting pond on a moonlit night.

I had seen a pond like that once.

"H-ow, how did it hap-pen?" she asks haltingly. Small ripples undulate, wrinkling the mirrored surface.

Mother and daughter stand leaning against each other, their eyes unblinking.

"Don't know for sure. They think, uh, it might be his heart."

"You mean, he had a heart attack?" Jamie looks incredulous. "He's been healthy. Never took a sick day."

"Whe-re have they taken him?" Nan asks. Her voice low, quavering.

"The Medical Examiner's, Denver Health. They said it's because the death is sudden."

The phone rings, earsplitting loud. A huge sound for the small room.

"Mom, you okay to walk?"

"Yes, yes." Nan straightens herself up, waves Jamie off and limps over to the sitting area. Jamie rushes for the screaming wall phone by the kitchen.

"Please, Ben," Nan gestures me to sit.

I perch on the edge of an oversized, overstuffed couch. Nan sits stiffly on the armchair, her eyes following Jamie. I look in the direction of the kitchen and spot Hank's thermos and lunch box on the kitchen counter. I turn back to glance at a worn magazine on the coffee table. Nan's 'Handwoven.'

Nan's a weaver, got her craft and the old loom from her mother, Hank had told me that July 4th. After we ate, he brought me into the house to show me that ingenuous contraption. A handsome piece of woodwork. Warm, smooth to the touch.

Hey, she makes good money at the arts and crafts shows, mostly before Christmas! He chortled.

Other than her welcoming hello, I saw little of the weaver that day. Like a tumbler with her hands full, she was in the kitchen while we were out in the backyard. She was picking up outside when we came into the house. She ate quickly, quietly, sitting by Jamie.

Under a discolored lampshade, a dreary cone of light sheds over the end table onto the armrest. A stereo cassette-and-CD combo sits on an oak case facing the couch.

That, a Christmas present for Nan. From me! Hank was eager to tell me, pointing to the set.

"Ben, B-Ben, " Nan calls softly. She is leaning forward in her chair, fixing her eyes on me. A quivering shine in her stare. "Ben, you know if, uh, if he'd suffered? Much?" she asks hesitantly.

"I think not," I say, swallowing.

"He went fast?"

"Uh, yes."

Maybe, they've got gentle lighting at the Medical Examiner's. Maybe, they'd have fixed his face. Maybe, mother and daughter, they won't see what I saw, not up close. Maybe …

Nan nods, then sighs.

I hear Jamie hanging up the phone.

"It's uncle Phil. He has just gotten off his shift. He's on his way here." Jamie bends down to tell Nan, face to face. "He's gonna, uh, gonna take us to, uh, to see dad." She chokes up, fighting back tears.

Nan reaches out to take Jamie's hand. They hold hands for a little while. Small sniffles, heaving lightly.

I tense up, wishing there's something I can say.

"Would you, uh, like some coffee, Ben?" Jamie asks, regaining her composure.

"No, no coffee. Thanks, Jamie."

"Tea?"

"No, thanks. I should be going."

"Yes, Ben, go get some rest. It's been a long night for you," Nan says.

She comes over, puts her hand on my arm. "Ben, I thank you for all that you've done for us." Her grasp is firm and steady. Her eyes, a sheet of shine once again.

I let out a breath.

"Dad's cell phone. Do you have it, Ben?"

"It belongs to Mile High," Nan interjects.

"I'd given it to the police."

Both of them turn to me with a baffled look.

"Routine, I guess," I say helplessly.

"I'd thought that it should go back to Mile High."

"Do-o they suspect foul pla-ay?" Jamie gasps, her eyes filming up.

"Not that I know of," I say, turning away. I want to wipe off the look of death on his face.

Jamie lowers her head sobbing. Nan puts her arm around her daughter's waist to draw her close.

"Ben, thanks so much for coming." Jamie lifts up her head, exhales, squeezes out a faint smile. "We, uh, we're gonna be fine. Uncle Phil will be here soon."

They usher me to the door.

"Bye now," Nan says in a hushed voice.

"Take good care, Nan. Take good care, Jamie. Let me know if there's anything I can do. Call anytime, okay?"

They close the door behind them. But Nan's calm eyes leave with me as I drive off.

They remind me of ma's eyes when my old man passed away.

Boulder barely stirs when I get onto Broadway. Turning into Baseline towards the foothills at Chautauqua, I walk briskly up the trail head.

Early yet. No hiker or jogger in sight.

Out, shadows of the night, out into the open air! I jog up the trail, my eyes on the Flatirons. Towering sandstone slabs. All three. Old crust of the earth. They take on the new day, the glow of the sun on their craggy, firebrick faces. Umber hued, soften this hour by a tinge of pink, the 'irons' sit upright, hunks of jagged peaks pointing up the pale morning sky. Their shadowed faces silhouette darkly against the light. Sloping troughs lush with evergreens gouge down the sides of the ridges. Sunlit, somber, the conifers fan their way down the slopes.

On the rise of the land below, luminous foliage of yellow and gold shivers in the air. A clump of aspens stands alone, naked white trunks resplendent with splays of golden light. And that, even before the sun has taken on fire. I walk up close to drink in the luscious light. A breeze whistling through. The quaking leaves sing like a thousand tambourines. A host of yellow butterflies take to the air, drift, twirl, and fall, littering gold.

A blur of the tawny grass undulates, rustling as I brush past. Something buzzing in my ear. I whisk it off. It's a smattering of bitsy flies, flitting, spinning loops. I pick up pace. Huffing along, moist breath on my face. The cool thin air tingling my nostrils.

Whoop, thump, whoop, thump, my footfall hits the ground. I follow the trail up the slope, down a gentle dip, then up again.

Just ahead, a blaze of fiery sumac gobbling up the hillside. An immense firecracker red explodes against the tall dark evergreens, splashing the slope a sudden red. I jog on. The path narrows, the flaming shrubs closing in, grazing my arms, blurring my view. I scramble for a way out.

Whoosh! Whoosh! A bright red cloud bursting before my eyes. It's the blood red glint that zapped through the dead eyes of the night! I jerk backward.

I blink. It's just a puff of the little red leaves flittering, brushing against my face. Twigs snapping. Panting, I beat my way out of the high color brush. Red blur in my eyes, I hasten to get back on the trail.

Look to the sun! Night's done.

Sound of a dribbling flow. Small trickles course along the silt bed, curve around fallen rocks. A blue jay dives down, takes a sip, flapping its wings. His mate nearby.

The trail winds up, leading to where the air sparkles, the scent of ponderosa smothers like a young buck's yearning. Dappling light and shade, the mountain folds me in to set me free. Little twittering. Fluttering among the branches. Scurrying afoot. On a lichen-encrusted boulder, a squirrel pauses, fluffs its tail, then darts off.

I look up to where the canyon walls rise abruptly. There, beneath the flanking cliffs, a crumbling footpath hugs the rocky face, snaking its way to nowhere. I'd seen it before. Still, I hold my breath. Worn down by foot traffic of old, what was once a level ledge is now choked with weed and vine. Seasons of freeze and thaw, growth and rot, have long eroded the path. Exposed roots dangle, scouting for a perch. Fallen rocks lie where they tumbled.

Yet, here and there, I see the hand of man. Loose rocks stacked to form the base of a narrow path. A toll road of yesteryears. Miners paid toll to walk to Nederland where they looked for work in a silver mine. Some never lived to return.

My heart beats wildly. Worn fingers of old scrabbling at crevices for a hold, then another, and another. A rock hurtling down, setting up a trail of loose stones. Cowering down, tucking in. Tired feet trudging, one gritty foothold, then another, bent backs strapped with ragged loads, tattered lives on tow.

Shadows of the dead straggling along, plodding on … I turn to leave.

On my way back, I take a detour to skirt around the flaming sumac. I hike down the slope in big strides. The sky is an endless blue, save for two crossing streaks of jet stream. The city below hums sedately, churning up dust of the day.

I look back to the day I stepped off the train at the Union Station. Coors Field was a new stadium then. There was bustling around town. Here, I would stay, I'd told myself. Here, not one bald cypress knee sticking out of the swamp. Or, another tulip poplar with yellow cups pointing up high.

Still, ma's watery eyes. They follow me where I go.

I'd wanted to tell her. How I'd wanted to tell her! But I was mute as a fish. Still, I see it inside my head, time after time.

Branches and twigs, slivers and splinters, blotches of yellow, splatters of green, all shrieking down, all at once … Flailing limbs, kicking the air. But you were up there! Up there, swinging the tulip poplar, reaching for that entangled kite, giggling like a clutch of chirpy sparrows before a summer downpour. All was way too late even before it had come to pass.

That killer rock lying in wait under the tree, could I have rolled it out of your way? Could I, Ellie? Could I have caught you in my arms and broken your fall?

I looked away from ma's eyes and clamped down the rumbling in my head. My eyes dry as the day-old pollywogs out of water, the screaming sky over my head.

The screaming sky always over my head ...

Now, the dark thing in that Lodo house ... I've an inkling that I'm going to get caught up in it. What's in store?

I feel helpless.

Am I doomed to fail?

A golden retriever comes up to me, sniffing, tail wagging. I bend down to pat her. "Good morning," says the young couple coming up from behind. "Good morning." I nod, rising to leave.

Sunny voices, brisk steps, bobbing baseball caps coming up around the bend. Four teenagers with day packs. "Hiya!" one calls out. I wave back.

Overhead, a lone falcon soars. Big sky. Clear bold light. The Flatirons butting up, pointing to a dauntless new day. For a moment, time stands still. I take in a deep breath, inhaling the great big openness ...

Then I let go. I let go of what has been holding me down. I'm that lone falcon taking in the new light ... Soaring, gliding, gliding ... I'm set to follow my sight, to where it may lead me.

As if on cue, the blood-red glint in Hank's dead eyes surfs up, like a freeze-frame shot.

What hell have you raised, Hank?

My eyes follow the lone falcon, not letting go.

I walk into my cabin to the ringing phone.

"Be at the LoDo house soon as you can, will ya, buddy?" Toby says, loud and clear.

"Will take me an hour or so."

"Get goin, then."

3

I turn into the alley and pull up behind Toby's Mile High Truck. Hank's pickup parked in front, as if he has gotten here early for the same meeting. But the yellow tape POLICE LINE – DO NOT CROSS over the back door is a rude reminder. I hurry out front. Through the shop glass, a glimpse of her honey blond hair. Jed has his back toward the door. Toby beckons me in.

I'm honed like a newly sharpened knife. The night squirms yet under my skin. But in the broad daylight, all seems clear and calm in the gallery. The newly painted soft white stair-wall and charcoal gray gallery look fresh and inviting. Yet, what happened here last night grates on me. I know that within these walls shadows lurk, not dissipated by sun or passing years.

"Hi, Ben!"

"What happened here last night?" Toby flashes me a quick look, fingers twisting mustache. His round face looks relaxed, but his bleary eyes have an edgy gleam.

"Hmm. He was already cold when I got here. In the basement. I called the police."

Toby has it on his face that he wishes I quit looking listless.

"Know what killed him?" Jed asks, his eyes sweeping up the curved stair-wall.

"We'll know when the Medical Examiner gets his report out," Toby jumps in. "I'd spoken to his daughter. She told me that he'd died of natural causes."

"Uh."

"No break-in, right?"

Ashley glances at her carton boxes stacked at the rear.

"No, no break-in," I say.

"Why, then, the yellow tape and the chalk line?" Ashley asks. A twitch at the corner of her mouth. So she has been downstairs.

"I guess, uh, it's the procedure when death is sudden and the cause has yet to be determined. I'll find out if we can get the place cleaned up first thing Monday," Toby says.

"Is there cause for suspicion?" Jed asks. He glances up at the volume of space in the double-height gallery.

"Ben?" Toby squints at me.

"No, uh, no."

"No sign of foul play," Toby says. "Who could have guessed? The guy's been healthy, never missed a day of work as far as I know." He shakes his head, but the blank look on his face belies his concern. "Sad to have lost Hank. But we'll put every man we've got on the job. Wiring and plumbing are in. First and second floor are mostly done. Some trim work and cabinetry left to do. That's about it, right, Ben?" He looks to me to confirm.

"And the basement ..."

"That, uh, of course." Toby cuts me short.

Jed shrugs, saunters off to stand by the stair-wall that leads up to the second floor balcony. He takes a step back, tilts his head sideways to study the curvature that spirals upward. He ambles halfway up the stairs to look down. "Go on, go on," he says. He then walks up to the old brick wall, newly sandblasted, runs his hand over its surface, rubs the residue off with his other hand. His smooth face untroubled by the reason that has brought us here.

Cool eyes watching, Ashley watching her husband as if she's a bystander from outside looking in.

Jed Roen. He was scrutinizing the timeworn face of the old brick wall the day he came to inspect. Hank was speaking to him about some construction details on how to do the curved stair stringer: For an application such as this, Mr. Roen, ... The way I would go about doing this, Mr. Roen, as I have done in so many instances working with Mr. Weber, Sr. ...

Toby was there, too, clipboard under his arm, smirking away.

Well, he's big, that Roen. He's principal architect of LoDo Tower. Hank told me afterwards. Then his voice trailed, losing steam. The foreman job had gone to Stan, a new hand.

"There," Toby turns to Ashley, "You've my word that we'll do our very best to get your studio done in time for the opening."
"October 16," she says firmly.
"Way to go, Toby. Get word to Jim Weber about this, huh?" Jed says as he struts down the stairs, hands in khaki pants' pockets, loafer heels squeaking the newly polished hardwood floor.
"Su-ure thing, Mr. Roen." Toby says jauntily.
Her husband turns to her smiling, teeth white and nose sharp, "Hon, it's settled then."
"How's his family? Toby said you've gone to see them," Ashley asks, her back to her husband.
"They're managing."
In that dim room choked with grief, mother and daughter stood clutching each other, lest they fall.
"Please give them my condolences."
"Ready to go, hon?"
"Get some rest, Ben," she says at the door.
That flicker in her eyes. She seems to be conscious of it and turns away.
"Here's a set of keys for you." Toby hands me a tagged key ring with two keys, front door and back.

I stay back to lock up, and to have another look at the basement. The midday sun slants down the stairs into gloom where the back door shuts out any hint of day. I sidestep his chalk line figure, reach up to grab at the pull cord of the bare bulb. The yellow filament burns weakly.
All's quiet. Not even the slightest drift, the tiniest heave to wrinkle the air. No other shadow but my own, the puddle under the dim bulb. Still, I strain to peer into the dark.
What fury was that which had gnashed the night and chewed up a life? The day has come with nary a whisper to give a clue of

what might have happened here.   I turn myself inside out, listening.

Ashley comes to mind.

"I'll be working down here a lot," she had said shortly after we started on the job.

That day she came to go over with Hank the basement layout she herself had put together. Hank walked by her side, studying her sketch, taking notes on his clipboard pad.

"Back here's where I'll do my dyeing."

She walked towards that part of the basement directly beneath the front entrance upstairs. There, a grimy brick wall stood matted with cobwebs. There, the sun that crawls in from the back door would not reach.

"I do fabric design." Her voice, a breath of fresh air in the windowless basement.

"Exposed ducts on the ceiling with exhaust fans to run directly over the burners, right about here, yes? Lots of venting. Through the side wall, perhaps? And here, the washing machine, dryer, and laundry sink against the back wall.   Warm fluorescent tubes overhead. Ah, the furnace? Hank, where do you think the furnace ought to go?"

I was on my knees nailing down loose treads on the basement stairs to make them serviceable before the new stairs go in.   I stopped hammering, peered down through the broken banisters.

The afternoon sun had crept in and lapped over her footsteps. She was tracing the path of her work routine, walking the concrete floor stained with warehouse grunge. She would have her big work island stand right in the center. Over there, a fabric bolt-rack and shelving units against the side wall opposite to the stairs.

Job for a carpenter. I tried to see what she was seeing.

"What's under the stairs?"

She was standing in front of a door not five feet tall. It had a big padlock on its latch.

"That? Stored junk, probably," Hank said. "We'll clear that out soon as we get to the stairs."

I walk back upstairs. The bare bulb that has been burning in my head melts into day. The sun has punched in through the three glazed-in holes on the gable under the pitched roof. The glow lifts the eye to the volume of space above the gallery. Much like that day.

That day I was making my way up the stairs to her office carrying a new window frame. Jed had come in to show a prospective client what he did to breathe new life into an old building. "The intent here is to create a sculptural form, a visual focus for the double-height gallery." He gestured grandly towards the curved stair-wall. "The eye follows the sweep upward to take in the volume of space in one breath. Hmm …"

"A small space, really … But we'd given it an immense openness. It invites the eye to view the exhibits in one continuum of space, from the gallery up to the second floor balcony."

From the concave-shaped balcony overlooking the gallery, he mused over the transformed space in a baritone voice. "While we'd reworked the interior to suit today's purpose, we're committed to preserve the historical façade and the scale of the existing building. The glass entrance here, uh, is where we'd taken an exception … Old and new, the call is to make the architectural elements mesh well to give the juxtaposition a sense of contemporary aesthetics."

Bunch of bull!

What historical façade? I had seen that block of old houses in the days when the Coors Field had just gone up. They were a mix of tight offices with grille doors and barred windows, refitted small warehouses with makeshift loading docks. Much of the original architecture had already been gutted out even then. What was left was a gable roof here, a cornice there, and narrow windows on the upper floors with arched lintels.

There are the brick and mortar commercial buildings still squatting squarely by the curb, staid buildings from the late 1800's and early 1900's that had already gone through renovations over the years. Up and down the few square blocks, there are now a brewery pub, a bookstore, eateries with varying degrees of facelifts, their interiors updated.

This house at the end of the block, the first day I laid eyes on it I could see that chipped and weathered as the stone façade was, the exterior was still discernibly Victorian. The corniced eave of the gable roof was gone, but there were the carved lintels on top of the windows and a pediment over the entry door. But when I stepped inside, I said to myself: Whoa, what had happened in here?

Four bare walls, cracked plaster on three and one of ragged bricks. The place was picked clean to the bones, stripped of moldings, baseboards, window caps. On one wall, there was the outline of a missing fireplace, its opening boarded up.

"What a dump!" Hank muttered, coming up from behind. He shook his head, eyeing the dilapidation. "This joint had gone to the dogs a long time ago." He was scuffing his work boots at the dirt over the wood plank floor.

"I know this area. Got my first summer job here, fixing up an old hotel down the block. My old man, hmm, he said to me: Get that scaffoldin up, do what they ask ya to do, son, and learn yarself a trade. Jus don't ya go messin around after yar day's done. That edge of town by the stinkin South Platte and the rail yard, nothin doin there but em warehouses and flophouses."

"Well, he said nothing about the whorehouses, but guys blabbered, ya know. I could see for myself, too, the goings-on in the streets." He grinned, "Heck, my old man ought to know that I cared for none of that stuff. I wanted my pay and, uh, to watch the Union Pacific locomotives pulling in a long line of freight cars, coal cars, flat beds. Stock cars, too. Yep, ya could hear the horn blowing before they even made the bend into town. Those days, they called this area Lower Downtown, just coming out of skid row. Now, everybody calls it LoDo. Umm, Denver's born-again strip of prime real estate."

I cocked my ear to a small sigh quavering like an echo as he spoke. It's the emptiness, I'd thought.

"Well, hmm, at least the tearing down part's been done for us, more or less," he chuckled, looking sour. "Can of worms. Old houses."

"Well, the boss makes the call," he continued. "Norton Development owns this block and, yep, quite a few of the commercial buildings around here. That's how big these real estate folks are!" He nodded. "This here's only part of a huge development project in the works. What do ya know? Heard that Jed Roen's a college buddy of Michael Norton III. Good chums to this day. Norton wanted him to head up the Lodo Tower design team. Heck of a deal, won't ya say?"

I climbed the squeaky straight-run stairs to the second floor. The newel post had its ornamental top missing; a couple of broken banisters hung from the handrail. The landing led off to a narrow hallway which ran the whole length of the house. Light filtered in through the three small dirt encrusted panes at the front end. Tiny dark rooms crammed along the hallway, a larger one tucked at the rear. The doors were gone, hinges off. A railroad apartment, probably original to the house.

What place was this, pigeonholes for rooms?

A flophouse?

I heard Hank coughing below. He was yanking at the back door when I got down the basement. Daylight flung in through the open door and set off a rush of scurrying.

A filthy hollow the basement was, littered with debris. A dank odor came from the sooty brick walls, from the concrete floor stained with spills and smudge. A broken down furnace leaned against a side wall. Loose pipes and cracked chases slung down the ceiling joists laced with cobwebs.

"Holy mackerel! We sure got our work cut out for us," Hank growled.

"Piece of cake" was what he told Toby the day of the teardown. "Could use more hands though."

We got Joey that afternoon. But, then, we always had Joey anyway, the odd job guy, the errand boy, the cleanup guy, Hank's shadow. He had been tagging alongside Hank for as long as I'd known the both of them.

Hank shrugged. That was that.

Took us a good three days to clean up the mess. When the dust finally settled, the straight-run stairs that had led up to the dark hallway was gone. Pigeon holes gone. Gloom gone.

Past noon now, the gallery is awash in reflected light. It is a buoyant light that lifts you, holds you in a lapse of what had come to pass in the wee hours. The place is cleansed, made whole by this light. A car horn toots, startling me. I look out the street. Cars streaming past.

Time to lock up.

I step outside, crouch down the front door to access the lock at the bottom frame. Getting back up, I happen to look inside. I flinch, do a double take. The gallery's shrouded in fog! Not the light-filled space I'd just walked out of.

Before I can make sense of it all, something compels me to look up. On the floor above, against the light filtering in from the three glazed-in holes, I see a glimmer of a silhouette. Quivering in the gloom, this tenuous form hovers along where there was once a hallway. I hold my breath, shut my eyes to let the vision pass.

In the blink of an eye, the glimmer dies, the silhouette vanishes into one of the pigeonholes where there ought to be no pigeonholes. The grip has loosened. I let out a sigh.

The space is once again bathed in a serene light. Gone are the upstairs hallway and the pigeonholes. The curved balcony overlooking the gallery floor is as I know it.

On my way home I stop by the Home Depot to have a duplicate of the back door key made.

4

Heavy steps stomping down the alley.

"So it's tr-ue, wh-at I h-ear?"

He calls out to me as I stand at the back door landing. He's eyeing the yellow tape I've ripped off. "B-but, h-his pickup, it's he-ere ..." He waddles down the steps, drops his lunch tote and the tool he's carrying to barge into the basement.

He sees it in the paltry light.

"O-o-oh!" he cries out. Short stout form plunks down the floor, crouches over the chalk line figure.

"Heart attack, dey say, and ya found him, huh?"

He turns to me, lips trembling, eyes red. "Ya coulda let me know, ya coulda, hmm, ya coulda call."

"I'm sorry, Joey"

"His folks, dey o-okay?"

"As well as can be expected."

He lumbers out into the brewing new day, picks up his lunch tote and the bolt cutter. "What ya wanna me do wit dis? Hank wanna me bring from da shop Friday. I plain forgot."

"I'll take it. It's for the padlock under the stairs."

"We'll get to it, yep, in good time," Hank had said about the bolted door under the basement stairs. "Top down, like I always say. Start with the top floor. Besides, let's not mess around with that rickety stairs for now. We've already gotten it serviceable."

"Would've gotten to it sooner if we'd some real help," he said one day. On another, he grumbled, "Gotta sandblast the lower part of that brick wall after the stairs' been taken down. Gotta seal off the upper floor good. Gotta ..."

Toby had wondered out loud when he came by why the sandblasting had to be done in two rounds.

"Don't ya think I wanna sandblast the whole darn wall in one go," Hank muttered the day the sandblaster came to take care of the upper wall.

"Judgment call, right, Hank?" said Toby with lips curled. "Heck, it'll only set us back a day or two."

Hank growled under his breath and walked away.

I looked up the tall wall and saw Hank's reason for making that call.

"My old man, he worked for Mr. Weber all his life." Hank had told me not long after I started at Mile High. "I followed him into the trade and learned from the best." He took a bite of his sandwich and looked me in the eye. I saw that he wanted me to know that he had been to the mountaintop.

"Yep, from Mr. Weber himself," he said, nodding his head. "Ya don't see him around these days except, maybe, at the groundbreaking of a big job. He handed his company to Jim Weber, Jr. a few years back and called it quits for good. My old man, he quitted shortly afterwards." He took a last gulp of his Big K and swallowed hard. "Um, he died before he could sit back and watch the world go by." He crushed the empty can with a firm squeeze, dropped it into his lunch box.

"See, old Mr. Weber's a building engineer. Tons of experience. Just look around town and ya can't count all his buildings with the fingers on both of your hands. We ought to take a ride one of these days and I'll point them out to ya. Tell ya how we put them up." He was sitting on his wood stool, an elbow resting on the particle board cluttered with work orders. He glanced over the blueprints of the job at hand and muttered, "A cinch to put up, these warehouses."

As we stepped out the trailer into one snowy November day, a plane roared off from the DIA nearby. Through the drifting flakes I watched a blast of exhaust shooting into the white air.

"I learned from Mr. Weber how to brace a wall as we bring her up," he spoke into my ear, pointing to that free-standing warehouse wall propped up with timber as we walked towards it. "Those mason guys aren't going to do it for ya, at least not the way ya want it done. No, sir."

"What do they know about building, those guys sitting in the office, huh?" He raised his voice in the jet engine boom. I heard the hard edge loud and clear.

"Those days, when I put a call through to Mr. Weber with a problem, he'd say to me, 'What do ya think, son? Let's hear it.' And he'd stop by any time. Not like what they tell me these days over the phone, 'Hank, uh, I'll be by tomorrow, alright?' And, Jim Weber, the new boss, ya don't get to see him at all. Not like his old man." He shook his head as he stared into the fuzzy whitescape.

I'd thought of saying, "Those guys do bids. They bring in jobs." But I said nothing.

Then, too, losing the LoDo Tower supervisor job to Stan was eating him up. And with it, every other little thing. Just the other day, Takeo from Sunshine Electric hollered up from the basement, "Hey, Hanko san, I don't see none in em plans! Ya wanna me run wire for light under em stairs while I'm at it?"

"Nah, forget it, just do what the plan says!" Hank bellowed from the top of the stairs.

"It's no business of mine, eh, if nobody think of putting a light in that hole."

"But we're going to take the stairs down anyway," I said.

He was mum.

He was spared that chore.

I look at the numbered markers on the floor and see what had been scattered there—the chisel, the hammer, the screwdriver. Over there, the toppled work lamp. Shattered glass from the cracked lamp litters the floor.

A life was snuffed out here. The chalk line figure on the concrete floor does not begin to tell the story.

"What for, em numbers?"

"To show where Hank dropped his tools."

"What tools?"

"Morning, guys!"

Toby's at the door. He steps in, rolled-up blueprints in one hand, camera in the other. "Take this," he tosses me the roll. "Hank's copy, got it from the pickup. First thing, that old stairs gotta go. I'll get Billy right over to give you guys a hand."

He starts clicking his camera, flashing over the chalk line figure, pointing close-up at the numbered markers, then a panoramic shot over the floor. "For the office," he says.

"Hey, Joey, go ahead and clean up before the subs show."

"Ben, think ya be ready for the sandblaster day after tomorrow?" He's surveying the basement walls.

"Okay if I let you know later today?"

"Three weeks to go, huh? Count on ya, buddy, to wrap this job up." He heads out the door.

In the alley, the sound of motor starting up.

"He a takin Hank's pickup," Joey mutters, poking his head out to look. He scoots back in, goes quickly to squat over the chalk line figure, one hand over its shoulder. "Dis ain't Hank, jus chalk line, dat's all."

Then, he gets up, goes about picking the markers up from the floor, muttering to himself.

He spots the flashlight in my hand and says, "Ya need a bigger light. I go get one from da job across da street if dey ain't usin it. Be right back."

I run my flashlight over the pint-sized door the height of my shoulder. A two-panel door that opens in the center. The boards on each panel clamped down with battens across the top, bottom and in the middle. Hasped and padlocked, a barrier to keep something in, to keep out of sight.

For safekeeping?

But what's in there?

Hank's wasted face jabs my mind, fingers like talons clutching gold ...

I rub my finger over the brass padlock. Tissue-thin scales flaking off, like dandruff. I run my hand over the wood above and below the steel hasp across the door panels. Same dry tissue peeling off onto my hand.

I step back and make out a scaly patch the size and shape of a handbill. Whatever it was that was pasted onto the door had been sloughing off over time. Close up, it is a strip of yellowed tissue with faded red ink brush strokes scrawled over its entire length. The writing looks like oriental calligraphy.

Under seal, this door? I hold my breath.

Klop! I put the bolt cutter to the padlock. Yank off the padlock, unlatch the hasp.

Pulverized flakes fly in my flashlight. The hinges screech. The doors creak open to a black nook under the stairs.

A trap?

Danger?

I peer in, listening up. My heart like still water. No eddies. I crouch down, clamber into the dark belly, flashlight scouring. A waft of old rot hits my nostrils. I gasp for air, coughing. Cobwebs brushing against my face. Crawly things skittering about, overhead, underfoot.

I bump my head against the underside of a riser, tripping over some squashy bulk. My flashlight swoops down over a tied bundle of old newspapers. I crawl back out, dragging along an entangled rag.

"Holy cow, can't see nodin in der! Here, gotta ya a lamp!"

Back on my feet, huffing, catching my breath.

"Ya okay?"

Joey looks at me darkly.

"Ye-eah."

"What's in der?"

"Old newspapers."

"Gotta be kiddin!"

I clip onto the door the lamp he has brought. He pokes his head in.

"Maka no get-go sense! What for, da lock? Nodin in der but em old newspapers and dat buncha rag."

I pull out the bundle of old newspapers, ripped and soiled, bristling with silverfish. I glance at the faded headlines and the smudged text. All in Asian writing, columns and columns of the small character symbols.

"Lemme take it to da dumpster."

"Leave it by the dumpster. I'll take a look later."

Joey picks up the bundle at arm's length and scoots out as fast as his legs can carry him.

I pick up the rag that I'd dragged out. A length of tattered cloth. Dull black, mildewed, stiff with dirt. A quickening stirs within its folds—a multitude of squiggly things slithering for cover in the light of day. I drop it, pick it back up, trailing dirt and more as I shoot for the door. A smattering of little brown things spilling down the floor, rolling whichever way, then a lump of wood and a stick clattering down.

Joey at my heels, hollering, "Whoa! What's dat?"

I'm about to toss the whole squirmy enchilada into the dumpster. I stop short, drop it onto the ground and stomp on it.

"Ya pest, ya dead!" Joey jumps in, stomping.

"Done killing?"

Joey grins. I gather up the worm-eaten cloth and spread it out on the ground. A patchwork of rectangular panels, threadbare, stitched together to make a big rectangle. A shapeless garment of sorts. It has a neck hole trimmed with a band, a pair of twisted ties, one along the open seam, the other on the side seam.

A robe, for draping over the body?

"Don't ya mess around wit dat filty rag! Dump it out quick," Joey says.

Without much ado, I gather up the infested cloth and chuck it into the dumpster. I pull off my T-shirt and slap it against the wall. I tousle my hair good before slipping the shirt back on. Then, I spank my jean legs clear of dirt.

"Hey, Joey, do the same. Get the bugs off you!"

Back inside, I pick up from the floor a small chunk of wood. Sculpted like a man's fist without the knuckles. Painted red. I rub the dirt off with my sleeve. The paint has been worn off where the hump is, the wood dark brown and smooth. Below the hump a wide slit opens into what looks like a grinning mouth choked with dirt and white clingy web. A shriveled spider sac lodges at one corner. Little pale midget spiders jiggling inside the dark recess. I run my finger over the lump and trace a carved line framing the opening like a pair of curled lips.

On the floor is the dropped stick. It looks like a chopstick topped with a small wood knob. I strike the knob against the hump.

Bok-ok-ok .... A resounding knock on hollow wood.

A small whimper echoes back, followed by a muted groan that sends shivers. I spin around, peer into the nook under the stairs. My eyes swim in the dark. Cobwebs tickling my ear. A spider slinging in the air.

Clink-clanking at the door, I turn to look. Joey has just stepped back in with a banged-up aluminum pail filled with water. He sloshes his way to where the chalk line figure lies. Bristle brush in hand, he drops onto his knees and splashes water over the floor. He has his head bowed, but I can hear him sniffling.

I pick up the push broom to sweep up whatever else that had fallen off the rag. A scrap of tattered paper gets snagged on the bristles. I bend down to dislodge it. What catches my eye is the smudged red ink on it.

I snatch it up, a shred of tissue-thin paper. I smooth it out on my palm, and see that it is splotched with faded oriental brush strokes.

There is not another scrap of such paper in sight.

Joey spots the little brown pellets on the floor.

"Em things, what're dey?"

I pick one up.

"A wood bead. See the hole going through it?"

Nearby, a strand of faded red twine with a couple of strung beads. I pick it up.

"Em beads, what for?"

"Got a hunch they are prayer beads."

Odds and ends. Toss them out?

Instead, I slip the beads into my jeans' pocket, and put the

small wood block, the stick, the scrap of Asian writing neatly
folded inside my lunch tote.

Stepping out for a breather. Ashley's white beetle is not in its
parking spot.

I sit myself down on a step at the landing, unroll the blueprints.
Hank had dog-eared the Building Section Plan showing the
elevation of the brick wall and the two flights of stairs. The new
basement stairs are to have an I-beam as central stringer and
butterfly steel fins to support the wood treads.

There's your job, Hank had said, finger tapping the detail
drawing of the tread fittings. A notation reads: "Anchor treads
onto existing wood stringer along brick wall."

Good for the wall, good for the stairs, Hank might have said.

Back to work. I thump up the old basement stairs. Top down,
Hank did say. Grabbing the handrail with both hands, I give it a
hard push and a harder yank. The whole thing flexes and sways,
the treads and risers heave and creak.

Rickety old bones, groaning old bones.

I stand, my head just clears the gallery floor. Something jabs
my eyes. It's a splinter of light that refracts from the beveled edge
of the glass door where the sun hits. I blink as if I've just opened
my eyes to light.

As I turn away, I spot a slit between the wood stringer and the
brick wall where they meet. The wood is not warped but appears
to have been jimmied. Clean wood shows through the split along
the edge. I run my finger over it and feel the grit from when the
upper wall was sandblasted. The gap is just big enough for a
dollar coin to slip in. Gotta get it filled when we put up the new
stairs.

Well, what's got to go has to go! Starting at where I stand, I
yank at the top section of the handrail with a crowbar to dislodge it
from the banisters. I then knock the banisters off their base with a
hammer. All the banging silences the nagging questions in my
head—Why the lock on the door below? Why the bother when it's
all but empty inside?

Joey goes about splashing water from the pail and scrubs at the chalk line. Bristle brush chafing. Chalk line, that's that.

"Yoho, guys!" Billy bellows at the door.

"This here's where Hank fell, eh?" He looks down where Joey squats, where murky gray water puddles on the floor. "How ya never know what's comin to ya around the corner! Hank ole pal sure didn't."

"Like I always say, gotta live the day like it's gonna be your last. Yessiree!"

"Watcha steps, Billy!"

"Gotta take it easy, pal, ya hear?"

I tear loose a section of the handrail and let it clatter down.

"Man, oh, man! This babe's comin down? Lemme give ya a hand, Ben. Got an extra crowbar?"

"No, Billy."

"Oh, yeah? I've got this baby here."

He pulls a hammer from his tool belt, tosses it up the air, catches it on the head as it comes down.

"Whoa, whoa, yeah, yeah! Lemme give ya a hand," he hollers. "This here's where I'm gonna start if it's alright with ya, Ben."

Swinging his hammer, he strikes out a tune at the banisters as high up as he can reach. He taps his feet to a fast beat, and rocks his hips to the banging rhythm.

"Yo-ho! Yoo-hoo!" he belts out as he strikes hard at a banister yanking it off its base. Then another, and another. He stops, hops up to grab at the handrail.

"Ben, ole Ben, this babe's comin down fast!"

Billy is a stringy, bouncy sort of guy with a booming voice. He has a way of filling up the place when he does come around. For one who had allowed no radio on his jobsite, Hank could do nothing but yelled, Billy, shut your trap!

Joey gets up from the floor, works his push broom over the floor. Thinning out the wetness, spreading dirt. Not a trace of the chalk line left, only a wet cloudy patch on the concrete.

Billy bops about to sidestep the wetness, kicking into some fancy footwork. He kicks his heels, right-right, left-left. Swings his hips, right-right, left-left, right, left, right …

"Bum-bra-la BUM-BUM! Aye, yo guys, thi-is heere's R-red Ho-ot Sal-sa!" He whoops with glee, goes on swinging, one hand waving his baseball cap, the other twirling his hammer.

Joey cackles as he trains he eyes on every step of those rocking boots tap-tapping away.

"Red hot! Me, r-red ho-ot dancin sa-alsa ..."

My head is scrambled, easing throbs about the dark hole below.

One riser, one tread at a time, plying them loose, unscrewing the fasteners, detaching them from the stringer against the brick wall with as little marring as possible. Skilled hands of old had put them up, crouching where I crouch, one tread, one riser. An outline of clean wood is traced along the stringer marking where it had been hidden.

Bum-bra-la bum bum ... Salsa beats bouncing in my head.

I peer down the hole below. Light strains down. Gloom recedes. The storage space looks like any forgotten nook which dusty past is being cleared out.

Plunk! I let drop a riser.

Plunk! Plunk-plunk! Treads and risers thudding down, pounding up dust.

"Yoho, gotta eat. Lunch time, guys!"

People at the door looking in. I walk gingerly down the half flight of stairs. Billy yakking at the door, gesturing. Joey sitting mum on the step outside. I head up the alley. The bundle of old newspapers by the dumpster is nowhere to be found. I look into the dumpster. It has been emptied. The collection truck must have rumbled through without my hearing it.

Lost for good! Should've at least taken a look at the dates.

The noon sun is bright and the sky clear. No white beetle.

Risers and treads, banisters and handrail sections in a tumbled heap. What's left is the outer stringer where the storage planks are attached and that pint-size door still hanging on. I prop a ladder up the opening and unfasten the outside stringer from the subfloor above.

"Wanna me bring this baby down?" Billy asks, grinning ear to ear.

I hand him the sledgehammer and he pulls out a dust mask from his back pocket. He springs into action hollering, "Here comes the one-man wrecking crew! Yoho, yoho, stand back!"

Joey and I stand by the door and watch. Blow by blow, whack after whack, stringer and planks come crashing down in a rush of loud clacks. My head pulsates as if I've been roused up from a bad night.

I survey the wreckage of the day. Nothing to salvage. We start hauling the discarded wood out to the dumpster. Pile the refuse into a big old plastic bin. Takes two to lug a load out. One trip after another, the afternoon rattles on …

"Man, this gotta be the last load!" says Billy.

The bin buckles, more refuse gets piled in ...

"Yippee, quitting time! I'm outta here."

"See ya tomorrow, Ben. Hey, Joey, ya comin?"

"Nah, Billy, ya go on!"

The sun filters in through the dust haze. A dull wedge of light washes over the lower part of the brick wall, over the dirt floor that was hidden under the staircase. It stops short of the dark reaches at the back. Still, the air radiates a soft gold, dispelling gloom. The basement has taken on an open feel as if a chokehold has been lifted. There is now a lightness to the place I hadn't felt before.

"Like nite and day, ain't it?"

I walk over to where the dark nook once was, scuffing dirt. My shadow falls ragged on the uneven floor. I scrape my work boot against a rough edge where the staircase enclosure once stood.

Joey stands by with his push broom. He's eyeing the spot when Hank fell.

Before calling it a day, I stand a ladder against the stairs opening, climb up to nail a length of the orange plastic safety fence to cover it up.

Push broom scouring the floor below.

I glance around the gallery floor. No sign of Ashley. Her

cartons are still stacked at the far corner. Reflectedr light through
the glass front lends a quiet glow to the empty space. A loaded
dump truck rumbles past. The rush hour traffic is building up.

"Looka here, Ben!" Joey calls out as I climb back down the
ladder.

I see it right away, in the mute gold of the hour, this patch of
reddish brown bricks swept of surface dirt. Set in a small
rectangle, the crumbly patch is slightly sunken. It looks like it had
been forgotten the day the rest of the floor was cemented over.
Out of sight, out of mind?

"Old house gotta old brick floor, eh?"

I kneel down and put my hand against the flat brickwork. A
chill shoots up my spine. I pull back, as if scalded by an icy
mountain stream under a bright sun.

"Hey, what's da matter? Em old bricks bite?" Billy chortles.

A damp chill that lingers ... I shiver, staring down at the patch
of old bricks, and listen up. Only the sweeping sound of Joey's
push broom heckling.

The last rays of the sun have shifted to the center of the room.
In the dwindling light, the patch looks just what it appears to the
eye, the remnant of an old basement floor settled with years and
dirt. But I'm piqued. I've this nagging unease because I don't
quite know what to make of the scalding chill.

Why is there the lock for this hidden patch?

"Long day," sighs Joey. He stands his broom at one corner
and looks around the empty room. Walking out, he shies away
from the spot where Hank fell.

I shy away, too. But it is from that patch of flat brickwork. It
gives me pause.

"Hank told me about em whorehouses," Joey says, lifting his eyes
up at the backside of the old houses along the alley.

"No kiddin!" Billy says, his mouth stuffed with his last bite, dropping crumbs.

"Yep, Hank says, look for yaself, see dat big window?" Joey points to the big in-fill on the wall. "See, em bricks and mortar, color different."

"I see, yep," says Billy.

"Hank says, dis be a window to a parlor. See da arch on top? Em fancy whorehouses gotta upstairs parlor and downstairs parlor wit fancy lookin windows." Joey pauses, munching words and sandwich.

"Pianos, too. Dey gotta pianos, and piano players, and singin, and drinks to go around. Lotsa drinks. Gals. Lotsa gals. Fancy gowns, with em big umbrella skirts," Joey pops the last morsel into his mouth and starts to sway about on the back door landing.

I hop up the steps, chuckle and wave him off.

Billy breaks out in a mighty whoop, kicking up his scuffed boots, "Hey, sounds like ya been der, pal? Hee-a-haw! Gotta be heaven, hee-a-haw! Tell me more, pal." He doubles over, spilling his Big K soda.

Joey stops, turns away. He picks up his empty lunch tote and stares into it.

"Umm, em gals in em fancy houses, dey be classy ladies," he mumbles, "Nah, dey don't care none a my kind. Dey be entertainin folks wit money, senators and em sorts. Know somedin? Ya gotta pay em in gold and silver. Dat's right!"

"How the hell do you know?" I ask, aiming my apple core at the dumpster, shooting it in.

"Hank told me."

"Hey, pal, ya're right, us folks ain't gotta no chance," Billy hollers. "Don't stop us none from dreamin. Ain't dat so? Hee-ee-yeah!"

What does Ashley know of this house?

*   *   *

"Is this the original floor?" asks Ashley.

She stands looking down at the patch of uneven brickwork on the floor. Jed looks in, but he hangs by the door, his silhouette against the wan morning light, cool and remote.

"Suppose so," I say, shining my flashlight over the patch. "Could have been a flat brickwork foundation. Might just be how it was done back then."

Still, Jed hovers by the door. He does not come in to look at how the bricks were laid jam-packed against one another without grout joints.

I'd called Toby to get word to Ashley about the patch of old flat bricks under where the old stairs once stood. It's going to show under the new open-riser stairs, I told him.

"Hmm, what a transformation with the old stairs out of the way!" says Ashley. Her voice is low and flat.

I glance at her. A silvery glow to her honey blond hair in the soft morning light. As if she has brought in the moonbeam. But her face is pale. She shifts about listlessly.

Jed steps in after a while, yawning. Ashley shoots him a baffled look.

"Next door, hmm, what's the basement floor like?" he asks, looking down at the brickwork.

"Concrete slab, just like this one here. Same in the ones I've seen down the block," I say. "Poured, uh, I guess, around the same time when they were being converted into warehouses."

"As I thought."

"In the 30's and 40's. I gather it was then that the street was turned into a warehousing block," says Ashley.

"What a no-brainer! Whoever did the job didn't think of pouring under the stairs," Jed snorts. "Shoddy brick-laying there." He points to the offending patch with his chin as he purses his lips. He flicks a speck of dust off the lapel of his jacket.

Neither of them ask about what was in the locked closet that was once tucked under the stairs.

"You want to have it re-surfaced? Cement it over?" I ask Ashley.

"I'd sooner leave it as is," she says after a bit. "A historical footnote to the house, uh, like this wall." She nods at the old brick wall. "Besides, any re-surfacing is going to show anyway."

"Well, Ash, that's it then?" Jed says. A quick look at his watch. "Got to run." A light peck on her cheek as he heads out the door.

She stands still, staring down at the flat brickwork. Sound of a car motor starting up. Time to leave, she walks to the door.

"Good day, Ben."

I see the dark cloud hanging over her head.

Not my place to brood over her dark cloud. But I hear it loudly in my head: What of the dark cloud now, Ashley?

The rumbling in my head …

It's only the crackling noise of the rosin paper as I tear off one length after another. Then, there's the ripping sound of the masking tape. Measure by measure, I move up the ladder until the wood stringer against the wall is well covered and taped over. Then I go around the front to get into the gallery. Throwing a tarp over the orange safety fence that cordons off the stairs opening, I pull it taut and seal it all around with tape.

Gus is unloading his air compressor and blasting tank from his van when I get back into the alley.

"Got the place ready for you, Gus!"

"Ya're a pal, Ben!"

He walks in, surveys the basement span of the tall brick wall and the other side and back walls with his megawatt work lamp. Then he turns to double check his equipments.

"The finest grade, same as what I did upstairs." He gives me the thumb-up sign, but his eyes shift ever so slightly.

"You're a pro," I nod, a little embarrassed by his need to have to reassure me. I then proceed to move my day's work out into the alley.

Gus suits himself up in his protective wear, pulls the hood over his head. Blasting nozzle in hand, he goes about his job as if he were beachcombing the wall.

A bitch of a job really. But heck, it gotta that I'm into it like she's a bitch in heat! I'd heard him tell Hank last time he came to do the upper part of the wall.

I set my table outside to sand down the ends of the oak treads for the stairs. Tread after tread. Behind goggles and dust mask, I'm in a world of my own. Good way to drown out the noise inside my head.

Still I hear the whirring of the orbit sander and think it my moan in the night. It was when the silvery moon was full over my bed.

I pause, glance down the alley. There, the picture slips back into mind of her hobbling in the snow, her eyes lit with tears.

The vision is a bad dream, and I'm as restless as the Chinook roaring down the slope.

5

"The Lord is my shepherd, I shall not want ..."

Rest in peace, Hank. I look past the small crowd gathered at the gravesite to rows upon rows of headstones on the drab green lawn. Orderly lines.

One life not so orderly, perhaps?

I want to forget his dead face, forget those tight fists clutching a secret.

"Dad died of a heart attack. They call it myocardial infarction, acute coronary. That's what his death certificate says." Jamie called two nights ago.

But his face tells more. It tells what might have caused his heart to stop. Looks to me he was thrown into a panic, and died of shock.

"I'd stopped by the police station to pick up the tools he'd left behind."

Yes, the tools he had brought with him that night. For a night job. Stealing hands jabbing my mind.

Christ, her dad's gone!

"I, uh, I'd thought of burying his screwdriver with him, but mom said no. No more tools, she said. I've to agree. Dad worked all his life ..."

Nan stands by the gravesite, a graying woman in black, steady and composed. She's holding Jamie's hand who looks totally out of it, pale as a sheet. Phil by her side, eyes downcast. Next to him, two fidgety boys making eyes at each other. The same two boys I saw the day of the cookout at Hank's.

Nan. She has this faraway look as if she has just lifted her eyes from her ancient loom and sees a new world.

When the time comes, she dutifully bends down, scoops up a handful of soil and casts it over the casket as it is being lowered into the ground. Head bowed, she is mouthing quivering words to herself. As she turns away, I see that she moves with the lightness of someone who has just stepped out of a long wedge of night into day, looking a little stunned, a little lost.

I know that feeling of lightness. It was as if I was tripping air, tipsy as a cloud of miller moths being chased out of hiding into the sun. I was holding ma's hand on our walk home after pa's burial. The bounce in her steps made me think that she had felt it too. Ellie hung onto her other hand and skipped along. Teddy walked on ahead, straight and tall, not slouching.

Back at the bungalow, ma threw open all the windows, front door and back, to flush out the cigarette stench and the alcohol smell. From then on, we all seemed to breathe easier, talk louder and laugh more readily. Though she had to hold down the same two jobs to keep us going, ma bustled about with a sparkle in her eyes I hadn't seen before.

Nan nods as Mary Lou from the office comes up to say goodbye after the ceremony. She glances at the bouquet of white lilies Mile High sent, but her eyes quickly follow a formation of migrating geese squawking the sky. A faint smile crosses her lips.

"Toby has said he'd be here, it being a Saturday and all." Mary Lou says to me. But she has stopped turning her head to look for him.

"Hmm."

Nan walks up to the small group. Bud and his old man Fred from Wilkins Drywall introduce themselves, mumbling, "… good man … miss him, yeah, miss him." Eddie hobbles up to her, nodding, offering his hand. He looks a bit gaunt, out of his painter's overall and no bandanna over his thinning hair. Electric

Bob himself from Sunshine, Chuck from Peak Plumbing, Teddy Simm's foreman Gabe, they come up to Nan and Jamie. A somber Billy tags behind. "Ya take care of yaself," he says to Nan, squirming, fidgety in his shiny black leather jacket. Nan is meeting her husband's buddies from work for the first and, likely, the last time.

Joey, she knows. She takes his hand, looking into his eyes. At a loss for words, he lowers his head, turns away sniffling. Stiff in black tie and full black suit too snug to be buttoned up, his face shines with sweat. Billy eyeing him, bites his lips to swallow a snicker.

"Thanks so much for coming," Nan says to each of them, her eyes gleaming softly.

As they leave, she exhales, lifts her eyes to the sky once again to scan for wings in flight. She holds onto Jamie who is dabbing her eyes.

"Look up there, Jamie," she whispers.

I look up too, inhaling the blue skies.

Early fall colors on the cemetery grounds. Clumps of aspen along the perimeter, specks of yellow flittering against stark white trunks. Where the land dips, a lone weeping willow slumps by a pond, sallow green branches swaying in the breeze.

Here, not a bit of sogginess to stifle the air, the air not screeched with cicadas to deafen your ears, your ears not buzzed by mosquitoes, your feet not scratched by weeds, not stung by horseflies even as your heart cries out for Ellie. Ellie, all alone, where the trees are dark and the rain squalls loud.

Sleep on tight, Ellie, sleep on tight!

"Borrowed from my coz." Joey tells me on our way to our parked cars. He looks at his black suit. He loosens his tie, takes out a handkerchief to wipe his brow and neck. "José, same name as me. Dis what he wore da day he got married."

"How come we call you Joey?" I ask.

"Hank call me Joey day I come work for him."

"You want to be called Joey?"

"Everbody call me Joey dese days, ya know," he says looking straight at me. "It's alright. I know me, José."

6

Before they quit, the steel fabricator's guys and I, we stand to admire the labor of their day. The central stringer of the basement stairs has been installed, its angle of incline runs exactly parallel to the old wood stringer along the brick wall. Flanges to support the wood tread extrude from the I-beam member like ascending pairs of outstretched wings ready to take off.

So it stands, the schematic backbone with evenly spaced vertebral discs. A skeletal form waiting to be fleshed out with treads, treads to be buttressed against the old brick wall. New stairs, old wall, shoulder to shoulder, I can almost see how it might look when done.

Leveler in hand, I crouch, I stand, I get up the ladder to mark where the treads are to butt against the old wood stringer. Cold steel, warm wood, one tread at a time.

Not a pin drop, nor a spike to prick my nerves. All's quiet in the basement but for that hankering inside me.

I hear her pattering up in the gallery. I crane to look through the opening. A flurry of motion. Shifting shadow underfoot. A soft melody rippling the air ... I strain to catch every pulse of her rhythm. Like rain drizzling over leafy branches, over needled branches. Sound of a purling brook chasing clouds, the dingy basement opens up to blue skies and sunny meadows.

The rattling of cardboard boxes puts me back to where I am. Standing by the raw steel sculpture, I swallow hard to resist calling out, Ashley, come look at this beauty!

*   *   *

With the stairs' going up, my job's winding down. Today, I'm down to counting the treads to be bolted. But what of the dark stirrings that have gotten under my skin? There has not been a wisp of anything. Nothing.

But then, I've been distracted by every snatch of sound that drifts down the stairs—Ashley unpacking, Ashley on her cell, Ashley letting someone in the front door. She is ramping up to get her studio ready for opening this weekend.

I stare at the patch of old brickwork under the basement stairs, feeling unfinished.

I re-position the ladder, climb back up and resume bolting the oak treads onto the flanges. Each tread butting up against the wall stringer. Just so, for anchoring to the old brick wall.

Ghrrrrr … Each grinding squeal dispels all that's in my head.

Satin light falls on the semi-glossy wood treads. A shade lighter than the old wood stringer along the brick wall. A subtle contrast. I run my hand over the varnished tread, over the old stringer sanded and vanished. Eddie's fine hand has given both new and old wood a smooth sheen.

The slit at the top of the stringer where ya can drop in a dollar coin, I'd puttied in some wood filler, he'd told me.

A truck rumbles into the alley. Ignition off. No more blue skies and sunny meadows.

"Got ya the furnace and the machines, Ben," someone calls at the door.

I step down from the ladder and walk out.

"Morning, Chuck."

The Peak Plumbing and Heating truck sits right outside. *Ka-plung!* His guy is putting down the loading ramp. I look inside the truck. A high-efficiency furnace strapped to one side rail. A

80-gallon water heater strapped to the opposite rail. Two huge Whirlpool cartons, commercial washer and dryer, stand at the back. An oversized two-compartment stainless steel utility sink with drain board on either side sits between the heavy cartons.

"Gonna be a busy day," says Chuck nodding towards the load. "Ya in charge now, Ben?"

"Yes."

He steps down to check the gas main by the door.

"Want to go over the layout?" I ask.

"Let's." He turns around and calls out, "Hey, Lew, I'll be back for the unloading in a bit."

"Okey-doke," Lew says. He is undoing the strap on the furnace.

On the way in, Chuck pulls out his tape measure to take a quick sizing-up of the doorway. We walk to the rear of the basement. He looks over the rough-ins he had put in at the time when Hank and I were gutting out the second floor. Old pipes had been taken out and new ones installed for both plumbing and heating. He takes note where the electrical outlets are located.

"Furnace against the wall. Boiler at the corner." He tape-measures the space for fit. "I'm gonna run the gas connect this way out." He points to the ceiling with the exposed joists for a straight run out to the main.

Back to the rear wall, "Washer and dryer here. Lotsa ductwork." Again, he looks up the ceiling for the most straightforward way for intake, for vent-out. He pauses, scanning the floor, looking distracted.

Looking for something, Chuck?

"What about vents for the two exhaust fans?" I ask, looking up the ceiling. "One fan overhead right about here, the other over the middle of the room."

"Uh, that too." He sounds far away, his eyes on the floor.

Three's a crowd in a basement crammed with machines just off the hand truck. Shifting into place with hauling strap, one slow piece at a time.

"Need a hand, guys?" I offer.

"Na-ah, bu-ut th-anks," Chuck says, panting.

"A te-am, we're, Ch-uck a-nd me!" Lew sputters.

Out of the cartons, the machines stand gleaming white on the floor. Chuck checking measurements. Lew chortling, "Gotta ya a laundromat in here!"

I dye cloth, Ashley had said.

"The lady dyes cloth," I say.

"Ya can say that again!"

"Alright, that utility sink gotta go in over there," Chuck says surveying the remaining space at the back wall. He whips out his measuring tape again, puts it against the wall. "It gotta fit. It better." A sigh of relief.

"The wall mount faucets, right about here, and the drain out, and clearance below the sink."

"Hey, Lew, let's wait on that sink. Won't get to it today."

The master plumber paces the floor, eyes on the ceiling, making sure he's got the job laid out in his head.

I pick my way through a jumble of ducts, elbows and clamps. Flue running and pipe fitting take off in a hurry, clink-clanking away.

"Shucks, aw shucks!" Lew mutters.

"What now?" Chuck turns around.

I shift on my perch up the ladder beneath the steel stringer. *Ghrrrrr … ghrrrrrr …* one bolt at a time, onto one flange, then another. Between bolts, the din throbs like a hangover, clamping tight, shutting off every tidbit of sound that might have wafted down from above.

"Sure gonna wake up the dead!" Lew hollers, grinning.

D-dead … d-dead … d-dead … echoes from afar, reverberating in my head. I spin around. Chuck's putting the concrete cutter to the wall, tunneling away. Red clay dust spraying over his goggles.

In this vacuous state of numbing noise, my eyes glaze over. Seeing red, I jerk back. Gripping my drill, I hang onto the ladder and wait for the sensation to pass. Under the day-glow fluorescent tubes, the afterimage is a blur of red fuzziness.

The little red fox?

The other day, I spotted a rush of stunning red fur scampering up the slope behind my cabin. Like fish to water, I took off after her. To have a better look. Nothing more. In the blink of an eye, her bushy white-tipped tail disappeared under an outcrop.

Red, a flash of red.

Again?

Red, then, it's all about red—red sumac leaves flittering over my face on the Mesa Trail, a bright red blotch zapping the dead eyes of the night.

Red and tantalizing. What visions are these?

My eyes are tearing. I step down the ladder and walk outside.

"Ya alright?" Chuck calls out after me.

I walk past him sitting at the back of the truck, feet dangling, heels kicking the tailgate. "Llew-ellyn. Call me Llewellyn," he calls out to me in a singsong pitch. "Llewellyn, my mom likes the sound. Music to her ear, she says. Welsh, ya know, huh?" He smiles giddily. "Says I oughta be in the movies, she does." Squinting at me, his boyish round face lights up a megawatt, freckles and all.

I smile back and wave him off. He chomps on his sandwich. I walk down the alley looking for a quiet spot to eat my lunch. Chuck sitting inside the cab, talking loudly on his mobile.

Her white beetle. I slow down as I stroll past it.

I sit on the steps down the landing of the house next door. A bike is chained to the railing. First time I see it. The place is empty now but probably not for long. Toby had come by yesterday for a walk through with somebody. Mile High must have gotten the job as it had the others down the block. Looks like I will be around here for a while yet.

The afternoon wears on. I put my leveler to each tread, shimming, bolting, checking the sightline each step of the way starting from where I stand at the bottom of the stairs. The routine plays on like a reel of slow motion film. The noise grinds down to a drone, broken only by a loud clang now and then.

No refuge amidst the hubbub of working around flues and ducts and pipes. No retreat into my head either. All thoughts are blanked out by the commotion.

"Gonna, uh, call it a day," says Chuck looking at me through an open riser after what seems like an interminable afternoon.

"About time!" Lew exclaims, jumping to his feet.

"Gonna finish up tomorrow," Chuck says. "One more run for the two exhaust fans, and putting up the sink. That's about it."

I walk over and look at his installations—the air intake, the return, the vents, the connect to the gas pipe, the long ductwork that journeys the ceiling, the minimum use of elbows, the clean-cut holes where the flues vent out.

"Everything's to code," he says.

"I'm sure, Chuck."

There is order and economy to his installation. I see the grit and the years behind it.

Lew is picking up the tools, putting aside the ducts, vents, clamps for tomorrow. Chuck and I step out into the alley to look at the vents on the exterior wall by the back door.

"Furnace vent, dryer vent. The vent for the fan will go in to the right of these two." He points them out to me.

Past four. The sun has cast a rich gold on the weathered brick wall. He takes off his cap, rubs his hand over his crew cut. The shade of gray on his hair has taken on a silvery sheen. His cheeks are ruddy but his eyes are puffy.

"Know what?" He turns to me. "My old man, uh, he died of a stroke at sixty. I'm fifty-nine."

"Ya know how old was Hank?" he asks.

"Fifty-six."

I shut my mind to blank out that haunting mask of death.

"Hmm."

As if to deflect his own thoughts of mortality, he says with a chuckle, "Funny thing. My old man in his last years took to speaking Lithuanian. We didn't know what he was mumbling about. Aunt Jurgita knew. They had grown up together in the old country. Funny how when one gets old one slips back to the language one grew up speaking."

"Uh-huh."

Lew is sweeping up the floor with the push broom when we step back in. Reddish brown clay dust collecting below the wall.

"Inspection day after tomorrow, okay?" I ask Chuck.

"Okay by me."

"Take care, Chuck."

"See ya tomorrow."

"Have a good evening!"

"Ya too." Lew winks, grabs the tool chest and dashes up the landing steps. Chuck lumbers after him. His steps are slow, his shoulders drooped.

The mellow sun streams in through the open door. It flows over the spot where Hank fell, over the patch of floor bricks, near hitting the back wall where the newly installed machines stand. The area is now washed in a reflective glow, but for the shadow of stair treads over the floor bricks—the slats looking like a short barricade.

Holding something down?

The day's racket over, the room has taken on an unsettling calm. I listen up to the sound of footsteps and voices from upstairs.

A vehicle passing through the alley. A draft sweeps in, kicking up a convective swirl of dust that rises like a gleaming breath. I hold still. The air current dissipates. The breath expires. The billow of light spiraling out.

Lying under the stairs, my back cool on the flat brickwork. Good light to fasten the lower treads at this hour. At this hour, too, the old brick wall has taken on a warm flush.

Ghrrrrrr ... drowning out all thoughts of eavesdropping. I angle the drill to tighten the bolts.

Drilling stopped, I perk my ears to catch the snippets of conversation that drop like eager morsels from a table.

The blushing light on the brick wall is fading fast. For the lowest tread where there is no clearance to use the drill, I try on a couple of vise-grips for size. I reach up from underneath the tread to tighten the bolts onto the flanges. Getting back up on my feet, I wipe the sweat off my brow with my sleeve.

Standing at the bottom, I look up the flight of treads along the I-beam stringer, along the wall stringer. I follow those two vantages to check the parallel edge of the ascending treads. As I step up, I test the steadiness of each tread. Nice and firm. When I get to the top, I eyeball the flight of descending treads. The sightline is straight and even.

My day's done. I pause yet on my way down for the arresting voices that ring out from the gallery ...

"Oh, here ... extend that telescopic pole ... the steel cable ... the hook ... anchor onto the grid above ... up the balcony." Ashley's voice huffing away.

Sound of tissue paper rustling.

"Whoa, what's th-is?" a thin voice asks.

More rustling.

"Indigo, here, a river of light, of motion. Let's get it up ... "

Shadows shuffle past the stairs opening, carrying a rolled-up bundle. Footsteps tottering up the second floor—Ashley's light patter, followed by sneaker soles squeaking against the polished wood floor, yip-yipping like prairie dogs barking.

"Ca-careful now ... uh, got it?"

Shifting, dragging, lifting.

"Ho-old on ... "

"I've got it!"

Sneakers hurrying down the spiral stairs.

"Hee-re it comes!" Ashley calls out.

Flu-umpf!

Sound of a sail unfurling, catching the breeze.

I step up to be at eye level with the gallery floor. A pair of jean legs prances about a length of fluttering blue cloth that has dropped short above the floor.

"Whoa, oh, whoa!"

Ashley pattering down the stairs. I retreat.

"Here, Kara, my River Indigo!"

There is a tremulous ring to her voice, like wind chimes shivering in the night.

I hear Joey stepping into the basement.

"Ya about done?" he hollers at the bottom of the stairs.

"Ju-ust about."

Footsteps tripping up the balcony. She and Kara. Voices muffled. The wind chimes sounding like fuzzy echoes. Muted rustlings of tissue paper, like a breeze wafting through the woods.

I walk back down.

"Nice stairs," says Joey.

"Em machines are big," he walks over to check them out.

"Looka like Chuck and his guy had a full day."

He glances at the ductwork up on the ceiling.

"They did."

"Yar day good?"

He is pushing his brush broom across the floor.

"Guess so."

I put in a call to Toby to confirm the plumbing inspection for the day after tomorrow. Then I start to pick up my tools.

"Hey, I met dis Chopper today, a kid outta school." Joey shifts around. He rests his broom, spins a finger to show a copter propeller whirling in the air. "Real name's Chester, eh, but everbody call him Chopper cause what he wanna do is fly a chopper one day. Come outa Cin-nati, Ohio and gotta guard job at da Tower site, checkin up on who comes and who goes. Glad to be here, he says, cause he looks to go ski when da snow comes."

"Goodnight, Joey," I say to him at the door.

I slow down as I walk past the front of the house on the way to my pickup down by the rail yard. I glance through the glass with its dark reflection of the passing cars. In the dim interior, the length of cloth hangs tall. Silent and still, it takes center stage of the gallery floor.

River what?

I look above the glass front. *Studio Indigo*—the copper sign in shiny cursive hanging over the glass transom. I never fail to look at it each time I walk past.

She shone, too, the day she saw it.

That day the guy from Denver Metal Works brought it without the proper brackets to anchor it over the glass transom. Be back in an hour, he'd said.

She asked me then to give her a hand to stand it against the wall. She was admiring the warm glow of new copper against old bricks.

I thought it beautiful too.

Ya can't bottle life, ya hear? Ma calling out over our laughter as we tumble down the front stoop, empty jar in hand.

Crickets chirping, legions of fireflies dancing ... Ellie running by my side.

Stars above, stars below, we drift into a cloud of twinkles. Little fluttering about our heads ...

Burnt-out flies dead at the bottom of the jar by morning. How is it that I see it clear as day even before the night's done?

Only ma's words reverberate: Ya can't bottle life ...

"Fireflies don't die, fireflies don't die ... " Ellie protesting.

"There, by the bushes!" she whispers into my ear. "When you see them, you get them inside your head, and they live there forever."

She hands me back the empty jar. I reach out for her hand but it's not there.

"Look, over there!"

Flickers of light in the dark, free and clear. Twinkles of life that don't die?

I turn to Ellie, but I can't see her face. I grope for her.

Ellie! Ell ...

I open my eyes, stark awake.

The convective spiral of dust gleaming in the basement light has turned into the fireflies of my dream.

Something that don't die?

Or, won't?

*　　*　　*

The window washers have just left, the professional floor cleaners are finally done. Every nook and cranny vacuumed, the basement floor wet vacuumed twice over. The place is spanking clean, top to bottom.

End of day, it's the hour for the final walk-through.

"Well done," Jed says cursorily after we had a quick tour of the place. He says little, staring out the glass front at the rush hour traffic, or stepping aside to answer his string of cell phone calls. He seems not to have noticed the length of indigo blue fabric taking center stage in the gallery, his wife's signature piece for her studio's opening.

"Glad to have met your expectations, and glad to be of service," says Toby in an emphatic tone. He beams, obviously pleased with his own words.

She seems not to have heard the exchanges. She does not look at her husband. She paces around, stops to answer her cell phone but once. Her eyes linger over the tall brick wall, following the curved stair-wall up to the balcony. She looks down the straight run stairs to the basement.

"Handsome stairs, Ben. How it transforms the space! So bright and airy. I look forward to working down there."

A shadow crosses my mind—a glimpse of a dark tunnel, a beckoning light at the end. I twitch and turn away.

I'll be keeping watch, Ashley.

"Thank you, Ben, for all that you've done for this place," she says with a smile.

"It's my job."

My pleasure, I may add.

"One more thing," she asks, "Would you mind coming by next week to put up two work tables for me?"

"Not at all." Toby's quick to reply. "Ben will be right next door."

At the door, she gives me a warm handshake.
I hear a loud flutter. A caged bird beating its wings to get out.
Noise in my head, again?
Then, there's that glimmer in her eyes.

I hear her soft footfall, her lingering refrain. Her smile staying with me whichever way I turn, the smile that had once shone through the plaster haze ...
Her hair, as luminescent as morning mist over a mirror lake up in the mountains. A serene break amid breathless heights.
An errant breeze skimming over the placid lake, wrinkling the mirror.
I stir, not letting go of what comes to me in a dream ...
Only in a dream.

The sound of raindrops hitting my window, waking me. I sit up to look out. The shadowy piñons shuddering in the wind. Sheets of rain slicing the night. I sit up for a long while.
The rain finally lets up. A lone owl coos from afar. A hazy moon shivers through the rain-streaked pane. It casts a pale spell over my bed through a sheen of writhing liquid silver.
I loathe to lie down for I want not the restlessness that aches the night. And the night thirsts on ...
Quench my night, quench my night ... howls the coyote on my bed.
Night after night ...

7

"All that money and no kids, huh?"

I hear Mary Lou muttering as I walk into the office Monday morning. A couple of guys hanging around her desk. She sits in front of Jim Weber's glass panel office.

"Three wives, not all at once, I mean, uh, and no kids," someone chimes in.

"Too young to go."

"I say, it's weird, that house, so soon after Hank ..." He stops short.

What? It feels like a hammer has dropped on my toe, numbing and tingling all at once.

"Morning, Drew," he says, looking behind me.

Drew the manager just walks through the door. "Morning, you all," he says on his way to the coffee machine down the hallway.

The phone rings. "Hold on, Ben." She looks up at me as she picks it up, "Mile High, what can I do for you?"

More ringing.

"Harper, line 3," someone calls out from the back.

Harper goes back to his desk. The other guy follows. I stand, a fish out of water. Toby has not shown as yet. I have not been to the office since the day I was hired. The times when I did come in it was to go around to the shop at the back to do a special fabrication or to pick up a tool.

"Jim coming in?" Drew asks as he walks past Mary Lou's desk with his cup of coffee.

"Suppose to." She puts down her receiver. "He's got a 10 o'clock."

"You heard?" she asks.

"We all heard." Drew shrugs.

"Don't know if Jim was there. He'd got an invite."

Another death at Ashley's. Who died? Who?

Drew glances at the wall clock. It says 7:40. He heads for his office next to Jim's.

"Morning, Ben," says Toby, walking in. "Come on back." He motions me to follow.

I stand at a loss in front of his cluttered desk, one in a row of three, backed against a wall lined with filing cabinets. Above the cabinets fat and thin rolls of blueprints stack into wall-mounted cubbies labeled A to Z.

"Got something for ya! Pull up a chair."

He sits down, pushes aside file folders, ring binders, loose sheets, trade catalogs to make space on top of an inch-thick stack of blueprints lying flat on his desk. He thumbs through them, pulls out a thin set, turns the sheets, one after another.

I sit, shifting in my chair.

"Tenant finish, next door to Ashley's. Jewelry designer's studio upstairs, art gallery street level, and, uh, a frame shop or some such in the basement."

From a floor bin, he picks up a thin roll marked 'Ben' and hands it to me.

"Got questions? Call. I'll get ya the timeline soon as I get the subs line up, uh, couple of days."

He swivels his chair to face the computer on his desk return, signs in, turns back to face me. "Joey will give ya a hand. Ah, the keys!" He pulls out a drawer, jingles around, picks out two keys on a ring with an address tag.

I sign them out in his ledger and return him the keys to Ashley's. He looks at the tag, signs them in. He looks over to the coffee machine.

"What happened at Ashley's?"

"Man, where've ya been? It's all over the news."

Two plump fingers twisting mustache, he gapes at me. He rolls his beady eyes and says in a flat voice, "Michael Norton died there Saturday night at her opening."

Where've I been?

I was replacing the missing shingles up on my roof. That done, I did the same for my shed. Then I stripped and re-caulked my windows. Then I put in new weather stripping on my door. I looked up from my chores and Saturday had slipped by.

On Sunday, I split firewood. Swung my maul, drove it into the log. One swift blow, a sharp thud. Strike after strike, log after log, I heard only the sound of wood cracking. Pulsing heat ran through my body. I paused, wiped the sweat off my brow.

A loud caw came from some flapping wings riffling over the treetops. Two squirrels chasing down a tree. A stunning blue sky above, a strand of white cloud.

A wisp of her honey blond hair.

I turned quickly to the stack of logs in my shed. Firewood that came free from cutting down neighbors' diseased trees this side of the mountain. Picking up another log, I set it on the splitting stump, letting go my wandering thoughts to the breeze.

I throw the thin roll of blueprints onto the passenger seat and start the engine. I fidget with the tuner knob of my radio that has a bad antenna. It pops off, drops to the floorboard. The static grinds on. I turn off the grating noise.

A running shade of white speeds past—a Light Rail crossing Speer! I slam on my brake. LoDo's not more than a couple of miles away but it seems to be taking forever.

A Mile High truck is parked across from the house. I pull into the alley. No white beetle in its spot. I tear down the steps. The door's locked. I press my ear to the door, hearing my own ragged breathing. I scurry out the alley, round the corner to the front.

"Closed" says the sign behind the glass doors. I look in. Her starlit River Indigo looms, center of the gallery, running its nowhere course. Cobalt blue it is, as drowsy as my torpid dreams.

What has she done to her hanging cloth since I last saw it? From the grid ceiling, she has directed halogen spotlights onto her piece of dyed art and pulsated it with fan-driven motion. Shades of blue undulate in cascading ripples, starlight glimmering, melting into day.

As I turn to leave, I'm caught by a red glint quivering at the back of the gallery. It hovers in the dim light. It shudders forward, seeping through the blue cloth, diffusing into a bright red haze.

I press my face hard against the glass, blowing steam. I wipe the glass with my sleeve, peering in. No, it's not the sun's glare on the shop glass! Nor a spark thrown off from a sunlit windshield rolling past. The glow is radiating from a shadowy figure ... a silhouette of a young girl ... her slender form draped in red, full skirt falling from a slim waist, gliding, swaying like a willow branch caught in a breeze ... now holding her head up to River Indigo ... now crossing her arms to clutch her elbows ... now turning her back to Indigo ... her hair in sweeping curls cascading down her back.

She shivers, as if she has just stumbled in from nowhere and is stunned to find herself in a strange place.

"Hiya, Ben!" Someone yells from across the street.

I hold still, staring hard.

Your face, let me see your face!

"Ben!"

"What's it, Ben? What ya up to?"

He comes up from behind, looks in where I look.

I strain for a glimpse of her face through the fogged-up glass, rubbing it again and again with my sleeve. She holds still ... Just then, as if someone has lit a match to the celluloid film I'm watching, my red aura singes in smoke! I bang my head against the glass.

Oh, blast!

M-miss ... don't go!

"Ben, hey, what's with ya? What ya lookin at?"

I look up.

River Indigo flowing still, but the starlight has faded. The morning sun has slunk into the gallery.

I spin around. Rico skulking at my elbow, squinting into the shop window.

"Did you see?" I cry.

"See what?"

You blew it! Yo-ou bloody hell lit the damn match!

"Get lost, will ya?" I snap.

"Ya're nuts, man. Ya know?" He turns to strut across the street, throwing up his hands, "NUTS! J-u-s-t nuts!"

A new hire from Mile High steps out of a row house across the street. He is gawking my way.

"Hey, what's up, Rico?" he shouts.

I step away from the glass. My reflection snarls back—fireball eyes, hair on end, nostrils flaring, mouth pulled into a growl.

No-ot … n-not my face! I stumble backward, breathing fire.

A news van with satellite equipment on top pulls up the curb. Like a spinning top that has hit a snag, I totter, near losing my balance. Someone with a camera gets out of the van, slams shut the door. "I'm gonna get a shot of the front, then pan down the street," he says to the driver. "Take her around the block, will ya?"

Sound of the van pulling into traffic. I eye the guy standing by the curb. He points his camera up at the 'Studio Indigo' sign, lowers it to study the various angles of shot at the glass front.

I trudge back into the alley, tail between my legs.

The girl in red, who is she?

The redness that has been steeping and brewing in my head since the night of Hank's passing is all about her then. Now, this vision of her in red … ethereal, unearthly. How could such dread come from the sighting of one so delicate? She, no more than a lost soul caught up in a time warp.

The fleeting red burst in Hank's dead eyes—did he catch sight of her when he took his last breath?

How could this be? He was struck down by a fury. An absolute fury that gnashed and gnawed, that had leapt up from an old wound past healing.

But, she's so very young, a wisp of a girl.

I break into a cold sweat. Plunking down on a step of the landing, I crouch over to bury my face in my hands. Something nudges against my haunch as I sit. I slip my hand into my back pocket. Snug inside are my surreptitious key to the back door and the handful of prayer beads—those tumbling, rolling beads which came to light one dust-filled morning. I keep them with me always. I fish them out each time before I throw my jeans into the washer. I would make a fist over the key, roll the beads in my palm, feel their roundness, their smooth sheen. Then I put them all back into my laundered jeans. A queer comfort they give me, key and all.

"Have you seen Ashley?"

A girl is standing astride her bike up the alley. The one who worked with Ashley to put up River Indigo the other day.

"No," I say, getting up on my feet.

"Door locked?" Her eyes shift from me to the door, then dart away just as quickly.

"Yes."

She is about to push on, but she stops. Getting off her bike, she leans it against the railing. A backpack nests in the handlebar basket. White letters on her maroon sweatshirt: Metro State.

"I've seen you around."

"I'm Ben."

"I'm Kara, Ashley's student assistant," she says. "Looks like she won't be coming in today." She fidgets, her eyes shying away from the door. "I heard that a workman died in there, b-before Michael Norton. You know about that?"

"Yes."

"How did he die?"

"Heart attack."

"When?"

"Three weeks ago."

"U-um."

She looks wary. She takes off her helmet, shakes her crop of short brown hair. A hint of a dimple on her chin, but there are bags under her eyes.

"I'll be working in there, twenty hours a week. It's, uh, just a bit unnerving. Two deaths in such a short time." She throws her head back and sighs, "Uh-uh, first time I ever saw a dead body."

"You found Michael Norton?"

She nods. "Ash-ley and I," she says haltingly. "We were about to leave. Ashley said she'd run down the basement to make sure that the back door's locked. She was gone a while. Then I heard a choking sound, like 'ugh, ugh.' I ran down. There she was, slumped against the wall, shaking like a leaf. At her feet was Michael Norton, all curled up like, uh, like a fetus."

"Ashley cried: Ca-call 911, send for the ambulance."

"His face, you saw his face?"

"N-no." She shakes her head. "He, he had one arm over his head, and a hand tugging at his shirt front. Like so ..." She clasps at her own chest.

"Come, sit down."

I step aside for her. She sits bolted upright. Her eyes shut tight.

"Take a deep breath, Kara. Breathe out slowly. E-easy."

"Why just the two of you, Kara?" I ask as soon as she opens her eyes.

"We were, uh, looking around, taking a breather after the party, picking up after the caterer's left. The place was empty, so quiet you could hear the fan motor humming over River Indigo. It was dark out, we were like, uh, moving about on a lit stage. Then we turned off the lights except River Indigo's, sat in a corner, sipped champagne, and waited."

She slumps down, resting her head against the retaining wall.

E-easy now.

"Waited?"

"We were waiting for Jed to come back for her. He had taken Mrs. Norton home. He told Ashley that Kate Norton had said that she saw Michael leave the party with someone else."

"Hmm."

"After midnight, Ashley was still trying to reach Jed. Phone was dead, battery low or something. So I offered her a ride home. Then, uh, then this ..."

Kara inhales deeply, blows it out slowly. She wants to talk.
"As we were waiting Ashley asked if I'd seen whom Michael
was with. I said no. She said she didn't either. But she went on to
say that it was strange because each time she looked, he was
standing by himself. Just not Michael, she said. Jed had told her
that Kate was miffed because Michael was hovering over a young
girl the whole time. Only Kate saw them together. Said the girl
wore red. Hard to miss, don't you think? Likely story, Ashley
said. Then, she was quiet. Very quiet."
I squirm. A little spark pricks at my scalp sending chill down
my spine.

Footsteps thumping up the stairs. Joey peeks through the
banisters, calling out, "Dere ya're. Been lookin for ya."
A small echo bounces off the bowed walls stained with water
marks. Even with the small front window open, a stench hangs in
the air, dank and foul. Dead rat or bird or some critter up the
rafter, I figure. Strewn about, a broom head without a stick handle,
crushed soda cans, McDonald wrappers. I try to keep my mind on
the job. The floor board creaks.
"Ya okay?" He steps up, steals a look at me.
"Why, Joey?"
"Nodin."
I look up. A full moon of a brownish stain stares down the
sagging plaster ceiling into an empty plastic pail. At one cobweb-
laced corner, a crack runs down the ceiling.
"I was across da street. Rico and Wes over dere say ya not
lookin so good dis mornin." Sheepish eyes peeping up at me.
"Dat house next door, u-uh ..."
"Yes?"
"I ain't gonna go in dere no more." He lowers his voice to a
whisper. "It's spooked. First, Hank, now, Mr. Norton. And dis
mornin Wes a tellin us old news about another Mr. Norton before
dis one died in dere way back. Grandafarder Norton. Now,

grandason. Died in same house not their own over so many years. Weird, won't ya say?"

Cla-atter!

The tape measure I'm pulling out springs back fast and hard, hitting my hand. Joey jumps up, bumping against the wall I was about to measure.

Are you done, Joey? Same tickling, choking lump swells up my throat as when I turned on Rico earlier.

What has gotten into me? I shoot down the stairs, Joey at my heels.

"Ya gotta be careful, Ben."

What da ya know, Joey?

"Ahem! Toby wanna me give ya a hand wit dis place. What ya wanna me do, Ben?"

Go away Joey, just scram!

Joey stays, keeps his mouth shut, eyeing me. He tags three steps behind. I look around the space, an empty shell dimly lit with dirt encrusted fluorescent tubes, peeling paint on dingy walls, worn floor littered with debris, rickety stairs.

I unroll the plans, tack them onto the wall facing the front window framed with metal security bars. Shadowed grids cast down the floor beneath the window. Enough reflected light for me to study the drawings: Joaquin Fine Jewelry Design on the top floor with built-in cabinetry along the walls, Polk Fine Arts Gallery on street level, a custom frame shop in the basement.

This job keeps me close by.

Joey comes up from behind, shoots me a quick glance. I look at my watch.

"Let's start with propping up the stairs, both flights. You ready?" I say.

He grins, as if I have just given him something to make a toothache go away.

"Gotta ya some studs and the saw down the basement."

Joey's an old hand, and a pal.

Early afternoon, stairs propped, we start tearing down the top floor. I locate where the studs are, then whack at the wall with a sledgehammer. Plasters crack and crumble. I pull off the loose pieces. Joey shovels, dumps the rubbles into a big trash bin. One load filled, he hoists it upon his back and hobbles downstairs. Back up for another load, hauls it out.

Dust shrouds the air. Fuzzy behind goggles, mum behind dust mask, the hours wear on.

Grandafarder, grandason. Die in same house ... Grandafarder, grandason ... die ... die in ... same house ... house... Joey's voice croaking in my head like a frog on a sweltering summer night.

My goggles fog up, sweat biting my eyes. I pull my dust mask off. Sneezing, puffing dust.

Joey, too, shines with sweat.

"We needa air," he says.

Out in the alley, he says to me, "Somedin more." He looks down, eyes blinking off sweat that streaks down his brow. He wipes with his sleeve, smearing his face. "Wes, he says da grandafarder Norton died in dat basement too. His broder a police officer, he hears it at da station."

He looks up at me and mouths his words slowly, raising three fingers. "Dat make three, ya know. Down in dat basement. Give ya da creeps, don't it?"

At four sharp, I get out into an alley steeped in golden light. A patrol cruiser exits the alley dragging its shadow.

No white beetle.

My pickup was parked smack against the wall since morning. Toss my cap and clipboard onto the passenger seat, I pull my sweatshirt off inside out, wipe my face and arms with it, then slap the dust and dirt off my T-shirt, my jeans. I put on a clean sweatshirt dug out from the duffle on the cab floor. I'm about to walk out.

"What about lockin up? I ain't gotta key." Joey calls out. He is standing by the dumpster with his last load.

I turn back, hand him the key.

"What's wit ya, Ben?"

"I'm alright." I turn away from his frown. "Thanks, Joey, for helping out."

His eyes are on my back as I head out the alley. Something hits me. I stop short, spin around, and dash back into the basement.

"Forgot somedin?" Joey yells, scampering after me.

"What ya doin?"

Inside the basement, I pace the dirt-filled concrete floor. No sign of brickwork, not under the stairs, not anywhere. But then there is no sign of an enclosed storage space under the stairs. Either somebody did a good pour job at the time the place was refitted for warehousing, or there never was any flat brickwork laid when the house was first built.

"What ya lookin at?"

He drops the trash bin, his eyes scanning the floor after me.

"Nah, nothing. See you tomorrow."

I walk past him, hop up the alley and head out.

8

On Market, three white-haired ladies in pantsuits and walking shoes huddle in front of the house, heads bobbing in hot chitchat. One looks up, shading her eyes from *Studio Indigo*'s coppery shine, the other two peering into the glass front. Just a bevy of magpies, long tail feathers twitching, chattering over thrown peanuts. A couple of passing cars slow to a crawl, heads turn to gawk.

No white beetle parked in front either.

Heading west towards Speer, I walk in the late afternoon sun. Its path angles a long wedge of shadow onto the side of a staid old building. Above it, a tangerine glow tinges the ocher brick facade a burnt sienna, highlighting the gray concrete lintels, casting sheen onto the window panes. I squint towards the street's end. There, a low-hung sun flushes the sky a brilliant crimson, threading gold through strands of purple clouds. There, the Front Range lie silhouetted against the day's torching flame. There, nesting in a valley, one little cabin awaits me.

Gonna be a long night.

Turning into 14th, I pass by the LoDo Tower site. A loaded dump truck rumbles round the corner onto Speer. Another is making its way out the gate, kicking up a dust cloud. Mack sticks his head out of the Mile High trailer stationed by the curb, grunts into a bull horn, "Chopper, told ya to hose it down!"

A redhead at the guard post rushes over to turn on the hose, spraying into the dust cloud. "Yo, watch it, kid, ya ain't gonna give me no shower!" yells one hard hat. Chopper cackles like a chased chicken, flapping about to dodge the wind-tossed sprinkle.

"Wet em ground before em trucks drive off, not after. Kiddo, when ya gonna learn?" Someone hollers as he's climbing into a truck. Others chortle, a safe distance away from the shower.

I walk up the chain link fence and look down at the gaping hole that has been opened up, shored up. Two hydraulic excavators sit idle after a day of clawing and gouging. On the staging strip, Simm's crew is packing up, hard hats mottled with dirt tucked underarm, strapped to the waist.

A van pulls up. "Get goin, Tuck." Tuck is rinsing his sweat towel under Chopper's hose. Chopper waves to the guys in the van, chuckling away.

Call it a day. Tomorrow will come. There will be more digging, more shoring. More tomorrows. Piles going in, foundation wall going up, a tower will rise.

No more tomorrows for Michael Norton, though.

I see his soaring vision on the big sign board posted high at the site entrance—an artist's rendition of a sleek curved glass tower, capped with a pitched solar roof. By elevating his glossy tower over LoDo's historic buildings, he gives a spangled feel to a revitalized community of art galleries, trendy shops and restaurants. A foothold on the fringe of downtown, it is a stone's throw from Coors Field and all that is happening in town.

Will his dream come true now that the man's gone?

"Gotta take it one day at a time, right?" A voice booms from behind.

"Hi, Mack."

He, too, is looking up at the sign board tower.

"See me up there. See, that yellow dot of a hard hat, up there in the penthouse?" he quips, lips pursed in a smirk, finger pointing to his fantasy.

"Uh?"

"Heck, no, Norton Development's not gonna pull out!" He turns to walk back into the trailer.

Ripe rays and lazy long shadows, Larimer Square is sedate with a late afternoon ease. I pick up a deli sandwich, a cup of tea

from The Market and sit at a sidewalk table with a leftover
newspaper.

"Da-arling, shan't we, hmm …?" he mumbles, unfolding the
map insert from a guide book.

"They call this tee-a?" she says after a sip. "Darjeeling, so-o it
sa-ays," she reads from the teabag label.

"Hmm, try the scone, da-arling," says the mumbling voice.

I turn my back to the young couple from another shore. At the
table across, someone glues his eyes on his laptop screen, taking
slow gulps from a tall cup.

I scan the paper. Michael's death is a recapped news item,
bottom of page one in today's paper. Michael Norton III, age 36,
civic leader, real estate developer, scion of an old Denver family of
railroad and mining fortunes, passed away last Saturday evening
during an opening reception at an artist's gallery and studio in
LoDo. The cause of death is as yet undetermined but thought to be
of natural causes.

A sad coincidence for the Norton family is that Michael
Norton Sr., grandfather to the deceased, passed away at the same
location on October 24, 1895, at age 35. The Market Street
address was then the famed establishment of a renown madam.
Norton Sr., a prominent business man, was a vocal advocate in
purging Denver of its red-light reputation. He was expected to be
appointed U.S. Senator at the time of his death. Record showed
that he had died of a stroke and cerebral hemorrhaging.

The girl in red, was she there, too, when grandfather Norton
died? Her red gown, could it be a period costume? Was she a
madam's girl?

Page three reports Michael's dedicated efforts in city planning,
urban renewal, and preservation of historic districts. It cites some
of Norton Development's vast holdings of property in the city and
elsewhere in and out of state. The company was started by his
father, Michael II, a consummate and reclusive tycoon.

It was widely speculated that Michael III would run for mayor
in the coming year's election. He had often spoken about his
vision for Denver. In this respect, he was more like his
grandfather in his civic endeavor and political ambition than his

father who was a singularly dedicated entrepreneur. He is survived by his wife, Katherine, and his mother, Mrs. Evelyn Norton.

Two deaths in the same family, hundred some years apart, in the same house.

I pick up to leave.

At this hour, Speer is thick with traffic both ways. I cross at a traffic light to the median where the Cherry Creek separates the north and south bound lanes. A cyclist with a courier satchel zips past me, bearing down a ramp onto the paved trail that runs along the creek. I saunter down after him and stroll in the bronze light by the sleepy creek. Dammed and embanked into an urban stream, it crawls through town without color, without pulse. Climbing vines straggling a burnt russet cling onto the embankment wall like ripped curtains.

Ahead, an elderly man walks his little poodle. The thump of my work boots startles them. Man and dog stand still, eyeing me. A honk and a tire screech from the traffic above jolt us all. I turn back. A little yipping starts up at my back. "Hush, Fluff. It's alright."

Up on Speer, I retrace my way toward I-25. Traffic rushes past. I walk on. Up the flyover, I stop and look down at the rail tracks crisscrossing below. Boxy condos stack up alongside all the way to the Commons Park.

The roar of the traffic on I-25 drumming the air. Closing my eyes, I try to picture the rolling valley it once was—fescue and yucca, bunchgrass and sagebrush, sparse cottonwoods canopied over pitched tents by the South Platte. Headwaters stream-fed on snowmelt, that sparkling river winding down the Divide's eastern slope. Over range and plain, it courses through town to this day with a murky thirst.

What fills the eye in the valley today is the immense Pepsi Center with its pie-top roof, the Sports Authority Field with its curvilinear top. Then, there are those hoops and loops punching the sky, the Elitch's spiraling, twisting roller coasters, and that needle tower with plunging cabs. Past season now, all stands still, empty of thrills and squeals.

I hang around awhile to catch the fiery moment when the last light burns its way behind the blue mountains. The range darkens in a hurry as if a pall has been dropped. Down here, the soft glow of twilight lingers. I get off the flyover and head towards the Confluence Park.

Dusk falls. The park is empty. A breeze kicks up, dropped leaves rustling under the light cone of a pole lamp. I sit down on a cold bench, tuck my hands under my arms and look at the tumbling waters below.

I walk briskly down the ramp to the river's edge. I loiter at the confluence point where the Cherry Creek spills into the South Platte. A stretch indeed from yesteryears' prairie to today's recreational landscape known for city kayaking, kids' splashing.

My footsteps rouse the resting ducks on a pebbled wedge of the river bank. They waddle away with a flap of wings. Some take to water with little trailing ripples. The South Platte flows along the constructed banks, churning short splashy rapids on a rock-studded ledge, spitting froth under a hunter's moon. I stand and gaze into that gushy stretch of the river, whiling time, feeling the pull in my heart to where my night will lead me.

A strong pull, indeed, from one so frail.

But I'm the one pushing, I tell myself. Like water over boulder, the fear that had sprung up on me this morning has been washed cleanly out of mind. What stirs inside me now is a longing for another glimpse of her.

Who is she, that willowy girl that comes in a red haze?

She who has come across space and time. Back from the beyond, she has come. Damn it to hell, she has come! What has she come for? Why hadn't she slipped into oblivion when she gave up the ghost?

I cross over the pedestrian bridge to the REI grounds dotted with landscape lights and moss rocks. Thick evergreens, lean aspens cluster together. Needled branches, stripped branches quiver. I, too, quiver. An errant breeze has wafted over my heart.

The historic red brick building looms over a platform by the water. I step down, lift my eyes to the bejeweled city that rises up by the water's edge. Overhead, the Hunter's Moon. Big and pale. The autumn chill starts to bite. I inhale deeply, filling my lungs with the tinkling air to brace myself for the night.

Time to go.

Along the dimly lit street, Studio Indigo is a lone bead of light. The glass door is being held open by a man in a chauffeur's uniform. I walk alongside the empty buildings, turn into the cross street. There at the corner, I keep watch.

A silver-haired lady in a black suit staggers out of the door, her head bowed, a hand raised over her eyes. Jed Roen stands by her side, nodding attentively, ushering her to the waiting limousine. Behind them, a leggy woman, tall in spiky high heels, sashays down the entrance step. Under the streetlamp, her glossy black suit has a wet look as if it has been doused in a downpour. She fusses over her fur stole draped over one shoulder.

Ashley follows them out, a plain dark figure but for her shiny blond hair. It occurs to me that, on this night, the bereaved mother and widow have come to see where Michael fell, to chew the cud of their sorrow. And Ashley has dutifully relived for them the frightful scene of that night.

The chauffeur hastens to open the limo door. While the party of three is getting in, Ashley turns to step back into the studio. The bright light inside goes off. She reappears at the door as the limo is pulling away. She stands motionless on the sidewalk.

A part of me has already rushed to her side, but another is holding me back. Too long I ponder. She walks stiffly to her white beetle, her crumbled shadow under her feet. The motor starts. She drives off into the night.

I walk hastily into the alley where I had left my pickup since morning. Her back door light is on. I step down onto the landing, take out my surreptitious key and let myself in.

The night basement is a gloomy place. A dusky beam slips down the stairs casting faint slats of light onto the floor. River Indigo's halogen spotlights have a long reach. I flip on the light switch by the door. A day-glow fluorescence floods the shut-in space wall to wall. I look over the floor. No chalk-line figure. Kara had not mentioned where Michael Norton fell. But my eyes are drawn to a spot below the brick-in window now covered by a big square of her fabric art.

I switch off the jarring light. The far corners of the room drop off into a pithy blackness. The small space is suddenly boundless, and unsettling. I grope my way from the foot of the stairs to stand over the suspect spot. I shut my eyes to try to see, but a fog has crept into my head. I sense not a thing.

But this much I know—three lives had ended in this basement, swept into oblivion. Three that I know of. Then, there is this girl in a daze, the girl in red. She who has come out of darkness.

I open my eyes, scramble up the stairs. Like a gypsy moth, I go for the flame. Not minding the little stars over River Indigo until I spot my shadow slinking along the gallery wall. I drop down, chest flat on the floor, and scoot back to retreat behind the curved stair-wall. There I am hidden from passing eyes on the shadowy street. There I crouch, my eyes fixed on the spot where she had come through this morning. I hold still, listening out for any stirring. Any stirring at all.

Not a ripple in the air but Ashley's little theater of running blue ripples and twinkling starlight. In the night, the fan motor purrs like a loud kitten.

Are you here, miss?

Not a flutter in my heartbeat.

Her silhouette smothering against a red haze, her fleeting presence already burnished on my mind, I hold my breath and wait.

Who are you, miss?

Silence.

I lie there for a long while, replaying in my mind every turn, every sway of her svelte form. Her red gown shrouds her in a mist. She glides along, now raising her head, now bowing. A stray lock of hair brushing against her hidden face.

Why have you come, miss?

A pair of headlights on the street glides into the gallery, up the wall, scrolls over the ceiling and slips back out. I slide back downstairs, sit bolted upright on the bottom step, and cock my ears. My eyes sweeping over the cold floor.

Hank's wasted face hangs over me. So is the untold story in his clenched fists. His uncanny death, and the two Michaels', lay before me like pieces of a jigsaw puzzle.

Outside, a rumpus of shrieking and thumping on the dumpster lid.

Damn alley cats!

The night wears on. Sitting in the dark, what meets the eye melts into gray smudges—the fabric pieces that line the brick wall along the stairs, the big square piece that drapes the back wall over the brick-in area.

So I wait, swathed in this gray hangover with no break.

I get up, stretch, walk over to the center of the room where Ashley's work tables will stand. I picture her working. Down here, by herself. I begin to fidget.

Pacing the floor, I hope yet to get a feel for the girl in red. I draw a blank.

She, the missing jigsaw piece?

My eyelids grow heavy, my hands clammy. A dankness has seeped into the air, and with it, a whiff of mustiness. The place is suddenly bleak. And I, totally down.

Call it a night now.

Peace. Peace be with you, miss.

9

"**I**'m Ruud," he says, giving me his hand. Sign on his truck: Ruud Restaurant Supply, Colorado. The elderly boss drives his own truck to deliver two work tables.

"Short-handed," he says.

He stares at the brick-in window on the back wall, then turns to look down the alley.

"I grew up north of here, 27ᵗʰ and Larimer. Way back," he mutters. "Lotsa changes in these parts over the years. Skid row turned warehousing district, hmm, and now LoDo."

"Let me give you a hand."

I'm keen to look at the work tables that Ashley had asked me to put up. We unload the two cartons from his truck, carry them into the basement, one carton at a time. Humped with years, Ruud is still a tall husky man with lifting power and a knack in negotiating corners. We lay the cartons against the side wall.

"Thanks," he says. He takes off his work gloves and wool cap and stuffs them into the pockets of his denim jacket. His bald head shines under the fluorescent lamps.

"So, this here's where it happened, eh? Where the two Nortons passed on?" He walks around, trudges up the stairs to have a quick look into the gallery. "Done up nice, this place." He turns around, walks back down. "Hmm, the whole neighborhood done up nice ever since Coors Field went up."

I bend down to cut open a carton, rustling to get the packing material off.

From his shirt pocket he pulls out a receipt for me to sign. He looks around, seemingly lost in thoughts.

"Something, uh, about this house …"

He walks to the back wall, lifts up a corner of Ashley's fabric hanging to reveal the brick-in area hidden behind.

"I'd peeked in once from the outside, through a window that was here. I was a kid then," he says, turning back to face me.

I sign and hand him the receipt. He tears off a copy for me, folds his, slips it into his pocket. He has a pensive look in his eyes. A ruddy color has come over his lined face. He turns his back to the door.

"There was this chanting I'd heard coming out the street front of the house on my way to school every morning." He pauses, listening up to the past. "Throaty sound, murmuring like. My old man told me that it was a Japanese Buddhist temple. Kids I hung around with used to leap up the ground to try to catch a look through the window. It was way too high and they saw nothing. What a racket they made!"

"But what did you see?"

"When I peeked in the back window? That afternoon, I cut through the alley walking home from school by myself. The other kids went down the rail tracks." He turns to gaze at the back wall. "Golly, I heard this knocking sound *bok-bok-bok,* and this chanting voice that flowed like tap water gurgling. It came out of this window here." He points to the brick-in wall. "One clear voice, not a bunch of voices like in the mornings. I ran down the steps and peeped in. I saw this Asian man with a shaved head, bushy dark eyebrows chanting in front of the window. The sun was on his face and he had his eyes closed, his mouth shaping monotones like *ami… uh-uh, amita uh…tabha, uh… amitabha … amitabha …* That's it!"

Eyes gleaming, Ruud is rapt with what he has to say.

"His hands were raised at chest level, in one he held a stick with a round knob. As he went on chanting, he hit the knob against a lump of wood he held in his other hand: *bok-bok-bok …*"

Ruud brings his hands up to show me what he saw. "That lump of wood was painted a bright red, a slit carved in the middle like a mouth from ear to ear, like a fish's gaping mouth when it's out of the water. He was beating rhythm on a wooden fish head!"

"The old man bowed low to the sky, then moved away from the window. He started to walk, slowly, round and round in a circle in the empty room. *Bok-bok-bok*, chanting away, keeping his eyes shut the whole time. The mid-afternoon sun had cut a swath of light in the dim basement, bright as a mirror. So he walked, into the light mirror, out of the light mirror, in his loose black robe, black cloth slippers, light and dark and light and dark. A long strand of shiny beads hung around his neck."

Ruud stares at the floor, retracing the old man's meditated steps etched in light and shadow still sharp on his mind. He is lost to the beating rhythm and chanting that echo from the past like a haunting refrain.

"The next day I passed by the house, there was a padlock on the front door," he says after a long pause.

He tells it as if it had come to pass just yesterday. I look at him, an old man nostalgic for the moment he had stumbled upon as a child. He sighs deeply. It's as if in telling what had captivated him for so long he has finally relieved himself of a charge.

Now, he has passed the scene to me. He has brought me a link to the past of this house as if he knows that I've been looking for it.

"What was the floor like back then?"

"A dark sheet of gold," he says dreamily.

"Wood, wide plank," he corrects himself after a bit.

So, a Buddhist monk had left behind his prayer robe, a wooden fish, and a strand of prayer beads before he moved away. Left them under lock and seal. Something behind the pint-sized door he wanted to bar from the light of day? Wanted to safeguard?

What for?

So, that crumbled worm-infested rag was the prayer robe I'd unwittingly tossed out for good. Then, there's that tattered page of faded Asian writing I'd picked up. What words were those when they were legible words?

I'm not one for religious faith, and much too skeptical to believe in anything other than what I know to be factual. Yet, I know what I know and that makes me uneasy. I have come to realize that there are far reaches of one's consciousness that at times intrude, that strain comprehension.

From this day on, when I put my hand on that scrap of worn wood I've kept, I will hear the wood fish calling out the beat: *Bok-bok-bok.* When I touch the dull beads, I will see that they had once shone with prayer. Now, more than ever, I want to reach out, across time and space, for that other-worldly existence that has meaning beyond my grasp. I want a feel of that reality.

Inside my jeans pocket are the few loose beads I hold for safekeeping. Intuitively, I turn to look at the patch of old bricks under the stairs where I'd found them.

Tired beads, tired bricks.

What's that?

I hold my breath as I try to catch a wisp of a stirring. A scent, perhaps.

I draw a blank.

"An historical footnote," Ashley had called that patch of flat brickwork the day she came by to look at it. "Just like the old brick wall."

So, this patch of bricks is here to stay.

What, then, to make of this tenor of a haunting agony that had exploded and simmered in the basement the night of Hank's passing? It has gotten under my skin. And I know not what is to come.

For she has risen, the girl in red.

And Ashley has moved into her *Studio Indigo* ...

So, I know that my job is not done even as I lay down my leveler. I look at the two work tables I've just put up. They stand side by side in the middle of the room, Ashley's work island, the satin finish of the stainless steel top gleaming quietly.

Something else's eating me up. It's this sense of defeat. It's as if I'm seeing Ellie fall, all over again. See her fall before it had even happened when it was already too late!

Any reprieve for me?

Ever?

I turn to look out the open door. Still listening up for her white beetle to pull into the alley.

I walk up to the big square piece of fabric that is hanging over the brick-in window. The blotchy black and gray that I saw in the night is seen in daylight as a grainy asphalt road surface etched with two sets of tire treads crossing each other. One is deep grooved, a heavy truck tire rendered in tar black; the other, in dusty gray, a skid mark of a smaller, worn tread. In the path of the truck tire, a rusty big nail lies in wait, sharp end angling up.

Black and gray, spiked with rust, it is clearly a study of threat, of imminent danger.

What had driven the artist to see impending danger? When did she work on the piece?

I walk out into a pale noonday beset by a dark feeling about the deaths that had come to pass in this house. At least, the ones I know of.

Ruud's voice reverberates, "Before it was a Buddhist temple, everyone knew it to be the fanciest parlor west of Mississippi ... "

Surely, Ashley must know.

"Ya done next door?" Joey asks. "Wanna eat?"

We sit out on the steps down the landing outside. I stare at the empty spot where the white beetle used to sit. Joey fidgets, chomps on his sandwich. He takes a big gulp of his soda with his mouth full.

"What's it, Joey?"

"Ben, next door, hmm, it's jinxed."

"Huh?"

"Wes told us dis mornin he heard Mr. Norton died on account of blood vessels burst in his brain. Knocked him cold on the spot. What's more, he heard from his broder who works at the police station dat da grandafarder went da same way, a hundred-plus years ago. Wes heard dat and told us."

"Chance a dat happenin to two guys in da same family to die in da same house not yar own? Kinda spooky, won't ya say?"

He turns to me and says, "Gotta tell ya, Rico says ya looked shit the other day when he found ya in front of dat house. Sure glad ya done workin in dere."

"Uh-huh."

Joey noisily crushing his soda can, drops it into his lunch tote.

"Ya worry about her in dere alone? The lady boss," he asks, eyeing me.

"Got to get back." I stand up to leave.

Dusk deepens into night. And the night stretches on, growing murkier by the hour. Only the alley cats' shrieking breaks the lull. I sit, all keyed up, on the bottom stair. Keeping watch, feeling the damp chill sapping my energy.

Yet, I listen out for her, the girl in red.

I get up, and start pacing the floor in the circle of prayer that Ruud had put into my head. I walk around the work tables which I had set up in the middle of the circle, an island of calm cool shine. No word of prayer or lilt of chant comes to me.

Still, I should like to think of Ashley working on this island of prayer.

I point my flashlight to the back of the room. On the wall shelves above the washer and dryer and the sink counter are rows of gallon-sized wide mouth jars with lids. In them, scraps of tire treads, rubber soles, seashells galore, coral fragments, sea sponges, bottle caps, clumps of coconut husk, bristle brushes for artwork, for wood painting, jute ropes of all lengths and thicknesses, twisted wires, rusted screws and nails of all shapes and sizes, bone fragments, wood chips, jagged stones, pea pebbles, tubes of iron filings, and all other imaginable castaways or collectibles. A curious cache indeed!

Then, there are bottles and tin cans with labels that read: Cochineal, madder root, indigo, marigold, saffron, birch bark, mint, rosemary, acorn. I gather that these are the mediums for her natural dyes.

All these, her whatnots, give clues to her work. I want to see more. More of her art. More of the artist.

As I climb the stairs, I train my flashlight onto the old brick wall where she had lined up pairs of fabric hangings in successive eye level elevations. In each pair, one is a mirror image of the other. One is in sundrenched colors with a background of muted earth tones. The other, in black and white. Twosomes of little amphibians in each pair of wall hangings: Warty cinnamon brown toads all puffed up, leaping frogs in moss green with black stripes, cavorting salamanders with bright yellow polka dots, dazzling orange lizards flicking their long tails, neon green snakes slithering about, forked tongues licking air.

Mating couples, I supposed. The fabric is crinkly, nubby, crimped, and coarse textured to imitate Nature's hand.

I turn to the mirror images. Flimsy silk pieces, shades of black and white. They look like photographic negatives of what has been executed in color. Either black silk bleached white, or white silk dyed black, the monochromic effect is striking. Here, the little cold blooded creatures take on ghostly forms in shades of gray. Pallid against a dark background, these creatures look like they have their daylight drained out of them and are now suspended in a shadowy zone.

I'm caught off guard by her artistic vision. I find it captivating as it is disquieting.

Up in the gallery, I scurry past the spiral stairs to head for the rear wall. There the starlight over River Indigo dissolves into a twilight gloom. I stand behind the curved stair-wall where I cast no shadow, where I pause to look around.

What I see nearly takes my breath away. Looming over me on the back wall is a host of huge hydrangea blooms, clusters of petals luxuriating in shades of soft blue. Full summer splendor rendered in shimmering silk, a show of Nature's opulence, at once tender and bold. The specter is downright surreal, the effect intoxicating.

I take it in, take it all in ... I'm that toad sitting at the bottom of a well pining for the sky.

She had once remarked to me, "Ben, I see that you like working with your hands. I do too." She smiled, summoning up sunny skies. I had no idea then what her hands can do.

I've forgotten myself. I dash up the spiral stairs to the second floor balcony and slip into her office. With my pocket flashlight I scan the framed photographs on the wall in the small sitting area. There is Ashley beaming, her hair close cropped like a boy's, standing next to an elderly Japanese man in kimono. There is Ashley sitting by a low table holding up a piece of blue and white cloth in a checkered design. I gather that it is the same piece of cloth that is framed below the photograph. The inscription reads: Block printing, tenugui, Tanaka Workshop, Kyoto, March 2002.

I stare at the staid square pattern of that block print. It is as far removed from the exuberance of the hydrangeas as can be. The hand that had exercised restraint and geometric precision now celebrates with freeform and revels in being outright sensual.

More, more of Ashley ...

Next to the block print is a framed piece of brown-and-white cloth of many a stylized rocking horse running in diagonal lines. The inscription reads: Wax resist dyeing: *Kuda Lumping*, batik in tree bark brown, Denpasar, Indonesia, June 2002. Above it, a photograph of Ashley sitting on the ground under a huge shade tree, working on a piece of cloth that was draped on a wood frame.

There are other photographs on the wall, some with signatures: Ashley and somebody draping a skinny girl in billows of indigo sheer; Ashley and somebody looking at fabric samples; Ashley standing at a store front to watch the hanging of a sign that says *Studio SOHO*; Ashley wearing shoulder-length hair, looking stunning at a function.

On her desk, there is just one small faded photograph in a tarnished silver frame. It is that of a young girl in baggy overalls standing by a thick-limbed draft horse. She is no taller than its muzzle. She has one hand reaching up to touch the horse's mane, the other holding a brush. On her face is the sunny smile I have come to know.

You sno-oop!   A hollow voice booms.   An echo out of nowhere.

I near keel over as if knocked down in one fell swoop by an unseen hand.

It's just me ... buckling under with shame.

Whoa, I've turned my night watch into a night prowl!

I dash for the stairs.   Scrambling down, I've a distinct sensation that keen eyes are watching. Stealthy eyes. I stop short, turn around.

On the old brick wall, there is not another shadow but my furtive own. Cold sweat pours down my back. My head throbs. As if I've been blindfolded, I grope and fumble my way out of the dark basement.

A dead silence cries out after me in stifled screams ...

10

I look out my bedroom window at a powdery white dawn. On the spine of the ridge, sparse conifers stand starkly against a wakening sky. Silent and still, the scene spreads out like a panoramic photograph negative.

I step out onto the porch, take in a deep cold breath, pulling a dull pain in my abdomen. A westerly wind has sent snowdrifts onto the plank floor. The season's first snowfall carpets the ground, broken only by a huge rock outcrop to the west where the slope dips abruptly. Close by, hoarfrost glistens on naked aspens, spoonfuls of the white powder settle at the crotches.

The snow must have come during the wee hours and is gone before daybreak. That frosty nip, that laden air, I'd smelled the wetness on my way home just before midnight. A corner too sharp here, a brush too close to the rock face, I sped up the dark mountain road to flee from my night's trespassing, from trailing eyes within. I was running away from my low self.

In the murky pre-dawn light, I'm still shaken by my adventure of the night. It was a transgression I hadn't known that was in me to make. I'd let my curiosity get the better of me. I'd snooped on Ashley. And that had nothing to do with what has been rattling me about the house.

Get out, Ben, your job's done. I hear a Mile High voice channeling Toby.

Stay, an impassioned voice says. Warn Ashley.

There's a presence in your house that is not of this world. A young girl who is dead but not gone.

How do you know?
I saw her. She has come to light.
You mean you saw a ghost?
Yes. She wears red, and she's restless.
Still, you snooped for yourself, says a censoring voice. What are your needs, Ben?
Peace, I want to make peace with myself.
Quit your night visits! A girl's voice interrupts. It has a hollow ring. An echo from the beyond only I can hear.

I break into a cold sweat. The echo rumbles on, but I turn a deaf ear. The pain in my abdomen gnaws.

It's the morning chill, I say, fighting back the creepy feeling. I zip up my jacket and walk briskly around to the back of my cabin. I hear a soft crunch on the fresh snow. A pale moon peeks through a strand of thin cloud. In the dimly reflected light, a troop of deer, a buck, some doe, trudges up the craggy whiteness to the spine of the ridge. There they stand, under the silvery pines to wait for sunrise, to catch the first warm glow of day. A couple of magpies ride piggyback on the buck, not pecking for fleas or ticks, just staying put.

I, too, look east.

I trust the coming of each new day, like the deer heading up the ridge in the morning, by habit or by instinct.

But I can be thrown off, like the flash of premonition that struck to confound. In the blink of an eye, I lost Ellie.

And guilt is a cat with nine lives.

Lunch break. I don't see the white beetle or the bicycle in the alley. The white beetle has been coming each day at regular hours. So is Kara's bike seen most afternoons, cable-locked to a rail post. The alley looks deserted today.

I've not gone back to the house since the night of my prowl. I've gotten myself into this damn-if-I-do and damn-if-I-don't thing. And it's tugging at me.

"Ya look awful, Ben. Got a bug?" Joey asks. He's squinting at me under the noon sun.

"I'm okay," I say testily, shifting my butt on the step.

Joey eyeing me. I gaze up at the swath of blue sky above the alley. The air is crisp and cool.

"Ya gonna watch news tonite?"

"What news?"

"Norton funeral today, goin on rite now, dey say, at da catedral by da capitol."

"I've got no TV."

"Ya kiddin? Me and my boys, we watch games, shows, everdin. My wife, she calls us couch tatoes." He cackles, chomps on his sandwich.

"Hmm."

Salami sours his breath as he turns to me, making me queasy.

"Say, what ya do evenins? Weekends?"

"Read. Go hiking, do some odd jobs."

"What kinda job?"

"Cutting trees."

"Getta paid?"

"No, do it for the firewood."

"Hmm. Ya ski?"

"No."

"Ya know Chopper? Kid from Cin-nati over at da Tower gate? He gotta weekend job to help out wit em chairlifts at Vail. Real happy about it, cause he wanna ski bad. Says he'd jus love to learn to ski down em mountains."

"Hmm."

"Ben, ya not eatin?"

"Um, lost my appetite."

I stand up to stretch. The dull pain in my abdomen has come back. Might have gotten a stomach flu or something.

I get off the Turnpike at Westminster to stop by an electronic store. A whole bank of muted television screens all tuned to the same channel: Multiples of the same faces reading the local news, same pictures popping up, same reporter on site.

"Sir, what can I help you with?"

"Uh, just looking. Thanks."

"Let me know if you need help."

He saunters off. I hang around.

Just now, a video segment of "Short Life Writ Large" about Michael Norton is streaming across the screen. It runs through his charitable foundation work, his civic appearances. Then a replay of the live coverage of the Norton funeral service: A panoramic shot of the gleaming white Cathedral; stained glass windows filtering rays over the candle-lit alter, over the casket bedecked with white lilies; clips of the governor giving eulogy, the mayor giving eulogy, a senator somebody giving eulogy, the archbishop saying prayers. The camera pans over the family, over the dignitaries. Among a sea of faces, I catch a cameo of Ashley.

On my way back, the snippet of her somber, vacant face weighs on my mind.

I wake up raw as a cucumber. Coyotes yelping through the night, wild and wary. My nerves are frayed.

"Whoa, what cries in the night?" asked my one-time neighbor around the bend, a newcomer to these parts. "Sends chill right through you ... those animals, scruffy, ugly, they look like dogs but they aren't dogs, they come even during the day, staring up at you with those steely eyes ... Can't even sit on your porch with a cup of tea." He had moved here to tend to his sick mother, even got a job at Macy's in town. Then I didn't see him anymore. "Back to New York City, says he can't take it no more," another neighbor told me.

Stepping outside, I take in a deep breath, blow it out slowly. The cold sharp air rouses me up as much as the dull pain in my abdomen. I press hard over my belly with both hands, then letting go. The pain stays, not churning but not going away either. I pace about on the porch, looking out at the thin blanket of snow that came in the night.

The sky at daybreak is an expanse of lucent gray, broken only by a bank of purple clouds to the east where a slit of intense pink is peeking through. A hint of blue fringes the high clouds. Magpies fluttering among the piñons, sparrows chirping under the brushes. I'm restless for the new day.

After tea and toast, I head out for Brainard Lake with a snug feeling inside me. Just think, a stone's throw away and I will be looking to have my head cleared of grime, looking to get recharged after a long workweek.

The Peak to Peak is a lazy byway at any hour. It's nothing but a lonely stretch this early. I coast along, a flat winding ribbon of light where the cool sun hits. The road up to the lake is passable but much of the ground is snow-covered. A lone car is already parked in the lot. I pick up my daypack, poles, hitch my snow shoes over my shoulder and set out heading towards the Mitchell Lake trailhead about a mile away.

I follow the snow packed path, crunching through the woods. Snowdrifts pile high here and there. The morning sun shoots slivers of gold through tall dark conifers. A chill wind rustling through, shaking down little puffs of shimmering snow. I stray off the path, put on my snow shoes and continue on.

On the way up, I look out for a glimpse of Mount Toll in the distance. It comes into view, that weathered peak above the snow fields, its rarefied look a stunning sight. Not huge, a hunk of an old rock nonetheless, butting up against the sky.

Where the woods thin out, I gaze up at a clear blue sky, soft sun on my face. It is a short and easy hike to the Mitchell Lake trailhead but I'm surprised that it tires me out. I sit down on a boulder to rest, still thinking of hiking up Blue Lake to have a good look at Mount Toll. There, overlooking the pristine lake, the pyramid rises majestically above the snow bank. I've always been awestruck by the play of light and shadow over its striated snow-swept face.

Today, I'd have to pass. A queasy feeling wells up inside me as I stand. The ground is sloping away, the tall conifers whirling, their tips pitching together then pulling apart. Clutching my poles,

I find myself slumping against the nearest tree for support. Gotta hold down that light-headed feeling.

The way back is long and arduous. I trudge down to the parking lot, barely making it to the restroom before I throw up.

Darn that stomach virus!

I get into my pickup and head home. Walking up to my cabin, I pass by the shed of cut logs.

Tomorrow. I'll split log tomorrow.

Right now, I turn in.

I'll sleep it off.

The coyotes howl through the night, taking my breath away. Shadows that roam, tramping over coniferous slopes, slobbering from boulders to brushes to my door steps, they come yowling into my sleep. I shake myself awake with a shudder because one doesn't always know the ways of the wild. Like one can't fathom the ways of the dead that don't pass on.

I look out the window into a starlit night, listening out to the long howls and the short yips far and near. My primal fear tells me to stay out of the dark, out of the way of the undead.

I toss and turn in my sweaty bed, burning a fever. I get up to have a drink of water. Clasping my hands over my abdomen, I crawl back to bed to wait for dawn.

Kaplonk! Kaplonk! Blow after blow, I let my maul fall, striking the log. The wood splits, falling away. I stand another log up. More blows. More logs.

The sharp pain bolts me up, shooting at my right side. Red light flashing in my head, I roll out of bed, pull on my boots, grab my jacket and stumble out of the cabin at four Monday morning.

It jolts me to think that Sunday had slipped by as I lolled around in bed. I had laid down my book, looked out the window at the clouds scudding past, breathing shallow to ease the stubborn pain. Between dozing and waking, I turned to look at my waiting pile of logs and thought no more of firewood.

Still, I didn't think of appendicitis.

Be cool, now. Hang tight.

I crawl into my pickup and wind down the dark canyon road.

Eyes fixed on the high beams, I make my way to the Boulder Community Health Emergency Entrance.

"Looka here if dis ain't Ben Ballad," says Rico as he walks in the job with me. "Hey, ya ain't gonna bite my head off, ain't ya? Like ya wanna to that day I saw ya in front a next door." He winks at me, steps aside, sizes me up and down, nodding his head. "Good as new, eh, man?"

"Thanks, Rico, for standing in."

"No problem, man, job's a job, here or across da street."

"Ya back so soon?" Joey asks, tearing down the stairs. "Toby says take yar time to get well." He looks me over. "A busted pendix, ha? Ya can die from it, ya know. My oldest boy, Pip, he gotta it when he was a wee fella. Almost lost him. Nobody knew a din till he hollered big tummy ache and puked up bad. How ya feelin? Dey clean up yar insides good?"

"I'm fine."

"Ya don't look so good," Joey says. "Gotta take it easy."

"Better than I saw ya last, Ben," says Rico fixing his eyes on me. "Man, I tell ya next door's jinxed. Ya die or ya getta sick just bein in dere. Hey, Ben, ya come out better dan Hank, or em two Nortons. Ya come out wit yar life, man!"

"But em ladies in dere looka okay, Rico?" Joey says. "Seen em in da shop real busy like, happy puttin up silver bells, tinsels, em holiday stuffs."

"Funny, eh? Seen em myself, too. Dey gotta no ugly lookin faces, not like Ben's I saw. Maybe, da jinx getta em men only. Won't boda no ladies. Like some voodoo curse done special for some folks only. Who knows?"

"Hope ya're right, Rico, cause I like Ashley and dat girl student. Dey say hi to me when dey see me. Have a good day, Joey! Ashley woulda say wit a smile."

"You guys got this place clean up good," I say.

"Shoulda see da loads we dumped out!"

"Started changin out em bad studs on da top floor. Ya gotta see."

"Ben, ya gotta let Toby know ya're back, so he won't duct yar pay no more." Joey says.

A small beckoning sound of a motor in the alley. I look out the back window. The white beetle has just pulled in, its door swung open. Her honey blond hair steals the shine from the morning sun. The shine falls over the shawl collar of her camel color coat. She walks sprightly towards her back door. I retreat from the window.

By noon, I see that Kara's bike is cable-locked to the railing at the back. Life's going on without a hitch. I missed three days of work and made it out that the roof had caved in while I was gone. I chuckle, the tug at my heart easing up.

"What so funny?" Joey asks.

"Nah, nothing."

A slow grind day. Replacing bad studs, the job's as dull as that pile of lumber stacked at one corner marking time for it to be used up, or hauled out.

Nail guns popping ... My eyes fog up behind the goggles.

Toby pokes in through the noise. "Hey, buddy, glad to have ya back!" He looks around, picks his way about the floor, looks up the plaster ceiling with the water stain from the roof leak.

"Roofers coming tomorrow. Gotta get her closed up before the snow. Here, brought ya the timeline."

The day has finally come to an end. Like a dead battery looking for a recharge, I trudge past her glass front. Slowing down, glancing in. People bustling in the gallery. The door opens, silver bells tinkling at the door handle. I walk on.

The picture of the little girl standing next to the draft horse slips into mind. Her smile that shone in the dark now glows under the sun.

I shudder still at my transgression of the night.

Nail guns popping through the night ... Coyotes howling at my feet ... My nights are as restless as my days are a humdrum. Each day I walk past Ashley's glass front without looking in. Yet I can't help watching out for the white beetle's coming and going.

Roofers thumping overhead. Glad that we're having a spell of dry November days. Inside, Takeo's doing the wiring and the lighting rough-in; Chuck and Lew are working on the plumbing rough-in, running flues for the heating. The job's moving along.

I call Toby Monday morning, "Will it work for you if I take a couple of days off around Thanksgiving? Wilkins Drywall isn't coming in till the week after."

"Sure, Ben. I'll get Rico back. Just tell him what ya wanna get done. Thanksgiving's a slow week anyway."

11

It's a long way home after seven years. The distance is taken in miles as well as in years. But then I've never quite left. What had come to pass a long time ago out in the field under a tulip poplar follows me where I go.

Dreams sometimes toss up a whole new outcome: I run after the falling sky and catch Ellie in my arms. She's laughing, the kite flapping in her hand. Flashes of green and gold dancing about us. I, too, laugh out loud. Jolted awake, I would find myself sweaty on a wintry night up in my mountain cabin a long way away.

Still, the southern country has a hold on me—the smell of sodden air, of hay, of cattle, of small chicken farms, the sight of droopy willows along stream banks, of sandhill cranes that come to winter, their honking fills the air.

Deep fall now, I will not hear the cicadas' deafening hum. There will be no fireflies either.

Still, ma would want to ask: Can't ya get a teachin job out West? Don't yar bachelor degree in education from UT mean somethin? I'd thought ya like teachin. Ya'd put in four good years at Dyer High.

I'm a carpenter now.

Ya make out alright, Ben?

I'm alright, ma.

Past midnight, barely a wink at a rest stop. I push on. Tailing headlights dwindle, recede into a dark pall as the road behind me fades away. High beams shine my way. In the dead of night, my foreboding over the deaths in the old house stews like fermenting plums that lay waste on the ground.   Bleeding ... bleeding drowsiness, spilling blood.

But there was no blood spilled in the deaths that I know of.

What about the girl, uh, the girl in a red haze?

I shift in my seat to shake off the drowsiness and the unease. Long road ahead.   Why am I taking this trip now?   What am I running away from?

Hazy night, quarter moon shy behind filmy clouds. I lower my window to let the whistling wind clear my head.   A sharp cold abrades my face. My eyes water. Raise the window.   I look up at the bleary moon that has emerged from behind the clouds, its silvery sheen graces the ink-blue sky.

Teddy's on the road.   Takin a load out west, ma had told me on the phone.   Gonna be back Thanksgivin Day.

Teddy, you looking at the moon?

Must be hard, to be on the road so much.   Sarah doing well with the new baby?   A girl, I think.   Their fourth?

Sarah in her white wedding gown with a bulge showing below the high waist and full gathers?   Pretty empire waistline, ma had whispered to me then, a twinkle in her eyes.

The motor droning, lulling me ...

Sound, any sound to distract.   A soft hum, the beat of velvety footfall drifting down from above ...   snatches of a melody that had lit up many an hour of mine in her basement.

Then, that patch of old bricks under the stairs slips into mind. I squirm, gripping the steering wheel.   I listen out to the sound of the engine to drown out the noise in my head.

The highway stretches from night corridors into bright concrete ribbons of a mellow afternoon with aqua skies and scant clouds. On either side, blurry trees with thinning canopies dot the harvested fields edged with drainage ditches. The rich brown earth is laid fallow ready for planting. Through the bug splattered windshield I look for the dirt road to turn into.

Still a dirt road, Teddy had told me.   Nothin much happenin around here.   Our house's bigger though.   I'd just put in another room.

I can see it now. At the end of the dirt road is this house which was once the small cottage we had moved into. Ma had taken us out of our ramshackle bungalow shortly after that fateful day so we wouldn't have to look into the field at the heartbreak tree with a missing limb.

I slow down, looking out for our dirt road, go past it and drive on.

A couple of miles or so, I turn into another dirt road. The old dirt road where I had stayed away ever since ma moved us out. To my right, the nightmare field. Now a pasture. A spread of tawny green meadow where cattle graze in the afternoon sun. By the edge of the field is a longish shed with a John Deere tractor sitting inside. Bales of hay stacked outside. A water trough nearby.

No ancient tulip poplar in sight, nor any straggly cottonwoods that had planted themselves in the ground over the years. As ma had said, when no one's lookin. Ma knew because she had grown up in that bungalow where gran once lived.

Inside my head, that one killer tulip poplar lives on. The cottonwoods, too, straggly as they were. The field of my loss stays, though it had sometime been our field of fireflies that stretched interminably onto the star-studded skies.

Those evenings, too, were forever, Ellie by my side.

I look across the road to where our old bungalow once stood. A tool shed stands in its place. Young cypresses line a short gravel drive leading up to a tidy little brick house with a white picket fence, a garden in front and a big garage to the side. Picture-perfect in Spring when the flowers are in bloom.

But in my heart there is always this broken bungalow with the stomping steps down the front porch.

I pull in to ma's smiling face. She's sitting in a lawn chair on the porch, rocking a worn bassinet with one hand and keeping an eye on the three romping boys in the front yard playing tag.

"Been lookin out for ya comin down the road, Ben."

"Hi, ma."

"So good to see ya."

We hug. She hangs on for a bit, looks up smiling through glistening eyes, fishtail lines fan out the corners. I smooth back her stray hair, gray now, but her cheeks are in high colors.

Over turkey dinner with the rambunctious boys at the table we can all see the distance we had traveled. The oldest is seven. "That's how long ya've been away, Ben," ma says. "Don't stay away for too long now," my big brother tells me. He is huskier and gentler now than I've ever known him to be. Sarah heaps food on my plate. She smiles, looking over her shoulder at the baby in the bassinet, turns around, passes food to ma, speaking softly to her, "Ya like the cornbread dressin?"

I stay the day after Thanksgiving. Teddy tells me, "I aim to buy those couple of acres behind the house. Lookin to start a little organic herb and veggie farm, rear some chickens for eggs, some goats maybe. Sarah wanna learn to make goat cheese. A bit of a slope but got a pond down below. With the work I'd put into the house I'll look to mortgage it for a loan. The trucker I work for is just hangin on these days, the gas price as it is. We get by right now, with Sarah workin in the school cafeteria. The boys are growin up fast. I wanna be around."

I know the slope at the back where the cottonwoods cast huge shadows. My brother has his work cut out for him. "With some terracing, it'll work out just fine," I say, giving him a pat on his back.

We sit out on the porch, ma and I, in the afternoon sun.
"Ben?"
"Ma?"
"Ya got a girl?"
"No, ma."
"I see ya fidgetin. Thought ya might be missin someone. Anyways, son, think about bringin home a girl next time ya come."

"I've got yar Shakespeare and modern poetry books all packed, ready for ya to take with," ma says at the door.

"Thanks, ma." I see that she still thinks of me as the English teacher at Dyer High. I carry the box out and put it on the cab floor passenger-side.

When I'm done with saying goodbye to Teddy, Sarah and the boys, ma comes up to me with a bunch of cornflowers she had picked from the sunny side of the house.

"Take this," she says, putting the flowers in my hand, avoiding my eyes. I put my arms around her, feeling her little tremble. When I let go, she turns away quickly but I see that her eyes are red. She smiles, waving as I pull out. "Take care." I see the words on her lips.

I stop by the cemetery, walk the winding path up to where she lies. I bend down to pull the weeds off the top. Looking up, I see what she sees. Same old shade tree, but it has grown tall and broad. The leaves are turning, some have fallen, but I can still make out the shape of the full crown. Through the thinning canopy the sun shimmers down an olive-green filter tinged with orange and gold.

Rustling, a crisp coolness sheds over us. I lay down the bunch of little blue cornflowers ma had picked for her.

"Bye now, Ellie."

12

An overcast sky blankets the city. The sun slits gold through the slate clouds holding out promise for a mild day. I look forward to be back on the job. Yet, I'm not sure where I'd left off. Just got the feeling that I'd run off in a hurry.

I glance at the box of books on the cab floor that had traveled back with me. It has taken me seven years to reclaim my past. But then I always feel that I've never quite left.

I think she means to tangle my eyes too!—a line drops into my head out of the blue. From the old Bard. Did I fish it out to give myself a rush? Something that no dumb casements or the best frame job can speak to me these days.

I park my pickup by the rail yard, grab my tool belt and lunch, and hasten along the few blocks to LoDo. Traffic's building up. A Mile High truck drives past. Someone sticks out a hand. I wave back.

Tangle my eyes? Whom do I've in mind?

The young girl who's dead but not gone?

The house has a hold on me. I'm that hapless prowler looking to foray into the dark. Looking for her, a soul lost in time, not letting go of what was and what was not, where past is present is past … And, I'm as trapped as she is.

What of Bottom's saying in *A Midsummer Night's Dream?*— *The eye of man hath not heard, the ear of man hath not seen …* I'm saddled with this urge to see, to hear what there is that only I can. Then, what? What can I do to give her peace, give myself peace?

Then, there lurks in me this feeling of doom ... *El-lie* ... *Ellie!*
Here's Ashley. She who lets her heart hang out in her art.
She's standing now but I've a hunch that she's about to be caught
in ... a flash flood?
I intend to keep an eye out for downpours.

The scant morning light barely skims the roofline as I turn into
the gray alley. A chill wind whisks through, kicking up dust.
There it is, the white beetle sits brightly in its spot like an
apparition that has come out of the dark. I try to absorb the sight
of its being there, seven-thirty in the morning, Monday after
Thanksgiving.
I slow down as I walk past her back door. The ventilation fan
is whirring, spinning light splinters. The door lamp casts a weak
glow. No bike on the railing. I twitch, bite my lips, walk hurriedly
onto next door.
A heavy start for a new day. It's as if I hadn't gone away. I
skid right back into my old rut, ruminating over red haze and dark
fears.

The white beetle gleaming under the noon sun. Kara's bike is
here, cabled to the railing, another bike is locked alongside, one I
hadn't seen before. Ashley's back door stays shut.
I eat quickly and stroll out front. Joey is across the street,
hanging out with Rico and Wes. Lupe, tall as a lamppost, hangs
out with them. He's new, has been working with Wes since Rico
took my place the days I was gone.
The sidewalks at midday bustle with holiday foot traffic. I
have eyes only for next door. Over the glass transom, the *Studio
Indigo*'s copper sign is festooned with a swag of evergreen and
loops upon loops of filmy foil ribbon.
"Here?" a man asks, turning to his companion. She nods, her
eyes bright with anticipation. They are about to enter when the
glass door swings open, a cluster of tiny silver bells tinkling at the
door handle. A strain of Bach's violin drifts out, mixed in with
soft murmur. An elderly gentleman in a trench coat steps out,
toting a platinum foil gift bag.

"Happy holidays, sir, and thank you. Come back soon," says a smiling young woman in a slim red dress. She holds open the door for him. He tips his bereted head to her, his red tartan scarf drapes over one shoulder.

"Do come in, please." She turns to greet the visitors at the door. The couple walks up, steps into a spirited ambience of festive red and holiday green.

Red and green? Where has River Indigo gone!

"Hiya, Ben!" Rico calls out after me. "Sun's out! Brought out da crowd. Brought ya out!" He grins. "Em shops done up real Christmasy, eh?"

Quitting time. The white beetle stays. So are the bikes. I saunter out the alley. On second thought, I head down the street to the LoDo Tower site. Mary Lou had sent word that my paycheck from two weeks back has been waiting for me there.

The western sky is streaked with a palette of brilliant pink and gold and turquoise. Below this radiant light, purplish clouds tinged with a burnished copper hang over the mountains.

I turn into 14th and walk up to the trailer. The trailer door swings open, a glum faced young guy storms out. He hops down the steps in a huff. A paycheck envelope sticks out of his anorak's kangaroo pocket.

"Hey, Chop, what's up?" Someone yells. Bob, AJ, Toro, and a couple of others are standing by the entrance. Lunch totes at their feet, they are taking off their bright orange safety vests with reflective tapes. Cato and Buzz are throwing bright blue tarps over the bundles of re-bars on the ground, over the stacks of form boards piled high along the chain link fence, holding them down with loose rocks that had been dug up. Someone's mongrel hops upon the heap, stomping down air pockets under the tarp.

"Down, Knuckles, get ya down," Cato calls out.

Knuckles wiggles up to him, wagging his tail, lifting his head up for a pat.

An orange caisson drill rig sits at one corner of the site, at the ready for tomorrow's job. Caisson tubes under clear plastic wrap stacked on one side. On the other side, sewage pipes and water pipes laid end to end. Looks like the excavation is about done and the foundation work is getting started.

"Over here, Chop!"

Mack is on the phone when I step into the trailer. He sits at his desk spread with dog-eared blue prints. Empty soda cans strewn about. Receiver propped upon his shoulder, he bends over his rolodex, thumbing listlessly through the well worn name cards. "Yeah, yeah, the kid's got a blabber mouth. Hmm, we all heard. But what the fuck do we guys down here care about who skis with whom? Sorry, Mary Lou ... So, word came from above Drew, eh? Sounds like, hmm, somebody's wanna put the lid on whatever. Ziploc. Mum. " He glances up at me. "Gotta go."

"Hey, Ben. What's up? Oh, yeah, got your pay."

He rummages through his top drawer and pulls out a paycheck envelope and hands it to me while he picks up the phone, finger ready on the push buttons.

"Know what, Chop? Wanna think about goin back to school? Young guy like ya, oughta learn a trade or somethin," says Bob. I nod to them as I approach the guard post. Bob nods back. "Say, Ben, Ya're a master carpenter, ain't ya?"

Chopper spins around, eyeing me. Jumpy. He looks flustered, his eyes big, his red head a bright spot among husky dusty men.

It seems not right for me to just skip. I stop by and listen in. Bob and a couple of others are Mile High old-timers. They are old enough to be the kid's father, except Cato and AJ who are in their twenties.

"Good luck, kid, move on, ya hear?"

"We'll miss ya, Chop, " AJ puts his arm around the kid.

Knuckles comes prancing about, wagging his tail.

"Too bad, uh, Vail's done hiring for the season," Chopper says with a sigh and a shrug. "What Mack said, um, is that I play hooky," he goes on, raising his voice. "Two Fridays in a row, he said. Well, that Friday after Thanksgiving, only some of ya guys turned up that day, right? No big sub was gonna show anyways, right? They gave me no warning whatsoever. *Blo-onk!* I got the boot right in my face!" He feigns getting hit in the face, stumbles backward, tripping over Knuckles. The dog growls, hops off, tail between his legs.

"Ooooh, so sorry, Knuckles!" Chopper bends over the mongrel, cradles his head with his hands, rubbing him ear to ear.

"Coulda have a word with the kid so he won't do it no more," Bob mumbles.

"When ya get caught ya get caught, that's that," says Toro who has been quiet all this time.

"Man, two Fridays, that's all, I swear!"

"Stay out of trouble, kid."

"Good luck, Chop."

"Bye, ya guys!" Chopper says, head down.

The crowd scatters, scuttling out the gate. Knuckles trudges after Cato, a muffled grunt lodged in his throat.

"See ya, Knuckles!" Chopper calls out. He looks up at the sign posted high at the entrance. There is the pictured Tower, a crescent wedge shooting up the sky gleaming like something out of this world. "Bye, Tower," he says under his breath.

"Take care, Chopper. You'll do alright," I say.

"Right on, Ben," he says breaking into an impish grin. "I'll do alright."

At daybreak, the light snow that has fallen overnight has tapered off to a thin powder. A patchy fog has moved in to hang over the dark mountain road as I head down. A white gust puffs over the snow-dusted conifers, their pyramidal tips swaying, catching the paltry morning light. The foothills are shrouded in a blur until I get onto the Turnpike where streams of red taillights and yellow headlights set the wetness aglow. The hum of the day has begun.

The white beetle is already in the alley as I walk in. A scant white powder covers its hood. Footprints on the snow lead to her back door. Her ventilation fan is droning, splitting light.

My back door's ajar. Joey rushes up to me with the news. "Ya know Chopper got da boot yestaday?"

"Yes, I know."

"Ya know what Chopper says? Chopper says he gotta hunch what gotta him da boot," he looks sideways and mutters under his breath. "I saw him yestaday after da guys left. He says it's on account a Mr. Roen, da arkitect. He says he saw him and Mrs. Norton, at da chairlift at Vail. She da wife a da Norton who passed away. Told everbody too about seein them, oh, coupa weeks back. Sure I didn't tell ya?" He looks at me, puzzled. Then it comes to him. "Ah, must be when ya're away!"

"How does Chopper know she's Mrs. Norton?"

"See, when Chopper gets up to Vail what he does is stand by his coz Dean at da chairlift station to help skiers getta in em chairs."

"Still how does he know she's Mrs. Norton?"

What business of mine anyway?

"Chopper says he heard Dean says, Mornin Mrs. Norton, when he brought da chair around to her and Mr. Roen. Dean told Chopper dat he saw da Nortons all da time on the slopes last year and da year before. Everbody know em, da Nortons. Big house, big parties. Mr. Norton, he's gone now. Chopper says of course he knows about dat."

"Hmm."

"And showin off like to Dean, when da two a em come next round up da lift, Chopper says, Hi, Mr. Roen. He says da arkitect looka him thru his goggles and ask, where I seen ya before? Chopper says, it's me, Chopper, from Mile High. Huh? Mr. Roen says, Ah, Chopper. Dat's me, I stand at da guard post at LoDo Tower, Mr. Roen, Chopper says to him."

"So, what?"

"Oh, yeah? When Chopper came in yestaday mornin, he told everbody he saw em two again at da chairlift dat Saturday a Tanksgivin weekend, real chummy like. Maybe, dey don't wanna nobody know about em up at Vail."

"Hmm."

Somebody's want to put the lid on the thing. Ziploc. Mum, Mack had said.

Joey's thoughts turn to Chopper. "Ain't no big deal, Chopper says. Mighta jus work out he a gonna get hired in some ski resorts. Learn to ski real good, ride a ski mobile, drive a snow cat, work da machines, may even become a ski patrol one day. I says to him, Chopper what about summer, what ya gonna do summer? Says to me he a gonna get job, any job, sticks around for winter. And snow will come, eh? Jus a screwball kid, dat one!"

It is high noon but the sky is dragged low by the layers of leaden clouds forecasting more snow on the way. Pallid light filters down the alley, gray and mute. A blanket of chill air is bearing down. The melted snow from this morning quickly refreezes into ice. It crunches with every grinding tire that comes through, every footstep that treads past. Shiny puddles here and there. The two bikes are cable-locked to the railing. The white beetle is in its spot.

I eat by the open door at the landing, keeping watch.

A small crunchy sound coming up from behind. I turn and see her plodding gingerly towards her white beetle, in slip-on flats too thin soled for the iced-up ground. Slim black pants, her arms crossed, tucked in around her three-quarter length camel coat. Scarf draped over one shoulder trailing behind. Her eyes fixed on the ground, she is watching every step with care. She wobbles. I come right up the steps. Our eyes meet.

"S-sorry to h-have startled you," I mutter.

"Hello, Ben!" Her lips quiver. She looks pale, dark circles around her eyes.

"Hi, ho-ow are you?"

"Fine, I'm fine."

"It's slippery. May I?" I offer her my arm to usher her to the white beetle.

"Tha-anks!" She takes my arm with haste as if she's in a bit of a hurry. She has no gloves on.

She's slight as a bird that perches upon my finger, wings trembling. A small gust tunneling through the alley would have swept her off her feet.

A sight flashes through my head—she is not about to take off. Her wings are clipped. She has gotten her wings clipped!

Stop this!

I shudder. She looks up puzzled but says nothing.

We pick our way to her white beetle, a distance too short.

"You need winter shoes with rubber soles," I venture to say.

"I know."

She sounds far away with her head bowed. When she looks up, I see a brooding shadow in her eyes. Dense and deep but for a desperate pinhole light poking through, staring straight out.

A beckoning light at the end of a tunnel!

Same pinhole light I saw inside my head the night of Hank's passing.

Am I looking at a reflection of what she sees?

Ashley, don't look! Whatever it is, is not of this world!

A thousand magpies flapping their wings, cawing over my head!

I shut the car door for her.

"Thanks, Ben."

"Take care."

She lowers her window, looks up with a wistful smile. The brooding shadow and the pinhole light in her eyes are gone. An impenetrable veil has been drawn, shielding her from what's out there.

Out there, her husband and the newly widowed Kate are making a smooth run down the Vail slope?

Or, is there some inner agitation that she's hiding from view?

I watch her drive out the alley. Something gnaws big at my guts, darkly menacing. I turn to glare at her back door.

Snow is in the air. May even be snowing in the mountains right now. I'd earlier thought of getting back to my cabin to catch the last light of day. To sit on my porch, watch the snow drifting down, white powder shifting on the plank floor with each sweeping gust. All is quiet and calm, a sweet breather of the day.

I would then tread up the ridge at the back of my cabin to take in the falling snow. Be it butterfly flakes peeling off a darkening sky in swarming whiteness, or a champagne snow shimmering in the air, I would take it in, take it all in.

Wet chill on my face. I shiver. Time to get back down. Shed my clothes in front of a crackling fire. A tongue of flame leaps up. It shoots at my nakedness, lighting a fire in my groin. All hell breaks lose! Fiery tits charge up from the blazing bosom to lick the air, spitting more hot tits. Ten thousand fire ants crawling under my skin ...

I keel over, flushed with want. Tears welling up my eyes.

Instead, I'm plodding along the sidewalk. Rush hour traffic rolling past. A loud honk. The smoldering fire that has been twisting in my head dies down in a hurry. My cabin is far away. I'm where I need to be.

I can almost see her now, soft silk scarf languishing over her shoulders. Steadying herself on my arm, she trembles still. The lightness of her weighs heavy on me ...

I pick up my pace, impatient for darkness to fall. My night mission is pressing.

Ashley has seen what I saw—the pinhole light at the end of a tunnel!

And, the light is beckoning ...

13

The fading light casts a pallor even as the shop windows shine, and the streets bustle with rush hour traffic. The wet asphalt surface throws up a dark sheen, glittering yellow and red. Pedestrians hastening their way. Up and down 16th Street, the Mallrides shuttling along.

Strolling on, whiling time. I pause as I come to the cross street, not knowing where to turn. A car horn toots, a corner too sharp. I tense up.

How much longer?

Dusk falls. The air's damp. Snow's on the way. No more thoughts of sitting out on my porch to watch the snow fall on the mountainside.

A while longer and the lights on the gallery row will dim.

On the prowl? Again?

I turn a deaf ear, pull my jacket hood over my head, tuck my hands inside my pockets. I cross the street and walk on, passing by a big display window decorated with lighted garlands. An open book on an empty armchair sits by a fireplace lit with flicker flame bulbs. I walk tentatively up to this historic building, push open the front door and enter a real-life storybook picture—this warm, well-lit place filled with books, tabletops of them, shelves upon shelves of them, and the buzz of people, and the aroma of hot coffee, and Victorian floor lamps casting soft glow over readers in cushy chairs, on plump couches by the stairs, and the stair rails bedecked with garlands and bright red bows, and the charm of it all, finding myself in here, out of the cold, out of the rushing sidewalk, out of the earshot of a vexing voice with questions I can't answer.

Sitting down, I cup my hands over the steaming hot tea, take a sip and munch on oatmeal cookies. Light chatter around me. A young couple poring over magazines on the next table, looking up to exchange glances. A rush of warmth comes over me. It's the comfort of being near people, of forgetting about marking time before nightfall.

Up the carpeted stairs, I try to make light my heavy work boots. Milk white glass pendant lamps staring down the high ceiling. Remind me of my old schoolhouse lamps. Upstairs, I glance over the Colorado History shelves, the fiction shelves. Flipping through the pages, words float past my eyes, I take in nothing.

I stand gazing out the tall front window into a blurry night. A vaporous moon, a dreamy glimpse of silver behind a misty veil. My day hangs over me. My night is yet to begin. I'm that precarious boulder on a thawing slope …

The road I'm to take is the one less traveled, darkly bowed in undergrowth. Unbowed, I'm to set foot on it, believing the difference I can make.

For her. And *her*.

I'm haunted by *one* who had long passed on but is stalking still. May *she* have peace. And Ashley shall have her peace.

People dwindling. The store's closing. Time to leave.

I walk hurriedly. Shimmering snow drifting under the hazy glow of street lamps. A breeze rushes past, puffing up a flurry. My eyes water in the cold, my breath steams up my face. Cars roll past, headlamps burst into twirling crystals pitching luminous long beams into the night. Along the gallery row, dusky lights diffuse into the soft whiteness. I turn quickly into the alley. Under the meager backdoor lamp, I pull out my surreptitious key.

Out of a white night into pithy darkness, I pause to get used to the night basement. Still I want no jarring fluorescent lights to drown out the slightest wrinkle in the air. This night is unlike any other. This darkness grips you. It snuffs you out like a candle, leaving no trace of smoke, leaving you dazed. But I'm no candle. There's no snuffing me out. I've come to look into darkness, into that elusive tunnel where at the end a light beckons. I want to see what Ashley has seen. And, more.

A long night ahead. Heartbeats marking time. The gloom will lift. The blur in my eyes will clear. So I wait.

In time, a fuzzy light steals in at the top of the stairs. I hold my breath. A luminous red glow has filtered through the murkiness. The upper part of the old brick wall has put on a deep rouge.

I jump out of my wet boots, drop my damp jacket onto the door mat. Like a squirrel chasing up a tree, I dash up the stairs in my socked feet, thinking only of her. She who walks in a red haze.

Up in the gallery, a brilliant red glow torches center stage where River Indigo once rippled. Reflection from the glass front doubles the florid glow. I'm taken aback. Ravishing flame-red flowers that smite, fresh dew glistening, softly beguiling ... Wholly disarming. Huge amaryllis blooms they are, locked in an enormous embrace. All that, flourishing in a glimmering silk panel, hung in a cylindrical column ceiling to floor. A shaded halogen floodlight filters down from above, bleeding an intense red gloss, vivid yellow stamens holding out life.

Looming large, utterly compelling, utterly stirring, this visual drama bowls me over. This, a blown-up photographic transfer, a screen print, or whatever it is, dazzles from different viewing angles to entrance the eye. At the risk of being spotted from the street, I sidle up for a breathtaking look.

A squirrel out squirreling, once again.

I retreat quickly to crouch down at the rear corner behind the spiral stairs. There, I lift my eyes up to a shining sea of hydrangeas. Clusters of soft blue petals luxuriating ... in a cool bright luster! I recall that it was an unlit corner that I had sought to hide from passing eyes on the street. I peep behind the wall hanging. Fiber optic lighting has since been taped to the back wall to give the blossoms that gossamer, translucent look.

I'm a carpenter with a fire within, all too eager to succumb to every call to dream. I now see that I'm burning for something quite beyond me. I work with my hands, my head, but little heart. What Ashley has rendered is larger than life, full of gusto and tenderness. Surreal, almost lyrical. I'm awestruck by the ephemeral beauty that she has conjured up and made timeless.

I stay crouched for I don't know how long.

Like a derelict watchman, I slip back downstairs, pace the floor in my socked feet, throw my flashlight aimlessly from wall to wall. Squirreling or not, I want to have a quick look around.

Since the last time I was here, the basement has been worked in quite a bit. Fabric bundles everywhere, on the counter by the wash basins, in a basket cart by an ironing board. Silk cushions stand on wall shelves, of big red amaryllis, pink amaryllis, pouting hot lips blowing kisses, abstract brushwork of purple and orange on brown. On the work island, subtly colored tie-dyed silk squares and folded oblongs stacked in piles. Rows of silk neckties, silk bows laid out neatly. On a wheeled garment rack, a black silk robe hangs, a pair of twisted red lips on its back. Twisted to scorn? Next to it, a rich brown silk robe with a deep crimson rift cleaving down its back, splattering blood. A maroon silk robe, a burst of purple petals over a white lightning bolt zigzagging down its back.

You watching your back, Ashley?

I clip the flashlight back on my belt and plunk myself down on the bottom stair. Burying my face in my hands, her colors on my mind. Big, bold and indelible. On my mind, too, are the torn petals, the splattered blood. The ripping violence they project is a stark contrast to her vision of vibrant sensuality that graces the gallery upstairs.

Ashley, the provocateur, as incendiary as a smothering fire waiting to erupt, unfathomable as a volcanic pit.

Not yourself, Ashley?

Then, there is this frenzy pace of work. What's driving her?

Inside my head, a dot of light quietly poking through. That very desperate light at the end of the tunnel. My heart races. A sigh weaves through the air soft as a butterfly's flittering wings.

I leap up, spin around and stare into dimness. My knees grow weak.

Who-o s-sighs?

A slight flux in the air, a thin rustling, a footfall faint as a petal's landing ... Then, a wisp of body scent seeps into the air. Ever so faint, like that of a rosebud about to bloom. The sensation lingers as I hold my breath. The air has taken on a teeth-clattering chill even as the furnace is on.

I perk my ears up to every pulse, every lilt, every cadence of silence ... I catch a skipped beat of my heart.

"Are yo-ou here, m-miss?" I whisper.

I've thrown a pebble into the pond. It's been swallowed up without a plop. A long while passes. I stand still. A flux of a motion brushes past. I turn to look.

She glides past, sweeping along in a big red gown, toward the back window where there has been no window. She stands by a Victorian settee below the window, lifting her head up to a star-studded cobalt sky.

I walk up gingerly behind her. A half moon beams down, lending a cool aura to her slim silhouette, a soft glow to her crimson gown. For all that's stunningly beautiful about her ethereal presence, there is something remote, something steely that keeps me at bay. Even the bright coppery tresses that cascade down her back hold a glacial sheen.

At her feet, there is no shadow.

"Who-o're you, m-miss?"

Silence.

"M-miss?"

I edge closer. She turns sideways as if to balk at my dare. I can't quite make out her features. Only that I feel I'm looking at a columbine in early bloom.

Go away! I hear it in my head. A faraway voice, calm and cold. But still, a girl's voice.

Go away!

I step back at her command. But I fix my eyes on her. My puffing breath in the bone-chilling cold intruding ...

She turns around to face me with those lucid eyes out of

nowhere. They shine like dark water, reflecting nothing. Blazing starkly, they brand into my head. My heart leaps up my throat.

Am I to die?

"M-men have d-die here," I stammer.

She stands unmoved.

"Wha-at did t-they die for?" I bolster myself up to ask.

"A guy died here," I turn to look at where Hank fell, at the foot of the stairs, "he stole from you, miss?"

G-O-L-D ... Pikes Peak gold! An echo booms from the pit of a hollow. Her eyes glare at the spot where Hank fell.

My legs buckle and I keel over in a thud. Up, get up! I tell myself. I scramble to get up and look directly at her.

A l-lost soul.

"An-another died wh-where you're s-standing, miss."

She stares down at where Michael Norton fell. She stands still, fluffed up in her blood red gown, erect like a hawk over her prey. Yet, a flinch ever so slight belies her stance. From that little tremble, I sense that a grievous wound has been ripped open. A seething rage shrieks into the air, croaking, howling ... A thousand crows cawing, their flapping wings blacken the silvery night. I cower down, hands over my ears.

In that deafening siren, I hear not of danger but of anguish. Anguish over an unvanquished, crushing grievance. I shudder to see how tormented she is, and how frail. She looks more trodden than menacing.

I strain to catch her face, framed by her coppery radiant tresses. A delicately chiseled face. One that I have seen before. Many a time I have stopped to look at the little blue and white columbine on the side of the mountain where the sun lingers.

She yawns now, like a child who's about to droop, the back of her hand smoothes over her dainty mouth, then letting it fall over her gown. Following the sweep of her hand, she looks down ... gazes at the fullness of her skirt. All of a sudden, she doubles over, scoops her skirt up in a bunch and raises it to her face. A quick glance at one side of the window, she stumbles backward. She looks down again at her skirt, seemingly stunned by what she sees that she has on.

Oh-ooh! Ai-ai-aiyih! Oh, oh, ooh! She lets out a wail so agonizing I can't even bear to hear from a wounded coyote.
Mountain lions stalking near ...
The utter despair in her cry cuts me up.
Then I hear a sob, such a heart-wrenching sob that I'm moved to want to comfort her.
Pluff! She drops to the floor, crouching into her big red gown. Her face's buried in its thick folds, her lustrous hair flowing over her shoulders, heaving, sobbing.
"M-miss, is there an-anything I-I can do?"
"I'm Ben, miss."
She sobs on. I kneel by her side, encroaching onto what has been keeping us apart. The icy grip that has been holding me back is melting. I'm struck by how small she is in that trembling heap of cloth. And how sumptuous that cloth! Under the clear half moon, I can make out a weave of raised curvy floral lines, bright scarlet against a deep crimson background, intricate and big-proportioned, dwarfing her slight body.
Slowly she stirs. She raises herself up as if awakening from a deep sleep. She looks up at me with eyes as blue as my indigo dream. They are sparkling clear, without a trace of tear.
Did you see the floats? A girl's voice asks.
Did you? Oh, did you, this afternoon?
Decorated floats, the pa-rade, you see them? Her tantalizing eyes beg to know.
You see the silver serpent? Si-ilver-silver serr-pent. Si-ilver-silver serr-pent, she starts to croon, trilling this strange refrain. A warbler, ever so delightful.
I'm completely thrown off, taken aback by the intense longing in her wispy voice, her brimming questions. This young girl, barely a woman, blown in from a time long gone and demands to hear about the fun in the streets she had missed that day.
What day? What year?
"What pa-parade, miss?"
Yo-ou know, the grandest Parade of the Festival!
"The Festival?"

Yes, yes, ye-es, the Festival of Mountain and Plain. Weren't you there? Weren't ...

Her voice trails. The flow has hit breakwater. The ebb is rushing out to sea. Her lyrical blue eyes fading fast, like jewels being washed out with the tide. Her long tresses drifting away, its luster dissolving ...

"M-miss, ple-ease stay!" I cry out to the evaporating haze.

She's gone.

The night has shut down. The gripping chill has yet to dissipate.

I've yet to say to her, "Peace be with you, miss. Eternal peace."

I kneel motionless on the cold floor where she has stood. I want desperately to retrieve every moment of our encounter, to gaze at the moon through the brick wall where she has shown me a window. I want to savor every tenor of my crossing over to her world. A world beyond reason, beyond grasp. But no less real while it lasted.

When I finally get up to leave, it is back into a night of shivering flurries under a bleary full moon.

And I'm as empty as I was before I walked in. Only more forlorn.

Galena

14

He calls himself Ben. He gawks at me with burning eyes …

Eyes I'd seen in town. Guys came down from the camps got them. Eyes like cats' on the prowl, lit with fire, unblinking. Once, looking west from Harrison towards State, I saw those cats, singly, two's and three's, slouching along rough plank sidewalk, slinking against tight buildings packed in a row.

Thud-thud-thud …

Over here, lil girl! One leered at me with what passed for a smile, brown teeth bucking out, the few he'd got left.

I ran around the street corner, my eyes wide open.

Before long, they got pulled into the clapboard salons with crooked windows. You could smell the sultry lot a mile away, sweat soured with much want.

Look here now, those muddy boots of his on the mat wet from trudging the sluice. A grubber!

No, he ain't gonna grub *my* gold!

One more time: No, he *is not going* to grub *my* gold!

Might just be that he's got a found nugget in his pocket and stumbles into the wrong place for a laugh. Can't he see this is no place for the likes of him?

Just you wait, ma'am will have Big Roy cuff your neck and throw you out the back.

Pikes Peak gold! I've got my twenty dollar coins. How they shine, those double-eagles! How they sing in my hands! Listen, ah-h, the sweet, swe-eet jingling!

I close my eyes when Michael rolls a tingling cold one up my thigh ... twirling it up my curve ... up to where I brim over and ache for more.

High up in the Brown Palace, the window looking west is aglow with the orange sun. You get up to leave, wanting me to button up your fine linen shirt.

Stay, Michael, please stay!

I hang onto the silken thread that spins us into a cocoon of whims and fancies—nursing our appetite, feeding our hunger.

Spin away! Oh, spin away!

Michael, when am I gonna, ah no, *going* to be seen by your side?

Silly girl, you coo into my dreamy blue eyes, your breath hot on my face, murmuring ...

Yes, sweet Michael? I drink deeply into the cup of dreams you hold out to me. How I get caught up in a giddy spell, conjuring wildly of love and the good life!

That other grubber, he came one night with chisel and all and stole from me. He was grubbing for my double-eagles. My singing double-eagles, ah, how they glitter in my hands!

He fell off the cliff. The one they called Hank.

Pa, too. The new one. He tumbled down the gulch, yowling like a hurt coyote. I saw him hit the rocks that jutted out crooked and sharp on the side of the cliff where the afternoon sun got shut out at three. The torrents carried his ragdoll body downstream to be fished out where the water slowed. In one piece or not, I wouldn't care.

I told Sheriff Burke I saw him lose his footing on the ledge made slippery by a handful of loose gravel. I'd never want to take another look behind that ugly big rock where tucked a bed of crunchy pine needles. There, looking up, I hung my eyes on a straggly lodgepole grappling to make it through another season.

Nobody asked why I was up there. Sheriff Burke narrowed his eyes a tad, looked down at the clog-clogging shoes on my feet, and said in his phlegmy voice that I oughta be in school.

Ma, stone-faced, said nothing. She'd been stoned-faced ever since the day that the new pa came into our lives. Maybe even before then.

He was no pa to me. But they didn't know the half of it, like they wouldn't know how the too-big shoes came to be on my feet. My new pa had said he ain't gonna let my pretty little feet get cut up no more. Lil girl, ya too pre-eetty to go walkin with no shoes on, he'd said.

Afterwards, I'd be keeping my eyes open to see what girl got no shoes, a swollen cheek, or, a black eye so I'd stay out of her way. What nobody could see was that I, too, got a black eye. Only it was inside of me. That was how I paid for those shoes.

Everybody knew that my own Pa died in the fire. The big one that turned day into night, and night into screams that could wake up the dead.

P-pass the pail! Hand to hand to hand, splashing, sloshing, the water got hauled up the line from the river to the men up front. Same river that was much cursed for having been fouled by animal waste and mine tailings. A big jerk rippled downhill, toppling pails, spilling water. Men yelling, clambering up, pulling back, held off by the shooting tongues of fire and the blinding, choking smoke.

The wind kicked up something fierce, lashing the whole cinder-dry mountain to hell, spurting ambers, hurling fireballs that leapt from tree to tree. Swishing, crackling, the tussock hill came flaming down the slope. Animals scurrying, screeching every which way.

I could feel the heat down by the river. My cheeks burned, my eyes watered. Through the smoke and frenzy, I saw the fire engulf the shanties where the China folks live on the far side of the mountain, whipping them to the ground in the blink of an eye. No water line was going up that way. Long day into night to night to night ... The loud cries at last dwindled to a blood-curdling whimper. I shuddered at the piteous sound but the silence afterwards was even more chilling.

I looked up at Ma. Her eyes watered too. And they kept on watering long after the smoke had cleared and the smoldering had died.

They found my Pa dead by where the tool shed once stood at the bottom of the hill. They said he died from too much smoke in his lungs. He lay face down, half buried in the charred rubble, clutching a borrowed pick axe, his battered lunch pail nearby. Ma said that the smoke had probably keeled him over, but he was trampled to death. When they picked him up, he'd got no face left, just a crushed mask of dried blood and dirt. His limbs were stiff and limp at the same time with more broken bones and loose joints than folks cared to know.

Eleven China men, eight China women, ten old burros also died in that fire. They didn't count the dead China kids.

That was the day I turned twelve. Afterwards, Ma never quite seemed to know how old I was, or much of anything else, drifting from chore to chore, forgetting meals, wearing too thin for the weather. There were days I found her crouching on the ground, sweeping dirt with her bare hands, mumbling to herself.

That man who had come to call himself my pa walked up to her then, gave her a whack on the head and kicked her in the butts. Hard. Ma pitched forward, got back on her knees sniveling, not looking up, not looking down, just staring straight into somewhere faraway.

Knock some sense into her, he'd say. He'd then slant his eyes at me, smiling his twisted smile.

There were times I saw Ma fixing her eyes at the charred mountains like she was looking for something. Nothing there, no deer, no fox, no coyote, no mountain lion, not even a pika. Just humpy slopes stripped of brushwood and bunchgrass. Burnt-out lodgepoles stood here and there, most laid where they fell. But when the snow came, I saw what Ma was looking at—there'd be a tiny red dot under a sharp rock outcrop among shifting blotches of shadow from the clouds.

One day, I hiked right up below the cliff and spotted her, a China woman, loitering under a steep rock outcrop on the side of the mountain where the shanties once stood. She was perching on a bitsy foothold, swaying like she was a half-broken branch in the wind. Her hands clasped tightly around a red cloak she had wrapped over her body. This was odd because all China men and women wore grubby black. There she was, a searing red thing stumping about, going nowhere. Her long black hair tousled about, not twisted into a braided bun like I used to see the China women around here had on their heads. Long black hair tossing in the wind hiding her face. I got goose bumps looking at her.

Others saw her, too. They said close your eyes when you chance upon her and she would go away. Truth is, she had never gone away for me. This woman in red, staggering in the soot, in the snow, haunts me long after I had left the mountains.

They said this woman clear lost her mind after her husband died in the fire. She went out one night and hung herself on that rock overhang which jutted out like a big knife.

Next morning, the China folks cut her down from the loop she had coiled and knotted out of her own tattered black tunic. She had bundled herself up in a worn red blanket snatched from the fire along with her month-old baby girl. She got no kin but they who knew her said that the dingy blanket was the one she had come across the ocean with. When they got the blanket off her to clean her up, they found purple cane marks on her body riled with blisters and open sores. Her breasts sagged with milk had bite marks on them. Who did that to her not ten days after her husband was gone? The China women asked among themselves, and words got down to the General Store where I caught them. They said that her hands were badly cut and bruised, caked with blood and dirt, three finger nails missing.

Under the hanging rock, they dug up the baby girl from a hole where a charred tree once stood. Over her tiny mouth and nose, there was the purple mark of her ma's small hand.

The China folks picked up what scraps they could and re-built their shanties far away from that side of the mountain. What they had left behind were the two bodies buried together under the hanging rock wrapped up in that soiled red blanket.

I heard more. A China woman bent with years, wobbling on a walking stick, bony hand clasping her granddaughter Ah Jin, told of an old China folklore that one who died wearing red would a restless ghost be. The old woman coughed and mumbled, chopping and spitting sounds between her few gummy yellowed teeth. Her narrow slit eyes blinked at us folks in front of the General Store where she and the little girl came to comb the gravel for the few dry beans that had spilled from the sacks. Even Stinthal came out to see what was going on for the China folks almost never came this way. Gotta be starvin, he said and walked back in.

Ah Jin, her coal black eyes darted up at the white folks standing over her. She tweeted for her *Poh Poh*: She so vengeful, she got bad, bad fate. She, *aiyah,* damned to living hell!

Others said the poor dead woman went plain nuts and grabbed the only thing she had to cover her body without her black tunic. But that shriveled old China woman kept shaking her balding head wrapped in a black headband. She sighed, slobbering sounds like *aiyah, yumkung, yumkung!*

I was caught up with staring at her face creased and crinkled like scuffed leather on worn boots, and wondered how one could live to be so very old. She must have been young once, like Ah Jin with two dangling braids which swung about her head every time she turned around. I was caught up, too, with the bit of faded red twine unraveling at one of her braids' end.

I let the old China woman's jarring words flitter into thin air. Calling to mind only when …

Oh-ooh! Ai-ai-aiyih! Oh, oh, ooh!
Wh-at what have I got on me?
RED, as red can be! Oh-ooh!

Sleep, only if I can … ah, close my eyes and doze a wink!

*   *   *

Inside me then, the sap of life was running like snowmelt in Spring. I was throbbing something fierce, aiming to bust out of my skin. As soon as I grew into my shoes, I went flying up the yonder hills.

A green fuzz had begun to spread over the charred mountain, but I stayed clear for the shrieks of that big fire still rang in my ears. I kept my distance from the hanging rock which jagged up on the far side like the blade of a knife. Still, my eyes went searching when I found myself drawn that way. Then I turned away quickly and ran as fast as my legs could carry me.

I rambled up our hill to where the lodgepole pines thinned and the ground stubbed with gray-green tufts. As I headed up, the dusty camps that squatted all over the nearby hills shrunk to no bigger than my fingertips. Down below, brown clouds hung over Leadville, made dirty by chimney smoke from the smelters. They called our town the Cloud City. I wondered.

But it was up here that I saw real clouds. White and fluffy, and the sky was blue. Oh, so-o very blue! The air sparkled. I took in big gulps of the tingling coolness. A little pika squirreled about, came out to sun himself on a boulder. I sat down and munched the week-old bun Ma brought back from Stinthal's. When he tossed her the leftovers it was his way of telling her that bake day a-comin. Stay back tonight, woman, uh, to scrub the floor!

Overhead, a lone eagle soared.

Get ya under, pika, get ya under!

I climbed up a flattop boulder, pivoted on my toes and twirled and twirled. I flung open my arms to catch the breeze. Breeze swishing my skirt, kissing my face, my hair a run of coppery gold over my eyes. I started humming the little ditties Ma used to hum when Pa was around. Tunes I hadn't heard cross her lips since he was gone.

On a day like this, I wouldn't want to be cooped up in that one room cabin Mrs. Burke called school. Kids there not standing up to my shoulders. That turned-up nose of hers pointing down at my shoes, eyeing me the way Sheriff Burke did the day my new pa fell down the gulch. She had this look as stiff as the bristle brush in her hand. She handed me the brush while the other kids went outside to play.

Scrub, girl, scrub like you be scrubbing the blackness off your soul, she said. The smirk on her thin face squeezed the last bit of air out of the tight cabin. There ain't no blackness in my soul, I retorted with my eyes. Still I had to put myself down on my knees and scrub the timber plank floor.

Swish-swoosh-swish-swoosh ... I worked the bristle brush as hard as I could, scrubbing out her face. All the while, I was hankering to get out. Away from those cutting eyes. Quick!

Just then, I heard the chug-chugging of a train pulling out of the station down at Leadville.

Sleep, only if I can close my eyes and doze a wink!

But I'm set to go wide-eyed and wakeful, stumping along on legs no longer mine, holding onto a husk of a body, going nowhere, festering, rotting away ...

One day, down in Arkansas Valley, I was bouncing in the meadow sprinkled with summer flowers. I was here not three days ago and it was then a spread of drowsy green. Something magical must have come tickling overnight and the whole field sprung to life with colors and tipsy nods.

There I saw him plodding ahead, walking stick in hand, a burro by his side carrying a load of wooden boxes, poles, a bag, a woolen jacket strapped on top. Even from his back, I could tell that he was not from these parts. He had on a loose white shirt, breeches, knee high socks and hiking boots.

I ran to catch up with him. Surely he'd have heard me coming up from behind though I flew like a breeze, my hair chasing after me. You could see the flowers fluttering and swaying as I swept past. He might even have caught sight of me as I made the bend. There was just nobody else. What a pity, on a day like this!

Mister, where ya headin? I asked, looking up at him.

His eyes were on the mountains that loomed ahead. Snow-capped, craggy white and shadowy blue, butting up against a sky the color of a robin's egg.

The flowered field where we were standing was as vast as the sky, and it rippled in the breeze. Everything dazzled and danced under the high noon sun. I wrinkled my eyes, and found dozy gold under my eyelashes, a glittery shine inside my head.

Surely he'd want to take in the sight, or he wouldn't have come this way, I'd think.

He halted his burro and paused.

Miss, he nodded, tipping the brim of his straw hat.

First time I ever heard me called Miss, and that without the fuss of what I'd got on for what I'd got on was a torn blouse and a frayed skirt. Miss—that tickled me down to my toes! I fidgeted, feeling scrawny and unwashed. My brow glistened with sweat, my copper-bright hair wind tossed, wild about my head. His eyes stayed on my face as if he'd caught something and couldn't let go of it. I felt my color rising and that was not from the sun.

Just up that way, young lady, he said pointing to the mountains. Fine day, isn't it? I'm looking to take some pictures.

Take pictures?

He might not have heard me for he'd lifted his eyes to the towering Mount Elbert, turning slowly towards the sprawling Mount Massive. In the shimmering light, the mountains seemed so near and yet so far away. He held fast his gaze, taken by the mighty hunks of the weathered rock that had bucked out of the earth way, way back. He stood there, straight up as a young lodgepole, utterly awed by the light-splotched range where brightness shone in soft shades of white and pink, and shadows straggled a deep purplish-blue.

While he stood spellbound I stole a look at his face. In his eyes, I saw a soft gleam which reminded me of my dead Pa. But his face was smooth, without the knitted lines Pa wore on his weathered brow. His voice was deep, not hoarse like Pa's.

From his faraway look, I'd a hunch how he might be feeling that very moment, himself planted firmly on the ground yet hovering in the air—a speck of dust under a boundless sky!

Pa had told me once: Em mountains got a way of makin ya small and big at the same time. Small in the scale of things. Big, too, cause they set ya free. Jus lookin at em, ahem, ya're already breathin easy and, yeah, feelin mighty grand too.

And I'd said, Glad to have em mountains, Pa.

Slowly, Mister came back down to earth. Where we stood we could catch sight of a tumbling flow as the Arkansas found its way down the slopes to course through the dark green woods and the sun drenched valley.

Overhead, a couple of eagles glided in easy circles.

Swish! One swooped down the river and lifted off with a wriggly silvery tail.

Where ya from, Mister?

Denver, miss.

What have ya got there on that animal?

Oh, my camera, stand and some plates.

We walked on. He led the way, walking at a brisk pace. I tagged along. He didn't seem to mind.

Pictures? I'd seen pictures of Baby Doe Tabor all over town.

Hmm.

What's a camera?

It's, um, a gadget, like a tool, I use to take pictures with.

Mister, you won't mind if I watch?

No, miss.

He didn't say much, like my dead Pa.

We came to a stop by the sloping riverbank where he unloaded the burro under a stand of trees where hoppers leapt and mayflies glimmered over the shiny water.

Mister, don't let the animal drink from the river. It's got sick mine tailins. Most water around here's bad.

He looked into my face and nodded.

He brought out his three-legged stand to a clearing away from the trees. He used his feet to test the ground looking for a level spot before setting up the stand. He then set a box with a glass eye atop the stand.

Miss, this here's a camera, he said, pointing to the box.

I went up to look at the little black box that was to take in what the eyes see.

You mean it can hold all this?

I stretched out my arms to show how much.

You'll see, he smiled as he slid a plate into the camera.

He turned to look at the sun, then towards the range, then into the back of the camera under the cover of a small black blanket. He did that at each turn, removing one plate and sliding in another. He said he'd take the plates back to his studio in Denver and turn them into photographs. He'd feasted his eyes, and now he was to take the feast back home.

Miss, what you see this bright summer day will be printed on a piece of paper. One day, perhaps, you'll get to hold them in your hands, to look at whenever you fancy—Mount Massive, and that Mount Elbert clear yonder!

Oh, truly!

Yes, miss. Here's my name card, look me up when you get to Denver one day, he said.

You're jesting, surely, sir? I thought.

But he handed me a small card with printed words and a drawing of that black box camera. I saw that he had a gold band on his finger.

What's your name, miss?

Galena.

Pretty name!

No, it ain't.

Oh, why?

My Pa called me that cause he ain't got no luck with his diggin. Got no silver, not even a smidgeon. Said all he ever got was lead. That's me!

Galena has a beautiful shine, miss.

But it ain't silver.

Hmm, but you've got sapphire eyes!

What's sapphire?

A precious gem, miss. It's as blue as the sky on a beautiful day. Like today.

I turned away to hide my blush, glad that the sun was on my face. He wandered off to pick one sprig of the blue flax and handed it to me. Out of a whole field of red paintbrushes, purple lupines, yellow daisies, he picked me a heavenly blue flax!

Mister, flax blooms for only a day!

But your sapphire eyes will last, miss, he said, smiling.

His smile made me feel on top of the world!

I'd just turned thirteen, head full of dreams. There was a gushing inside me like the yonder Arkansas tearing down Mount Elbert to find its own valley.

That night, a swarm of mayflies flitted into my dream skittering over the bright water before they dropped.

I gotta go, Pa. I told him that morning I slipped out of camp. I told him in my heart where he'd always be. Just like the mountains.

I stood at the foot of our hill looking across the Arkansas Valley. Bye, Elbert! Bye, Massive! My eyes grew misty and the mountains shimmered.

Good luck, girl, they said.

Pa, other mountains are calling out to me. Gold and glitter awaitin me out there. I just know it, Pa.

Can't I go back? Can't I? Can't I?
Back where? Where, oh, where?

I'm going nowhere, getting no rest.

Only if, uh, if I can doze a wink ...

Never mind I can't doze a wink! Never mind I've got stumps for leg! I stir, thud-thudding along ...
Ah, raging red is my gown, consuming me, goading me on and on ...
Blazing big, that torch inside me ...

I grit my teeth, hell-bent rankled by the big burn inside me.
In the drowning darkness, seething, churning, churning ...
If only I can lay me down ...
No, no! Got to look for something. Something I'd lost?
But, what?

A dim past flickers ...
Stoke, stoke, stoke, smoldering, fuming ... stoke, stoke, stoke ...
Rage, oh, rage!

AMITABHA, A-AMITAHBA, A-AMITAHBA ...
BOK-BOK-BOK-BOK-BOK ...
AMITABHA, A-AMITAHBA, A-AMITABHA ...

Damn you, Buddhist monk! Damn your chanting! Damn your wakeful beat! Damn your cursed robe cast over where I lay!
Call it bloody mercy or what you will. It ain't no mercy when every part of me is put in a stupor but my one burning wish.
And it keeps on burning ... burning big!
Don't you know that I'm cloaked in RED? That bloody RED is all but a yoke that has set me a charge.
Don't you know that no prayer of yours could have extinguished that blazing charge of mine?

My one and only charge—to go back.
Back to the light! Back to life!
You didn't know, did you? Or, you plain didn't care?
Damn your Amitabha! Damn your bok-bok-bok living hell!

Deliver me! Oh, please deliver me!
There are flowered meadows back in the Arkansas Valley, and ah, my bosom mountains to behold!
See, I've an unfinished life to redeem, a life of roses and double eagles!
MERCY! OH, MERCY!

Ben?
Was that you who came one day? Came and threw open the door cursed with chanting. Cast off the damn prayer robe that was holding me down, threw away that rotted-out wood fish with the hellish wakeful beat.
I see that you have kept a chip of wood and a few stray beads in your pocket.
Why? Ben, why? What good would those cursed things do you?
Rid of them, will you, Ben?
Begone Amitabha!
Begone bok-bok-bok-bok!

I shiver ... Out of the stupor, through the fog, I see it now—a pinhead of a light flickering at the end of the tunnel.

There was once a tunnel ... gritty with coal dust ... A door at the end ... opening to a carpeted hall. Alabaster lamps softly glowing ... Stares that came my way lit up like night owls' eyes. A snicker here, a smirk there soured the air, the air reeked of condescension. My face hot and cold. I held my head high, and walked up the carpeted stairs, taking care not to let my soiled slippers show.

Ben, you're no slobbering cat. Look at you, you've got gentle eyes, not a cat's eyes after all!

Pining eyes. Ben, you've got pining eyes. A lover's eyes. Like mine. Ah, a heartbreak to behold!

15

A star on my palm! A lone bead of olive oil glistening under the kerosene lamp bright as a star plucked out of the night sky ... though it be that little window of a night sky! I reach for my flask of rose water, sprinkle a few drops over the little twinkle. I smooth the scented ointment over my feet scarred with old cuts and hard times. Over my chapped heels, I rub in a little paraffin. Ah, nothing a little pampering won't heal! I slip into my silk stockings and step into satin heels paid for with my precious gold pieces.

I count them out with care, *clink, clink, clink* ...

Eyes light up as I enter the parlor. *Swis-sh, swa-ash,* I sashay around the parlor in my new silk gown, the luster of morning glory blue. The swirl of my lace bordered skirt catches every eye and turns them green. Or, sets them afire. I shrug my shoulders, twirl around, showing off my lace embroidered bodice, grosgrain ribbons streaming down my waist. I raise my hand to sweep up a stray curl, my lacy cuff flutters about my wrist. Surely, someone ought to know the cost of Flemish lace, huh?

Ben?

He stands there starry-eyed. Back so soon? I quickly wipe the surprise look off my face.

Come, I'll show you around. I give him my hand with a smile.

He shrinks back, shivering like Madam's poodle after a bath.

I laugh, little silver bells tinkling. He braces himself.

Miss, yo-ur name ple-ease?

I slip away without a word. Smiling all the same. He stays close behind.

The whole house is in full swing—supple bodies, slim bodies, flowing gowns, fussy gowns, bulging waistcoats dangling gold watches, deep pockets heavy with jingles, slow on easy chairs, soft on thick carpet, heads light on cigar fume, woozy from one too many shots of whiskey, faces flushed in the glow of the fireplace, eyes shifty, smiles too eager, hearts tickled with every passing adulation.

In the front parlor, the professor plays the piano with a broad smile and nifty fingers. He hums, his head bobbing with the rhythm, bowing low when a handful of silver coins tinkles into his tipping glass. Much obliged, much obliged, he mouths the words. White teeth gleaming, his eyes narrow into slits as he watches the tipping glass filling up before the night is done. I wink at him and he blows me a kiss, his brown face shines to please. Same as every other face around here.

"Humoresque" drifts in the air, the air droning with murmur and twitter. A burst of laugher gushes out, little titter swells like a songbird chorus. A server comes in, a bottle of Magnolia Whiskey and Old Fashioned glasses on a silver tray. Someone asks for champagne. Glasses clink, another round of laughter follows, then another.

Hey, the night's young! A groggy voice calls out.

A fine-suited gentleman is being ushered in. A noisy taffeta gown sweeps past to greet him. She's all but a rush of lightning purple, heavily scented with lavender. A heart of diamonds gleaming on her chest. Gold coins bulging in her secret pockets.

She spots me, her eyes roll up and down, counting the gold pieces I had to shell out for all those yardages of silk and lace and the seamstress's top price. You see, the seamstress gets paid, too, for fawning over me.

Ma'am blinks, a perfunctory smile curls her lips mouthing, Darling, shouldn't you be up in your room?

Ah, she's just doing what Michael asks her to! I smile, put a finger to my lips in a gesture of hush-hush.

To stay put in my room's so without cheer, sweet Michael. Wish you were here! I whisper to myself.

Overhead, the chandelier sparkles, splintering rainbow slivers in your eyes, in the gilded mirror above the mantel. A mirror full of flowers in crystal vases, candle flames dancing on silver candelabra, lush crimson damask drapes on every window ...

Ben stands at one corner, surveying the walnut paneled room. He makes his way to the wall, runs his hand over the rich dark wood. He walks over to the fireplace, gazes into the mirror. He takes a quick step back, steadies himself. I walk up behind him.

Inside the mirror, a black hole. His own face, the only face, a mere shadow, staring out. He grimaces, steels himself, as if he has been expecting it to be so all along. He turns to study my face.

Something on your mind, Ben?

But I, ah, I'm taken up with pining for my Michael. No other care in the world but my sweet Michael!

I walk away from the mirror to get back to the gaieties of the evening. He stands, dazed still.

Ben ... O-oh, Ben!

I slip out the parlor, gathering my skirt to take my steps down to the billiard room below. He follows. On the way down, he pauses to examine the brick wall alongside the stairs.

Ah, Ben, you've got to watch a game of billiards! Ma'am has the finest pool room in town.

Sounds of ball knocking, handclapping and giggly cheers weave through the air as we descend into a haze of cigar fume under the brass pendant lamps. Green glass shades cast a cool light on ruddy pudgy faces, on rouged cheeks and pouty red lips, on shiny lashes hiding tired eyes.

Bending over the green felt table, one balding gentleman, cue in hand, beady eyes squinting, aims to shoot. Other players watch. Giggly girls hang by the rails, holding onto their drinks, taking little sips. Little sips only, one drink a night, Ma'am has been drilling into their heads.

One coyly lowers her torso, near spilling out her creamy white bosoms. Eyes shift and gleam, mustaches twitch. A player drops his cue, quits the game in a hurry, walks off with his girl.

Aren't you seeing your Michael tonight? Someone with sly
eyes leans over and snickers into my ear.

Silly goose! She knows jolly well that I see my sweet Michael
in the afternoons. I turn away, pursing my lips.

Ben?

He walks up to the rear window. He peers out into the dark
alley where hacks for hire stand waiting. A driver is squatting by
his horse holding his place in the line. A hack comes to the door,
its gas lantern lit. Someone has called for a cab.

Ben stands there for a good long while looking out into the
moonlit night. Then he goes to the side of the window and picks
up a fold of the drapery. He runs his big hand ever so gently over
the silk damask of scarlet against a deep crimson, studying its
floral pattern under a wall sconce.

Come, Ben!

Look no more, please ...

He pauses, rears his head up as if something has come to mind.
He heads for the door.

Enough for a night, Ben?

He turns around. A quizzical look on his face. He reaches
into his pocket and brings out a fist. He opens it to show me
what's inside.

Rolling in his palm are a few of those damn prayer beads!

All goes black.
My feet wobble, trudging on ...
The chanting, the beat start up all over again, like a rising
tide, folding me in ...
Amitabha, A-amitabha, A-amitabha ...
Bok-bok-bok-bok-bok-bok ...
Amitabha, A-amitabha, A-amitabha ... bok-bok-bok ...

Begone!
No more Amitabha!
No more bok-bok-bok-bok!
No more, I say!
I'm on my way!

*   *   *

I'm on my way ...

I've always been on my way ...

I haven't forgotten my Pa cradling Ma's red chapped hands within his own. In the curl of smoke from the burnt-out hearth, he bowed and smooched them. I'll make good by ya, he sobbed, don't ya go washin no other folks' clothes no more.

That was two days before the big fire which gave him no chance to make good his word. Not that he had much of a chance before then. I could hear the strain in his voice at the end of a day as he slumped down by the big outcrop at the back of our cabin: Darn, darn, darn! Tons of dirt and no ore! Ma was inside our cabin, tending to the pot of thin soup at the crackling hearth.

Both of us, Ma and I, saw the sky fall when the Tomkins Hardware man came up one day and took back the tools, pick axe, spade, hammer and all, worn as they were. We heard his gruff voice: Can't grubstake ya no more ... ya got no good claim ... bits of cheap ore ain't gonna pay to put the roof over yar head. Ya a hired hand now, ain't got no use for tools a yar own.

Ma quickly slipped out back to dig at the plot that was hacked into the rocky slope where she had managed to squeeze out a few mean spuds and a handful of lean beans in the summer months. Galena dear, she mumbled to me, biting her lips: Wish ya get to eat fat spuds one day ... and, uh, beans that are juicy and firm, yeah, like those back in Kansas Territory ...

Ya, too, Ma, I'd said to her as I hung by her side burying my face in the thin folds of her skirt.

Ma stopped digging after a while. She laid down her hoe, bolted up and raised her filmy eyes to the flat land on the other side of the mountains only she could see. A sweaty strand of her hair fell out of her head kerchief. She swept it back with her dirt encrusted hands, smearing her face. Then she broke into camp songs. A line here, a phrase there, *home on the rocky high range*

... rainbow's a bridge across my heart ... silver sparkles in my eyes ... Softly, then loud, louder. *My cup's full ...*

She stopped abruptly, ran her sleeves over her soiled face and walked back into the cabin with her head bowed so I wouldn't see her tears.

I haven't forgotten the seasons of knee-deep snow and long cabin nights when the cold wind whistled through the cracks and my stomach growled, and the sound of my new pa snoring which was better than not snoring.

How much longer? How much longer do I've to wait before I clear out of these dark days and darker nights?

Oh, be quiet, you hooting owl, lest you tell me right this minute!

Geese flew north, geese flew south, squawking down the sky across the Arkansas Valley. Flapping black dots journeying past, spreading out into a wide V, folding back up into a narrow V.

Take me, oh, ple-ease take me! Anywhere, ya hear! I screamed my lungs out at the bunch of soaring dumb birds fast fading out of sight.

That night, I dreamed I could fly. Up, up away into the clear blue sky!

But I'd to stay put, wait out my time. I squatted behind the sacks of beans and flour and devoured every scrap of the old *Heralds* and *Chronicles* which found their way up the General Store, picking out words I could read and poring over sketches of new store arrivals: A lady's ball gown with an embroidered bodice, a full skirt with a train behind, long silk gloves and a pair of satin heels to match; summer bonnets with fancy crimps, sun hats trimmed with taffeta ribbons and rose buds. That, a para-sol?

Stop messin with em wrappin papers, garl! Stinthal barked. Maka yarself useful other ways, huh?

His salivating dog's eyes licked at my budding bosoms. I threw down the papers and ran out the backdoor, his eyes burning after my back.

Hey, woman, come over here! I heard him hollering at Ma.

I took to my feet and tore down the gully, scraping past prickly brushes, setting off a trail of loose stones after my heels.

I'm on my way ...

Gosh, everyone had been saying that it was gonna be the dandiest Parade the town had ever seen!

I started out just as the birds broke into their twittering at daybreak. My heart went aflutter, hurrying me down the path to get to town. As I ran, the pine-scented air charged up against my face. The cool breeze tousled my hair but I didn't mind a bit. I had my hands over my skirt, holding onto the crust of old bread I had tied underneath.

Deer scrambled up the slope as I flew down. Crows took to the air, *caw, caw, caw*, wings flapping among the lodgepoles. A hare dashed across my path, scurrying into a hole under the brushes. Golden rays splintered through dense needles lifting me out of the shadow. On a high perch, a finch broke out into a string of whistling, trilling notes.

Beau-ti-ful day coming up!

Down by the Depot, the South Park stood on its track. What right mind will be leaving town today? Of all days? The bench outside was empty. A trainman was standing on a step ladder with a bucket, washing car windows. Another was climbing up the locomotive. I walked around the rear end of the car to the side away from the Depot. I looked up the steps where passengers got into the car. A small folding gate with a latch stood at the top of the steps. I went up against the first step. It came near up to my waist. Without a stepping stool, I gotta hoist myself up.

I ran along the length of the car, jumping up in the air trying in vain to snatch a look inside through the windows. Then I stepped upon the ties and started to skip and hop along the track. The crust of bread bouncing under my skirt, bread crumbs falling down my legs.

Ooops! I flung my skirt about to loosen that scratchy feeling. Giggling aloud, I ran on.

Choo-choo! Choo-oo! The train running on in my head.

Breeze on my face, a warm rush rising inside me.

Hey, gal, off the track! A trainman shouted from behind.

I stopped running, turned around and mouthed the words without making a sound: Hey, take me out of here, ya hear?

I got off the track and kept running. I turned into East 9th Street, and headed toward Harrison. Store fronts were decorated with red-white-and-blue buntings, and the Court House had the tallest flag flying. Folks everywhere. Town folks and camp folks eyeing one another. Folks pouring into Harrison from the side streets. Heard that the stage coaches had brought in lots of folks from out of town, and trainloads from Denver, too.

I watched where the crowds gather and they all seemed to be gathering at this end of town. I could hardly wait, counting the hours when Harrison would come alive with the promised show.

What's a Parade, Ma?

Ain't never seen one, Galena.

Won't ya come with me?

Nah, ya go on and have some fun.

Ya gonna sit by Pa?

She nodded.

I could just see her, sitting by the big outcrop of moss rock where Pa was laid to rest. She'd be telling him things the way she used to, in her soft voice. Little cheery things like: Ain't it a beautiful sunset, dear? Remember when we rode out here? Our first sight of the mountain sunset, and ya called it magical. It still is, dear. Over there, ya see the magpies flappin about the bushes? Makin such a racket …

High noon, the crowd thickened, lining both sides of the street. Never mind the jostling, I stood my ground right up front.

Oh, look! Tabor's Light Calvary!

Heads turned, cheers rose.

Mr. Tabor gonna be here?

Nope, Aunt Mape, he a long gone a Denver.

Oh, my! That so.

Here they come!

My heart throbbed at the sight of the dashing Light Calvary—their blue tunics, red trousers with one gold stripe down the side, shiny brass helmets with chin straps—marching to the band music of trumpets and flutes and horns flashing in the sun.

Ain't dat da biggest drum ya ever seen, Addie?

Moss, ya're a pumpkin.

I inched away, lest people mistook them for my kin, scrappy camp folks nudging up close.

Hey, what's comin up?

The most beautiful tune ever to pulse the air, weaving through the oohs and aahs, came straight up to me as if it were crooning and trilling to me and me alone.

Hush up! Listen!

It sounded like a lone bird in the woods calling out, warbling for his mate, like oh where, oh where's my love?

That's Duncan playin his bagpipe! Someone who knew spoke from behind.

Ma! Man wearin skirt? A squeaky voice said.

Son, that's a kilt, a Royal Stewart kilt he's wearin. Mr. Duncan's leadin Mr. Tabor's Highland Guards. See, the regiment comin up behind him.

Highland Guards? Dey all be wearin skirts, huh? What're em pouches danglin in front a em skirts?

The knowing voice said no more. He had moved on.

The guardsmen marching past, in their pleated, what, uh, kilts of red-and-black checkers, knee-high socks with tassels swinging every step of the way. They tipped their bonnets and smiled at the crowd.

Ah, but it was the bagpiper's tune that spoke to me. It spoke to me like a running brook that pulled down the sky and took with it the shivering sun and the downy clouds. It ran me over with a softness that was wholly new.

Maybe, not so new. I thought I'd seen glimpses of it in Ma's eyes when she looked into Pa's in the sundown light, sparkling ever so softly. Like stars twinkling.

Other marching bands came along. The sound soon grew jarring to my ear. Trumpets blared, cymbals clanged, drums bonged. A bunch of jingle-jangle that went on and on.

Gal, ya havin fun?

I looked up. A red-face with a frazzled beard was blowing hot foul air into my face. A jumble of stained teeth in his mouth. I squeezed my way out of the crowd.

Come back, gal! Lemme show ya a good time, he grunted.

I shoved myself into a pack of kids hopping alongside the Parade. I hopped along, fretting about my spoiled fun.

Someone hollered: Fire trucks! Fire trucks comin up!

I could hear a horse neigh, and the sound of hoofs hitting the ground, and the clanking and rattling of wheels and a dog barking. Loud whistles and cheers rose in the crowd rushing up from behind.

Sis, hey, sis, ain't ya too big to run wit us? A little fry with a loud mouth bustled up to me and yelled into my face.

Ya, wa-ay too b-big!

We wanna no gal around, ya hear?

Yeah, get lost!

Shut yar mouths, I screamed back at those bobbin heads above the din. Ugh, snooty town kids! But I slowed my pace and fell back a bit. I turned back, looked around. No red face, no bearded red face, in the crowd.

I stopped running when we passed by the brick building that was Daniels and Fisher department store. Shopkeepers hung about the sidewalk, chatting, taking in the Parade. Behind them, the doors of the store stood wide open. A tall gentleman with white mustache, bright green bow tie and a starched white shirt, kept an eye behind his back to take note of who was walking past.

I stepped upon the sidewalk, got a foothold and craned forward to look out for the fire trucks. The plump woman by my side shifted her bulk and looked me over out of the corner of her eye. She waved her pink handkerchief about her nose throwing off a heavy sweet scent.

She gonna sneeze? I edged away from her all the same.

Cheers and clapping sprang up as the first fire truck rode past, pulled by two handsome horses, one black, one white. Bright red, big wheeled, the truck had a shiny brass plate on the side which read: *City of Leadville F. D.* The firemen wore jackets with bright brass buttons and box caps, two rode standing on each side of the truck. The firemen waved to the crowd.

Howdy, Fire Marshall!

The Fire Marshall nodded and waved to both sides of the street. More cheers!

Hey, Jimmy! An elderly man shouted excitedly to the driver sitting next to the Fire Marshall. The young lad waved back with a sunny smile. A dog rode in the truck.

Spot, hey, Spot!

Didn't Spot get run over last year?

This here's a new dog, ya dope!

A couple pushed their way up front, stretching out their necks for a better view.

See our Junior, pa?

Not yet. He's with the hook and ladder company comin up.

Next came a truck, carrying ladders, long hooks, sledgehammers and other tools.

Ma, there's Junior! See him?

Hey, Junior! Over here! The couple waved to one of the firemen riding on the side of the truck.

The truck that followed carried coils of hose, a hand pump, stacks of buckets and six more firemen.

Buckets.

Busted buckets, banged-up pails, clanking tins—the water line heaved uphill. Smoke and heat. The fire that raised hell on our side of the mountain, torching day into night into day into night ... The fire that snubbed out lives and charred the hearts of those left behind. The fire that took Pa away. Took Ma, too, in a way. Left me burning to get out of here ever since.

I turned away from the Parade and stole behind the shopkeepers to take a look into the shop windows. The canvas awnings above the windows were drawn up. The sun glared down, washing the glass in a sheet of shine. I looked in and saw this soft white summer gown on a dummy body form. It had a lace collar, lace embroideries over the shoulders and the torso, and little buttons running down the front. From the waist down, lace embroideries sprinkled like falling petals over the skirt. I could not tear myself away.

I stuck my head inside the open door. On one side was a pale yellow gown on another dummy body form. But I was struck by something else. At the back, a full length mirror stood on the floor facing the door. In it, I saw the reflection of a young girl in a scruffy dress which hung limply on her matchstick frame. She stood dark and drab, her back against the outdoor light. But for her head, her head was a fuzz of golden light. A halo ablaze, doused by the bright sun.

Me! That was me! My hair was a blaze of rose-tinted coppery gold! Not like what I used to see in Ma's fogged-up cracked mirror I held in my hand, or from peering into the shadowy stream on a clear day.

Galena, ya got a name that says lead, but ya got yar Ma's hair. That's yar gold, child, Pa had said to me once.

It came to me then how Pa had looked when he touched Ma's hair. He ran his fingers gently through her tangled curls specked with dirt. He tousled mine, grinning away. But he kissed hers, misty eyed and breathing steam.

Will someone look at me like so one day? I felt giddy just thinking of it.

Off you go, girl! Shoo, shoo!

I turned to look. A shop lady was coming after me. I stood rooted to the ground, too shaken to move.

Others spun around and they, too, came after me. Mother hens, two, three and more, clucking, flapping their arms at me like I was a stray cat. The gentleman with the green bow tie turned around and watched. I saw his white mustache twitch as he glanced into the store. His eyes softened. He must have seen that

I was drawn to the mirror.

Ladies, ladies, he hushed them with a gesture of his hand. They held back and looked to him.

Miss, good day! He said as he stepped aside to let me pass.

My first Parade came to an end as I stepped out of the store. I cut through the procession and walked across Harrison, holding my head high all the way back uphill.

When I came into town times afterwards, I never did go back to look at myself in the mirror, or to gawk at the gowns on the dummies. There was a whole lot more to do!

There was this special colored picture of Baby Doe in a salon window right on Harrison. It made my heart stop every time I passed by. I would linger, press my face against the glass and let her eyes speak to me, eyes as blue and clear as the mid-summer sky. They looked at me and said: Galena, life's sweet, go for it!

Yes, ma'am, oh, yes!

Then I asked: What's Denver like?

She said no more. But I knew that she shone in Denver, and went on to shine at the nation's Capitol, a place called Washington, D.C. I read about it in the old newspaper scraps that had found its way up to the General Store.

There was just a hint of a smile on her lips. I pored over her lovely face, her cheeks were flushed like the pale pink blossoms that hugged her bosoms. She had her shoulders bare, and they were round and creamy white. Her reddish gold hair was piled up in curls. Reddish gold just like mine.

Not quite. Mine was shaggy and unwashed. I saw my dark reflection on the glass and looked away.

After that, I would go by the Clarendon and be dazzled by the bright lights inside. At the street corner, I would keep watch over the guests coming and going, and the white-gloved doormen bowing as they held open the doors. There I saw how a lady would step on and off a carriage, how she would gently lift her skirt, drape her stole over her shoulders as she lightly took the gentleman's offered hand.

I would walk on to the Tabor Opera House next door to look at the playbills, reading some but mostly just gawking at the drawings. Leaning against the door, I would try to picture the evening crowd gathering inside—ladies in flowing gowns and capes, and gentlemen in theater jackets and polished shoes. I might then hop on over to the Grand Central Theater to look at more playbills.

I never did seem to get enough of the town. There was the Saddle Rock Café where Baby Doe met Mr. Tabor, the Silver King. There was the Tontine Restaurant on East Chestnut where I had many a time peeped through the gauzy curtains at the candlelit tables. There I saw how a lady would pick up her fork, hold her knife, and, ah, how she dab her mouth with a piece of white cloth the size of Ma's head kerchief. Only nicely ironed and white and new, for sure.

The sun had swung west and the sky was on fire. Time to go. I had to drag myself to leave.

Goodnight, Mrs. Tabor, I said to her as I ran past the salon on my way back.

I headed up East 7th Street. Passing by the Depot, I saw that the South Park from Denver had arrived. Passengers were getting off the train. I ran on. When I got up the hills I looked across the valley at the sprawling blue mountains yonder.

The sun had flushed gold behind Mount Elbert and Mount Massive. The hunks of old rock looked awesome and dark against a flaming sky freckled with purple fish scale clouds. I started to climb. Hurry! The sun would go down in the blink of an eye.

Our side of the mountain looked west and had the last light. But shadows rolled down the slope like a hand that dropped over your eyes. Then, before ya could take three deep breaths, darkness would fall in one big swoop.

I ran, fast as my legs could carry me. Looking up into the deepening blue sky, I called out to the first star of the night: Star light, star bright, keep me safe tonight!

16

All aboard! A-all abo-oard!

Mornin, ma'am, goo-od lookin mornin, ain't it?

Mornin, sir! Have yaselves a nice trip!

Watch ya step, ma'am.

Footsteps thumping up the steps. My heart raced like a hare with a fox at my tail. I popped my head up to peep at the front entrance of the car. Now! I got up from crouching under a seat at the rear end. Last thing I wanted was to be caught hiding. I sat myself down by the window and lowered my head.

Oh, please, let nobody see me just yet!

Ticket? Yeah, my ticket. Um...

I'd dig my hands into my pockets and fumble around, looking puzzled.

Mister, I don't seem to, uh, find it, uh, on me ... Swear I'd put it in my pocket, uh, must have dropped it somewhere.

I was running the scene through my head ...

Flu-ump! Thum-ump!

O-oh, my foot! My basket, I drop my basket!

Myrtle, Myr, ya alright?

Oh, blah, I twisted my ankle! Pick, eh, pick up my basket! And em stuffs that fell out ...

Ma'am, ya okay? The trainman asked. Mister, lemme give ya a hand and get ma'am settle in first. That alright?

Next thing I knew the trainman was standing at the rear entrance. He must have gone around the back and gotten in from the other side, same way I did.

Can ya make it, Myr?

Sure I can.

Sound of shuffling, scraping. I slid myself down on the seat.

How about right here, mister?

Myr?

Will do, yeah, thanks, captain.

Captain? I near giggled out loud.

A loud bang.

Amos, leave that case be, go pick up my things. See the loaf of bread on the landin? Quick, folks comin up!

I heard quick footsteps down the aisle of the car. From the corner of my eye, I caught a flash of the dark blue uniform. I held my breath, sat very still. Go away, go-oo away!

How ya get in, gal?

I bit my lips and was slow to look up. The trainman stood over me, squinting down, frowning big. The morning sun had slanted in through the window, setting me on fire. I broke into a cold sweat. I gripped my seat with arms like sticks and went mum. All that I'd wanted to say flew out of my head.

Got ya a ticket?

I squirmed.

No? Gal, ya gotta get off.

My eyes pleaded: Please, mister. I've come a long way. I, uh, I gotta get to …

Where ya gonna go? He asked as if he had read me.

Denver, mi-ister.

By yaself?

She's with me, mister. Someone answered over the beat of snappy heels. A young man with a cowhide hat walked up from behind.

Hello, there! He lifted his hat and tipped his head towards me, flashing a twitchy smile without showing his teeth. His lips were thin like his voice, and he got unblinking eyes. He stared at my face, my hair, my body, then at the little bundle by my side. Reminded me of a fox's steady gaze out of a thick brush.

Mister, I'm gonna get her a ticket to Denver.

Allow me, miss? He gestured with his head at the station ticket booth and winked. Two thumbs tucking at his shiny belt buckle, he shuffled past the trainman to strut down the car without so much as an "excuse me, mister." I saw that his pants were skin tight and he wore polished cowboy boots.

Gal, the trainman said as he looked at me darkly, it ain't no business a mine, but young gal like ya oughtn't a goin to no big city by herself, and not with no stran-ger. His voice tightened as he went on. Go on home, gal. Don't yar folks miss ya?

I turned my face to the window so he wouldn't see the tears welling up my eyes. I looked out at the sparkling sunshine. A blur of the slick evergreens looming over sparse bushes flecked with green. Nearby, a clutch of sparrows chirping, rousted out of the junipers by a sudden breeze. My heart went thumping like a chased hare charging down the slope ...

Ma, I gotta go.

Silence. Just as I wondered if she had heard me, she mumbled, Whe-ere to, Galena?

Denver, Ma.

Must ya, huh? Ya know I won't be comin along, dear. Gotta wait for yar Pa. He's gonna be back for his lunch pail anytime now. His pick axe, too. She stared blankly at the squashed pail and his rusted pick axe with a broken handle. She had kept them by the door for him.

I turned to look out back. The setting sun had hit the slope and threw orange rays over the moss rock where Pa used to sit, so the lichen looked a tad greener, the brown red and the black glinted with mica specks. He was put to rest beside that big outcrop. Nearby, the little plot where Ma had worn her knuckles out over a few strings of lean beans and a handful of mean spuds was now overtaken by stubbles of weed just like the dug patch over where Pa laid.

But nothing was forgotten. Not on her good days. I had seen her sitting by the big rock, her eyes shut to the late day sun, humming little scattered phrases of the camp ditties she once knew so well. Her flushed cheeks shone with sweat. Or, tears?

No matter, it ate me up all the same.

I threw my arms around her and hung onto the rhythm of her breathing. I couldn't let go of her warmth, her smell. She ran her hand gently over my hair, and kissed both my cheeks.

I'll be back for ya, Ma, I whispered into her ear before letting go.

She fumbled about her skirt, took out a little packet wrapped in yellowed newspaper and pressed it into my hand. I opened it and saw the four dollar coins, the four dollars she earned in two weeks, sometimes longer, for baking, cleaning, washing at the General Store and, damn, for lying down for Stinthal!

I thought of the crusty old bread that Stinthal chucked our way to keep us going. An anger leapt up to churn inside me, and I breathed hotly.

Ma, remember ya told me to eat fat spuds? Promise ya, I'll get to eat fat spuds. Ya, too, Ma.

I had meant to sound cheery. But I saw the tears in her eyes.

Stinthal came in the night fouling the air with his beer breath, and he came most of these nights after his wife got sick. He tossed Ma about in bed, belched and moaned, before settling down to snore. I rolled into a tight bundle in my corner of the cabin and covered up my ears. Sleep came as if to a burrowed pika under a boulder.

At the crack of dawn, I slipped out with my little bundle. A pika on the run.

As I was leaving camp, I turned to look for the sun to rise on the burnt-out side of the mountain where the slab of rock jutted up, where I had once seen the China woman in red stumbling along, going nowhere. I took to my feet and ran.

I ran in the dusky gray light. I ran in the pale white light. Soon, a glimmer of sun slit through the lodgepoles. A gentle light showered down the needled branches, showing me the way down the slope. In the blink of an eye, the spread of the hillside was at my feet. It shimmered in a silky shine as if I was looking through many a spidery web stitched together and thrown to the air. Down below, the town was wrapped in a thin haze. I could barely make out the spire of the Church, but I knew down there at the Depot the South Park was waiting for me.

I paused and looked across the Arkansas Valley. The white mountains dazzled in the wakening light. They rose above the mist and floated in the air. The air gleamed like a big dewdrop so you saw the mountains closer than they really were, like they were at the tip of your outstretched hand. I knew better because I had walked a whole long day and did not even get to the foothills. Beneath the mist a fuzz of tender green had sprouted through. Spring had breathed a new life into the valley.

Ah, how I wish my photographer friend of that one summer day were here! To catch sight of my mountains this very moment. To have his breath taken away.

Gotta go!

Bye, Elbert! Bye, Massive!

My eyes grew misty and the mountains shimmered.

Good luck, girl, they said.

I did not once turn to look back to camp, to where our little cabin perched by the big outcrop. But I shouted out loud to a waft of the errant wind, Ma, ya take care, ya hear?

I squirmed as Tight Pants sat himself down beside me. Perhaps, it was that big smirk of his, or the smell of tobacco about him. Or, something else. I pulled Ma's old shawl over my shoulders and wrapped myself snug and tight.

Choo-choo! Choo-oo! Chuff-chuff-chuff ...

The slow engine was starting up. Whistle blowing, wheels grinding, screeching the rail. We were chugging out of the depot, *chuff-chuff-chuff* ...

Fly, oh, can't ya fly? Go with the sun, ride with the wind, get me to Denver, quick!

But my eyes lingered. The mist was burning off, the air quivered like a puff of lustrous breath, lifting the day. Even the tall dark conifers had a wash of light over their tips. The sky had opened up to a clear blue, the white mountains sun-blushed, and the Arkansas a silver ribbon winding down the high grounds, glistening through the gentle green valley. For a moment, my heart stayed put.

Summer flowers any day now, and butterflies will come ...

By now, Ma would have gotten the message I'd sent her with the wind. I turned back to look for our hill. But we had rounded a bend and what I'd left behind was gone for good. Snuggling up against her shawl, feeling her close ...

Jack, call me Jack, Tight Pants tapped my shoulder and gave me his hand. Eyes like a fox's. They fixed on my face. I felt like a butterfly with a wing ripped even as I was about to fly.

What do I call ya, miss?

Call me Lena.

Please to meet ya, Lena. He-ere's yar ticket.

He handed it to me. It said: Denver, One Way, Eight Dollars.

I reached down my pocket and held onto the four dollar coins Ma had given me. It would have taken Pa, bless his soul, near three days' earnings to pay for this ticket. My hand shook holding this bit of printed paper that was about to give me a new life.

How am I gonna pay? I looked out the window, pushed the thought out of my mind.

Thanks, Jack. I stole a look into his eyes and saw a glint of steel even as he was smiling.

Smile back, I said to myself. I didn't want to be that hurt doe. She had one hind foot caught in a trap not meant for her. It was a loss to the trapper and a bigger loss to her. Worn with kicking, she froze as I went gingerly up to her. Her glazed eyes told me she had lost her will to fight. My fight had just begun.

Tight Pants smiled some more, chewing his thin lips and asked, Lena, this yar first time to Denver?

Yes, I said in a bright voice.

Well, well, ya gotta let Jack show ya what a swell town Denver is. A wow town, lots a wha-wha, ya'll see!

Hmm.

Why ya go to Denver, Lena?

To look up a friend.

Oh, yeah? Who? Hey, I know people, I know Denver like the back of my hand. He flipped his hand over and over, to show me how he knew Denver.

What ya do for a living Jack? I was about to ask. Then I saw that his hands were clean, no cuts, no chaps, only tobacco stain on two finger tips.

Tsk, tsk, tsk, a tongue was clicking nearby. I turned to look. A couple of squirrels sat across from us. *Hee-a-hee!* They snickered and turned their heads our way, making to look like they were trying to catch the view out of my window. The woman squirrel had on a pretty blue bonnet but her face had the color and the look of sand, and her man got no eyebrows, making him look like a frog.

Footsteps thudding up from behind, a guy with a thick felt cap and puffy eyes sniffed his way up to where we sat. He looked me over good, twisting his curled-up whiskers with two fat fingers. Jack sucked in a breath, wrinkling his nose and hissed between his teeth. Sounded like a rattle snake without his rattler.

What can I do for ya? He asked loudly, making big his thin voice.

The guy thudded his way back without saying a word.

Chuff-chuff-chuff ... The train was on a climb, heaving up to where it was snow-packed. It got to that we were clawing our way up the blinding white slope steep like a wall on one side, but when ya turn the other way, looking west, ya saw the widest spread of gentle green valley down below.

Just when ya think ya could go no higher, we headed one notch up closer to the clouds.

Oh, hang on, hang tight!

It was like ya were on a sling, seeing nothing but up or down, and ya were about to fly off the edge of the world the next breath ya took. I shuddered and grabbed onto my seat.

Awesome rocks loomed ahead. They popped up at every turn glaring at ya. Spur after spur stood above us, peak upon peak reared up yonder, then getting closer, and closer until we come to snake our way beneath the towering white spires.

I took a peep at Tight Pants. He had his hat pulled over his face against the glare. I let out a sigh, feeling at ease even as the big white cragginess was closing in outside my window.

Climax, Climax comin up! The trainman called out as he walked up and down the aisle. Folks this here a Fremont Pass, top a the Divide. What's a Divide, ya wanna know, don't ya? It means that some a the runoff from the snowmelt on this ridge right here a gonna find its way out west to California, and some down south to the Gulf a Mexico, cause, folks, this here a where the water divides.

How high are we? Someone asked.

11,325 ft, mister.

Whoa!

Yeah, man, that a Continental Divide! Tight Pants said smugly, one eye peeking out from under his hat. He nudged up close, leaning over me to look out the window. His thigh rubbed against mine. My cheeks burned. I shifted, tucked my shawl in tight.

Cold, I said.

Gal, ya gotta mind to get off here? The trainman asked standing over us, his eyes shot straight at me. Ya gonna hop on the train right here at this stop to head back to Leadville later this afternoon. Fourteen miles back to where we started. Ya won't wanna nobody to bother ya no more.

I saw the growl on his face as he glared at Tight Pants.

Outside, there was this small station hut, and a blowing whiteness that huffed up to a big blue sky. Here, ya couldn't make out where the land ended and the sky began. One wrong step, I'd surely fall out of this world. I was not about to budge. I bolted straight up on my seat and shied away from the eyes under the trainman's cap.

Getta lost, man! Jack snarled. She gotta ticket to Denver, and that's where she a gonna go.

Jack showed his fox's teeth, small and sharp. I turned to look out the window. I wanted to wipe those teeth off my mind. Out of the corner of my eye, I saw the trainman walk away. Doesn't he get it that I can't turn back? Won't turn back? *Tsk, Tsk, Tsk,* squirrels smirking.

I'd heard the camp folks say that it took five days to go on foot to Denver. Five long days of trekking over mountain passes, down gullies and canyons to follow the rivers into valleys and plains. The nights were long and cold because yar growling stomach gnawed at ya, keeping ya awake. Yar feet felt like mush, bloodied and sore. And wild animals stalking yar scent, howling and yelping so yar hair gotta stand on end.

Robinson here, looka west, folks, watcha out for the Holy Cross comin up on that mount yonder!

A bit of jostling followed as passengers from across the aisle bent over to vie for a good view. The squirrel couple was quick to make the sign of the cross as a huge snow cross came into view in the distance. It stood out on the dark rugged face of the mountain as if a hand had put it there.

Keep me safe, holy cross! I said in my heart.

Chugga-chugga-chugga ...
No turnin back at Kokomo!

Winding downhill, chugging through the canyon, a tail wind whistling us along. Trees shook and clouds rolled up over the snow-capped ranges that stretched on forever under the endless blue sky.

No turnin back at Frisco!
Chugga-chugga-chugga ...

At Dickey, a burly unshaven man with a head kerchief got off the train. He had a rolled-up bundle slung over one shoulder, a tin cup and a walking stick tied onto it that went *clink-clink* as he hobbled down the dirt road. Ya see his type all over the hills looking for work. I'd seen them up our hills in better days.

No turnin back at Dickey!

At Dickey the rail took a turn. So did I. By now, Leadville was no more than a dot on my mind, but for Ma. Stinthal would be hollering at her this very minute, Woman, wheere's that garl a yars? This here's the bake day and she ain't nowhere to be found? Who's gonna tend the fire? Ya hear me, woman?

Ma would be kneading, a dusting of flour fly up her arms, powdering her face. She would punch down hard at the dough, *pou-pou! POU!* Never mind that Stinthal huffing and puffing over her.

Ma! I'll be back for ya! Just ya wait.

A river! We came upon a river and pushed on along its bank, going with the flow. Shivering in the sun, the snowmelt ran clear and full, splashing froth over the bedded rocks. Little canals branched off along the way like slithering snakes. People squatting down by the shallows looked up from their pans as we made our way downslope.

That a what ya call a sluice. That wood trough, see? Use a wash for a gold. The man squirrel said to his woman as he pointed out the window. His woman was rummaging her carpet bag and had no eye for gold or sluice.

Yep, that a it, the trainman said walking down the aisle. Been seein more folks a pannin these days, ever since more and more mines about Leadville gotta shut down. Silver gotta no pay these days, hmm. Over there, see how they a come over the mountains, that little band a folks lookin for hire!

I looked to where he was pointing. A ragged bunch, sure looked like folks from my parts, trudging along the river bank, driven out of the hills by empty stomachs. A little girl tagged behind her ma who was carrying all she owned strapped onto her back. A pot dangling out of the bundle. The little girl stopped and gawked at the passing train.

Coulda be me, if Pa's still around!

Chugga-chugga-chugga ...

Gotta get out, Ma. My luck had run out in em hills, Pa told Ma two days after the Tomkins man came and took away his tools.

Ya a hire hand now, we'll see about it come next summer, Ma muttered with her head down.

The mountains have a way of breakin yar back, I thought. Yar heart, too. I bet Ma had no idea how life would turn out when she first came out of Kansas Territory with Pa. She was seventeen and newly hitched. Oh, yeah, Pa must have talked her in good!

Galena dear, she'd talk to me when I was toddling at her feet. Leadville's Magic City! She'd say. Oh, yeah, there's silver waitin in these hills. Ya hear men strikin it big every day! Our turn will come, baby. Yeah, it'll come.

Those days, her footsteps were light and there was music in her voice. But then I thought I heard her sigh when she turned her back.

It's my turn now, Ma. I'm gonna strike it big. Wish me luck!

Tight Pants's sour mouth was next to my hair and he was blowing moist breath over my neck. I fidgeted and shifted away. He leaned back, pointed his chin out, stretched his neck and let out a big yawn. He dug his hand into his jacket pocket and took out a snuff tin. Rolling a pinch of loose tobacco between his yellowed thumb and his yellowed forefinger, he sniffed it with his eyes closed, snorting loudly. Then he put it into his mouth, tucking it between his cheek and gum.

Like the smell? He asked, eyes narrowed into slits.

I shook my head.

Ya gonna get used to it, he chuckled.

Fat chance, I said to myself.

I looked out at the mills that dotted the slopes, spewing smoke. Logs piled up in the rail yard.

Lumberin country, someone said.

Jack chewed his tobacco and after a while spitted out the little moist lump onto the floor.

Mind ya not doin that, the man squirrel said, scowling at Jack.

Jack shrugged. Mind yar own business, he shot back.

Chuff-chuff-chuff… A slow crawl up steep slopes. The river ran on down below. It ran out of sight as we wound our way up.

Chuff-chuff-chuff... Lugging ahead, pointing up and up.
Tall thick conifers fell back, stand after stand, running through light and shade. Snow caps shining through. Rearing tall, they jutted into the sky.
Whoa! Sky so blue I felt queasy looking at it. Slopes dotted with boulders rolled down into snow fields, fell into valleys thick with conifers. Conifers fanned out, thinned out, as they sprawled into grassy plains. Purple and blue, layer upon layer, yonder ranges pushed through bands of light—a lighter shade, a brighter shade, another lighter shade.
Peering down, I saw blotches of shadow over the land where clouds traveled. Eagles soared beneath my feet, spreading their wings wide, oh, so wide!
Wish I can fly!
Fly, oh, fly!
Gosh, I'm near touchin the sky!

Boreas Pass, folks, the trainman said. Second time around, we a here on the spine of the land where the water divides. How high? Folks, 11,481 feet high!
Holy cow!
I feel sick, the woman squirrel whimpered, nudging her head against her man's shoulder. Her bonnet came undone. She sat up quickly and fussed over her hair.
Wanna eat? he asked her.
Nah! She was fussing over her hair still. Then, she turned to fuss over her bonnet.
Fussing, eh? Not when ya're on top of the world! I pressed my face against the window.
Gotta take it in, take it all in!

A deep breath, and Pa's low voice hummed inside my head: Galena, ya golden girl! Ya're fifteen and ya're gonna shine!
Shine like Baby Doe, Pa?
Shine like gold, my girl, and ya gonna outshine Doe!
I'm gonna shine like the sun, Pa.

Out the window, the sun shone like I'd never seen it shine before. Golden rays shimmered through air thin and cool and still. Like ya had just opened yar eyes to a bright new place, like ya could walk right out into it and that once outside ya would become this light. Ya be all golden, and be sparkling in yar mind and in yar heart!

Pa, ya called me yar golden girl?

Tight Pants let out a loud snort and brought me back to where I was, sitting next to a snorer who had no use of the golden light. And, he was drooling.

I once saw a fox slumped by the trail like an empty blood-soaked gunny sack, red fur matted darkly in the sun. Drooling, his jaws hung loose and set, and his eyes did not blink even as my shadow came over him. He was blanked out by a sling-shot to the neck. I took to my feet and ran.

Denver ... then what?

Tight Pants was puffing his thin lips. The rumbling of the train drowned out his snoring.

Past noon now. I pulled out the crust of old bread from my bundle and nibbled on it. A tap on my shoulder. The trainman handed me a bun.

For luck, he said in a low voice, looking me not in the eye. I held my breath, gaped at him. He walked away before I could say thank you.

I looked at the bun he gave me. It must have come from his lunch pail, put there by loving hands. I took a bite. Soft and chewy. In it were bits of dried sour cherries.

Every bite's for luck, every bite's for luck, every bite's for ... I need all the luck there's to get.

Soon, I looked out the window and saw that we had stopped by a place called Como.

Looka here folks, the stone roundhouse ya all must a heard about, the trainman said. See, a turntable with tracks inside! That a way, the locomotive can turn around and come back a out after work a done on it.

I looked out and saw six huge door openings in a curved stone wall. Two locomotives sat inside the roundhouse.

Every bite's for luck, every bite … I kept on munching and staring out so I could forget that Tight Pants' by my side.

Welcome aboard, mister. To Denver, aye? I heard the trainman say down the steps.

Choo-oo choo-oo!

The snow glared like a bunch of sun slick pine needles poking ya in the eye. I shut my eyes and let my body rock with the motion … sun and shade rumbling past … rumbling past … two small finches circling in my head, singing to each other … Pa's starry eyes melting into Ma's face, her hair glowing in the moonlight even as the hearth fire had died and the cabin cold, and I dropped off to stroke the belly down of a robin chick …

Shades dappling past, a running bright sun came over my lids. I opened my eyes and caught the most wonderful sight. It was as if the mountains were stamped down on all sides and the earth opened up to a spread of grassland where herds of cattle and sheep grazed, and the rivers took sleepy wide turns, and creeks ran off where the land sloped. A buggy carrying a load of hay made its slow way on a path that cut through the fuzzy green fields. Huts and sheds dotted the land. There were much stirrings by the river banks—folks panning, kids fishing, cattle drinking. The sky was a dreamy blue and everything glimmered under the sun.

Lookin good. So-o good!

Plains! Surely Denver can't be far off. I told myself. The picture stretched on for miles. At a bend, I got a glimpse of the white mountains looming ahead and my heart sank. We started to climb again, but not before I turned to have a last look at the green pastures below. I wondered what life would have been like if Pa and Ma were to put their roots down in those fields instead.

Maybe, that was what they'd left behind in Kansas. Maybe, they never had it in them to ranch or farm. I knew in my heart then that it could not have come to pass just as I knew it was my lot to head for the light where I knew I was gonna shine.

How much, oh, how much farther? How much longer? I leaned back, closed my eyes.

A rub against my thigh, a tight squeeze of a hand over mine. I threw the hand off me and turned my back to Tight Pants.

Through half-shut eyes I peeped at the mountains closing in. Mountains, more mountains? Too much mountain! Make way! Open up, let me through!

Ma, when ya rode out of the flatlands, didn't ya shudder when ya first laid eyes on these breathless mountains? Here, ya could almost hear the shadows fall because yar heart would bump and skip like a lost hare, and ya couldn't do a thing but stand and watch the heavy gloom slide down the timbered ranges into gorges ya knew not how deep.

Ya didn't want to know, did ya? For a cold fear would creep into your dreams and ya would wake up shakin, pinin for planted fields where yar eyes could sweep over the endless croplands ...

Ya sold off Scotty and our wagon, why? I heard ya ask Pa once.

Like him, I'd sold myself to the one dream I had and there ain't no turnin back. I've gotta make good, Ma, and I ain't gonna let nobody break my back, or my heart.

And, ah, how I ache to shine!

But, I've got a darn fox at my heels. Gotta get away.

How? Where to?

We climbed over eyefuls of conifers which sloped down the mountainside in thick folds, the sun skimming over their tops. We shoved along steep embankments streaked with snow, and looped our way around spurs.

Spurs. Ah, more spurs!

I told myself then: Ya wanna only to look up when ya gotta this high. Let yar eyes swim in the sky, for if ya look down yar heart would surely stop, because ya might think ya gonna fall and ya never gonna land on yar feet again.

Flat land! How I pine to walk on flat land!

Kenosha Summit, folks! How high? 10,130 feet high, folks. Looka over there, ya see Webster? They gotta minin camps over these hills above Webster, the trainman said, walking up and down the aisle.

Webster? Tight Pants jerked himself up, turned to wink at me with dozy eyes. Ain't far from Denver. Promise ya, I gotta show ya my town. He reached out to grab my hand, squeezing it.

Folks, uh, folks ... The trainman called out as he came up to us. He glared down at Tight Pants. Tight Pants let go of my hand. I looked away. The trainman walked back without saying what he was about to say.

Then we came down. We came gently down. We came rolling down. I hung onto my seat. Tight Pants hung onto me with one arm over my shoulders but he was sliding off the seat. I put his arm back where it belonged and rolled my eyes.

Lena, eh? His thin lips curled up. He was smirking, but he kept his hands to himself.

At Webster, I saw a stagecoach waiting at the station. Somebody clattered off the train and boarded it. I saw it drive away as we took off.

Choo-oo choo-oo!

From here on, folks, we're sixty miles to Denver! And ya gonna see some dandy sights this stretch a the way.

Six-ty miles to go! It had taken me years to come this far! My heart pounded wildly.

What awaits me at the end of the line? But I want to think only of getting there fast. Lightning fast.

Is it true of what I hear? That the Tabors have gone dim these days? On account of the price of silver having gone south?

Hey, Denver ya're a big town, ya shine still, right?

South Platte comin up! Someone in the car said. I looked out the window and saw the river. It was running high, flushed with snowmelt. We were going with the flow, making our way into a narrow gorge.

Quick! Show me the way to town, South Platte, ya hear?

Huge boulders humped up along the banks, by turns closing in, then sloping away, then closing in again. The sun was shy in the deep gorge. Still, straggly cedars, lean pine saplings and scrubby tufts thrust out of the rock crevices where the sun hit.

Go for the sun, yes, the sun!

I looked up at the tall rugged ledge, then at the brimming water below.

Hmm, one little slip was all it took! I thought of my new pa's one little slip on a high ledge that sent him plunging down the fast river below. A slip that set me free.

Hey, think not of slippin! Life's just ahead! I told myself.

Chugga-chugga-chugga ...

I near jumped out of my skin! We were at a snail's pace next to the rushing flow. Muddy yellow water with a tinge of dull green and where it hit rocks, churning up froth. Rays of light sliced the spray tossing up rainbow colors. Where the droplets fell, a wriggly circle of foam fanned out, broke up and hurried on its way.

Gotta run like the river!

Creeks flooded with Spring runoffs dumped in gushes along the way. The river swelled, bursting over its banks. Ya could hear the roar of the flow. Two boys stood fishing around the wide part of a bend where the water slowed. They looked up at the passing train with wide eyes as though they were seeing it for the very first time.

Then it came to when the banks widened some more and the river turned lazy and slow.

Make haste! Make haste! My heart was yet riding the roaring flow.

Are we there yet?

Folks, Estabrook! Best spot for a fishin. Here ya see the biggest trout, and folks come here a hunt for deer, bears, and yep, big cats, and small games, too, the trainman said.

Guess not, I grumbled under my breath.

Ya said somethin? Tight Pants asked, rubbed his woozy eyes and blinked.

Nah! I turned away, wondering how one could sleep so much. I won't close my eyes now, not even a wink.

We rode with the river. We snaked our way, rounding bends and crossing bridges where ya looked down at the gushing water and yar heart would miss a beat. Shadows bore down upon us and the river got squeezed, tumbling over smooth boulders, splashing along banks as we headed into yet another gorge.

Not again!

Canyon walls butted up, tall and steep, bare but for the scattered stubbles among the weathered rocks, and teeny trees, wind-beaten, clinging onto their perches. The jagged ridge rammed high into the sky. The sun shafted down, splitting light and shadow in a sharp wedge over the craggy scarp.

Down below, dark water rolled over a bed of river rocks, sloshing up wiggly white foam. A wind howling through, taking yar breath away.

I closed my eyes.

Chugga-chugga-chugga...

Ma, this here gotta be the bottom of the canyon. When I get out from the bottom, it's gonna be going up, right?

Comin through, Ma, I'm comin through!

I'm gonna be in the Queen City! Queen City of the Plains, ya hear, Ma?

We chugged along the edge of the slope. The slope eased up a bit and pines and spruces sprung up on the hillside making ya feel there was life around after all.

And, yeah, I spotted the twitching tail of a fleeing deer!

Still, spurs sprung up atop towering peaks just a stone's throw away.

Dome Rock! The trainman called out. Folks, looka yar right, see that a big round rock squattin up there?

I looked. Enough rocks already! I sighed.

We crawled on, winding with the river, winding without the river. Then, we started coming down. We came down easy, then we came down on a roll, then we came down easy again.

I looked to where the sun had slunk over the westward mountains. A big orange glow washed over the land as far as my eyes could see. Rolling flat land! Out of the canyon into the plains, I had left the mountains behind for good! I hung onto the window and turned my eyes to the open country. Open country with open arms, I so wanted to believe.

Folks, we're twenty miles to Denver, the trainman said.

Choo-choo-oo!

A huge flock of birds leapt up, little black dots blotching the golden sky. Lark buntings? Never saw so many of them! They swirled overhead, swooped down onto the ground, sprung back up, flapping their white-patched wings.

I just knew it, they were here to wish me welcome. Only the *chuff-chuff-chuff* drowned out their song.

We traveled along the west bank of the river. Soon, it was taking us past farm lands with plots upon plots of greens and irrigation ditches branching out of a canal which took water from the river. The water gleaming in the late afternoon sun.

Soon, we were chugging along a bridge crossing what the trainman said was Cherry Creek. Soon, I saw a jumble of pale city houses in the golden light.

I knew we had arrived even before the trainman called out, Folks, Union Depot comin up! I knew it for my heart had started to go *chugga-chugga-chugga* ... I knew it because Tight Pants had waken up, grabbed my arm and hung onto it, all the while smirking his thin-lipped smirk. I did not want to look into his eyes. I did not want to feel sorry for having sold myself for the price of a train ticket.

Thank you, mister, I said to the trainman at the foot of the steps. I'd meant more than just thank you, but I could say just that.

He looked at me darkly beneath his cap, his brow knitted. Perhaps, it was the shadow of the car behind him. I heard him mutter, Take care, gal. Good luck, gal. He, too, looked like he had something more to say. But he bit his lips and forced a smile.

I nodded because my voice was stuck in my throat. I swallowed hard, looked him in the eye and thought only of Pa and Ma, and how their lives had been bare-knuckled hard. That way, I got all pumped up.

Gotta make my own life! Gotta make good!

Back at the camp they used to say: Down in the mine shaft, ya look up and see the light, ya know ya ain't alone. Deep in the belly of the earth where ya can't see the fingers on yar hands, ya wanna out, ya go look for the light, go look for the light at the end of the tunnel.

Ah, I'm headin for the golden light! It's out there waitin for me. I just know it.

But, not this way, my sweet Michael, not the way I've to walk the tunnel to come to you. The tunnel's for coal carts. Look, the coal dust's soilin my satin heels, brushin over my new satin gown! Why can't I walk in from the broad daylight like everyone else goin into the Brown Palace? Why do I have to come by way of a tunnel?

Yeah, I see you cringe when I drop my g's, or when I say ya, or ain't, or gonna. Then, you smile as if I've amused you. At least, Ma'am would say, Lena, you smart girl, now say your g's, say you, not ya, and it is aren't, not ain't, and going to, not gonna to.

Yes, ma'am.

Oh, how I want to shine!

And, shine I will!

17

So I arrived the Queen City a pawn. A pawn to one who didn't work with his hands for a living. What's gonna happen to me? A question too late to ask. I shrugged it off. I'm in Denver now, ain't I?

I turned to look west. The sun had sunk behind the faraway mountains. My heart sank with it. A golden pinprick lingered at one tip of the purple range—a golden kiss, my goodbye kiss.

The range sprawled in quickening darkness. I was filled with a sudden yearning for home. The flowered meadows, the tumbling waters, the hills of ponderosa, the pine scented air had all but slipped away in one day. Me, a butterfly no more ... flitted away in the sundown light. My eyes grew misty.

And, I miss my bedroll in the cabin ...

Before I could look around, before I could slip away into the crowd, Tight Pants grabbed my arm and shuffled me through the packed hall. He had me out of the Union Depot and onto the street in no time. I turned to look back. The hall was big, and the crowd had no face. Help?

Lena, don't ya even think of that, he hissed, glaring into my eyes.

I wriggled to pull away. But his grip was tight, jostling me along. I spun around, looking to dash off. My eyes fogged up amid the din of people gathering on the curb. Carriages trotted past. A horse drawn street car was picking up riders. Tight Pants shoved me past the line of people waiting to get on. He hustled me across the street. I dragged my feet.

Dusk fell, fast and heavy. The streets were shadowy under the gas street lamps. People stared at the pair of us. Some walked up, slunk past as Tight Pants hooted, Get lost! Move!

I sighed. Night's falling fast. What am I gonna do?

The City that had sprung up before my eyes was a wilderness of its own. I'd seen camp cats slobbering, stalking Leadville at sundown. Animals that prowled the city streets I knew not how loud, how foul. And I knew not what hidden corners to watch out for.

There was no starlit path to lead me back to our cabin where Ma would wait up for me. The streets here, looking dark and mean. I shuddered.

Ma, I miss ya!

But I ain't that hurt doe. I'm caught but I ain't gonna be a prey. I'm gonna fight. A break, give me a break!

Wait for mornin, maybe?

Ah, everything's got its own time. Flowers don't bloom before Spring, pods don't burst until ripen, and caterpillars turn into butterflies only when they get their wings. My time's not yet, but it has to be soon. Very soon.

Whoa, like now!

The looks of those men! Their eyes got tongues that go slurp, slurp ...

The trainman had warned me, didn't he?

Shoulda bellow and bawl! Shoulda yank loose! Shoulda run for my life! Shoulda ... shoulda ...

Now I'm trapped in a pit. How to get out?

Even before I stepped into Jack's filthy back room with a mucky pane for a window, I was sick to my stomach. We had come up by the stairs at the back of the building. Jack squirreled me past men hanging out front where ya could hear the hullabaloo spilling out into the street. Unshaven men, dusty hats tipped over bloodshot eyes, fingers hooked onto holsters, slunk about in the murky light, puffing smoke, spitting tobacco.

I looked up at the big black letters on the white sign in front of the building: All Hands Billiard Hall.

Jack ole boy, what ya up to? A gruff voice barked.

Sonofagun, come over he-ere! Another bellowed, swilling out of a bottle.

Be down in a jiff, Jack yelled back.

Lena, this here's my uncle's joint! He said in a singsong voice as if to make nice this dingy place. Hey, I'm just helpin him out these days! Gotta business of my own, ya know? He winked at me with that ya-know look as if I'd got something to do with it.

The room was dark, the air reeked of tobacco, alcohol and sweat. A whiff of the sickening sour stench came right at ya. I choked for want of air.

Ah, mountain air that tingles as ya drink it down, air that fills ya up and gives ya charge! Air that I'd left behind!

He put a match to the kerosene lamp that sat on a rickety table. It lit up my stony face, my bitten lips. I turned away from his hot eyes, but his hot body was edging close.

I step away from the pile of crumpled bedding on the floor, and fixed my eyes past him at the chair with a broken back. On it sat a battered wash basin. He comes up to grab at me with sticky fingers. I push him away.

Pok-pok—sound of knocking at the floor from below. Someone was poking a cue up against the floor board.

Jack! Hey, Jack!

Pok-pok!

Come on down, ole buddy!

Pok-pok!

What chick ya got with ya up there, boy?

Pok-pok!

Jack let go of me and stamped his foot down hard. Pipe down, ya all! He knelt down and screamed at the floor board. Then he got back up and stormed out, slamming shut the door.

CLICK! I heard a key turn in the padlock outside.

I threw myself at the door, banging, pounding. The door shook, the latch rattled but would not budge. I kept on hitting until I scraped my knuckles and got splinters. Then I kicked and kicked and kicked …

Too late, it's all too, too late! I gritted my teeth.
Thu-ump! My feet gave way. I plopped down onto the floor,
buried my head into my bloodied hands. Blackness swarming over
my eyes ...
    I had leapt, eyes wide open, into water way too deep, way over
my head. A way out! Gotta find a way out!
    Sound of knocking balls bounced off the downstairs walls and
shot straight up in a din of hollering and cursing and whacking.
The kerosene lamp dwindled, burned out. Darkness crammed into
the small room, and the four dingy walls spun round and round.
The loud racket from below rose and fell as if on cue.
    I crouched down a corner, squeezed myself into a tight bundle,
and stared woozily at the gray pane of night outside. The city
seemed far, far away.
    Gotta get out! Gotta ...
    The ruckus from downstairs rumbled on ... My eyes grew
heavy, my body heavier. I slumped over, dropped off to
somewhere even darker.

    Animals came mauling in the night. I gulped for air, heaving,
kicking, thrashing ... They kept coming ... dragging me down to
where I didn't want to go.
    No, oh, no! NO!
    Yelping, gurgling, groaning ... yelping, yelping, yelping ...

    I opened my eyes to a milk-white pane of light. I bolted up,
shaking like a leaf. Not a stitch on me. Stiff and sore all over,
soiled through and through ... I choked back a shriek of anger.
Tears streamed down my cold cheeks.
    What came in the night tore through me and left me sullied and
bruised. Tight Pants sprawled by my side, snoring. I saw that he
had no pants on. My ripped underpants, my torn blouse, my
rumpled skirt strewn about the floor. The pocket of my skirt had
been emptied.
    I tiptoed to the corner where I'd left my bundle. Gingerly, I
slipped into my only change of clothes. I got on all fours and
reached for Jack's pants tugged under one leg, pulling at it lightly.

He stirred, spewing groggy sounds, chewing his thin lips. I shrunk back. He turned over on his side, bringing his leg with him. I snatched up his pants. The floor board creaked. An empty bottle rolled.

I was that desperate squirrel searching for a quick root. I dug into his pockets, emptying both, taking what he'd taken out of mine. And more.

Scrambling up on my feet, I plucked the key from the table, grabbed my shawl, my shoes, and shot for the door. There, I paused long enough to empty the pockets of his jacket hanging on the door peg.

Click! I locked him and the beastly filth behind forever.

Loud snoring at my feet. Foulness laid like strewn carcasses. Two half naked bodies slumped against each other on the floor. Crumpled pants scattered about the narrow hallway. I picked my way out, mindful not to trip over the empty bottles.

I clutched my pocket, dashed down the stairs into the street, turned the corner before glancing over my shoulder. No one was behind, no one was about. The pale morning light was spilling down the empty street. I scurried across to the sunlit side of the street, lifted up my head, let out a big sigh.

I ran, fast and furious. I ain't gonna let nobody see my stains lest somebody was out early to spy on girls with night stains.

The night had ripped through me like a train with busted brakes racing downhill. I'd crawled out of the wreck. But I've yet to crawl out of a most hideous hurt. Hurt where you can see, hurt where you can't see, it being a hurt that won't ever heal.

Oh, bloody hell, don't I know?

I took a pause, knelt down to quickly put on my shoes. I yelled out in my heart: Get ya to hell, Jack! I ain't gonna let nobody break me. Not ya, Jack, and not nobody! Not ever!

Never mind the racking pain roiling me inside and all over. I picked up my feet and ran. Let the breeze toss out the grime in my hair, scour clean my face, my body.

Run, run, run …

I left behind the grubby street with the two boarded up shops.

The signs read: Cigars and Tobacco; Davis Drug Store –
Medicines, Seltzer, Mineral Waters, Sodas.

I kept on running.   My pocket was heavy with dollar coins
which clinked: *Shame, shame, shame! Jack sold ya! Jack sold
ya!*

Shut up! I screamed.

It sickened me that Ma's four precious dollar coins were now
mixed in with Jack's soiled ones.

I heard neighing and smelled horses. Across the street was the
ELEPHANT CORRAL. HORSES FOR SALE. I walked up. The
horses were feeding outside the shed. *Splash! S-splash!* Someone
was throwing buckets of water into the shed. Little brown foul
streams ran down a drain outside. I took the door key out of my
pocket.

Plop! I dropped it down the drain.

I continued on down the street, turned the corner, down
another street, turned another corner. I was heading towards where
there was a loud rattling and a whole lot of bustling in the air.

I stopped, dug my hand inside my pocket to fumble about the
coins.

The name card?

Gone?

My photographer friend gave it to me.   He who gave me
sapphire eyes and offered me a sprig of blue flax for keeps. That
one glorious summer day two years ago!

Bloody Jack took it! Didn't see it anywhere. Coulda be in his
shirt pocket he rolled over on.

Pity! I shall miss that tattered piece of keepsake held so dear
for so long. But, mind ya, I can recite the printed words: Allen
Bristol, Artistic Photographer, Portraits and Sceneries,
Stereoscopic and Plain Views, All negatives preserved. Fifteenth
Street and Larimer, Denver, Colorado.

Ah, what I know by heart no dumb Jack can take away!

Horse carts trotting past. A milk cart driver stopped by the
curb, ogling at me.   He opened his mouth, gummy brown teeth
getting ready to buck out.

Hey, gal! Wanna ride?

Ya old geezer! I gave him a sharp look and walked on ahead. I paid for a bun and an apple at the corner food stall. Without raising her head, the old woman brought the dollar coin close to her eyes, rubbing it with two fingers before giving me change. I ate standing with my back against the building, keeping an eye on what came near. Then I moved out of the shade and walked down the street.

Clunk-clunk-clunk! I heard the bell before it turned the corner—the car not drawn by a horse. It came clattering down the street on rail tracks. Inside the long car, riders sitting in rows looking out the windows. It ran along the street broad with people and horse carts and carriages all going their own ways.

Trot-trot-trot-clonk-clonk-clatter-clatter-clatter...

A new beat of life! So, this here's the Queen City!

Em cars that rattle, they call cable cars, ya know. I rode in one, sure did. Ride so smooth, ain't no bumpin at yar rump, ain't like nothin drawn by a horse, ya gotta try it, ole pal! I once heard someone who came through camp brag to Stinthal.

Hmm, ten past nine!

I looked up at the clock with four faces standing at the corner of the sidewalk. City folks live by the clock! People coming down the cross streets need only to look up to tell the hour of the day.

I got onto the cable car that said: 16th St. & North Denver. In the open trailer, men in jackets, in shirts with vests, sat side by side on rows of benches. They turned and stared under the brim of their hats. I wouldn't care, I'd paid for my ride just like everyone else.

We clanked along, rocked a little, rolled a little, making our way up the street. I looked out both sides. Buildings tall and big, square blocks of them in stone and mortar lined the street, sharp angles rounded out with big arched doorways and little arched windows punched out the front, floor by floor.

Signs were everywhere—big letters posted above drawn-up awnings, gold letters pasted on second-storied window panes, a picture of a pair of wire-rimmed glasses hung over the paved sidewalk, and, over there, a two-faced clock stuck out of a red brick building!

I rode up, then down 16th Street. A light breeze brushed against my face, I raised my hand to shield the sun and spotted the Larimer Street sign. I got off and walked briskly up Larimer to 15th Street. I looked up and there it was. A sign atop a red brick building bore the big letters in black: A. BRISTOL, PHOTO GALLERY. My heart leapt up, beating like a bunny that had lost her head on a summer meadow.

Ah, talk of summer meadows!

Remember, Mister, the wild flowers? Colors that danced in the breeze. They were strewn about our feet and stretched on as far as eyes could see. Remember the big blue sky?

I was shabby then. But ya looked at me so, and yar look lifted me out of my grime and washed me sparklin clean just like the Arkansas runnin on ahead. Ya haven't forgotten, have ya, Mister?

Umm, it's been a long, long journey for me to come to stand before where ya're at, Mister. And, uh, I'm shabby still.

Far shabbier. I swallowed a tear and lowered my head.

I gotta feelin, Mister, same feelin I had that one time when I stood lookin up at Mount Elbert after a long day's hike. The flamin sky was eatin into the darkenin range … long shadows like talons clawin their way down the ridges … I was nowhere yet near the foothills.

Tall conifers blocked my view and gave me pause for findin my way forward. Another day, I'd said to myself then.

I'll be back, Mister!

She came to me in a cloud of lilac blooms, swaying in the breeze, perfuming the air. Like that lilac bush Mrs. Olivia Graham had it brought to Leadville for her. Big, full-leaved and heavy with buds, the talk of town. The long train trip all the way from the East didn't hurt it none. Said she missed lilacs in springtime something fierce. She had it planted in front of her handsome clapboard house on 6th Street, showing off her abundant silver dollars.

Say, ya seen the lilac? Seen the lilac, eh? Words swept up our camp like an upslope wind.

It was a very brief summer flowering. Even so, it was a big show of sweet lilac blooms ya could spot and smell coming down the street.

Then it stood without flowers the year after, then it stood with just a sprinkling of leaves the following year. Woman folks gotta their tongues wagging as they walked past the sickly bush: Too much prunin, I'd say. Nah, gotta be the soil. Sand and gravel won't hold water none. Nay, nay, it's the clay around here that don't drain water none, rot em roots in no time. Gotta be too much waterin! Nope, too little waterin, for sure. Look, how crumbly dry the soil! Ya dope, it's our long cold winter here that killed it!

How'd anyone know? I'd thought. Ain't this the first lilac shrub ya folks ever lay eyes on in these parts?

Anyway, the lilac bush died before the third summer was over. I gotta feeling that lilacs were finicky, not like the prickly bushes and the little yellow flowering weeds that covered the hillside after a brief summer squall. Those weeds, when ya pulled up the stalks, they broke right off, but they got roots that go deep down, and before ya know it, new stalks would shoot back up, and the little yellow flowers would take over the hillside.

I counted—four wire posts at the street corner where I stood. High wires spanned like strands of cobweb stretching across the streets, giving yards of foothold for sparrows to perch. They gotta place to rest. Not me. High noon now. Where am I gonna go when the sun goes down? A cable car rattled past with a sign that said: Elitch's Gardens. My eyes followed the wheels down the street, then turned aimlessly to some other wheels. It was then I caught sight of her.

Halt! Halt! The tall horsewoman in lilac called out, tugging the reins of the four-horse carriage she was driving. The white plume on her bonnet fluffed up as if a rare bird had just come to perch. She brought the carriage to a standstill in front of the stone building with the tall arched doorway. I looked at the big gold lettered sign above the door: People's Bank of Denver. She passed the rein to the young woman in pink with the broad brim straw hat sitting by her side.

The lilac lady pinched a small fold of her skirt with a gloved hand, lifting it up as she stepped down onto the curb. A burst of summer lilac blooms dropped in on the city! People passing by dropped their jaws. Wheels on the street slowed down. The young woman with the straw hat handed her a lilac parasol with a frilly fringe. She nodded, her white plume bouncing in the air, stealing glances around her. She walked in measured beats under the shade of her parasol, her drawstring purse dangling from her wrist.

I was not three feet away from the door. She glanced at me. Without missing a beat, she walked on into the bank. But I thought I saw her lips curl up a tad.

There, she's a lady like no lady I'd seen! I said to myself.

Sis, hey, sis!
Sister?
Oh, my! A squeaky voice chimed in.
M-me? Who calls? I looked towards the waiting carriage.
Chattering and giggling, four heads with abundant curls busted out the carriage window gawking my way.
Over here! A handkerchief waved at me.
I headed over, but stopped short on the pavement. Two gentlemen coming out of the bank stepped right into my path.
Well, well, look what we've got here, Mort! One gentleman gushed.
Whoa-whee!
Mort and the other gentleman paused, turning their heads for a quick look around. The carriage door swung open. A young woman in pale yellow gathered her gown, smiling broadly at the gentlemen. She held out her hand. The pair limbered up, they tipped their hats, and rushed to offer their hands to help her down the carriage. Another young woman followed, giggling as she stepped out. Her powder blue gown rustled, ruffles and ribbons

and all. People slowed their pace to watch. I was all taken in by the flourish.

What dash of colors, such easy manners! The young women dressed as if they were on their way to a garden party. Yet they dallied on the street. Little laughter ringing out, they met like old friends coming together. But then I saw the young women pull out little cards from their dangling purses to give to the gentlemen. Many little winks lit up their faces. The gentlemen stood at attention.

An old bent couple tottered past me. I heard the wrinkled wife huffing under her breath: Sin on the street, sin on the street, what in the name of God's going on here in broad daylight? Don't look, Hud, don't look! She tugged at her glassy-eyed husband.

Tsk tsk! You, yes, you! Hurry on! Get going! The young woman holding the rein called out to me. She glared down from her driver's seat, her eyes bright like a bristling cat's under the brim of her straw hat. But she was stone-faced. She gestured with her free hand, Off you go! Away, get away!

She stopped just as suddenly as she had started. She turned towards the Bank, and her eyes glazed over like a dazed doe's. I followed her line of sight and caught the lilac cloud gliding out the arched doorway.

She paused to open her parasol, twirled it a little so the frills fluttered over her head like a bunch of butterflies hovering, wingtip to wingtip. She walked up to the company gathered by the carriage. The two gentlemen took their hats off and bowed. She nodded, her eyes skimmed over their faces while she stole a look at me. Smiling as she spoke, she swept one arm open in a welcoming gesture, the other hanging onto her dangling purse. Smiling still, she waved her hand as if to say: Gentlemen, excuse me please.

She turned and walked straight up to me.

Hello-o, dearie! She said, her red lips framing each word. There was a high lilt to her sweet sound, lifting ya up with every word that came out of her mouth, holding ya in a thrall. She brought her parasol over me, giving me lilac shade. The sprig of fresh lilac pinned on her collar sent out a scent as ripe as the hour past noon. She peered into my eyes and took in a breath.

Ma'am!

I looked up at her. She got eyes, uh, like a raptor's, round and bright and sharp. There was a quick shiftiness in them as if they were busy taking stock. Unblinking, taking stock, shifting sideways.

Like Stinthal's when he weighed his sacks of beans with his eyes every so often. Or, when he looked me over, top to bottom.

Umm, eyes like those make ya wanna burrow or they could gouge ya out and leave ya in shreds. Ya ever seen a pika lookin up at a hawk?

My wo-orld, sweetie, whoever did *that*? She hushed her words as she raised a gloved finger, lightly touched my cheek and traced it down my neck. But her eyes were over my hair.

Wha-at?

Slap-zap! Slurp! Slu-urp! The storm of the night came raging back. My legs started to wobble.

The bruises, and those bite marks on your neck! Oh, dear-ie! She went on in a low voice, shaking her head. Her eyes told me that she knew a whole lot more about me than I'd thought. I dropped my head.

Let me take care of you, sugar. Come board at my house, huh? Her voice dripping honey. I looked up at her, at her fine horses, at the gay young women in party gowns who rode with her, at the smartly suited gentlemen by their side.

Maybe, this is what I've been lookin for—a way to shine!

I oughta burrow, though. The sun was shining bright. My eyes grew bleary over the trotting, rattling motion on the street. Everything spun and twirled, messing up what's inside my head.

I'm yar golden girl, ain't I, Pa?

Ah, how I wanna shine!

I oughta at least glance up at the young woman in pink with the straw hat before I stepped into the carriage. But then I thought only of putting my head down somewhere safe for the night.

I miss ya so, Ma. I miss our little cabin, my bedroll tucked at one corner. I miss the big moss rock with the lichen where Pa lay. I miss the sunset that torches the sky and make yar heart aglow …

Be back for ya, Ma ...

It hadn't even crossed my mind that Nina was kind. She did try to warn me. Didn't she? Nina, ya looking so pretty in yar sweet pink gown, pink ribbon on yar broad brim hat streaming in the breeze. Won't ya know that this scrawny girl has a head full of dreams and had come a long way just to squint up at ya?

I couldn't have known. Could I?

Nina, ya called it quits, ah, not three days after I came to the house, groaning and flailing in yar vomit and soil and blood. I shuddered and wiped yar tears as ya were being carried out. My hand trembled over yar cold sweaty brow, over yar face twisted with pain. In yar vacant eyes I saw that life was slipping away.

Why, Nina, why?

Are yar dreams spent, Nina? I asked, feeling a pang in my heart.

They said ya must have lost yar head to drink yar own douche. That stuff burns yar insides out, they said.

Stupid girl, ma'am said, flashing the white of her eyes.

I don't intend to lose my head, I said to myself as I glanced at the small bottle of white powder tucked in one corner of my wash stand. I'm waiting for the day to break out. But not this way.

There was a hush-hush in the house afterwards. Ma'am treated the officers who came to ask questions to tea and hot cakes. She invited them to come visit in the evening after their duties were done.

She had Nina's windowless room scrubbed and kept the door open for a whole day to air. The next day, she put another boarder in the room. Ma'am went about it like she had done it before.

I'll never, ever gonna let my dreams die.
I'm gonna shine!
And shine I will.

18

I dropped off to a groggy sleep as soon as I laid my head down. I only knew that I was off the streets where dark shadows lurked. Still, yapping animals tailed me without break. They came mauling into my sleep. I kicked and screamed, fighting off the slobbering beasts. Rumbling and moaning jolted me up. Like echoes from afar. I bolted upright in bed. The room was pitch dark, hot and stuffy. I held my breath. Nobody else in here but me. I let out a deep breath, lay back down. My body sluggish, my head woozy …

A bath, sweetie? The first thing Ma'am ordered when we got back to her house.

It felt good. So good, when I had warm water doused over my well soaped body. My body still sore but ya see no dirt, at least not on the outside.

Be still, *ja?* Said a big woman with rolled up sleeves and strong arms. She looked away from my bruises and scrapes, and she was gentle with those ghastly bite marks on my neck, over my bosoms.

You not have an ounce of fat on you, *ja?* She tried to make a joke, but she avoided my eyes. Afterwards, she wiped tincture of iodine over the bite marks. Her fat fingers lightly touching. I flinched at the sting. You'll be alright, she said. Rub your bruises, *ja?* Get the angry purple out quick.

She put on a clean apron and fed me in the kitchen. A hot bun, a small grain patty and some beans. While I ate, she busied herself

picking up the many soiled dishes and cutleries left on the table.
You, how old? She asked over the noise of the dishes.
Fifteen.
Your name?
Lena.
I'm Hannah.
Hannah took me upstairs to a tiny room with a bed. Ma'am
says put you in here, *ja?* Girls getting dressed poked their heads
out of their rooms like kept pigeons stuck in their holes. They
stared without a word. A girl in her underclothes bustled down the
narrow hallway holding a pin cushion covered with threaded
needles.
    I did not see the girl in pink with the wide brim straw hat.

    My eyes swam in the dark. Faint smell of alcohol mixed with
tincture steeped in the air. A slit of light under the door. Footsteps
tramping past. A husky chortle, some light giggling. Banging and
rustling in the rooms next to mine. Moaning ... More banging ...
    The house swelled and hummed. Waves of chattering, bouts of
laughter rose and fell. A drift of piano music. I hopped down the
bed, put my ear to the door. A girl's voice singing. Other noises
drowning out the tune. I tried the doorknob. The door was locked.
    I lay back down in bed and let the fuzzy sound carry me ...
    Chuff-chuff-chuff ... chugga-chugga-chugga ...
    No, no, don't sleep ... sleep ...

    A nest of little chicks chip-chirping up a tree, beaks open wide
to catch a wriggly morsel from the mother's beak. One chick falls
off, drops at my feet. I bend over just as a fox dashes up, snatches it
with his mouth and scampers off.
    Ya fox, ya dare! I spring up to give chase. He turns, stands his
ground, growling.
    All of a sudden, I feel the crush of his jaw. I go whimpering ...
    Oh, no, I ain't that little dropped chick!
    I stirred, my body a bunch of loose crackling twigs. I ached to
my bones.
    I woke up to a quiet house. No footsteps in the hallway. Not a

sound. The room I was in had no window. Faint light slipped in under the door. I had no idea what time of the day it was. I only heard my stomach making noise. I lay still, floating like. My mind, empty, floated along. It was as if I'd let go of what had been weighing me down for a very long time. And I was much too tired to want to figure out what was to come to me.

Stirrings about the house. A click of the lock.

Up, *ja?* Come eat, Hannah called at the door.

I ate with the girls in the kitchen. I looked up at the wall clock. Two. Daylight streamed in through the window.

I still did not see the girl who was in the pink gown with the straw hat. I asked the girl who sat next to me. She was in her undies. The girls were either in their undies or their nighties or half dressed. Eight of them, all looking a bit groggy and pasty.

Oh, ya mean Nina? She, late again, huh?

I did see her coming in when we were finishing up. She was in a worn cotton gown frayed at the cuffs. A bit snug, looking like she had outgrown it. Or that it was a hand-me-down. Her eyes were red and puffy. Been crying? She looked nothing like when I first saw her, so very pretty in pink, ribbon on her broad brim straw hat flashing a pink light. She did not look up, sat down and ate quietly by herself.

Nina, I whisper, getting up to walk to her. She kept her head down as if she had not heard me.

Come with me, Hannah called out just then. She took me to the room where I had my bath yesterday. She looked at my bite marks stained yellow with the iodine. You heal fast, *ja!* She washed off the stain with warm water and soap, then wiped dry the bite marks before smoothing an ointment over them. The ointment came in a small pot with a label that read, Zinc Oxide. Then she said, Ma'am will see you now.

Her room was at the end of the hallway upstairs. I slid in through the half open door. She was sitting in front of her dressing table in a slippery purplish-red robe that sloughed over her body like a half shed skin. But she sat up stiffly, looking into the mirror, her hands busy fixing her curls into a tight pile on top of her head.

A pink shaded table lamp fringed with dangling beads sat on one side of the dresser. The lamp's mirror reflection doubled the light in the dim room. As I walked up to her, I passed by a window draped in lace curtains. Wan light filtering in.

Ma'am?

Ah sweetie! It's polite to knock.

Huh?

Come here! She turned and fixed her eyes on me, head to toe. I inched my way up to her. Her eyes sharp and round and steady—the way eyes looked when taking aim at something with a slingshot. I saw that she was wearing a corset underneath. First time I saw a corset on a real body. I had seen only drawings of them in the old newspapers that Stinthal used to wrap up the goods sold at the General Store.

She turned to look at my reflection in the mirror.

Oh, my! Lena you tall girl! Pull up a chair.

Then she said, Look at yourself in the mirror.

At once I fell for my face in the mirror! Reminds me of a pink evening primrose in bloom. Looking shy and bold all at once. Ya see a whole lot of them on the stretch just below the rocky slope blushing in the late afternoon sun. My hair's coppery shine had taken on a rose tinge, warm curls falling gently over my shoulders. I raised myself out of the chair, pressed my face close up and saw, really saw the sapphires in my eyes for the very first time. In the pink glow of the mirror, a face I hadn't known before was looking straight out at me!

O-oh! I let out a sigh. I had forgotten that she was by my side, coolly watching. Then I felt her eyes studying me. Then I heard her laugh a shrill little laugh. The sound a bird made on having wrestled a worm out of another's beak.

Lena, turn to me, she said.

With her finger, she dabbed some red color onto my lips from a small pot with a lid. Upper lip. Lower lip.

Now, close! She pressed her own lips to show me how. Now look!

I turned to the mirror. I smiled in spite of myself.

Now, ro-ouge! Her high pitch voice sang as she dabbed a light smear of the lip color onto my cheeks.

In the soft pink glow, I saw the heightened color on my cheeks. A blush like no blush I'd seen. Except, perhaps on Baby Doe's cheeks in that colored photograph behind the shop glass up in Leadville.

Pretty?

I nodded. I couldn't wipe the smile off my face.

She picked up a silver lidded powder puff from a small round glass tub and dusted face powder over my face. Soft as a chick's down, sweet scent flying about my face. Puffing done, I was about to turn to the mirror when I heard her said, Now put that on! She gestured with her chin to a pale blue gown laid out on her bed.

I went over gingerly, looked at the glossy gown. So blindingly beautiful it was that I trembled at the thought of putting it on. I turned my back to her and fidgeted to unbutton my blouse.

After I dropped my skirt and about to reach for the gown, she said, Take it all off, would you, dearie?

Now, turn around, sweetie.

Again, dear. Slowly.

She did not take her eyes off my nakedness. She said nothing about my bruises, scratches or the bite marks. Her raptor's eyes full and hard. Unblinking, as if she was taking measures of my body, doing numbers in her head.

I stood there, like a sack of beans that Stinthal was weighing with his eyes. Only I was shy with bosoms and buttocks, and my lips were trembling. She curled her lips as if she got a sour plum in her mouth. Her eyes cold on me.

The air in the room was stifling. The ceiling was bearing down over me. I fixed my eyes on the window with the lace curtains. I had a mind to yell to any wings out there: Pick me up, lift me out of here, please, oh, please!

I swallowed the tears welling up in my eyes, and lowered my head. It came to me then that I well knew what I was getting into.

Now put the gown on, dear.

Turn around, she said. Not a bad fit, eh?

See those slippers over there, put them on.

She stared at my feet as I removed my crummy old shoes. I squirmed.

Fit alright? Walk up to me, hon.

I wobbled on the little heels. One shoe slipped off, baring my foot with the old scars and the new cuts from yesterday's running. I quickly slipped my foot back into the shoe. Her eyes wouldn't let go.

I stood there like a squashed pumpkin.

Didn't she frown?

You'll get used to them, she shrugged.

Ya mean the slippers? For I'd never gotten used to my hurt feet and the bad memories.

Or, what's to come in my new life?

Lena, you pre-etty girl! She said jauntily in a pitch that pierced my ears. Hon, you'll come down the parlor this evening. Show them what a beauty you are! Come, look at yourself in the big mirror.

She got up, beckoned me to follow. We walked up to a double door wardrobe that stood facing the bed. She swung open the door that has a mirror on the inside.

Standing before me, a girl in a shiny pale blue gown, pleats gathered at her small waist cinched with a ribbon sash. Her small white shoulders showed off nicely by the modest scoop neckline trimmed with ribbon and tiny bows.

Ma'am walked up to me, swept my hair back. There, more shoulders this way! And, darling, do hold your pretty little shoulders back and your chin up as you walk. You'll be just grand, dear!

She saw me glancing at her many gowns hanging inside her wardrobe.

Ah, sweetie, you'll earn enough in time to pay for your own wardrobe and more. With your looks, you be sure to ask for gold, you hear?

By the way, Lena, what you have on is on loan to you. She shut the wardrobe door and walked away. She went back to sit before her dressing table, her slippery robe falling off her sagging shoulders. I stood behind her.

From a locked drawer, she took out a gold necklace with a diamond pendant in the shape of a cross. She put it on herself, closing the clasp as she leaned towards the mirror. There, she caught the sparkle. Her eyes lingered over the glitter. Then she stole a look at my reflection in the mirror, locked the drawer and put the key back into her pocket.

A small silver framed photograph of a gentleman with a dark mustache sat under her table lamp. Her little perfume flasks and jars and the powder tub with a silver-lidded puff on top sat in a row in the center. To her right laid her embossed silver hand mirror, a silver hair brush and a silver framed comb. Everything gleaming so under the pretty pink glow to fool the eye and soften the heart. Mine.

Ah, just so you know, Lena dear, my house's the best first class parlor this side of Mississippi! I take in only the prettiest well-bred girls with fine manners, good speech and fancy gowns. I have the best piano player in town, and serve the finest whiskey and the best cigars. And, our gentlemen guests are the very first class gentlemen. They've got means and positions.

By the way, sweetie, you sing? Dance?

U-uh!

Never mind, Lena, you're a smart girl, you'll learn fast.

Here, take these, dear. She handed me a tube of lip color rolled up in paper, a small handheld mirror, a small pot of facial powder with a powder puff.

Wet the power and smooth the paste over where you need it, she glanced up into my eyes. I knew then she meant to cover up my bruises and the bite marks.

No biting my girls! So very ghastly, she muttered as I was walking to the door. I turned around and caught her frown in the mirror.

When I teetered into the parlor that evening on those pretty blue satin heels, I knew I had walked in with my eyes wide open. That shiny pale blue gown, once ya put it on, ya not gonna take it off.

Or, as Ma'am would say, once you put it on, you're not going to take it off.

*   *   *

I aim to shine. How I aim to shine! But I kept it to myself, biding my time.

I thought of Nina quite a bit. But I saw her only in that pretty pink dress, pink ribbon streaming on her broad brim straw hat, sitting high up on the carriage, reins in her hands.

I soon learned to turn a deaf ear to the girls' tittering behind my back, to the catty tales about who was seeing whom on the side, who was jilting whom.

I also learned that the bleary eyes that blinked over cigar smoke and whiskey glasses were blind to my sapphire eyes. Nor could they gaze at my coppery gold hair the way Pa drank in Ma's with his eyes. Dreamily, his smoldering eyes lit up our dingy cabin even after the hearth fire had died down.

Pretty head of hair you've got there, Lena!

That was all that passed those puffy lips.

19

I didn't count the trees. I didn't care to.

Dense and tall, needled branches all, splintering the sun, wavering the moon. I only knew that it would take me long days and longer nights to trek through the wilderness before I would be out of the woods.

Not quite as yet. But, in time, I would.

I gritted my teeth and kept my eyes pointed to Mount Elbert, to Mount Massive. Ever looming, ever bright and white! Ever beckoning, Come, Galena, come!

When I stepped out of the hired cab that longed-for afternoon, in my new gown and new broad brim hat trimmed with ribbon and rose buds, I knew I'd arrived. I looked up at the sign: A. BRISTOL, PHOTO GALLERY.

I had an appointment to sit for my portrait. But I knew not what to expect because I knew not what I'd really come for. Am I here to relish the memory of one summer day that seemed so very long ago? The day of blue skies and flowered meadows when I was offered a sprig of blue flax for keeps. The day I was told that I've got sapphires for eyes?

Or, am I here to keep a promise I'd made to myself? My mountains are just ahead, go for the peaks!

Galena, you gonna shine!

I walked in, sun and breeze in my head, in my heart. I was received by Mrs. Bristol at the door. Her smile was courteous and her eyes quick. She was big with child. But she moved about with ease, and with the look of someone who had long been minding the store. A gracious homesteader who knew her land and her charge.

Much obliged for your interest in Mr. Bristol's work, she said as I lingered before the hung portraits on the walls.

A portrait of Baby Doe called out to me. I walked up to her. Something compelled me to look past her rich lace and pretty blossoms, her bonnet of lush plumes, past her soft ringlets over her brow, her hint of a smile. It was her eyes! Her lustrous eyes gazing out wistfully as if she had looked into her future and saw what was coming.

There was soul in those eyes! Or, whatever it was that was shining through. Full of grace and grit. Ah, a serenely tenacious light! It lit up her face, lifting her above the material trappings she had wrapped herself in. I tried to absorb the beauty of that light. But it was beyond me. I lingered over the fluffy plume on her bonnet and wondered what bird it was plucked from.

There were other distractions on the wall. Photographs of stage performances at the Tabor Opera House and portraits of performers in costumes. Studies of gusto and bravado. But I was moved to go back to stand before what had so captivated me.

What's burning in your eyes, Mrs. Tabor? I pondered. For shining through was that undying, beguiling light!

As I finally turned to walk across to the opposite wall, I caught Mrs. Bristol studying me at my back. We both smiled and tipped our heads, dispelling the awkwardness.

There were the photographs of sceneries: Rock formations pointing up the sky, a river meandering through a meadow, a sheet of light washing down sheer canyon walls, panoramic views of mountain ranges. Breathtaking and grand, all of them.

But I did not see my mountains.

I walked back up to Mrs. Tabor. I knew then I would want to have my portrait hung right here in the gallery where people would walk in and catch sight of me.

They might ask: Who's she? Look at her eyes!

Mrs. Bristol showed me upstairs to the studio. Mr. Bristol

came out of the dark room as we entered. He had on black work sleeves, looking somber in a maroon bowtie, white shirt and suspenders. His hair was neatly combed, parted in the middle in a clean line. His eyes were as dark as a stream on a cloudy day. Not the eyes of the summer meadows I once knew.

Where had the fire gone—the fire that had leapt up as he held the mountains in a gaze?

Gone, too, was the high color of summer that had burnished his cheeks and made his brow shine.

And, where was that breezy smile?

A smile so like Pa's when he looked me in the eye and said: Don't ya blink, Galena! Look, the sun's smoochin the mountains goodnight! See that golden kiss? Pa pointed to a pin of light that pricked at the dark line of the shadowy mountains just before sundown.

Miss Saber, he greeted me without the faintest sign of recognition of the girl he had chanced upon that one improbable summer day on a high country meadow.

I looked up at him, You may call me Lena.

Miss Lena Saber, he said with a slight bow. Allen Bristol at your service. You've come to sit for your portrait?

I nodded, my eyes still fixed upon his. I felt the brim of my hat quiver. He must have caught it too. He glanced at me, at the curls that had fallen over my shoulders. He turned away quickly.

Remember me? Galena! Sapphire eyes! Remember? I clamored in my head. My eyes would not let go of his.

Two summers ago, Mister, on a flowered meadow in Arkansas Valley, you and your burro and your camera! Oh, I know, the winters in between were long and dark ...

Yes, as long and dour as the faces in the framed portraits that lined the wall in here. Stilted faces with squeezed smiles.

Will I, too, look like so in the portrait? I asked, sounding a bit sour.

Like how?

Uh, like starchy stiff.

Ah, how I want my eyes to sparkle! And to speak only as eyes can speak—as if I'm gazing up at a rainbow that arches over a rain-scrubbed sky, or smiling at my own face in the stream, or ogling over a couple of mating dragonflies in the air.

He looked as if he had read my thoughts.

But how can he when he doesn't even look me in my eyes?

Miss Saber, he said, you'll look as fresh as you appear before me today.

Will you put my portrait up in your gallery? The gallery downstairs?

If you wish.

I very much like you to, Mr. Bristol.

He looked at me as if my voice had awaken him.

Oh, yes, he looks at me now! But does he see *me*?

He sees a girl in her new cotton gauze gown trimmed with little rosebuds, white as snow, soft as a petal. Pretty as a picture, um, that's all. He can't possibly guess how she had paid for her outfit, can he? But surely he does see how she wants to shine!

Ah, Mr. Bristol, you will surely make me shine! Your eyes had told me so on the day of our summer meadows. Oh, yes, you will surely see Galena shining through! I just know.

Miss Saber, this way please, he said in a voice without color.

He ushered me to the sitting area where his camera and lighting equipments stood. It was an area flooded with natural light from the glass ceiling that pitched down to meet a bank of front windows. It had an open feel to it. He looked at me with an eye for the camera, studying the angle of shot as he adjusted the lamps to shine on my face.

Will he see me with the same eyes that were once under the brim of his straw hat? Will he?

I looked straight at him, and smiled.

Just then, he reared his head up from under the camera's drape cloth and held still, his eyes steady on me. I caught in them a glimmer, like a spark that leapt up from a fire flickering in the dark. He blinked and stared and blinked. Then he lowered his eyes and bowed to the camera.

Please look right here, Miss Saber, he said as he put his hand out to point to the lens of the camera.

Mrs. Bristol was standing by the door looking in. She stood behind her husband's back but she could clearly see my face. By her side, a toddler boy tugging at her skirt.

Mr. Bristol, may I see a photograph of Mount Elbert? Mount Massive?

Surely, he said.

He did not seem surprise that I asked. But he paused as if he was looking inside his head for something. He took a sprightly step back and walked towards a large cabinet against the wall next to the dark room. He looked at the labels on its many drawers, pulled out a drawer and took out two prints each the size of an eight-by-ten portrait. He held them in both hands and presented them to me with a slight bow.

For you to keep, miss, he said. Miss Saber, he added. A faint smile lit up his face. He seemed momentarily lost.

Thank you, I smiled back.

Mount Elbert, Mount Massive, ah, snow-clad and majestic, mountains of one summer day long ago, yet not so long ago. To hold in my hands! That was what you'd said to me.

Alas, these are but black-and-white copies of Nature's true grandeur! Out where they stand, they bathe in ever changing light and shade, peaks and valleys forever. A splendor indeed to behold! You do know, Mr. Bristol.

I looked up at him without a word. He caught in my eyes what I did not say aloud.

Again, there was a glimmer in his eyes.

Did he catch it? A glimpse of the sapphire?

Seemingly lost in thought, he looked as if he was trying to retrieve something that had slipped his mind. Or, buried in its recess. Just as quickly, he let go, not wanting to get to it, as if he did not want to believe whom he saw standing before him. Maybe, he did not care to know. Or, did he already know too much? The corner of his mouth twitched ever so slightly.

He gazed up at the glass ceiling. From some smoldering depths, a fire leapt up and re-kindled his eyes. He might have found himself, then and there, in the open country once again, high up where the air and sun sparkled and the spirit let soar! His eyes might have taken wings, flying over peak after brilliant peak, over shadowy gulches and tumbling waters.

Or, he might have gone back to the summer meadows where tipsy flowers danced. Only he would know. But I thought I saw a hint of a breezy smile flit over his face. If he had any question as to how a caterpillar in the meadows had come to be a city butterfly, he kept it to himself.

While I was watching my photographer, Mrs. Bristol, standing heavy, was watching the two of us, toddler boy by her side. My time was up.

Where the wild flowers had captured his fancy and delighted my heart, on a summer day when he offered me a sprig of blue flax for keeps, we both knew then, right here in his studio, that we had long left that moment behind for good.

And we had left Galena where she belonged!

You've sent for me, sir?

I see myself now as you must have seen me, in a portrait newly framed, hung on the wall in Allen Bristol's photography gallery— my eyes sparkling, speaking to ya. Uh, only to *you*!

I don't have to tell you how I'd been counting day and night, long days and longer nights, in truth, to have my portrait taken by Mr. Bristol so when you do come by, my sparkling eyes would speak to you.

Hmm, you say under your breath, jiggling your brandy, swirling the amber light in the glass. You raise your eyes slowly and look dreamily across the room.

There you sit in your cushy red velvet armchair, your back against the crimson velvet drapes drawn to shut out the afternoon sun. A slit of the golden light steals in above the window casting a ruby-garnet glow on the high ceiling, showing off the carved molding.

I stand over my shadow under the chandelier lit with so many electric lamps, like so many bright eyes gleaming over me. A rich glow washes over my soft white cotton gauze gown, the same gown I wore to sit for my portrait.

Lena? You say after a while, just when I feel the plush maroon carpet between us is beginning to stretch.

Yes, sir.

Come! Your voice is raspy, a little breathless. The air is hush, so hush I can hear the rhythm of your breathing.

I turn to walk up to the dressing table instead. Sitting down, I look at myself in the cool mirror. I fancy myself a drop of morning dew glistening through a soft red haze, my eyes still misty from the sun outside.

Ma'am has sent me in her carriage, you know?

Brown Palace, miss? The driver had asked with a bow.

I reach up to take off my fine straw hat trimmed with little white sand lilies, yellow mariposas and blue bachelor's buttons fashioned by the milliner's hand just for me. For that, I owe ma'am a bundle! Ah, I don't want to think about it now!

My hair cascading over my shoulders, a lustrous coppery gold halo glows in the mirror. I toss my hair to liven up the curls. Then, I lean up close to the mirror to moisten my lips with the tip of my tongue.

I see in the mirror the reflection of the dark wood four-poster bed with the heavily carved headboard.

Umm, I sigh, parting my lips!

I see you now in the mirror, bending over me, your eyes suckling, your warm cheeks nestling in my hair, fuming brandy breath down my neck. You finger my ruffled gauze trimmings, from nape to throat, then down front, lingering over the small swells of my bosoms.

Sapphire eyes! You murmur, gazing into my eyes.

How do you know? I want to ask, remembering when I had first and last heard them called.

But then I look into your eyes and see the same blue dream I see in mine. Ah, so very dreamily blue!

A pair of dreamers we are, my sweet Michael! I coo in your ear even as you are tinkling a few of your gleaming double eagles into my hand.

Turns out I'm the only one who dreams!
Ah, how I live and die by my dream!

20

Gotta get to the light ...
   Gotta ... Gotta ...

   Come by the tunnel, you say.
   I ask, Why? Why can't I walk into the Brown Palace like everyone else? I came through the front door that very first day. I did!
   Lena babe! You turn away, shaking your head, not a hair out of place. Slick chestnut brown hair gleaming like the brandy you nurse in your hand.
   I look at your handsome sideburns and see your angular jaws tighten.
   Most surely I want to come. Why won't I? Many a girl would kill for a chance to come to Mr. Norton, by tunnel or hell fire.
   Then I look into your eyes. They are as clear and blue as mine. And your voice, your raspy smoky voice, and your brandied breath over my mouth, they put me on fire, kindling big my dream for love. Yes, love, swe-eet sweet love!
   So, I manage a smile at the door and tell myself that you do mind loose tongues. Yes, sir, you do very much mind loose tongues.

   So, I come by the tunnel.
   Ma'am sends me to the Brown Palace in her carriage each time.
   You be sure to let Mr. Norton know that I take good care of

you, dear. Tell him I've put you in the room across from mine. A room with a window, no less! Oh, sweetie, how lovely you look! She says, her eyes spying on my new heels, counting out the gold pieces in her head.

I watch the carriage trotter away before I dash cross the street to the Navarre where I turn to look over both my shoulders before slipping in. I hold my head high for I've come in my prettiest gown, smartest bonnet and brand-new slippers. Another pair of new slippers. Ah, they do wear out fast!

I walk the carpeted stairs down to the Restaurant kept away from the noisy gambling halls at the lobby, kept away from the hushed-up rumbling in the rooms upstairs. Waiters in bowties and jackets stand by the door. They stare, turn their backs and snicker.

I walk the floral carpet down the hall lined with potted palms. I hurry past the high-back tufted-leather booths alongside the walls where gentlemen sit, cozy with their lady companions, nibbling late lunches over white linen tablecloths.

I look away, not wanting to see or be seen. Heads turn. How I wish the little milky globe lamps weren't so bright and the brass a tad duller! So eyes won't burn my way.

But I hear them, chuckling and giggling, wine goblets clinking. Same vibes as those that float around madam's house.

So, I walk the long walk, past the coal-burning heating stove with a shiny brass ornament sitting atop the cylinder of vents, past more booths till I reach the end of the hall where the alabaster statue of a nude stands. They call her the Nymph because she has barely a bosom. I go behind the Nymph to slip through a secret door into the tunnel.

There I pause, holding my breath in the sooty air, giving me time to get used to the dimness before I take another step.

Out of the tunnel, I wipe my face with my handkerchief, dust my sleeves and sweep my skirt before climbing the back stairs up to your floor where you sit in your suite, in that cushy red velvet armchair, jiggling your golden brandy.

As I come up to you, you glance at your pocket watch with the dangling gold chain. Then, you smile. You smile in spite of yourself, and I rush into your arms.

*   *   *

That tunnel's for coal carts!

Ple-ease, sweet Michael. See, my new slippers already soiled by soot and dirt!

Don't you get to ride the rail cart? He asks.

My heart sinks.

What I won't tell is the air in the tunnel, sodden with earth and soot and sweat, and men with blackened faces and bad coughs shoveling coal into ore carts to haul from one building to another to give heat.

And I, I come by way of the tunnel to give you comfort.

Haven't I left my mining roots behind for good?

No, I won't tell, or you might say, I thought you've known all about that.

So I lift up my fine linen gown, and by the light of a hung lantern, pick my way in the dirt to get into the repurposed cart with a blanket on the seat. So, with the railman watching, I ride the cart to the door that lets me into the lower level of the Brown Palace.

On my return trip, the ore carts would stand empty and the men gone but the one who runs the rail cart, for there are other riders, and they come at all hours of day and night in their fine gowns. I hear that it's the owner of the Navarre who had put the rail cart in the tunnel between his place and the Brown Palace. Here's a fellow who knows how to serve the needs of gentlemen with good names and deep pockets, especially those who have much to lose.

Sweet Michael, would you want me to take a room right here, at the Brown Palace? I ask, peering into your dreamy blue eyes while you rest your head on my lap, your hair slick and glossy. I smooth my hand over your distinguished high brow clear of lines. Got to be younger than my Pa, um, though Pa looked older than his years, his brow creased with worries as long as I can remember. Poor Pa!

Hmm, who asks?

Me, I ask. Say yes, ple-ease!

You close your eyes, dozing off. The sun peeks in through a slit in the drawn drapes. A dusky red glow infuses the air like the shine of a full-bodied port that softens your head, and makes freer your spirit.

Michael darling, hear me, please! Ma'am already has three girls staying at the Brown Palace to take care of business right here. They don't ever come to the house. I can stay in the hotel just for you. Just for you, as you have wanted. Only closer ...

You yawn, mumbling ... Um, in the house, um, you've your ma'am to watch over you ...

Don't you trust me on my own, Sweet Michael?

Hmm ... no, oh, yes! Yes, uh, I mean I like ma'am to take good care of you. Lena babe!

You pick up my hand, steal a look at my flushed face with your half-closed eyes. Smiling, you kiss it and close it with three gleaming gold coins.

Double eagles—big, cold, heavy and, ah, gorgeous in my palm!

Michael dear, you're *sweet!*

I'm blinded by the glittering gold. Bending over, I kiss and kiss you, laughing giddily, letting slip the pressing question I'd raised only a moment ago.

Come, Lena, you say, reaching out for me.

I see a spark of flame in your eyes and call it love. So, once again, I open up to you, trembling, heaving ... swearing undying love.

Come by the tunnel, you say.

How much longer? I ask, my face flushed, swallowing my pride, my hurt.

A little while longer, um, just a little while ...

So, another trip on the rail cart.

And another ...

*   *   *

Someone ya know gonna stab ya in yar back, ya know that, my
little pigeon?
   Ma'am a little pigeon? I near giggle out loud. I hear Carp's
deep voice in madam's bedroom as I happen to walk past. Carp,
handsome with the thick mustache. I stop and press my ear to her
door.
   I've heard that fella Norton ...
   What about Michael, huh? I gasp.
   That Norton, says he's gonna clean up. Yeah, that's what he
says he's gonna do when he gets to be Senator, Carp says.
   My heart near misses a beat. Michael's gonna be Senator? He
has not whispered a word to me. Not a word!
   We'll see! We're not without pull, you know. There're
lawmen not on his bandwagon. That Norton, he keeps his girl
here, sends for her when his fancy suits him. Oh, yes, he watches
his own back real good. That kind of a fella, you know, stabs first
before he ever gets stabbed.
   I press hard to listen, my heart throbbing like I've just raced up
the hill.
   Norton, uh, he's got a good hand. Something to say about
marrying into money! Ma'am chortles. I hear his wife's old man
is bankrolling him into politics.
   What's he anyway? Carp asks.
   Investment banker from the East, so he tells people. To the
papers, too. I hear what he does is to take other people's money
and do business with it. He's got good fortune, for sure. Done
well enough to pay his girl in gold.
   Ya got some, my pigeon?
   Ha, he gives not one coin more nor one less. Not the type of
fella who throws his gold at you for a bellyful of laughs. But, eh,
he pays well enough to keep his girl all to himself. That I'd say.
   Pays ya enough to keep yar mouth shut about his girl, huh?

Hey, the fella's got charm, what can I say! She chuckles.
Like me?
Oh, Carp, you're one of a kind!
What follows is the sound of rustling and thrashing and muted laughter.
I tiptoe away from her door.

O-oh, there's light! There's light at the end of the tunnel, I twitter to myself as I fly down the hallway, make a turn around to stretch my legs before I get back into my room. I near burst out laughing as soon as I shut my door.

Michael's gonna ... Nah, come again! Michael's going to be made Senator! I chew on each word to make sure that I get it out right.

I swirl around, bumping into my bed, my wash stand, my bureau, but I don't care. A blur of my coppery gold hair flying in my face, blinding me. I stop to catch my breath, but my head spins on like a top that goes twirling round and round.

I hear now your husky voice purring, breathless like mine: Lena my love, this is the day we've been waiting for! I will bring you into the light! You will be my new missus and we will head for the capitol.

My, oh my, o-oh, my sweet Michael!

Come by the tunnel, you say, just as you have been saying all along.

I draw a blank. I look into your eyes searching for that flame, that blazing splendor which I call love. Seeing me quiver, you smile that knowing smile of yours, and pull me into your arms.

Lena, oh, Lena! That's all you say.

So I tell myself: He's got to be careful, even more so now. The big day hasn't come yet. But it's got to be here soon, very soon.

Promise me the light of day, sweet Michael? I ask.

In time, you say.

Perhaps, it's the tone of your voice. Your two words grate like the scraping sound of Ma's rusty knife when she put the blade to

sharpen on the stepping stone outside our cabin door.
It goes: *Rasp, rasp, rasp* ...
Rasping against my heart.

Stump ... stump ... stump ...
All's dark. All's empty, but for the swarming in my head of all
the bygones that are now ... are not now ... now ... not now ...
I flounder, not knowing where to turn.
Until light comes in a flash and I stir.
I stir big!

21

M-miss? Miss?   Someone's calling under his breath.

But I hear him. I hear him amid the hoopla that is filling up the whole house. I look down the stairs and see him standing there in the parlor, his face drawn.

Aw shucks! Why's he here?

Be gone, *you*, be gone!

Does he not see what's going on?   All that bustling around him? His eyes wide open but he's not seeing, not hearing. Looks like he's got his mind fixed on something else, and he's listening out for it. Now, he's heading back down the basement.

What're you looking for, Ben?

He hears me! He stands still, looks to the top of the stairs as I back away from the landing.

Miss?

Hush up, now! I tell myself and hold still, so still that you can hear a pin drop. Ah, you're not going to hear me because I won't let out a breath.

Not a breath, um …

Something's drawing him downstairs.

Ah, bumpkin, I don't care what you're up to! This here's an evening for fun! I won't let you spoil the tidbit of it. The tidbit that's going to come my way just because you walk in here in your grubby old boots any time you fancy.

You see, I'm to stay out of this evening's party because my Michael says so.

But, Michael? I protest. Ma'am says that the party's just our way of turning a cheek to City Hall. After all, they call us soiled doves, say that we're to wear yellow to mark who we are. So, let's have a party, a yellow costume party! Ma'am says. A cheeky thing to do, that's all.

Your stone face tells me that you will hear no more of this silly party.

As you wish, Michael, I say, lowering my eyes.

The red glow in your Brown Palace room burns my face. I walk up to the window draped in crimson velvet. I have half a mind to push aside the drapes and throw open the window, take in the outside air, look up at the clear blue skies, and ah, look west to the yonder mountains!

I'll get to see the light of day. I will. And I'm going to shine!

But, they call us *soil doves?*

Fella wanna make senator, wanna make a name for himself, make it a business of his to clean up the red-light district. I'd heard Carp telling ma'am.

In my head, I see only the beautiful satin gown the seamstress is set to sew for me. Look, the color of sunflower, Miss Lena! She'd said this morning as she unfurled the bolt of golden yellow satin. What a gloss! It came all the way from France, Miss Lena.

I put down a Double Eagle for her payment.

A question drops into my head which I won't put to my lips: Will your girl in the closet ever get to see the light of day? Will I, sweet Michael, when you Senator be?

Coming to a year now, I've been walking the tunnel to come to you. For near twelve whole months, I've been waiting to walk in the light of day, waiting to shine. Sitting in my small room every day, waiting … pining for you, my sweet Michael.

Ah, the light of day has an awesome pull! You know that, don't you, Michael? I'd say you do, same as I. I see it in your

eyes, the hotly bonfire that is spitting sparks, crackling, spitting ...
We both want so much to shine, don't we?

What's his bet, huh? Why else would he be watching over his
back so? I'd heard Ma'am letting it slip behind my back.

Ah, Michael, what I won't tell is that when I'm shut up in my
room, night after night, I hear all the merrymaking downstairs—
the piano plays a slow piece, a fast piece, another fast piece,
someone breaks into song, others join in, feet tapping beat. Ah,
round and round they go, dancing and laughing and clapping ...
The whole house comes alive while I'm all cooped up, waiting to
shine.

In the upstairs rooms, there are the heavy breathing, banging
and moaning. I can hear them even with my head under the
pillow.

Mornings come, the whole house reeks with the odors of the
night—stale liquor, flat tobacco, spent perfume, sweat and urine
and douche chemicals, and now and then, a whiff of the sickly
sweet opium that Ma'am frowns upon.

All these, I won't tell, Michael. But couldn't you have
guessed, if you care?

Ain't ya gonna shine, girl? Get out, girl, fast as ya can! I hear
my mountains calling out to me, day after day. My eyes grow
misty when I turn to the two black-and-white prints hanging over
my bureau. Gray and dull and mute. In my heart, they are forever
pristine, forever majestic.

Shine I will, I promise ya.

So, I throw myself into your arms cooing, sweet Michael, will
you take me for a walk in the park? How I miss the fresh air! I
hear that there are fiddlers on the green and mandarin ducks in the
lake. Ah, mandarin ducks! What I hear is that they've got a green
sheen on their heads and over their wings, and they swim in pairs!
And, ah, I hear there's a fountain on the lake, spouting water?

I look up to you with pleading eyes. I see you smile, one
corner of your mouth tilted up. A wry smile? A smile
nonetheless, I tell myself.

Will you, sweet Michael? Oh, ple-ease! My lips curl into a pout.

You bend down, put your lips over mine.

That fire in your eyes, I call it love, darling Michael!

Pa, too, had called out his love without a word. The way he looked at Ma. The fire in his eyes said it for him.

Ben, I'm watching you!

From the landing upstairs I see you heading down the basement, past girls fluttering about. A swarm of yellow butterflies in palettes of buttercup, marigold and daffodil. Yellow ribbons streaming about bouncy curls. Hands busy pinning twists of yellow ribbon on the gentlemen's jacket lapels.

Not many gents coming in tonight, huh?

Ma'am has been expecting a big turnout. She had set the date of the party to follow the three-day gala in the City, ah, the Festival of Mountain and Plain!

Festival of Mountain and Plain?

I, uh, I draw a blank! What, uh, what of the parades and the races and the grand balls that everyone's been talking about?

Have they come and gone?

Already? Oh, darn, darn, darn! How co-ould I've missed it all?

What did Michael say about my going to the festival?

I draw a blank. Nothing comes to mind. Not a thing!

Ho-ow can this be?

An emerald gown waltzes to the open door. Ma'am opens up her arms to welcome the three gentlemen walking in. A big smile crosses her raspberry lips. Her big heart-shaped diamond pendant flashing on her chest. It catches the light of every eye, saying: This here's a classy parlor.

Girls flock to greet them, flaunting curls, making eyes, big yellow skirts brushing against trouser legs. One happens to look up the stairs landing. She gasps, her face white as a sheet, as if she has seen a ghost. She whispers to the girl standing next to her. The girl glances up sheepishly. She puts on this blank look as if she sees me not even though I'm standing in plain view.

Silly cows, it's only me, Lena! Well, yes, I'm not dressed for the ball! I shrug.

The piano is pounding out a fast tune, pumping the air with much excitement. Someone squeals above the strains, setting off a big roar of laughter. Two giddy girls hustle their guests up the stairs. One has her hand dipped into his trouser pocket while he has a hand over her bosom. They shuffle past me without so much as batting an eye.

You're not seeing, or hearing any of these. Are you, Ben? Your mind, um, is fixed on something else.

What's that something, Ben?

Down in the basement?

I'm not following you down, Ben. Not when the house is in full swing. Michael wants me out of sight. Got to stay put in my room.

I sit on my rocker, leaning back, and hum, *High in the Colorado Rockies ... mountain child, so soon I'll go back home ...* phrases of camp ditties stream through my head to drown out the noise of the goings-on downstairs.

I happen to glance down the floor. One of my brand new yellow satin slippers is resting on its side under my bed. I pick it up. It looks as if it has been trampled on, its little ribbon bow crushed.

Oh, no!

Now, where's the mate?

I bend down to look and find it under the head of the bed.

Who was in my room? Who shoved my slipper way up there? Such adorable heels, squashed!

I straighten out the bows, smooth out the toes, and step into one slipper, then the other. I sway about gently, close my eyes and fancy myself waltzing above a field of sunflowers.

What a pity! Michael would never want to see me wearing these slippers, or my dazzling sunflower gown.

Nothing yellow! He'd say.

Of course not, I'm no soiled dove. I'm your Lena, sweet Michael!

But, where's my sunflower gown?

I turn to my wardrobe. The door is open. Empty inside. Not a single gown hanging, no splash of color to greet my eyes!

No, this can't be my room!

Dark in here. The kerosene lamp on the table is not lit, but I *can* see around me. I can make out the little pink rosebuds on the milk-white glass shade. My pretty rosebud shade! I can make out the clusters of climbing white roses and twining green leaves on the tan wall paper!

I can see in the dark!

So, this here's *my* room? But, the walls are bare. No framed pictures hanging. My own cherished portrait by Mr. Bristol above my bed gone!

Gone?

Gone, too, are the prints of Mount Elbert and Mount Massive! They were hung above the bureau where I could see them as I lie in bed.

Who took them?

Why, oh why?

I stumble backwards, spin around. I see now that the room has been stripped bare as if no one's staying in it. My washstand's here but my washcloth's gone. The little crocheted doily under my lamp's missing. So is my bedside rug. My bed's without bed linen. The mattress has its underside turned to face up, its sewed-on tag visible: Jones Mattress Maker. I hasten to lift the mattress up to peer under. Nothing there? I push the mattress halfway off the bed frame, sweep my hands over the board underneath, looking for my hidden treasure.

Nothing!

My purse, nowhere to be found!

Oh, my Pikes Peak gold, my Double Eagles gone!

All gone!

I yank the mattress all the way down to the other side of the bed, flipping it over in a loud thud. Whoa, what's on the surface? A big blotch of a reddish-brown stain! Dark. Still damp. As if there has been, um, an ugly incident ...

NO! IT'S A KILLING!

It comes to me in a blinding flash—I'm being eaten alive, inside out! A fury has, uh, has gotten inside me, corroding my guts, gnawing me to bits ...

O-ooooh! Pain, oh, pain so huge, pain so wretched! I thrash about, retching, choking, wheezing ... Spit it out, spit it all out!

Mercy, oh, m-mercy!

Thud!

I drop onto the floor, scrambling to get away ... away from the wrecking pain, the wailing pain.

I look up into her many jumbled faces jostling over me, her raptor eyes glare like flaming torches, her raspberry lips clamp-shut into many blades. Her talons clawing over me, over my hair, over my flailing limbs ... tugging, dragging me across the floor ...

Strike after strike, lightning lashing down, thunderclaps exploding over me ... inside me ...

Thud ... thud ... thud ... thudding down into darkness. Darkness swelling up, drowning me ...

Oh, woe!

Woooe-wheee!

I lie whimpering, gagging on my own puke, spitting blood ... Roiling in sweat and tears, grime and slime, I hang onto my tattered nightdress. Floundering, I heave myself up to grab at a desperate cover, blindly snatching ... pulling down what's, uh, within reach.

A blood red sky crashing down over me ... I cling dizzily onto my last breath, holding tight, so tight, a dimly burning wish.

I run my hand down my thigh. Nothing. I feel nothing. Pinch it. No pain. I fold my arms across my chest and feel no warmth. I touch my face. Nothing, not even numbness. I clamber over to

my wardrobe, slam the door shut. I stand in front of the mirror and
see only an empty room. Empty and dark. I throw myself at the
mirror and pound on it.

    Woe, oh woe!

    I slump down the floor, wailing ...

There was this hurt doe panting and thrashing under the big
outcrop. A wild thing must have given her chase and she had
taken a tumble from high up. I went up to her and she froze,
glazed eyes staring up at me, one hind leg twitching away.

    I walked on. Not a few steps away, I turned back. She was
nowhere to be found. There was no blood trail on the ground, and
no drag marks.

    Oh, Ben, light of my life, get me out of here!

22

Michael?

Oh, Michael, I hear you!

I rush out of my room and look down the stairs. The hallway lamp is burning, casting a dim light into the parlor where I see shadows shudder.

Michael? Is that you?

Silence. All's quiet but for the little noises in the bedrooms. Footsteps. Someone slips out of a door, shirttail over his pants, jacket tucked under one arm. He brushes past me, stumbles down the stairs and heads out the door. Outside, hacks for hire wait by the curb for their early morning fare.

Are you here for me, sweet Michael?

I fly down the stairs and rush into the parlor. There stands my dashing Michael in his dark pinstripe suit, maroon silk tie, and bowler hat.

Oh, Michael!

I want to throw myself into his arms but I held back.

He's speaking to ma'am in a hushed voice. Clearly, she has not been expecting him. I see that her coiffed hair is undone, tied with a ribbon at the nape. She has her magenta robe over her nightdress.

He has never been to the house, she has said so.

Why's he here, at this hour?

I see that in his hand he is holding a bulging leather pouch. Ma'am gestures to receive it from him, her hand touching his. Michael recoils, clutching his pouch, his eyes guarded.

I tiptoe up to him. He sees me not.

O-ooh! I tremble and pull the red cloak tightly over my soiled nightdress.

Her faded raspberry lips are smiling. Those same raspberry lips that were spewing cutting words last I heard.

Do you know what has happened to me, Michael? *Michael?*

Ah, he hears me not!

Hmm, you know why I'm here, Michael says. There is a steely edge to his harried voice, and in his eyes, an icy glint like a big cat's staring out of the dark.

Mr. Norton, you know there's no cause for you to be concerned whatsoever, she says, looking up at him.

Michael is unmoved. He looks away from her.

What can I do for you, Mr. Norton, that I haven't already done? She pauses. Then, in an abruptly aggrieved tone, she says, You know, it's, uh, it's so-o dee-vastating! She pulls out a handkerchief from her sleeve to dab her eyes.

I have come for what belongs to me, he says curtly.

They're absolutely safe in my keeping. But, of course, I will hand them to you now, if you so wish, ma'am says.

He nods impatiently. Eyes like flint.

I trust, sir, you'll respect my business interests after you're appointed senator. Lena's gone, bless her soul. You see, um, that I've kept my end of the deal … ma'am chokes up, shaking her head while she steals a look at him.

Hmm, he interrupts her, wanting to hear no more.

So, *you* know, Michael.

Flashing back—a lightning bolt, a thunderclap, knocking me over …

What *do* you know, Michael? What *deal?* I shriek. A voiceless shriek that cries torrents down the gulch! It buckles canyon walls so no echo can travel back!

Yet, one echo darkly hurtles back … to taunt, just before …

It's a betrayal that gouges deep, oh, so bloody deep!

I'll wait here, he says as he turns his back and starts to pace. His shadow climbs up the wall, and the parlor grows small.

I won't be a moment then, ma'am says.

She turns to walk up the stairs, sweeping past me. I follow her up. Her room is at the end of the hallway across from mine. She picks a key from the key ring she keeps in her pocket at all times. She unlocks the door, taking care to shut it behind her. Behind me, for I'm right at her heels.

Sitting down at her dressing table, she lifts up the lamp with the pink silk shade, and pulls a key out from under the base. She unlocks the top drawer and takes out an envelope that has my name on it.

My head explodes. Blood in my eyes. The whole room spins, throbbing fiery red.

She pushes aside her bristle hair brush with the silver handle, her silver hand mirror, and spreads out the twelve photographs under the lamp like a small deck of cards. They lay, shining mutely under the pink glow. The glass-beaded fringe of the lamp shade trembling still.

She chortles as she savors them—the images of my date with Michael in the park!

Lena, what a little fox she was! There hasn't been one quite like her! Not ever! Me, I'm just here to take advantage of a rather unfortunate situation and see that my interests are taken care of. Norton and his wounded pride? Huh, he could've forgiven the poor girl's imprudence, for she knew not what she had done. What man is this who can't live with a little childish prank, huh?

She reaches into her drawer, retrieves a small envelope among her papers and the I-owe-you's. From it, she pulls out strips of negatives where little dark images had been captured by the camera. She fans them open and holds them up to the light. She scans through them. Her face is set like stone, but one corner of her mouth twitches.

Um-hmm! This is what's going to hold a gentleman to his word, though it may, uh, comes down to just being a matter of buying time …

She sighs, drops the negatives into the envelope, and stashes it back inside the drawer.

Woe, oh, woe!

How wily the world, ah, how heartless, how cold blooded!

Unwittingly, I'd set myself a trap. I'd fallen prey to my own desperate ploy. Desperate to want to know if you truly care for me. Desperate for a way out of my closeted life. Ah, to get to the light!

Michael, whatever photographs, whatever negatives, I would have gladly offered them all to you. If only I'd kept a clear head and knew what they meant to you ...

Would I've been spared? Would I, Michael?

Why ask a moot question, girl? A voice inside my head chides.

But, what of love?

Love? Didn't you ask for gold, girl?

Tears stream down my cheeks. Pain so huge, I reel with heartbreak and rage!

Ma'am collects the photographs and slips them into her handkerchief. As she looks into the dresser mirror above her perfume flasks, her cut-glass tub of face powder with the silver lidded puff, she pauses to admire herself, smiling her twisted smile.

I look into the mirror and see only one reflection—her blood-sucker's face.

No more of that face!

After she locks the door behind her, she reaches over to test the knob on my door, making sure that it is locked. Then she moves towards the stairs.

I once saw a golden eagle take to the sky from its perch on the cliff. Before its wings could carry it up high, a single shot rang clear out of the blue from another perch. The big bird was golden no more, just a killed bird plunging down the gulch.

I look down the steep canyon floor. Down where the sun's shy, there's this sprawled wreck in the red pool of my eyes!

Ma'am? No! Oh, no!

Cy-bil! Cy-bil!

Help! Get help quick!

Shadows everywhere! They come out of their rooms to crowd over the crumpled heap at the foot of the stairs.

Quick! A stealthy hand sweeps up the photographs scattered whichever way on the floor, stuffing them into a pinstripe pocket. The other hand is clasping a fat pouch.

I follow him with my bloodshot eyes. The thief does not spare a look at the wreckage from which he's pilfering. He surveys the floor, gets back on his feet and shoots for the door, nearly dropping his bowler hat.

My bloodshot eyes are on his back long after he's out of sight.

Someone's lighting up the house. Everyone sees the carcass plain as day, its head twisted, jammed into the lower tread at the foot of the stairs. Girls in their nightdresses half undone screech and scream. A couple of overstayed guests pull on their pants and scurry out the door. One hack driver rushes in to gawk.

The police! Call the police!

Get Big Roy!

The handler is not out front with the hack drivers. Someone has to yank him up from his cot in the basement. He rubs his sleepy eyes as he pushes his way into the crowd. He drops to his knees by the wretched clump, puts his thick index finger over its nostrils.

Ah-no! Ah-no! He hollers, shaking his head. He looks up at the stunned faces around him. Some lower their heads, others turn away whimpering. He crouches over the body, puts his hand over those staring dead eyes to shut them for the last time.

Make way! Make way!

He gathers up the limp bundle and walks up the stairs, nearly tripping over the magenta robe that is trailing down the steps.

Ya need to lie in yar own bed. Ya need to … He's slobbering his way up.

On the landing, Big Roy passes me by with that dead bird in his arms, its broken neck dangling. I'm about to cast a shooter's eye at my prize when I hear Ben mutter, I'm so sorry, Cybil!

Cybil? No, no, I'm not that dead buzzard!

I'm Lena! Le-ena.

I'm so sorry, Cybil! Ben mumbles still.

Buzz in your ear, huh?

23

I'm about to jump out of my skin! For days now, the dry autumn air has been parching my skin, scourging an itch all over my body. I'm that caged bobcat, pacing night and day, day and night ...

Rain has finally come this morning. I press against the window to peer up at the slice of rain-soaked sky. Droplets streak down the pane, blurring my view of the brick wall across the way.

But the pitter-patter does not drown out the squabbling in the hallway. Sadie's still squawking at Zelda over a borrowed dollar. Or, is it her missing hair pin this time? But it always comes down to a strapping buck named Dill who sneaks in from the back when Big Roy happens to be chatting up the hack drivers out front.

My eyes are bleary. Ma, ya looking at the autumn gold? There's no autumn gold here.

It's been over a year since I left, but it feels like ages. Ya missing me, Ma?

The air's damp now, but my itch stays.

Oh, get me out of here!

The sky breaks at noon, the rain slows to a drizzle. A faint light shines through the thinning clouds. That is when you ring up.

Lena, meet me at the City Park.

But, uh, it's drizzling! Sweet ...

As you wish!

Yes, yes, I'll come!

At three, east gazebo by the lake.

At three I come to you. I come in a light drizzle. I come in my gown of burnt-orange wool crepe and flowing cape to match. My bright coppery hair glows against the rich brown silk inside my hood. How I want to outshine the Fall colors in the Park! And most of all, be a delight to your eyes, sweet Michael.

The day, though, has been washed pale by the rain. Still, the evergreens stand tall and dark, wet and slick. Turning colors brush over thinning canopies that cluster about the grounds, sprinkling a variegated gold.

There, in the shroud of mist my love waits for me!

Here I come, my sweet Michael!

I step out of the hack onto the sodden grass. My slippers are soaked, and I cringe. The hack driver coughs. I see him squint as I sweep into the open air.

Darn day to walk in the park, miss, he calls out after me, shaking his head.

Where's the lake? I turn to ask.

That a way, miss, he stretches out his hand to point.

I don't like the snickering look on his face one bit. My eyes point steadily to the lake.

Want me to wait, miss?

No, thanks! I wave him off.

He mutters away, but I hear not a word. I'm listening out for the breeze and fancy it to be a fiddler's tune. Of course, there are no fiddlers on the green. Not on a day like today. Then, I hear the hack trotting off.

My cape soon glistens with a gloss like a touch of morning dew. Only it's three in the afternoon. For me, the day's about to begin.

I pick up my pace, kicking dirt onto the bottom of my skirt. I'd fancied wearing this new Fall outfit to an evening at the Tabor Grand Opera House. That is, if you'd have me by your side, Michael. But this afternoon's date comes first.

Ah, a little drizzle matters not a whit, so long as you're here for me, my sweet Michael!

I walk on, my feet wet and cold. The park is vast and deserted. An endless stretch of dull green grass spreads before me.

Where's the lake?

I've no eye for the yellow mats under the trees, color so bright the leaves have to be newly dropped. No eye for the troupe of chattering magpies hopping and pecking about the wet grass. No eye for the lone robin up on a branch watching me.

I push my hood off. Overhead, a white sheen shivers through the gleaming leaves, a smattering of yellow and orange among the dwindling green. Light so sheer it glistens as through dragonfly wings.

The mute sun is peeking through the thinning haze sending down gentle rays to smile upon me. I bathe in the breaking glow, feeling as airy as the finches' call. The drizzle softens to a blown kiss on my face. The sky's opening up for me!

Inside my heart, a brazen little lark bunting is trilling away. It fills me with song so big I'm giddy in the head.

The lake, two gazebos on its opposite banks, come into view all at once. A tall figure in a camel coat stands in one. I know it's him by his bowler hat. He has one hand resting against a post, looking out …

For me!

My sweet Michael!

I break into a run, my cape flying after me, laughter rippling through my heart. As I sail near, I catch your beckoning eyes. A twitch of an impatient smile crosses your face. I race up the steps into your arms.

All at once, you suckle my breath, inhaling me as if you've been waiting to come to life.

Oh, Lena! You sigh, your brandy breath moist upon my face.

You glow, girl, you murmur, caressing my hair with one hand, the other inside my cape holding me close. I feel on top of the world, rainbow over my head!

A rustling among the shrubbery not six feet away from the gazebo. You turn to look. I listen, my eyes shut. The tip of my tongue reaches inside your mouth, lingering, fondling. I hear your heart throbbing wildly.

Take me with you! I whisper.

Uh-huh ...

Oh, take me with you, sweet Michael!

Where to? Your voice is groggy.

To Washington!

Huh?

Senator Norton you'll be, promise me the Capitol now!

Hmm.

You put on this amused smile as if you've just laid eyes on me for the very first time, and you are stunned.

You love me, don't you, my sweet Michael?

Lena, you girl! Your voice has no warmth.

The fire in my heart flickers. Your silence blows like a chill wind. My cape has slid off one shoulder. I lower my head to draw it back on so you won't see the glistening in my eyes. You turn to look somewhere else. Maybe, a bird has flitted past.

We stand gazing at the lake, its surface a sheet of mirror, holding forth a translucent sky, bright and white and vacant, not a ripple to break its calm. We stand, together in our separate worlds.

The pale sun is heading west to the blue mountains smudged in haze. You look west too, not at the endless ranges yonder but at the gazebo across the lake. No one is there. I wince.

Young shade trees, branches sparse, rim the lake shore. A flock of geese, heads bowed, peck at the ground as they waddle along. One takes off, another follows, honking loudly as they skim over the water surface.

A stir from behind the shrubbery.

You didn't hear, did you?

Taking both my hands in yours, you bring them to your lips and kiss them, gazing dreamily into my eyes.

My sapphire eyes!

I, too, am lost in your heavenly blue eyes. I'm about to fall in love all over again when you suddenly step back and say, Lena, I've got to go.

So soon?

The bench is damp but I sit down for all I care. The ground beneath my feet is giving way. I swallow a rising ire. I hear your footsteps creaking down the steps. I look away but for a moment, then turn back to trail your handsome figure. You walk briskly across the stretch of grass to where a street hack awaits you by the curb.

Ah, you've been gracious! You didn't dropped me a few of your double-eagles for our afternoon together.

I tarry a bit to stretch my day's outing so when I stand up, I will be able to stand tall.

A breeze sends wrinkles over the lake. I sit and stare, looking for the mandarin ducks with the green sheen on their heads. I don't see any. A few of the brown-feathered ones squat under a tree. I spot them as they flap their wings when the geese get near. Those big birds keep on pecking, not looking, not seeing.

A dull day at the park. No fiddlers on the green, for sure. No other souls but those who could make use of a soggy afternoon away from prying eyes. Yet I loathe to leave. I take my time to savor the moment when I'm let out of my cage.

I was that child licking a found barley sugar bonbon. Even that carried a price as I had come to know so many years ago. Still, I lick with relish my dubious afternoon bonbon.

Clouds thickening. I look west. The waning sun is a whitish glow in the moisture laden sky. Dull rays scattering over the blue mountains far away. Empty and lost, I find myself squirming in my damp slippers. I stand up, draw my cape around me and turn to leave. The blanket of gloom is almost too much to bear.

A figure in a dark suit comes out of the shrubbery. He lifts his cap and bows. I pause on the gazebo steps. He looks up.

Miss Saber, says Mr. Bristol. Sorry to have startled you. May I offer you a ride back?

I, um, I … thank you.

He tips his head and offers his hand to lead me down the steps. We walk in silence, leaving me to ponder what he might have made out from the scene at the gazebo.

I had said this to him earlier over the phone: My gentleman friend and I desire artistic and spontaneous shots on this special occasion of ours. May I ask that you please not to make your presence known?

I glance back at the gazebo as we are about to step off the green. Then I turn to him and say, Mr. Bristol, I'm much obliged that you came, and at such a short notice.

My pleasure, he says. But I hear a wistfulness in his voice.

Then I say with my head bowed, Mr. Bristol, I'm grateful that you've stayed back for me.

Don't mention it, Miss Saber.

He helps me into the waiting hack. We ride in silence. I sit back and listen to the trot-trotting of the horse and glance out at the fine houses along the streets—houses where families live, where loved ones gather to say prayer over meals, say goodnight with kisses and hugs.

Camera? Where's his camera?

I turn to him. He sees the puzzled look on my face. Out of his coat pocket he brings out a small box, a red leathered box that he holds in the palm of his hand.

This here's a camera! He says with a hint of a smile. A Pocket Kodak. It holds a roll of film for twelve pictures!

Oh?

How unlike the heavy box he had shown me that very first time, and I already called it magic then!

I look at the little thing sitting in his palm, at the round hole in front.

A glass eye?

The viewfinder. Here, point and shoot, he says. He holds the little red box with both hands to show me how, looking straight down into another glass eye on top.

How do the pictures look? I ask, dying to see.

You'll soon see, Galena, Miss Saber!

He speaks into my eyes now. He holds them in a steady gaze, in the fading light. As he once did, under a bright afternoon sun. That day of summer meadows when he offered me a sprig of blue flax and called my eyes sapphires.

I feel a rare warmth that stirs deep. For I know now that there is a place where we both belong where neither passing time nor distance traveled can erase.

*   *   *

The pictures come small, like the camera they were taken with. I put each in the palm of my hand and pore over it. In that gazebo with the diamond latticework, I see the meeting of two lovers. Passion gleaming through the black and white prints, clear and tender and full of heartbreak. Those precious moments that had fleeted away are now images on paper. Ah, for keeps!

Still, I sigh with a longing for what had come to pass that day in the Park. Our embrace lingering in my heart still.

In the envelope there are also three strips of negatives, for all twelve pictures. The envelope is unmarked, save that it is addressed to Miss Lena Saber, hand delivered by an errand boy for me to receive in person.

24

$\mathbf{W}$hat's with Norton anyway? This cleanup business of his, huh? Says a voice thick with phlegm.

Well, the fellow wants to be senator. He's got to have a platform.

Michael, eh? I perk my ears as I walk past the parlor on my way to the front door.

Ahem, someone clears his throat.

More whiskey, gentlemen? Ma'am says in her singsong voice.

Heavy bodies shifting, the settee creaks. Girls twittering.

At the front door, I quickly sign a receipt for the errand boy. He hands me an envelope with no sender's name on it. I clutch the envelope to my pounding heart. The photographs!

The errand boy pokes his head in, eyes bright like a snooping kitten's. I give him a one-dollar tip and send him off.

I peek out of the corner of my eye as I walk past the parlor again. Inside, beady eyes ogle through curls of cigar smoke straight into the hallway. A skulk of foxes coming together to gossip about my Michael? Hatching some idle schemes?

I make it look like I'm heading for the stairs. But, I pause past the doorway and cock my ear.

That his girl?

Cute young thing, eh?

Ahem …

Well, the fellow wants to have his cake and eat it too.

Now, old Bob Hayes' got deep pockets and he's hell bent to want to clean up this town.

Yep, Norton may just have to do what he's got to do, with that father-in-law of his on his back.

Whoa, not so fast! We'll have to see about that!

Now, now, I can speak for all of us here, there's no finer establishment in town than this one here. Our compliments to you, madam.

A-absolutely!

To you, ma'am, and your fine house!

Ah, more whiskey!

A round of tweeting and chirping ...

Gentlemen, I thank you, one and all, ma'am warbles. We dearly love to keep our door open for you. Our girls adore your company, eh, girls? Ah, heaven knows, we count on your favors! She pauses to let her words sink in. Then she says, *Now,* more than ever, gentleman.

Madam's power patrons come over after a day's session at the City Hall. Jackets off, they let their hair down, prop their feet up, club around in her lounge made mellow with whiskey and cigar, belly-laugh and soft skin. The parlor is sedate with an unhurried ease. I can just see the pasted smiles and feckless eyes cozying into ready arms, flaunting pushed-up bosoms and pouting lips, fanning ... fanning the flame of desire with an eye for, maybe, a little tip on the side.

Well, I'm above all that! Way above ...

But, the question pops into mind: What will become of me, sweet Michael, when you have your day?

Michael? Ah, ma'am told me the other day that Councilman Becker had inquired about me. Do you know what that's all about, sweet Michael?

The sun outside is just so that a tongue of light slips in through the drawn drapes. It licks through the dusky red glow in the room and crawls onto our hot ruffled bed. You raise your hand to shield your eyes and wipe off the little beads of passion left on your brow.

Huh?

You heave a raspy breath ... your chest rising, falling, rising, falling ... I know then that you, too, must have heard the whispers along the hushed corridors.

Take me with you, Michael!

I'm going to shine. Oh, yes, shine I will! Please, sweet Michael ...

Ah, Michael, you keep your eyes shut because of the sun?

Ma'am comes in late one morning. I hop right out of bed. A call from my sweet Michael?

No, dear, not as yet.

Slumping back to bed, I rest my head on my raised knees and let my shoulders droop.

Ah, another long day coming up? I yawn, rubbing my eyes.

Lena dear! What do you think will happen to you when we get run out of here?

She searches my eyes while she reaches out to smooth my hair, running her fingers gently over my tresses. Luster of bright coppery gold.

Like mine, she mumbles, puckering up her lips.

These days, her luster comes from a jar of hair cream. She has her hair piled atop her head in a heap of tight curls. Ringlets like corkscrews fringe her powdered face, a touch heavy with rouge.

She turns to walk up to the wardrobe mirror. The big woman who shows up in there might have fared very well as a homesteader, hauling water from the stream, or baling hay. Strong limbs she's got, I can tell from the way she gets on and off a horse. So, don't let her fine silk gown fool you!

What will happen to you, uh, Lena dear?

Her hands busy now, coiling stray ringlets. The mirror catches the fire of her diamond drop-earrings.

She comes over to sit on my bed, waiting to hear.

Um, ma'am, I don't know ...

I catch her smirking at my bare feet. I throw the coverlet over them and turn away.

Ma would be tearing up the times she'd bent over my scarred feet. She would be wrapping my hurt with whatever scraps of paper and cloth that happened to come her way.

Ma, I got hurt somewhere else, too. Where you can't see, Ma. But I'd never said it out loud to her. No more heartbreak for her.

Then, I got my first pair of shoes. They allowed me to take off to roam where I fancied, where I could lose myself.

Will Michael take care of you? Ma'am presses on.

Yes, he will, I say cheerily, looking her in the face. I know he will, hmm.

I'm thinking that ma'am would go on to ask if I'd talk to Michael about letting up his cleanup thing, for my sake.

I'm wrong. Ma'am does not ask that of me. She does not ask how and when Michael is going to take care of me. And, she does not say: Oh, I'm *so-o* hap-py fo-or you, Lee-na dear!

She parts her raspberry lips gleefully enough, but her eyes are piercing.

Darn those raptor eyes!

You can almost hear her brain go clicking away, chewing on things that won't pass her lips.

Ah, how I'd wanted to show them to you the minute I walked in! But you pulled me into your arms and pressed your brandy breath onto my mouth. Snug and urgent, passion throbbing, as trilling as a tree swallow's morning song ...

I so want to be loved!

So, I know not what's coming when I smooth over the rumpled bed linen and spread out the photographs, eager for your eyes.

Look what I've got here, sweet Michael, something to remember our date at the Park!

You bend over me, over the photographs. You pick one up. I look up ... I'm taken aback by the dark cloud over your brow. The glint in your eyes sends chill—an icy blue chill that goes straight to my heart. My lips quiver, my smile flits away.

You drop the photograph down my laps and walk toward the window. You put on your trousers quickly, throw your shirt over your back. There you stand facing the drawn drapes without a word, but I hear the silent growl that is choking the room.

I, ah, I'd them taken to, uh, to remember our day at the Park, sweet Michael, I murmur as I crouch, small and sore, on the bed, the twelve photographs jumbled all around me. The bright glow in the red velvet room is dimming fast. A sudden chill has descended. I pull a sheet over my nakedness.

Who took them?

Mr. Bristol, a friend.

Hmm.

You do know Mr. Bristol. It was in his studio that you had first come upon my portrait.

You snatch a print and bring it up to examine, front and back. Then, another and another, dropping each as you are done. On each, there is a label below the image: Pocket Kodak. There is no studio label.

Who has the negatives? You ask, clenching your teeth.

I do.

You turn away. I kneel down to pick up the photographs which you had let dropped to the floor. It has not occurred to me that I should offer them to you since you frown upon them so. They are mine then, and mine alone. A keepsake.

You pace like a caged animal, then pause in front of the unlit fireplace. You bow your head in front of the gilded mirror above the mantel.

Has anyone seen them? You ask, turning around. You come to stand over me. Your brow knitted, your steely eyes glaring down. I shudder.

No-o! No, I say without blinking.

Why would I want to tell? I ask in silence.

The girls had giggled over them and I saw from their curled lips the grin of envy as they passed them around. Ma'am bit her lips. She arched one eyebrow and asked, Has Mr. Norton seen them? Her eyes narrowed into lizard slits over her cup of afternoon tea.

I gather enough courage to look up. A small twitch pulls at one corner of your mouth. You stare at me with a stranger's murky eyes.

Forgive me, Michael? I whimper, nearing tears.

Silence still.

Lena, you sil-ly, silly girl! You whisper after what seems like an eternity. Your eyes shut, you tuck me into your arms, grasping me tight, near squeezing the air out of me. The sheet over me slips down the floor. You run your hands over my nakedness.

Got to take you away! You murmur into my ears.

To the Capitol? To Washington D.C.?

I break out into my sunshine smile. You murmur into my hair, though I catch not what you're saying for my heart's bursting into song and my head's up in the clouds. Ah, I've skipped the storm and am now dancing upon the rainbow, chasing after my one cherished dream!

Oh, Senator Norton, my sweet Michael!

Hmm, not quite as yet!

But you will be. Everybody's been saying so.

Who?

Ma'am and the others.

Who?

Uh, the lawmen, the whole bunch of them!

Oh, Lena! Lena!

I'm already thinking of afternoon teas at the Capitol and grand operas in the evenings and the beautiful gowns and how you would sweep me off my feet to dance the night away.

I laugh heartily. I laugh till my tears come, lighting up my sapphires. You look into them as if you are seeing them for the very first time. Or, for the last time. For you hold them in a steady gaze for a long, long while.

I look through the tears and see Ma smiling and my mountains glittering.

Galena, ya gonna shine!

What's this? I look down and see an angry bruise on my waist. Ah, you did hold me tight, Michael! So tight, um, I'd thought I would crack like a porcelain vase.

Ah, how your eyes lingered over mine! As if you were loathe to let me go …

Oh, well, the bruise will fade!

Shine I will, just you see, my sweet Michael!

25

A knock on the door ...

At midday?

Our door's never locked noon to past midnight. Not today. Today, the house's empty, but for Hannah and me.

Hannah buzzes around the kitchen, her cheeks flushed and her brow shines with sweat. She squats down to scoop coal from the scuttle to add to the red hot hopper, then reaches up the stovetop for the tray of filled tartlet tins and slides it into the oven. She's baking up a storm of pumpkin tartlets! On the kitchen table, rows of piping hot ones are cooling on racks.

Yet, I smell no warm scent of cinnamon ...

Anyway, I want naught of cinnamon nor pumpkin taste. Nor the little ham-and-egg tea sandwiches looking pretty on a silver platter.

Knock, knock, knock ...

Coming, coming! Hannah cries as she lumbers out the kitchen, wiping her hands on her white apron. She is wearing black today.

Goodness, so soon? She mutters, dusting off the flour from her chubby forearms and rolls down her sleeves.

Michael Norton at the door! I take a step back. The thief of the night comes back in broad daylight.

What now? Have *you* no shame?

Lightning strikes, thunderclap explodes ...

Hell, oh, bloody hell!

The not-so-gentleman has the brim of his hat pulled over his brow. He glances sideways as he edges close to the door, getting set to push his way in.

Sir, do come in please! Hannah steps aside for the gentleman in haste.

I rush forward, but then I'm, uh, neither shadow nor murmur, just a wisp of nothing ...

The house's at the funeral service, sir, at the Fairmount Cemetery, Hannah says. She bows and makes the sign of the cross.

She sees your red-and-brown striped bow tie, brown tweed suit and immaculate white shirt. The gentleman's not attired for mourning, but house rule's house rule: Gents welcome. Always. She shows Michael into the parlor.

Please have a seat, sir. Mrs. Shore and the party will be back for tea shortly.

As she speaks, Hannah turns to inspect the gleaming silver tea service sitting atop a white linen draped table at the back of the parlor.

Mrs. Shore?

Madam's sister, from Leadville.

You walk up to the front window and peer into the street through the lace curtains. Then you turn to look over Hannah's graying head into the entrance hall.

You, a hound on a trail?

If you don't mind, sir, may I be excused? The party won't be long.

Hannah's got no eyes for his fidgety look, or a head to ask for his name. She thinks only of her batch of pumpkin tartlets needing to come out of the oven.

Good old Hannah! She sniffs her way back into the kitchen without waiting to hear from you.

But, of course, you don't mind, Michael, do you?

You slip out of the parlor and charge up the stairs, hat in hand, two steps at a time. You turn the knob on every door down the hallway until you come to that locked one at the end. You yank at the knob. The door glides open.

I wait inside.

You walk in, without a thought of how a locked door would yield. Or, how you may look to unseen eyes. Michael, have you forgotten yourself? Here you are, squinting in a dead madam's small dim room, looking to pilfer from her.

From me, in truth!

But what I've lost is lost for good ... like what's been thrown to the wind, or let down the tumbling water.

Woe, oh woe!

Michael, you don't mind that hung-over scent of hers that fills the air in the shut room? Her bedclothes, her powder puff, her perfume, her magenta robe hooked onto a wardrobe peg as if she's just taken it off—they give out a whiff of her presence though she's gone to the ground right this hour. Her presence, ah, it shrouds like a spell, a spell of charm which aims to dazzle, ah, to gall! She was a cheat who gave with one hand, and took away with the other.

O-oh, and that's not all!

I do know ...

Don't I bloody hell know?

Nice to have dreams, eh? Sort of like wishing for a rainbow, she says to me one day.

Uh?

Try pocketing a rainbow, dear! She says as she flashes the white of her eyes at me. Only fools believe in dreams, her look says.

Oh, yeah? My eyes retort.

I ask myself: What's to become of a dreamer without her dreams?

Ah, no, I'm not ever one of her horses that she brings out of the stable once in a while joy-riding the streets to show off her girls! I'm not ever into flaunting my pretty frilly outside and covering up my sores inside. For I want no sores. No sores at all! And, I know that I mean to shine.

Make it soon, though!

Make it now!

I'll live my dreams one day, rainbow in my pocket! So I tell myself.

Ma'am, eh? She ought to be thankful that she went fast and that her bedclothes were spotless to the end. I look at her bed now. It has been smoothed over where she was laid. Her embroidered velveteen shawl lies neatly folded at the foot of her bed as if she's just sent for the chambermaid.

I've been merciful. Haven't I?

Not she ...

Not you, Michael! You did more than break my heart ... The foolish thing I did, is it so unforgiveable that I'd to pay with my life?

Woe, o-oh, woe! I'm only whiplashing myself, over and over again, uh, gasping yet another dying breath ...

Light filters in through the lace curtains. There, you put down your bowler hat on her dressing table, and push the chair aside to get at the top drawer.

Darn! It's locked.

So, I slide the key out from under the lamp with the pink silk shade. The glass-beaded fringe trembles, but you have no eye for it. You spot the key and pick it up. You unlock the top drawer, reach in with both hands, shifting through her papers, bills, tearing open envelopes.

Not here?

You go on to rummage through the two side drawers. Her perfume flasks shake, her bristle hair brush and her silver hand mirror clatter. Your bowler hat drops to the floor. You pick it up, toss it back on your head.

You rush over to her bedside table, pull out a drawer, nearly crashing it to the floor. Little pill boxes tumble out, popping open as they land, scattering pills all over the dusty rose carpet.

Crash! The bedside lamp topples, its milk-white glass shade shatters as it hits the bed post, sending shards flying.

Um, you mind not a bit! Not a bit!

You head for her chest of drawers, rattling and knocking over a portrait of a younger, fairer ma'am, and letting slide the dresser scarf. Yanking out drawer after drawer, you thrust your hands in and rifle through her undergarments, stockings, blouses, collars …

I stand by the door and watch. There's nothing more unseemly than a gentleman going about his business of snitching from a lady, though she be a madam. Um, a dead one at that. If you were to glance at the dresser mirror this very moment, you'd see that what looks out is a rat, beady eyes scouring, pointy nose sniffing away.

It just doesn't become you, Mr. Norton!

Could I've been spared?

I think not, seeing you the way you are. Not even if I were to offer you my precious memento. Negatives and all.

Um, I see now, there can never be a question put to Senator Norton: Lena who? She, a tainted dove?

You turn to leap over to her wardrobe. Flinging open the door, you see yourself alone in the mirror. But, there, from the corner of your eye, you catch a glimpse of someone standing right behind you, someone the mirror does not see.

You spin around and glare. Such livid eyes! Your nostrils flaring, your mouth gaping, you let out a deep, guttural groan.

Ghrrrrrr …

Michael?

Ghrrrrrr?

You know me not, Michael?

It's me, your Lena!

Oh, no! Don't run away!

I've what you're looking for.

Here!

Walking up to you, I hold out my hand. In it, the three strips of negatives.

Say, are these what you're stooping so low to get, Mr. Norton?

Stumbling backward, you slam shut a couple of the drawers. A loud bang echoes in the tight space. You back into the dresser, grasping at it to steady yourself, shaking, heaving …

I take a handkerchief out of an open drawer and come right up to you. So close I can see your huffing breath in the cold room. You are panting like a trapped mountain lion I once saw. Crouched down in a pit, the poor beast was growling and clawing, alas, to no avail!

Oh, cat, you're done in! My little girl's voice rang out.

I saw then the utter despair of a death trap. And what a piteous sight it was!

Piteous me, too, the way I was wasted …

For what? For taking a nibble at a table not set for me. So a strong arm pounced on me and hurled me out into the cold with nary a flinch.

The mountains in me flattened. Shimmering no more. Breathtaking no more. Can't lift my head high, can't see the sky. Sodden and mired, I grit my teeth and hell-bent on avenging what I was robbed of.

Here, Michael, let me dab your shiny brow. It's moist with sweat. Your glistening sideburns too, and your dimpled chin. The dimpled chin I'd so adored.

Oh, Michael, you're trembling so! I gaze into your eyes, um, still blue, but gentle no more, beguiling no more. A cold fear has crept into them, shuddering, unblinking, shuddering …

I can't bear the way you look, Michael?

Ah, do you loathe me so? Let me stroke away that ugly look of fear.

I raise a finger to touch your eyelids. You shut your eyes and let out a sniffle.

Hush, hush, it's only me, Lena!

I'm what I'm because of you. You know that, don't you?

You keep your eyes tightly shut, groaning.

Wishing me gone? But I'm here for you, as always, Michael.

Panting still, you open your eyes at long last. I see in them what you see: A girl in crimson damask, a smile on her lips, a kiss, too. A kiss you used to relish.

But, rage's glowering, seething inside me. I clench the strips of film in my fist. I hold onto them like I was holding onto my last breath … because, ah-h, Michael, you hold them so very dearly. More dearly than you'd held my life.

My life, come to think of it, was no more than a glass of
brandy you'd picked up, eyed its amber gold, put it to your nose.
Bouquet, good, eh? Then, to your lips. Mellow on the palate, eh?
Then you put down the empty glass without a care.

Thirsty now, Michael? For what?

For the good life, like I used to?

Come, Michael, come downstairs with me! Come lie with me
awhile, the way we used to do on our many afternoons together at
the Brown Palace.

Here's this needle point settee under the window where we can
rest ...

Together now, we're together ...

Always will be ...

I put my head against your heaving chest, nestling close. I
hear your heart racing, about to leap out of your body.

Ah, a bunny scurrying for cover!

Be still ... I draw you into my arms ...

Oh, dear, your teeth are clattering so! You're shaking like a
wind tossed tree ... your face, white as a sheet. Your wheezing
breath, it puffs up a steam over your face.

Ah, Michael, don't whimper so!

Easy now, Michael, easy ...

26

A restless wind howls.

> *Woo-oosh-swoosh ... Swooosh-sh-sh ... Shhhhhh ...*
> *I grope on, going no-o-where ...*

> *Amitabha ... bok-bok-bok ...*
> *Amitahba ... bok-bok-bok ... Amitahba ...*
> *Dead end ... dead end ... dead dead end...*

> *No more Amitabha! No more bok-bok-bok!*
> *No-o-o more ...*
> *NO MORE!*

> *Girl, you're back!*
> *You travel now, girl, out of the dark.*
> *Shadow to light to light to light ...*

Ah-h! I choke up, staggering back. Away from the glass front!

A moving beam cuts a wedge into the night. Muffled wheels roll by. No clop-clopping of hoofs. Smooth and fast, color and dash, vehicles so sleek, way out of this world!

All that, in the blink of an eye? Ah, not so. But, how long was I gone? Ho-ow long?

More wheels speeding past, chasing lights on paved street. Where have the hacks gone? Where have the horses gone?

Drowsy sky above, sleepy stars let out dim lights. Once they were the brightest of twinkles up where the air sparkled and the sky was bluer than all the blue jays in the world put together.

Oh, hitch me a ride out! A ride out of here!—I'd called out as I flew up the dark mountain path into the twinkling high swarms.

Now, to the twinkles that twinkle not, I plead: Stars, oh, stars! Show me, oh, show me the way back!

Girl, you're back! You hear?
Out, get out into the light!
But, ah, it's a strange new world out there ...
And I, a wisp of nothing, no breath nor shadow.

Ben jumps as if he hears me. He spins around, cocks his ear. Miss?

I hold my peace. I'm watching him as he watches out for me. No doubt he has seen me teetering in the light of day. See, I've just awaken! I'm trying to splice light with shadow, shadow with light, and so much more ...

He comes out of the dark corner where he has been squinting at the itsy, bitsy lights twinkling down the wavy blue cloth in the center of the room. Lights that prick your eyes. He peers dreamily out into the night as if to escape the lot he is in.

Shadows approaching on the sidewalk. He flops down the floor like a dropped sack of grains. Flat on his face, he tries to hide from view. But he lifts up his eyes. A young couple sauntering past. They walk on, arms entwined, eyes only for each other, this crisp Fall night, in their own charmed world.

Ben lets out a sigh. He gets on his feet and shoots for the stairs to head down the basement. Glancing over his shoulder, he catches them kissing under the glow of the street lamp.

I raise a finger to my lips. Nothing. I feel not the touch.

Will I ever kiss again? Be kissed again?

Will I?

At the foot of the stairs, he stands leaning against the brick wall. Sleepy eyed, he stares into the pitch darkness. Now, he shines the light he holds in his hand over where the grubber fell, the one who came in the night to steal from me. Then he shines it over the patch of bricks under the stairs.

After a while, he drags himself out the door into the night.

Ben comes again into this other basement where there is no billiard table nor brass lamps with the green glass shades nor the dusty rose floral carpet underfoot. He comes in stealth, a coyote that keeps the night awake. Wary eyed, he turns on the little light in his hand to scour the floor ... the foot of the stairs ... the spot below where there was once a window. He comes up to her big work table cluttered with things. He sits down on her swivel chair, looks over her things, touches her things, sniffing around like a pup after a bone.

He walks around. He walks up to the sink counter at the back wall and inspects the empty wash basins. He rubs a finger over the side and points the light at his finger tip. A reddish tint. He puts it to his nose. He looks at her jars of odds and ends, studies them as if they are collectibles he himself would have kept.

M-miss? He whispers in the dark.

Are you here, miss?

But his heart is scattered. It sways with whatever wind that happens to blow his way.

He comes yet another time.

M-miss?

Are you here, miss?

But he's restless. He walks around snooping like a love-sick puppy. He goes upstairs to the room she calls her office. With the light in his hand he looks over her things. Always looking over her things. He studies her photographs. Then he tears down the stairs as if he is being chased by a lumbering bear.

Call it a night, Ben. Your heart is mush, and you've got fluff
in your head!

Cybil? No, no, I'm not that dead buzzard!
I'm Lena! Le-ena.
I'm so sorry, Cybil! Ben mumbles still.
Buzz in your ear, huh?

Still he comes back! Ben comes back with his head and heart
cleared of fog and noise. And he comes straight into my time ...
into the old basement where the billiard table is. He does not look
around. He hops right up the stairs, to the landing where the raptor
fell. He stands on the spot, exhaling slowly.
    What are you seeing, Ben?
    He hears me? He hears me not?
    He lifts his eyes up the flight of stairs, to the top where the
raptor is about to take off. He closes his eyes, takes in the scene.
He holds the scene in his head.
    Ben? I whisper.
    He's not listening. He holds absolutely still. Across time and
space, he's coming through.
    I draw a blank—his mind void, his heart purged!
    I've lost him ...
    He sees now. With his own eyes, he sees a silent, slow-motion
replay: On the edge of the upstairs landing, a tall figure trips over
a yellow slippered foot meant for a tumble. She hurdles down the
flight, head over heels over head ... limbs flailing... magenta robe
flip-flapping ... crashing down to where she crumples into a heap.
    Quick, a gentleman in a pinstripe suit and bowler hat, hovers
over the broken body, rummaging away, one hand gathering up the
strewn photographs, the other clutching a fat pouch. He gets back

up on his feet, heads for the door …

Ben catches that face!

A double take. He looks stumped.

He knows that face?

How?

A chorus rises—Ma'am? No! Oh, no! Cybil! Cybil!

Big Roy bends over the twisted heap, turns her over …

Ah, her face! Her raptor's face past midnight is raw flesh scrubbed of rouge and powder, lips a faded raspberry, gaping wide. Auburn hair strewn about her face. Her dead raptor's eyes stark open, catching nothing.

Ben's taking it in. He's taking it all in. He raises his eyes slowly … back to the yellow slippered foot. He wants to see more than just the foot. He wants to see who she is.

But he draws a blank. That someone is not in his sight.

Ben lets go. For now? But he's got a hunch. He turns to look for the young girl he had once caught sight of … as if he's ready to face a new day. A fresh charge has taken hold of his heart. And he has something else on his mind.

What's it, Ben?

Dark clouds gathering over his brow, he looks troubled.

Your name, miss?

Who're you, miss?

His voice like the bell tolling up the church tower in Leadville, waking up the dead …

It matters not, whatever the name, I sigh.

Ben comes back like a hound trailing a scent. But he can be thrown off, and not by me.

There he stands, gawking at the big red amaryllis that holds center stage up where she calls her gallery. He looks at it with the eyes of a lover thoroughly smitten by what has captured his fancy. More so, by what he's conjuring up in his heart!

There he slumps down the floor, near drowned by the sea of

blue hydrangeas that she has called up for a dreamer to dream. She, the honey blond, who works with her hands, long hours on end, till her eyes are bleary.

He staggers down the basement. Takes in a deep breath, exhales. He closes his eyes, opens his heart.

He catches my scent ...

He sees me now, through my red haze. He sees me in the full splendor of my crimson silk damask. I brush past him as I walk to the rear window. There I stand, gazing up at the half moon. The silvery shine lights up a trove of things called to mind. Things I seem to have missed just yesterday. Or, a lifetime ago.

The parade, yes, the parade! And more ...

Stay, please stay, miss!

Again, he comes back. He's not one to lose a scent!

Where had he seen it before? The crimson damask that relishes his eyes, that touches him with a swell of sadness.

A sadness that I own ...

He closes his eyes to see. Back to the time when he first stood facing the rear window, the rousing sound of the billiard game behind us. He picked up a fold of the drapery and ran his hand gently over the deep crimson damask weave, over the floral swirls in glossy scarlet. Then, he studied its lustrous silk texture under the wall sconce.

Now, back again to this night when he calls up the rear window. Yes, he calls it up! He calls it up all on his own.

There, he sees a drape missing on one side!

I stand, shivering. Pain wallops down once again ...

Steady, steady now ...

He's breathing hard. His eyes near pop out of his head. He sees me, all of a sudden, wrapped up in the crimson silk damask. Not a gown, but a drape!

A drape for a hasty, desperate cover ...

He stands, dazed by the harrowing sight. He turns around, his head spinning ...

So, he sees me now, walking in blazing red, on a blighted path going nowhere. Like that loony China woman in her red cloak, stumping under the big rock ...

You can't know! How can you? You're not from my parts, my times.

What do you want, miss?

How can I bring you peace, miss?

Miss?

His voice softens to a whisper. A lisp of tenderness passes his lips.

Pea-ce? A-ah-ah! Pea-ce?

Echo ringing in the air ... Pea-ce?

Surely, he does see that I was nipped in the bud. Gone too soon! Way too soon!

Can't you see, Ben, I've yet to shine? To return to the lush flow of pulse and heartbeat, the rhythm I call life.

Yes, life!

Rest in peace, miss.

His voice quavers. But I turn away. I turn to look for the dappling gold on my side of the mountain where the aspens quake.

Ah, a most ravishing sight!

The door opens without a sound. He leaves it slightly ajar. A slit of light cuts in. He shuts it out.

What's up, Ben?

In a flash, he bolts upright, eyes shooting clear across the darkness to the corner of the basement where I crouch.

But you can't see me! I'm swaddled in my eternal night, biding my time, forever biding my time ...

How much longer?

How much?

Ben's holding his ground, getting used to the dark. His eyes sweep furtively over to the patch of bricks under the stairs. He walks over to stand on it. Head bowed, he stands there a long while, listening, his hand dug deep inside his jeans pocket. A long dead silence. A-achoo! A-a-achoo! Ah, Ben, you're losing it! He, too, knows it. The sneeze that breaks his concentration gives me relief. He sighs, hangs down his head. He turns around and slips out into the tired night. I hear him lock the door from the outside. Darn him and his surreptitious key!

A puppy after a bone! Ben comes in yet another night to sit at her big work table. He looks over what's in front of him. He flips through the pages of a sketch book. He studies her pencil doodling—curves and stripes and zigzags and swallowtails and polka dots and squares, mirror images of shapes and more shapes. Something catches his eye. He reaches over to the pile of fabric by his elbow and pulls out a red square from where it has peeked out. His stares at the square. NO! He cries. It is a dyed pattern of a damask weave—stylized floral swirls of brilliant scarlet against a deep blood red! He sees now a copy of my crimson silk damask, a wretched drape, my desperate cover! He sees what Ashley must have seen! Eyes on fire, he glares around the room. But he sees nothing, he hears nothing. His heart is bog, his head is pulp. He stands up, pushes himself away from the table. He is quaking like a blur of turning aspens in the autumn breeze. Oh, blow, blow away, you! He pulls himself together to scamper out of the door as if a swarm of bees is after him. Ben, you're a rudely coyote that comes stalking, howling into my dream!

27

*Y*ou, *too, are back?*
You walk through the open door ... into my head lit with a blinding light. Everything bounces off a glare—colors fly, movements flow like streams, sounds echoing through air thin like nothing ...
Not a heartbeat, nor a breath, yet here I'm!
My eyes are on you ...

The light that drenches the air is as peachy as a mountain sunset where high clouds blush a deep rose pink and the sky streaked with gold. I hear a warbler trilling ... A fiddler plays a soulful tune. Warbling, trilling, she fiddles, dreamy-eyed. Her melody sends me a shiver. For I've just come to ...   I look around. Warm bodies bustling. Chatter hums and drones, laughter purling like a Spring brook.
This is now, this new place, all before my eyes!

You walk in, full of yourself, snazzy in your black suit and a black bow tie, your chestnut hair neat and slick.
Ah, no bowler hat?
You smile, ah, how you smile, your eyes beaming!
Heads turn.
Who's she by your side, Michael?
She, your wife, Michael?
She, with hair cropped like a lad's? She's got plaster on her face, Michael. Just look at her pasted smile and her surly eyes

with no sparks! Tall and skinny, sticks for arms, baring for all to
see, and whoa, legs that are not shy? She has on that slinky slip of
a pewter gown with a long slit at the back showing off her ankles
and calves.

Pewter with a shine, reminds me of that German stein ma'am
bought for her Carp with the sleek mustache. Yep, same one she
zinged at him in a fit when she caught him making eyes with
Ruthie. She raised a purple plum on his forehead that took a while
to ripen.

There, your pewter woman hangs by your side. She, wanting
to shine, naked legs and skinny arms?

I look at her and see that thoroughbred mare in madam's
stable—thickly maned, good thigh muscles, strong legs. A regular
show horse, that one.

Say, ma'am, somethin missin, the stable hand blurted out, that
mare, she's got a good kick, but she ain't got no fire in her belly.
No fire, ma'am.

Shut your stinking mouth, ma'am barked. The mare's a
thoroughbred and got plenty of stock for good breeding.

Look here, Michael, I've got fire!

Plenty of fire!

But she, she's got that mare's vacant look. She shifts her legs
as if her heels are hurting her. Smirking, her eyes scout about the
room. But you nary notice, did you? Your eyes, too, rove around.

"Michael!" She calls out. That honey blond in a little black
dress.

"Ashley!"

She who pleats and ties and dyes and washes, she comes up to
you without her rubber gloves and rubber apron. I see her now,
eyes not tired. The redness in them gone. She looks at ease. The
restless hum I'd heard buzzing in her head, revving up her heart
has let up, at least for now.

This evening, she's a show horse with shine. And I quite
nearly forget how she does get sick some mornings.

With open arms you take her in for a bear hug, smooching
both her cheeks.

"So nice of you to come, Michael," she says, smiling.

"Won't miss it for the world!" You say in your jaunty, raspy voice.

"Good to see ya, buddy!" says the tall gentleman by her side. Smiling broadly, he throws an arm over your shoulders.

"Hey, Jed, you did wonders with this place!" You say as you give the room a quick look around, but you turn right back to her.

"Fabric design, eh, Ashley? You're amazing!"

You squint at the play of the itsy-bitsy lights on the rippling blue cloth in the center of the room.

"Light and motion. Simply hypnotic!" Someone gushes.

"Fan-tas-tic!"

"What a collection!"

Ashley listens, nods. There is a glimmer in her eyes.

You perk up like a proud rooster. The brood that surrounds you go cluck-clucking away.

All dumb acts over nothing! Just scraps and pieces of cloth hanging about, that's what I'd say.

Jed is exchanging glances with the pewter woman. "You look wonderful, Kate!" He brushes her cheeks with kisses.

Smug and bored, I'd rather say, the way she sulks.

He bows to whisper into her ear. She throws her head back smirking, but her eyes light up.

A steward in a black formal jacket with tails walks up, bearing champagne glasses on a silver tray. Jed offers her one and helps himself to one. He puts his arm gently around her waist and ushers her to the spiral stairs.

There, he gestures towards the curve wall that sweeps up to form the second floor balcony. Her eyes follow, then turn to gaze into his.

You're busy shaking hands. People turn where you turn. Smiles flashing, aiming to catch your eye. You turn instead to Ashley.

You throb for her, Michael?

Still, your eyes wander. They flit over the girl fiddler with rosy cheeks and twinkling eyes, her ponytail dances with her bouncy bow movements.

She's still in her teens, Michael!
Like me.
A small party walks in just as Ashley turns to glance at the
cozy couple by the spiral stairs.
"Ashley!"
"Wow, what have you done, Ash?"
"Gosh, what a show!"
"Some gallery!"
"To Ashley," you raise your glass to toast.
Colors everywhere …
But I see red. Only red.
Oh, bloody hellish red!

So, I come to you in my blazing red gown. You see me now
through your raised glass. Your eyes light up, bright as the Double
Eagles you toss my way.

*Ah, the glitter of gold that blinds! Head over heels, I weigh in
for love and trade in my heart. For I only hear them jingling … I
hear not their jeering: Fool, you vain fool!*
*Still I go after them! I go after them the way I yearn for your
warm brandy breath over my mouth, the scent of our flesh, our
lingering moments …*
*Ah, all that I fancy are but smoke rings that evaporate in a
heartbeat when the golden afternoons begin to fade!*
*So, it comes to that gold's what I'm left with. Gold with its
undying luster! Got to take it with me.*
Ma, I'm gonna be back for ya!
Be back for ya, Ma!

*I heave myself up, clawing my way back … Back where?
Tumbling down … a gulch deep and dark. Thrashing, flailing, I
scream for my gold.*
*Gold, oh, gold! I grope for my double Eagles asleep under
my mattress where I'd hidden them.*
*Cold and hard, a big blur of the gleaming coins clinking into
my hands. Woe, oh, woe! I would've swallowed you, swallowed*

you all, if I could. If, ah, if only I could!
Gold, you go tinkling back into my purse. Tie it close, close to
my heart.
Rocky road back, full of bumps, Ma ...
Thud, thud, thud ...
I clutch my pain and my gold ...
Thud, thud, thud ...

I see the old flame leap up your eyes. The smothering tongue of lust in the red velvet glow of the Brown Palace, licking, suckling, licking ...

You hold your breath, gazing into my sapphire eyes the way you used to.

The steward comes by with champagne. You lift a glass from his silver tray.

"Miss," you say with a bow, offering me the sparkler.

Death by champagne? Once again, huh?

I glare, but you lavish your eyes over my cascading curls.

Girl, I ask myself, what more have you got to lose?

So, I quiver a smile and take the fizzing poison from your hand. The golden light bubbles up to snarl at my withered heart.

Heart? No heart, nor head, for both are gone. What's left? A burning rage that gnaws at my bones as I wallow in my crimson woe.

So, I put down the bubbling glass for I need no drink nor poison.

"Michael Norton," you say, offering me your hand.

You know me not? Now, surely, you're jesting? I turn away, laughing till I tear up.

"Miss?" You look into my eyes. Then, you grin and ask, "Are you with someone, miss?"

Ha, you ought to know!

You look at me now ... Ah, the same steamy eyes of those golden afternoons!

You mock me, Michael!

O-oh, you mock me! I tremble, seething.

"You're cold, mi-ss?"

I offer you my hand, you reach for it, then recoil.

"I-icy co-old!"

You shiver uncontrollably. You look to me with glazed eyes, blinking to stay awake. But you are groggy, your limbs heavy and slow ...

Come with me, Michael!

You sleep walk, away from the crowd, away from eyes that see not what they see. We walk down the stairs and move toward the window. There we stand looking up at the sickle moon, cold and sharp.

You've come to mock me. Haven't you, Michael?

From the hollow of my rotted-out hull, vengeance shrieks like a pack of howling wolves.

Clink-ink! Crash! You let slip the glass in your hand, splashing champagne over the needle point settee.

You've got blood on your hands! I screech from where there's no echo.

"Uh-huh?"

Thud, thud, thud ...

I hear it now, the thudding that knocks at my bones, thump after thump. I hear my retching—*Eeeeeetch ... eeeka, eeeka-eeeeeetch ...* A metallic burn scorches my throat. I'm spewing up a trail of blood and yellowish green bile.

Thud, thud, thud ...

Oh, I suffer abominably!

"U-uh, no, no, oh no!" You grunt as you turn to look up the stairs. You see now, a battered body being dragged down the stairs. You want to turn away but that soiled mop of coppery gold hair catches your eye. A piteous sight, eh?

You're shaking, Michael.

Thud, thud, thud ...

I'm being hauled down the stairs by an arm strong enough to wrestle livestock to the slaughterhouse. The other arm is gathering up a skirt with a tucked trim as it sweeps down the treads. A skirt too nice to wear to a slaughter.

You see me now, Michael? Uh, what's left of me?

Ring-ng-ng! Ring-ng-ng! Ring-ng-ng! Ring-ng-ng! Ring ...
The ringing phone jangles her nerves. She drops me and scuttles back up the stairs.

Wallowing in pain, I blindly jab my fingers over the brick wall, scrabbling for cracks in the grout, for gaps where the wood stringer butts up against the wall. Here, here! I pull out one slippery Double Eagle ... slot it in ... slip in another, and another, into any old cracks I can rake up with my scraping fingers...

Ya old brick wall, ya hold my gold for me, ya hear?

O-oh-ooh! O-o-oh-ai-ai-ai-aieeeck!

Sliding over the treads, I hurl my wrecked body down to the floor below. A big red blur beckons from afar ... I wriggle my way to where you now stand, by the back window where the damask drapes hang.

Fiery as fiery be, the crimson cloth taunts me, flaunting me a promise to return me a specter after, ah, after all's over ... I will then rise and walk like she—she who stumps along, high on that charred rock, in her red cloak ...

I squirm and heave myself up to tug at the drape, to tow in, ah, a lifeline so I would walk again!

I, uh, I'll be back!

Flump! The whole flaming sky crashes down over me ...

Bloody hell! My beautiful damask drape that came all the way from France, you've bloody hell ruined it!

A foot flies out of a skirt and kicks hard.

Woe... oh, woe!

Let go, girl, let go! What false modesty!

She tugs at the drape to yank it off me.

Which is worse, insult or injury?

I grab onto my lifeline, bloodied fingers clutching tight, hugging my nakedness, my pain ....

Girl, she yells, you're taking too long! Much, much too long!

The raptor casts a huge shadow over me. I gasp for air ...

She bends down and gabs into my face: Girl, you want to know who called? Ha, yo-ur Mr. Norton! He wants to know if all's well in the house. Guess what? The gentleman asks to speak to you. I said to him, So sorry, Mr. Norton, Lena can't come to the phone just now. You see, she's rather indisposed. Just so he gets the message.

Bloody hell! That's his genteel way of asking if I've done his bidding? I gave it to him alright! I gave it to him by asking for more than just his word of not shutting down my house.

Mr. Norton, I said, I'd appreciate if you count me some gold pieces, say, um, two hundred for helping you rid of your, um, what you call it, your inconvenience?

Oh, no, not much at all! It's, uh, it's just so very na-asty. I spare you the details, Mr. Norton. Never, ever, would I have done, um, such a thing if, uh, if you hadn't been so insistent ...

A deal then, Mr. Norton, uh?

To be sure, I'll get you what you ask for.

Uh, uh, huh!

She picks up the draped bundle and drags it across the floor. She drops it into the hole under the stairs Big Roy had dug the day before.

She cares not if my last breath lingers. She dumps dirt over me, over the soiled crimson damask that she no longer has use for.

So, in my death throes, I cling onto this desperate cover, spinning me a burning wish ...

Michael, you're heaving so ...

Sit and rest awhile. Here, on the settee. Don't turn away. I'm here for you, as I once did. Remember?

Spring's in the air!

I tear down the slope to romp in the meadows where hummingbirds flutter, butterflies dance, and, ah, dragonflies skim over the fast stream swollen with snowmelt. The sun's bright, the air tingles. I throw myself into this cool shimmering light, for this light washes me clean of winter's grime and lifts me up and gives me wings and let my laughter ring out like a lark bunting's song!

I crouch down by the water's edge to gaze at my sparkling face, my hair speckled with loose petals. I bow and put my lips down to sip in the wrinkling blue sky.

Whatever ya do, don't eat the wild iris, Ma tells me.

Ma tells me that when she still has a head for such things, when Pa was still by her side.

Why?

They'll kill ya.

Standing tall, a lone stalk of Shooting Star rises out of a ring of leaves. It holds forth a host of blushing pink blooms, heads bowed to earth.

Why ya called Shooting Star? I ask. Ya're looking down, not up. In truth, ya're more a falling star!

What Ma has said, I let drift off with the wind.

Someone rustling in my room, waking me. A candle flickers. A big shadow pulls up the ceiling. A fish-belly white filters in through the lace curtains. Ma'am comes in at daybreak bringing me wild irises in a bubbly bottle.

How could I know?

How could I, Ma?

Champagne for you! She whispers into my ear as I lie in bed.

Huh? I rub my eyes and yawn.

From Mr. Norton, of course, she says, business-like.

Oh my gosh! I open my eyes wide, and sit right up.

She has in her hands a bottle of champagne with a big gold foil bow and a gold-rimmed gift card. She brings it right up to my face. I'm too taken by surprise to notice her twitchy smile.

Mr. Norton had this sent over last night, she says with glee. You were already in bed, so I had to wait till morning to see your happy face. Well, this *is* the day!

Oh, yeah, the Festival!

I quickly reach over to light my bedside lamp. She fidgets.

Waiting, um, to see my happy face?

To Lena, Enjoy your day! The card reads. It bears no signature, but I don't care. You see, Michael, I've never seen your handwriting.

Do you mean that I can go to the Festival, sweet Michael? I scream for joy, jumping out of bed.

Shhhhh, dear, she hushes me up, putting a finger to her lips. You're waking up the whole house!

I twirl about giddily by my bed, crying out, Ah, the Festival of the Mountain and Plain, he-ere I come!

Ma'am stands in my path.

Oh, my sweet Michael, how I pine for you!

I stop short. Ma'am doesn't know that I haven't seen you since the day, um, since the day you laid eyes on the photographs. Does she, huh? All the same, here you're, sending me a gift. A gift to tell me you love me still!

When will I see you again, my sweet Michael? I'm dying to know.

But, ah, today! Today's the day for parades and fun in the streets!

I laugh, silver bells tinkling in my ears, giggly shadow twirling up the walls.

What gown to wear? I hop over to my wardrobe. From the mirror, I see ma'am pick up the sparkling bottle I've left on the bed.

Let's celebrate, Lena dear! She says in that syrupy voice of hers. Her cajoling voice.

At this hour?

Mr. Norton says enjoy your day! He's so-o adorable, isn't he? We're going to get to it right away, uh? I just can't wait, Lena dear!

She walks over to the dresser where she has two champagne glasses ready on a silver tray.

I fling open my wardrobe door and pull out my new velveteen gown. Under the kerosene lamp, the color glows like sun-kissed earth.

Perfect for a Fall day! Ah, the sun will light up the coppery shine of my hair!

I hear her pop the cork behind my back. She's humming. First time I ever hear her hum. A thick, guttural tune ... um, like that beer hall rumbling that spilled out onto the sidewalk along State back in Leadville. Walking, those days, I got eyes at the back of my head, and cocked my ears to the thumping on the timber plank sidewalk coming up from behind ...

I wish I'd kept my eyes at the back of my head just now.

To you, my special one, all the best wishes in the world! Ma'am comes up and offers me this brilliant, bubbling elixir, a cheery smile on her face. A hint of a tease in her voice. She arches her faintly penciled eyebrows and winks. Looks more like a twitch. She turns away.

She knows I'll soon take wing? She's sour, perhaps. Oh, yeah, I'll fly high! I smile, a little lark bunting on a high perch, stretching her sight. Then I glance down.

Madam's hair, dull as tarnished copper, hangs limp over her shoulders, yesterday's hair tonic matted like glue. Her magenta robe looks a little scuffed at the collar, a little frayed at the edge of the sleeves.

Bottoms up! She raises the stemmed glass to her lips of faded raspberry color. She empties the bubbles in a hearty gulp, eyeing me as she puts down her glass.

I miss her steely-eyed stare, so busy am I looking into the mirror with the gown against my body, swaying to and fro. The little lark bunting in me is so utterly charmed. Poor thing, she can't possibly imagine that she will be brought down from her high perch in the blink of an eye!

Oh, here, to a wonderful day! I beam, toasting to myself.

I drain my liquid gold with a flourish. A thunderclap crashing down, I reel over that certain aftertaste, metallic and bitter! Tilting the glass, I see the dregs at the bottom of the glass.

CLINK!

I let the glass drop, let slip the gown in my other hand. It crumples over the broken glass.

My next breath is parched, searing hot. A quick burn singes my throat, setting my insides afire ... I slump forward, my head hitting the bedpost.

DON'T EAT THE WILD IRIS! DON'T EAT THE WILD IRIS! Ma's words caw like a crow with broken wings, flapping wildly over my head ... My head pounds, *boom-bump-boom,* a crack hammer being swung at the rock wall, *boom-bump-boom* ... Ooooo-oh!

Wa-wa-ter! Quick!

Ple-ease!

I, uh, I don't want to be snuffed out ...

Ma'am stands darkly against the gray morning light. I stagger past her, stumbling for the door. It's locked!

Thump—I throw myself at it!

But, ah, this is a house that turns a deaf ear to the thumping and moaning behind closed doors!

Wo-oe-whee! He-elp! I tear at my scorched throat, rasping, heaving. My head explodes, HELP!

A voiceless cry!

She pounces upon me from behind, yanks me backward and throws me on the bed. I roll over, doubling up. I dig into my mouth with both hands, retching, coughing ... Nausea comes like a blinding blizzard, and I spew up a sickly foul trickle.

Gasping in pain ... through withering tears, I fix my eyes on her face. Like stone, she flinches not to see me suffer. Like nails, her eyes.

Life's unforgiving, dear!

I flail about, trying to snatch a corner of her robe. She steps back.

Wh-why? I sputter.

For wanting what's beyond your reach, she says coldly.

I open my mouth to gulp in air ...

A sudden jerk! She plucks me up and drags me over to a bedpost where she binds my grappling hands with the tie of her robe, tightening the knot around my wrists.

Woe, o-oh, woe! I thrash and kick ...

Quick! She leaps up and snatches the bottle. I see now that it's a Korbel, the champagne she keeps in her basement cellar. Michael drinks a French import, with stars on the cork!

Don't you look at me so! She scowls as she pulls out a vial from her robe pocket and empties the powder into the glass, then she pours in the champagne.

I'm only doing his bidding, your Michael's bidding, dear!

She fans the fire, lashing it into a frenzy: Your Michael's bidding!

How dire your need, Michael, eh, to want to sweep clear the path you walk on?

The raptor flaps her shadowy wings, fanning the heat. Her beak sharp, her words cutting. A deafening rage rumbles like a thunderbolt that won't let up.

She pries open my mouth, clamping down my jaw for the poison to gurgle down my throat. I flounder and spit, choking … drowning in fire. But she keeps clawing, gashing ...

Small stirrings outside, footsteps in the hallway.

Knock-knock!

Ma'am, are you up?

Someone calls for her, knocking at her door across the hallway.

The raptor holds still … not a squeak! She grips my foaming mouth with her talons till it's numb with pain. Then she sprints over to my washstand. She hops right back to stuff a washcloth into my mouth, gagging me.

The raptor squawks at me with her razor eyes: Now you go, easy!

E-EASY?

I'm being gouged out by hell fire!

The raptor springs up from crouching over me to stand by the door. Listening up. Chatter and footsteps down the hallway, then down the stairs. Then, the raptor slips out, turns the key in the lock.

Go-ld, go-ld, m-my gold!

I writhe in roaring pain—fingers wriggling, twisting, head bumped up against the bedpost to get close enough to let my fingers pull the gag out of my mouth. Panting, retching ... I heave and puke, throwing up a bitter hot gunk.

I tear at the knot tied around my wrists with my teeth, blowing corrosive breath. Fiery breath. The knot melts ... my hands numb with pain, but I'm free.

Free to take my last breath!

I flop against the bedpost. Looking up the dresser, I see my mountains ... Blue and white, touched with a haze of early Spring green. They're calling out ...

Come home, girl!

Ya belong here, girl!

I, uh, I'm coming ...

I slump down onto the floor and reach under the mattress to retrieve my gold.

My gold! My life!

Burning hot and cold ...

Sky so, so-o very bright ...

Shine ...   I'm gonna shine ...

Forgive me, Ma!

I ate the wild iris, Ma!

Ashley

28

Why does she send for me? This noon, a week after Michael's funeral.

"This is Mrs. Norton, Michael's mother, um ..." she said haltingly over the phone.

Her dazed look comes to mind. A small frail figure in black, mantilla draped over silvery hair in a tight bun at the nape. She staggered up to the casket, bowed for a final goodbye, one palpable moment, an everlasting communion.

"Hello, Mrs. Norton. How're you?"

"I'd like you to come by this afternoon, if you please," she said without pause, her voice soft and urgent.

"Of course. What time?"

"Would two suit you?"

"Yes."

"I'll send a car for you. Come alone, please."

For her, I would close up shop and more. I'm remiss not to have called her. Come alone, she'd said. Why?

I'm not close to my mother. The thought of her makes me think of muggy summer days and ants crawling over my skin. Even now, when she comes on the phone I'd drift off and let her sticky voice carry on—all about herself, whom she'd talked to last Sunday at Church, what they'd talked about, how happy or annoyed she was about this or that, et cetera, et cetera. "Pumpkin, are you there? Pumpkin?"

It's been a long road out of the Iowan cornfields, but the

swelter of summer still fogs up my mind when I look back. So, I look ahead. Tirelessly looking ahead.

Chores and deadlines, orders and numbers fly out of the window as the limo heads up I-25. On one side, a stadium with a curvy roofline. On the other, an amusement park to remind us that summer is always around the corner. The sprawling city is a dusty canvas of humdrum gray, gleaming towers rising above blocks of low risers, a church with a golden dome among the modern-day encampments. Living colors, natural light, the flow of traffic, a hive of industries, a real world out there. It makes me feel as if I've just looked up from my dye vat and see the world zipping past. Not toiling over pigments concocted from boiling madder roots, bleeding plants, or cooking barks, though I know the fun of extracting cochineal and, yes, fermenting indigo.

The limo heads out into rolling country. The scene before my eyes is surreal—radiant sun, the sky a larkspur blue, a faint streak of high cloud. Early Fall colors brush over the hillocks, palette as effusive as the brilliant light that permeates the air. A light so luminously clear that I see as if I've never seen before. A light that imbues you and make you feel that you can take on the world.

But then, here, where the sun is up 300 days of the year, a dark cloud has sprung up over my head. Here, I've been treading water almost from the start. But Jed, he's just swimming fine.

Out We-est? As they said back East.

Well, it dawns on me that I may have already dropped out of the professional network. Out of sight, out of mind—the fabric design and the couture art circle is finicky that way. I'd thought that business can be done on the internet, over the phone, text messaging, Fedexing of samples. To some extent, yes. I'd told myself that what I had set up in SoHo, I can do it all over again in LoDo. I'd overlooked the bit of shoulder rubbing and gallery hopping and palling around fashion shows. I'm prepared to travel, but I'm still waiting for the call.

Still, my studio has just opened. Give it time.

Neither Jed nor I'd acknowledge that I'm the one who has

more uprooting to do and has more at stake with our move. It may not even have occurred to him that I'd given up an established setup to come out here and to start all over again.

"It's for the both of us, Ash, you know that, hon?" he'd said then.

Of all the twists and turns that my life had taken, this is just another turn. I'd made light of it. Maybe, it's time to opt for less noise, thinner crowds, calmer life, and maybe more of each other. Then, too, I've been expecting a wonderful thing to happen to us, hopefully sooner than later. So, when it has come true that a baby's on the way I'm totally ecstatic and welcome the new dimension in our lives. A change, for the better, I'd hoped.

"Isn't that what you've been looking forward to?" Jed says. His voice, without color, without cheer. Not what he's been looking forward to after all, huh? I catch his eyes as he turns away. Without the slightest spark. My heart sinks.

Somehow, deep down I've already known. It has come to pass that I'm more than resolved and more than happy to have my child even if I were to be a single parent. This might even be a subconscious decision that has evolved over time. It has only come to look me in the eye now that the prospect may indeed be real.

What do I do? I take stock of my life. Always taking stock. I abhor even the thought of it because it reminds me of my cornfield days when I was day and night hatching a way to break out. I'm not a devising person. My trade calls for stocktaking. Not my art. My art takes me to a different plane where I can feel free. So I retreat to my work where I find solace.

But I've more on my mind. These days, I breathe and take comfort in knowing that there is a new life throbbing inside me. The feeling is absolutely exhilarating! I know I'll have to work harder to prepare for its coming.

But, what of the dark cloud?

Jed doesn't seem to see the dark cloud even after Michael's untimely death.

"Two deaths, Jed, in just weeks!"

"A coincidence." He shrugs.

Then he says, "Hey, Ash, try this one out, Mullen Roen Spiegel & Associates, Architects!"

Already? Jed Roen is moving on. He has quite forgotten his lean days grumbling about remodeling small restaurants and retail spaces, always wanting to catch the big fish. Well, the big fish did come to him through Michael and his Norton Development.

Now that Michael's gone, I don't hear his name pass his lips. It's as if Jed has crossed a bridge and is not ever going to look back. He spares not a thought about an old friend gone too soon.

"What about the old house?"

"What about it?"

"Where they died. Where I work."

"Umm ..."

"Uh, never mind!"

Jed has become distracted and absent-minded as of late. He seems to be mulling over something. I can see that even as we spend less time together with my load of studio work and his pressing deadlines calling for late nights. Then, there is this project of an art and culture center in Aspen where Kate Norton heads a committee.

So, Jed has morphed from the laid-back, easygoing guy I thought I knew to someone who is driven, flamboyant, and uncaring. I was puzzled at first. I'd thought that maybe his new position had brought about the change. But I'm starting to think that this is who Jed really is. He has shed his old skin and uncovered his true self because he thinks he has arrived at where he can let his hair down.

I begin to mull over what is left of our relationship.

Fall colors streaming past. I sit back to feast my eyes. When was the last time I looked at a tree? Really looked, I mean.

No eye for trees.

Eyes for each other only. We took long walks under lush green canopies ... under bare boughs hung over crunchy mats of dropped leaves ... We melted into sunshine, we melted into shade, we melted into an occasional smile of joggers and nannies pushing strollers.

You took no picture, though you had your camera with you. Yes, your camera always with you.

You don't trust leaving your eyes at home? I teased.

I knew then that you trusted your own eyes first and foremost and had wanted no lens or viewfinder to distract.

We only wished that Central Park would go on forever. It didn't. We both knew it from the start. We knew that we would likely not get to melt into another Spring.

Just make it sweet while it lasts ... I'd told myself even as I could see that a pallor had crept over your face and you were growing thinner and weaker.

Then the day came when you gleamed through the dark clouds, smiling bravely as we said our last goodbye. Long ago, even as the snow lingered and Spring was tardy.

I had since walked past sidewalk trees though I didn't think of them as growing, living things—dusty dull leaves, caged trunks, part of the street scene. Same for those in West Village where I had last lived. Jed and I. Dogs went to them as they would to steel signposts.

I'd not gone back to Central Park since.

The park is just too full of you, Haruo.

Here, on a private road at the outskirts of town where low hills stretch, clumps of aspen gold burst forth amid tall evergreens on the slopes where the runoffs course down. I let go of my heart, follow the hump of the land, the swale of the land, and climb over rock outcrops that thrust up against a clear blue sky.

The limo winds up mid-slope to where a tall sandstone wall imposes added security. We stop at a huge two-panel iron grille gate. The chauffeur keys in an access code on his remote. The heavy gates glide open without a sound.

I look out and up. Fiery red maples pitching tall along the gently winding drive, mature trees planted for the call of the season. They glimmer in the afternoon sun, casting warm glow against the somber blue spruces beyond. Warm glow over a dull pain for the loss of a friend. I would always remember him as someone who in the short span of our friendship had changed the course of my life.

Why does his mother send for me?

Hers is a mother's grief. I saw it plainly, the evening she came to look at where her son fell. She stood trembling over the chalk line figure. *Thud!* She dropped suddenly onto her knees, bent over to touch the cold floor with her hands. She held her palms down, over where his heart had stopped, where he had let go of his last breath. Sobbing quietly, her shoulders heaving.

Kate went up to her, helped her to her feet. She spoke not a word. Her face ashen, her eyes a watery sheen, her lips tightened, biting back tears. She stood long and silent. Kate, pale and fidgety, stood by her side.

They stood, like strangers at a bus stop. Her bus came, the mother wobbled away, carrying a leaden sorrow. Kate let out a sigh and scudded up the stairs as fast as her spiky heels could carry her.

But they had no idea. On that cold floor, the white of his eyes, the slack parched mouth, the twisted face ... Every time I step into my basement and look to the back wall, I see a wasted fetus on the floor below, old beyond its age.

I turn quickly to look out at the Fall day.

The autumn flame rolls by. A beautiful light, shimmering everywhere. Over the foliage, a sheer wash of gold makes vivid all colors and shifting shadows. I feverishly want to stay every glimpse. Call it a spell, call it whatever, I'm lost for an eternal moment.

The enchantment is broken when we come upon one stretch where gardeners strapped with leaf blowers put in their dogged bid to pick up after Mother Nature. A machine stands by, coughing, spewing smoke as it churns up what is fed into it.

Climbing now, under a crisp blue sky, over red canopies into piñon pines and spruces, an expanse of green and blue comes into view as the slope unfolds. The lay of the land, the layering of Fall colors take my breath away.

The drive follows a wide bend to reach a tableland that looks out to the city in the distance. Majestic blue spruces line the drive leading up to the stately mansion from another era. Openly grand and as timeless as the jagged peak that rears up behind it.

Man and Nature had come together to raise this landscape—a melding of resources, an eye for clime and site and for the vista that comes only with the passage of time.

What man was this who had visualized what's before my eyes today at a time when the mesa was just a plain Jane flat-top mound?

The limo rounds the circular drive before stopping at the front of the mansion. A massive fountain stands at the center. Shut down. Cast bronze carps in formation cavort over the bottom with gaping dry mouths. Weathered a green patina, they must have stood many a season, wet and dry. Tubs of tall ornamental grasses stand in their midst. Silvery plumes and tawny blades tip and bow in the breeze.

I'd seen the house when the fountain was spouting, in a photo copy Jed had gotten from the Colorado Historical Society. For architectural interest, he told me.

He read the caption out loud, "Italian Renaissance Revival built in the early 1930's by Michael Norton II on a mesa outside Denver. It is a bigger and grander version of the Norton mansion in town, originally the Hayes estate."

Then, he slipped it back into an inch-thick folder labeled: Norton.

We had never been invited to the Norton estate. Michael and Kate stayed in a penthouse in town which Kate laughingly dubbed their "pad."

"Hey, Michael, your old homestead's an architectural gem!" Jed said, fishing for an invite.

"Hmm, Mother lives in the old house."

"Some house."

"She keeps the hearth and her old flame burning. My old man, he passed away in the house."

Sounded like a cloistered domain.

"My old man married late. Mother married young. They'd a happy life together." He paused before continuing, "She's been looking after business ever since. I owe her a break."

His husky voice trailed. He came home, didn't he? With his third wife, after those footloose years abroad and his East Coast fling. He came home to take helm of what his old man had built during his long life, and to test his own political ambition.

"Like a wake-up call ... buzzes me no end till I get moving," he chuckled.

"Well, Councilman, how would Mayor Norton sound? Or, Governor Norton? Your grandfather, wasn't he a senator?"

The real thing in front of me is much more imposing—a rough hewn blond sandstone mansion with a Tuscan columned façade and an arched, recessed entrance, balustrades on the balconies, low-pitched slate-clad roof, deep eaves and beautiful moldings. Great height, classic symmetry. Lead glass window panes on the upper floor reflect the sun's glare in a watery sheen.

The Norton Estate. Whose name will it bear ... now that Michael's gone?

I walk up the steps to the front landing. A heavy feeling weighs me down. Inside these walls, a mother is in mourning.

Why does she send for me? Come alone, she'd said. A week after Michael's funeral.

The butler shows me to the library. Mrs. Norton sits by a window looking out into a loggia that faces an interior courtyard. A pink glow steals in through the row of deeply recessed windows. The copper-embossed coffered ceiling takes on a blushed tint. The room gives a cozy feel despite its high ceiling and immense proportions.

She turns and rises from her solitary wing-chair to greet me. I walk up to her, a small person in enormous circumstances.

"I'm so glad you came," she says, giving me her hand. Her voice is soft, her hand warm. She looks into my eyes.

What does she want to see?

She stands now, not hunched or bent as when I first saw her in my basement, and then at the funeral service. She has on a tailored black Shandong silk pantsuit. Her silvery hair is, as before, pulled back in a chignon. She looks younger than when I first met her. There are fine lines on her face, but her eyes are clear and bright, like her diamond ear studs. She wears no make-up and appears at ease in this stately mansion she calls home.

"Mrs. Norton, how are you?"

She does not reply. She glances out the window at the small multi-stemmed maples on fire. A little bird chirps and darts about the branches.

"The Amurs are bleeding so this year," she sighs. "Michael would have come home just to look at them."

She turns away, then back to me.

"Come, have a seat," she says after a moment of silence.

A hint of a smile. I'm relieved. I follow her to the maroon leather sofas in front of the massive black marble fireplace. A small fire is crackling. Scent of burning wood soothes like a mellow port. I take in a deep breath.

On the mantel shelf, antique silver candelabras stand tall amid a resplendent ivy spilling over its Ming blue porcelain planter. Looking down from above is a gilt-framed oil portrait of a seated lady in a tight-bodiced black gown. Her light hazel curls are gathered on top of her head. She wears pearl-drop earrings and a multi-strand pearl choker with a cameo brooch around her high collar. On her finger is a solitary wedding band. She has a faraway look and a stoic air about her. A full suited young boy stands by her side, a hand on her shoulder, gazing solicitously into her face.

She looks fondly at the boy.

"Michael's dad, nine years old, with his mother, 1905."

She turns again to the boy who was to be her husband.

"He was close to her. Born seven months after his father passed away." A touch of wistfulness in her voice.

There are two other ancestral portraits by the fireplace flanking the mantel piece. I am struck by the resemblance between the Michael I know and a gentleman of yesteryears. A maid comes in to place silver tea service on the coffee table. We sit on sofas facing each other.

"You care for tea?"

"Yes. Allow me, please," I reach over and pour us each a cup in her fine bone china.

She sips her Darjeeling, staring at me over her raised cup.

I glance around the period chamber of dark wood paneling lit with antique red copper sconces. Book cabinets with beveled French glass doors line the far side of the room away from the windows. Thick Aubusson rugs over the parquet floor. On console tables, Tiffany lamps glitter like bejeweled blossoms.

A bronze sculpture catches my eye. A Remington? So much gusto, so much valor riding on sheer grit, an Indian tribal warrior charges on a galloping stallion. What an irony, the tamest thing about him is the shiny spear in his hand! This spectacle of the Wild West, stout of heart and spirit, now stands a masterpiece. Just that, a masterpiece.

Over hot tea, the scent from the bouquet of white roses on the coffee table suffuses the air.

Why am I here?

"You wonder why you came?"

"Yes."

"Ashley, how well you know my son?"

"He's a dear friend. Michael is the reason Jed and I moved to Denver."

"Hmm."

She smiles faintly.

"Jed and Michael knew each other from college."

"I know. You?"

"I met Michael and Kate in New York a couple of years back."

"How do you find it here?"

"Denver's a break for Jed's career."

She does not follow up.

"How do you find, uh, your place?"

"My place?"

"That old house. How do you find that old house?"

"Gr-reat location."

I hold my breath for what I fear may come next.

"There had been deaths in that house ... Other deaths," she says under her breath.

She turns to the portrait of the Michael look-alike on the wall. A sunny face at first glance. Cloudless high brow. Clear blue eyes gazing loftily into a distant horizon. Chestnut hair and sleek sideburns. The gold chain of his watch looped out of his vest pocket, peeking out from under his brown tweed jacket.

Yet, there is this icy glint in his eyes, and this hidden scorn that lurks in the corners of his mouth, canting up to look like a smile but too frosty to call it a smile.

"My Michael's a split image of his grandfather, but for the sideburns," she sighs. "Same dashing blue eyes and, yes, that distinguished high bow. A more congenial look, though. My Michael has a less angular jawline."

She seems to be lost in thoughts.

Then, she mutters, "A curse, really."

Huh?

She turns back to glare at the Victorian gentleman. "It started with him. He passed away in that cursed house. Hundred some years later, only days apart, my son followed. Same house. Same cause of death. They, uh, called it natural. Brain aneurysm, massive hemorrhage. Both in their prime of life."

I hear the grievance in her voice. I had read that familial predisposition does exist for brain aneurysm, but it's not what I would want to bring up.

"Mysterious circumstances, the newspapers said," she mumbles.

"These similarities may just be coincidental, and most unfortunate."

It hits me now that the mother is beset by something which she finds troubling.

"You found Michael ... You, uh, saw how he looked."

She can't let go. But how does she know?

"I'm truly sorry for your loss, Mrs. Norton."

I glance at the rose bouquet, averting her eyes.

The blood curdling look on his face! I fix my eyes on the delicate blooms and push that look of horror back into the blur zone.

"Come with me, please."

She gets up and beckons me to follow. We walk past another portrait: Piercing eyes, frowning brow, gray hair and bristling whiskers. Robert Samuel Hayes, says the little plaque.

We turn the corner, enter through etched glass doors into a private study behind the two-sided fireplace. A portrait of a silver-haired gentleman in tuxedo sits above the mantel, a commanding presence in this secluded chamber.

Dark brown leather armchairs sit on three sides of the coffee table in front of the fireplace. On the table, red roses flourish in an antique pewter bowl. Old roses, a scent heady like no other.

"My husband. He sat for that portrait the year before he passed away."

A liquid shine lights up her eyes as she looks up at him. The gentleman looks down with Michael's kind eyes.

"Come, please."

We walk past the heavily draped windows framed with lit onyx sconces, past curved glass wall cabinets displaying trays of gold nuggets, crystals and mineral specimens.

She shows me to the back of the room where a huge carved mahogany desk stands a command post. Behind the desk, framed photographs cover the wood paneled wall—of oil drills and rigs, close-ups of men standing by the installations, panoramic shots over a vast sweep of land stippled with giant claw-like mouthpieces boring pipes into the earth, of excavators and tractors and earth movers on surface mines, of a conveyor and a cage lift in the hollow of an underground mine, of ground-breaking ceremonies, of ribbon-cutting ceremonies, in front of buildings, by train engines, at the mouth of tunnels.

I look for the man in the photos, he who did all those things.

"My husband was blessed to have passed away in his own bed."

As if this was a singular achievement of his.

She turns to the desk. A onyx desk lamp on a pewter base casts a mellow glow over twin framed photos. A young bride with her graying groom, smiling into each other's eyes. Confetti on her hair, over his shoulders. The bouquet in her hand as fresh as her looks. A young Michael beaming out of the other, in cap and gown, diploma in hand.

The desk chair has been pushed back as if someone has just gotten out of it. She sits down.

"Please have a seat."

I take the side chair. The desk is neatly laid out with a leather trimmed writing pad, an embossed pewter ink stand with twin pens and a rocker blotter, a corded desk telephone with many buttons.

"I'd like you to look at this."

From the top drawer she takes out an old manila envelope. She pulls out a small black-and-white photo and puts it down in front of me.

"Michael Sr. passed away October 24, 1895, age 35, in *that* house," she murmurs, her eyes shy away from looking.

I glance at the grainy photo, yellowed and curled at the edges. It hits me in a flash what might have been troubling her. There was the body, curled up on the floor, one hand over his head, the other clutching his heart.

Same posture of death, same spot, a hundred plus years earlier, as what I had seen that night.

"Mrs. Norton … "

In the photo, there was a settee under a paned window. A damask drape hung on one side. Its mate was missing.

"I found it in my husband's safe. It came from the Denver Police at the time."

"You, uh, you saw how Michael looked that night."

She takes out a new envelope from the drawer and clutches it to her heart.

"It's not natural, the way he looked … the way they looked." She chokes up, sobbing quietly.

"Mrs. Norton, I'm so very sorry."

She lowers her head and mutters to herself, "I'd left your personal papers as you had kept them until, um, until I read about the past, in the papers. Too late. Only if I had seen that old photo before, uh, before it h-happened. You knew something about that house, didn't you? Your mother knew, and told you? You bought that house some years back and kept it locked up."

She's heading for drowning waters. Then something hits her and she turns to me.

"Did you see her?"

"Who?"

"The girl in red."

A flicker of fear in her eyes. A fear as forbidding as it is incomprehensible.

"Kate said she saw Michael with a young woman in a r-red gown just be-fore he, uh ... "

"No, I didn't."

"You've never seen her?"

"No."

"Kate couldn't recall her face. Just the red gown."

"Hmm."

"Not since?"

"No."

"Would you please move out of that place?"

She looks at me intently.

"Huh?"

"It's an inconvenience, I know. There are other locations available on the same block. Norton Development will take care of everything for you."

"I've just settled in ..."

"Can't you see the danger?"

"What danger?"

"The house's haunted. Something, uh, dark in there. Sinister."

Her tone is grave and urgent.

So, she wants to shut the place down? Memory so tormenting that she wants it locked up. Just as her husband did.

"The house, um, does have a past. Like all old houses, I suppose," I say, helplessly.

"No, not like any other. It has a sordid past. There was a young woman in there, in that whorehouse, who had disappeared just before Michael Sr. passed away. She was rumored to be his girl."

"Um."

"Ashley, I'm only thinking of you. You, by yourself, in that house."

There is sadness in her eyes as she turns to me.

"Please think about my offer."

"I will, Mrs. Norton."

Deep down, I balk at the time and the energy needed to start all over again. Not now.

She grins as if she divines what I'm thinking.

"I appreciate your caring about me."

I speak my heart. She seems relieved that I see that she means well.

"You know Michael well?"

"He's a dear friend."

"You fond of him?"

"Very much so."

The Michael I knew was a big-hearted fellow. An easy charmer.

A pensive smile crosses her face. She is beaming through her tears. She has been safekeeping her husband's memories, and now, she has taken on her son's as well.

"Mrs. Norton, have you spoken to Kate about your fears?"

"No, it doesn't concern her," she says quietly but firmly.

I'd seen them together. The way the two women avoided each other's eyes tells me that there's a distance between them that no bond by law can bridge.

At parting, she walks me to the foyer. I take her hand in mine. Her hand is cold. She is about to say something. No words come. She knits her brow, her eyes glisten. I reach out and fold her into my arms. She nestles in my embrace. We both seem to have taken to this strange familiarity that has sprung up between us.

"Goodbye, Mrs. Norton. Take good care," I whisper into her ear.

The sun has swung over the house and casts its setting glow against the peak behind. Reflected light fills the air, tinged with the color of steeped tea. The cool air clears the head. But my heart weighs on me as I walk down the shadowed steps. Alone in that mansion, a mother is gasping for air.

A small gust rustles through the tall spruces, thick shadows shuddering over the ground. Spent reeds toss about in the drained fountain. Down the slopes, the maples bleed all over the tired blue spruces.

It's a long, long way to Spring.

On the way back, all that I think of is a loss that cannot be appeased. I think of Haruo. He, too, had passed on in his prime, but he did not go without taking leave. We had time for a hearty, gracious goodbye. Still, the mourning goes on. I remember how I had felt then, being left behind, grappling to feel whole again.

It is still new for her. In time, the pain will abate. I wish I were able to say to her: Guilt's troubled water, don't wade in it.

Over the years, I have learned to seek my momentary reprieve. Forever young and vibrant, Haruo, his skin, the touch of silk, his breath, a toss of warm sake down my throat, and in his eyes, a longing for hibiscus about to unfurl—these tantalizing remembrances I keep to heart, to distract, to soothe. Still, it has taken me a long way to get there.

A mother can surely call up her stock of fond memories to ease her to calmer waters. There, her turbulent heart would find peace. Peace that comes with lullabies, and sweet first words, and toddling first steps, and birthday treats ...

She will find her way there. Surely, she will.

Even so, in her bereavement, she extends herself to me, to want to keep me away from the foreboding she has called up from the dark side of the Norton family history. Her fear is as palpable as it is vague. Her sense of guilt, unfound as it is, racks her all the same.

She has taken me into her confidence. Whether she intends it or not, I'm beholden to her, for her well-being. Then, there is this thing that draws me to her. She makes me think of motherly love. The giving kind. The kind I want to nurture myself.

For now, if there's anything I can do to dispel the dark cloud hanging over her is to let her know that I'm safe and well in that house.

Take good care, Mrs. Norton.

29

I'm up to my neck in work. Long day into night, I finally drift to where sun and sea sparkle and a host of scents to enchant ...

Under a bright pole lamp, a sinewy bronze figure walks barefoot along the edge of the hotel pool, muscled calves bulge out under rolled-up sarong. Tall bamboo pole in hand, he drags a nylon net over the water surface where dropped leaves and insects float. Biceps flexing a smooth rhythm, broad chest heaving a silent song ...

A little twitter here, a string of high notes there, a predawn chorus weaves through the dark foliage, growing loud, wings flapping over treetops.

All at once, my head throbs. Drums and gongs and flutes and metallophones—gamelan music undulating the night where a crescent moon hangs, sharp as a silver kris in the sky.

Coo-ru-coo, coo-coo-ru ... little brown cuckoo doves, seed-pearl necklaces feathered around their necks, nest in pairs under the jasmine shrubs. Amid tender green leaves, dainty jasmine flowers send out fragrance by the mile.

Unseen, I linger in my watch behind the hibiscus trees, my face hot as the flaming blooms. Before sun-up, the bronze sheen of his biceps, his broad chest heaving ... mellow as a sip of the cream sherry that makes you thirst for more. My face, hot as a hibiscus bloom with no scent. No scent at all!

At Jimbaran Bay, the day after I arrived ...
Guten morgen! Dieter gone offshore, *ja?* One tanned wife

asked another as they lounged in ample bikinis by the pool. Under the fan palms that held still in a sultry afternoon, they ogled over sunglasses at a young man in a saffron-hued sarong not ten feet away. Sweat shone like dew on his bare back sun-buffed to a mellow copper tone.

Zap ... *z-zap* ... sound of garden shears snipping away, pruning bougainvillea vines. Deep muscles working, torso taunt, shoulder blades folding in, angling out, as if he was about to take wing.

Ja?

Nein, Nein.

Zap ... *z-zap* ... he stayed back to tease, body heat radiating, sizzling.

Flowers of no scent, tiny white bougainvillea blossoms, moored to dense colorful bracts. Orange and purple and yellow and magenta, clouds upon clouds of them that I saw burning in the reflection of their dark shades.

Eyes lit up, under a breathless sun.

Scentless hibiscus blooms, fiery red and luscious yellow, smoldering in the predawn cool. I slip away from behind the trees, flushed and limp. Hurry, I pick myself up to run down the beach to catch a breath of the sea! Or, I'd swoon even as dawn is about to break and the breeze a cool smooch on my face.

I look to the thin haze where water is sky is water. In the blurry white light where the rim of the world lies, a line of white foam rolls in. The ever widening surf pushes to shore, gently swelling, gently breaking. Closer ... closer ... sleepy waves lap, lapping up to me, spraying foam. I dig my heels in the shifting wet sand, trudging along the empty beach. Buoyed by the sound of the waves, the whole world to myself.

A pinprick of fire lights up the horizon etching a thin bright line. A tinge of gold washes up the sky, flushing it with a rose pink light. Down below, the waves swash in a sparkling glow.

A swell rises, rushing to shore, sweeping me off my feet, carrying me up high. Way up high ... Unbound, I reach for you. An eel craving for feed, mindless of bait and fate. In the deep of the night, all has slid to oblivion save the agitating flesh. You stir, your breath upon me. Your tongue slow and full. The wave crests over. It breaks, splashing, heaving ...

An amber sun dazzles like a blinding torch. Ah, no, it's a blaze of bright coppery hair! A face I see and not see, hovering over me, eyes like star sapphire staring down.
Yearning eyes ... Consuming eyes ...
I bolt up. Naked and alone. The sun cuts in through the slats of the black aluminum blind, infusing the room with a mute glow. The clock says 8:12. The alarm has not been set. I throw off the covers. My rumpled nightgown lies on the floor, a surrender of the night, the skin I shed.
I pick it up, slip it back on and listen up.
All's quiet in the house, not even a whiff of coffee aroma.
Jed's gone.
Gone?
Was he home at all?

I lumber into the bathroom. In the mirror, bags under my eyes as if I haven't slept at all. I cover up my mouth to hold down a swell of nausea up my throat. Bowing over the wash basin, eyes shut tight, I let ease the queasiness.
Groggily, I run my fingers through my hair, sweeping it off my face. Three long strands of hair come loose, entangling my fingers. I untwine them, lay them on my palm. Coppery gold, lustrous curls that singe my eyes and make me see red.
Uh-uh! I fend off the wavery light and slippery everything to tear back into the bedroom. I lurch towards the bed. I fluff the pillows, toss aside the down comforter, combing the sheets for dropped hair, long coppery gold curls from whomever Jed had dallied with.
In our bed!
Jed, oh, Jed!
Spotless sheets. I slump to the floor against the foot of the messed up bed. Resting my head on my raised knees, my cheeks a hot iron. No tears come. I cower down, my heart hurtling a

hundred miles a minute.

Muffled noise of traffic percolating outside. I push myself to stand on my feet gone asleep. Pull yourself together, I say, biting my lips. My mouth dry and bitter, I teeter into the bathroom for a drink of water. On the white marble counter laid three strands of hair—long, straight and honey blond.

Mine!

I tremble, let go of my glass, water and shards fly.

Swill … swirl the cotton cloths, one at a time, through running hot water before lowering it into the last rinse bath. Tossing, chopping, making waves … like a trawler plying its slow wake to shore.

I shift my legs to relieve the pressure on my back, staring at the wet pile, each piece awaiting its turn.

Steam rises up my face. The dye bleeds the water a smoky blue, shrouds and streaks agitating, dispersing. The cotton cloth hangs limp on my tongs, the wax residue about gone. I drop it into the drain basket hung over the adjacent basin.

I trawl in another. Then another.

I shift my legs. Going numb. My head groggy.

The bath drains. A blue vortex whirls around the basin's dark hole. Reflected light flickers in giddy circles, spinning glitters.

Some distant flurries light up, rousing me. That day, the cherry blossoms let go of their petals, gleaming pink and white, in a sudden gust. You could hear them sigh. Through the open window, they flitted in, quivering, sprinkling over the tatami mat.

Tanaka-san stood motionless, looking out at the wildly swaying trees. I looked up from wood-blocking my first tenugui.

I stepped out that evening into a courtyard carpeted pink and white. The trees stood silent and bare.

The carpet was gone the next morning. As if the windstorm the day before was but a bad dream, the ground was swept clean.

But there were a few flecks of pink and white still clinging to the lower branches.

Up close, I could see the sprouting green shoots.

I left when the leaves were still a young green. I wrote the following Spring to inquire about the trees. Tanaka-san wrote back: Sakura abloom.

Still, the cherry blossoms on my mind are those which had snow-flaked the air the day I began my apprenticeship at Tanaka-san's Kyoto Workshop.

I hold onto to you still, Haruo, the way I've been holding onto those shimmering petals long gone.

Much tenderness is within me, Haruo.

"What's tenugui?" Kara asks as she feeds the cotton cloths into the roller press. The steam hisses. The pieces come out perfectly ironed. She studies each before putting it down.

"They are the traditional hand towels of Japan. Stenciled, mostly. Sushi chefs wear them as sweatbands. I make them for napkins, placemats, guest towels. This batch is block printed. Like to try your hand?"

"Gosh, oh, yes!"

"You've seen the old wood blocked piece framed up in my office?"

"Yes, strong lines, bold colors!"

"Start with mixing a dye."

My cell rings.

"Hi, Alex! Hey, congrat! Heard your show's a smash. Sorry to have missed it. Ah, yes! Will get to asap ... Promise."

Another call coming in. I let it ring.

Still catching up on phone messages and e-mails. Business is picking up, but I seem to be dragging my feet.

Really ought to be starting on Spencer's silk ... Spencer wants "something wispy, breezy, yes? Morning-glory blue? Uh, no. A shade paler, like forget-me-nots ... See, Ashley?"

I see my raw Suzhou silk crinkled into lilac clusters by Shibori crumpling and resist dyeing into runny shades of French blue.

"Ashley, when did you work on these, the tenugui?" Kara asks. Her voice is strained.

"Sunday."

"Alone?"

She knits her brow. She shoots a sideway glance at the dark shadow on the floor only our eyes can see.

"Where, uh, did the workman die?" she'd once asked.

I shrugged and tried not to look at the foot of the stairs.

Kara comes down here only when I'm around. Each week, she puts in 20 paid hours as my assistant. The rest of the time she does her own studio work under my supervision. I have noticed that she plans her schedule so she stays up at the gallery, or works in my office when I'm not in the building. It suits both of us fine.

"Don't you think, uh, you deserve a day off?"

I hear her nervous little laugh.

A quiet moment up in my office. Batik is my topic for this evening's talk at the Metro State's Art and Culture Forum. The announcement says: For the general public. I browse through the PowerPoint on my laptop. Thumbnail images fill the screen, the harvest of my apprenticeship in a faraway land. All that and more have long taken root in my heart. Nature's hand has tutored me to give my art an emotional tenor and a dare with color and scale.

Of Java and Bali, tropical islands where passion simmers, and love has the sound of sweet pulsating melodies—*tjinta, kasih, asmara, sajang*. Lush green everywhere, earth red and brown, rivers brown and yellow, banyan trees thick with air roots, banana flowers hung like bleeding hearts. A thousand wings bustle, a million insects hum, day and night and day. Sizzling heat and sultry air, shadow and light and shadow, hanging bats and walking lizards, squawky birds and chattering monkeys ...

Monsoon rain buckets down, drumming hot tin roofs, drowning out cries of splashy kids and bristling cats, sloshing banana leaves to a slick shine, shrouding tall canopies in a misty green. The air shudders with a thick earthy scent.

I, too, shudder with it, blowing out steamy breaths.

Dousing fires inside hot bodies?

Hot eyes linger over wet blouses, fiery curry and red hot chili, cigarette smoke as pungent as unwashed socks.

What cigarette is that?

Kreteks, nona.

Huh?

Clove cigarettes, *nona.*

But there are fragrances to swoon for. White ginger flowers, petals of butterflies, flaunting a big luscious scent. Clusters of frangipanis swaying overhead, I pick a single blossom, tuck it behind my ear. Scent to beguile me into the silvery night.

A breeze drifts in through my mosquito net, wakes me with a huge bouquet. Darkly arousing, it's a hypnotic perfume that lingers to intoxicate, to seduce.

An ancient magnolia, *nona.* It blooms in the dead of night, full and white as the moon, to send out a scent to bewitch.

Selamat datang, selamat datang ...

A *njonja* comes up to me with a welcoming smile, sparkling a gold tooth and 22-karat gold earrings, a rope of gold chain around her neck. She walks in fragrance, strands of jasmine twined into her slick braided bun at her nape. Women in *sarong kebaya* sit on floor mats, *tjanting* in hand, intent on applying wax to the cloths. Someone melts wax in a *wajan* over a burner. Partially waxed cloths draped to dry on bamboo poles. Those nimble fingers have much to teach!

At noon, a waft of a honeysuckle breeze sails past carrying flavors that make your mouth water. Coconut curry sauce over prawns, fish cakes and saffron rice served with a spicy sauce on a sheath of banana leaf, a sprinkle of ground roasted peanuts for crunch, and, yum, those little skewers of chicken satay.

How I pine for a taste of the tropics wrapped up in little packets of roadside delicacy!

Back to the slides—flora and fauna curl and loop, arch and bow, colors to complement, colors to jar. The geometric lines and curves of *Ceplok*, the slanting knife pattern of *Parang* from Central Java, the intersecting circles and lines of *Kawung* from Jogjakarta. Sharp black outlines, stippled white dots that do not blur the eye.

Abundant browns and yellows and blues, wrought by artisans rooted to their land. And the land proffers up bark, root, wood, and leaves, of cinnamon, turmeric, mango, jackfruit, morinda, indigo ... Skilled hands extract the natural dyes, discriminating eyes bring out colors that run from brilliant to subtle, warm to austere. All for the artisans to render their craft in batik, in ikat.

I look up at my collection of wax stamping *caps* sitting on their handles upon my book shelves. I take one down, run my hand over it. Copper strips twisted and welded into curves and dots. Each *cap* renders an exquisite motif of flora and foliage, an artwork in its own right.

A tune floats into my head: *Benga-wan Solo ... Riwayatmu ini ... Sedari dulu jadi ...*

The river of nostalgia comes back to haunt. Inside my head, flowing dreamily, that sleepy river out of Surakarta ...

From the cornfields of Iowa to where I had not dared to dream, from a sweaty muggy kind of heat to the breezy drowsy heat by the Java Sea, I had gone far on a NYFA fellowship after NYU and Parsons. My world has grown larger and freer. I feel there is more of me to give ...

"Ashley, A-ash-"

I look up at her standing by my desk.

"Ka-ara?"

"You okay?"

"Ye-es. Yes."

"A-anything you want me to do?"

"No, uh, thanks."

"I'm gonna take off now. Look forward to your talk this evening."

Still, she stands there, a puzzled look on her face.

How I pine for the monsoon downpour! Cool drenching rain that splashes down in torrents, washing away grime in body and mind.

These days, monsoons on my mind only ...

Still, I heave a sigh of relief.

The butterflies inside me have already told me so!

Haven't I seen enough of my mom ever growing big with my younger siblings? She was laid-back about her pregnancies and saw the doctor only in her third trimesters. The twins' coming took her by surprise though.

I've been counting the days since my last menstruation but have been putting off going to the ob/gyn. Too busy trying to find my footing and to learn to live with the cloud over my head—Jed, the studio, and where I'm heading. Then, there is the pressure of fulfilling my orders and rushing to get stock ready for the holiday season.

Into my third month now, I finally pick up to go for the test, to find out the exact due date.

I step out of Dr. Kline's office into a golden Fall day with this quick hunger for papaya. Right this minute! I take off south on Speer, to Cherry Creek, to Whole Foods. There I pick the ripest papaya that I can lay my hands on, and have the produce guy slice it in half and scrape off the seeds, and yes, half that key lime, too, please. I stop by the Deli for some slices of the Prosciutto ham, pick up a bowl of salad, a ciabatta bun and a tall banana smoothie. I pile them all on a tray and head for a table outside.

Bright sun, crisp air, and the crowd thin, I'm ready to enjoy my lunch. Yum!

A little girl toddling after her mama looks up at me as I dribble lime juice over my papaya boat. I smile. She smiles back, nudging her head against her mama's thigh and reaches up for her hand.

Eyes like Josie's when Josie was little.

I scoop up one spoonful of the fragrant yellow flesh into my mouth. Sweet and mellow. I look down at my food, away from Josie's eyes.

Eyes that had followed me to the door the day I left home, eyes big with questions because of the bag I was carrying and the Sunday dress I had on.

Wa-it, wa-it for me! She cried, scattering her crayons and toddled up to me.

I dropped my bag, fell to my knees and put my arms around her.

Hush, hush, I'll be home soon.

Say goodbye to your mom yet, Mary Ashley? Dad asked in a hushed voice.

He waited at the door in his Sunday's best, a fish out of water. His eyes darted towards the kitchen.

I stood up and saw her coming down the hallway. I lowered my eyes so I would not see the dark cloud upon her brow. She brushed her cheeks against mine, her gardenia scent much too Walgreen sweet.

Bye, mom.

I stepped back.

Sure that's what you want to do, Mary Ashley? She asked, her glossy peachy lips mouthing something like, not too late to change your mind, not late at all. You hear, pumpkin?

Yes, mom.

In the kitchen, the twins were bawling in their high chairs. I could picture their teary faces smeared with applesauce. Mom did not budge. I did not rush back in. I did not want to see the stack of dirty dishes in the sink that was mine to rinse and put into the dishwasher. I turned to walk out the porch with Josie.

Dad took my bag and strode across the yard to the station wagon. Outside, he moved about snappily, not the gingerly steps he used to take around the house. Outside, there are no stray crayon stubs and beat-up John Deere toy tractors and Matchbox cars on the floor to look out for.

Then, there was mom's piano playing. Chopin's Nocturne forever which she had played for her Miss County Fair title the year before she married dad. Her fingers danced in the air, nocturne any time of the day, twins be hollering.

Luke and Paul were by the barn, saddling up Iron Joe.

Bye now, I called out to them, to the old draft horse.

The boys broke into a run, sending Iron Joe scuttling backwards. They rushed into my arms.

Must ya go, sis? Paul cried, blowing hot moist breath right into my face.

I'm going to school, boys! I said cheerily.

Mom says you're gonna be a nun, Luke blurted out.

I gave him a smooch on his cheek, then turned to Paul with a peck on his sticky brow.

School. Come on, it's school, boys!

Me, me, Josie whimpered, tucking to kiss.

I kissed her on both cheeks, then turned to look for Tommy's bike. It was not by the front porch.

Where's Tommy? I asked dad.

Huh? Must have gone to the library, he said.

As we pulled out the yard, I waved to Josie and the boys. They stood under the big oak, slowly waving back, falling back, out of sight as we rounded out onto the dirt road. I sat back to stare at the cleared fields on either side, bright with sun and great big openness.

Tall, scratchy stalks heavy with ears of corn gone. No more breeze rustling down the rows to shake up the shadows. No more sweaty brow and sticky feet in dampish sneakers. No more nagging thought of mother frowning and babies crying back in the house.

Will Josie need find herself a hiding place in there too? Not too soon, I hope.

A speck of blue caught my eye one day: A lone cornflower reared itself out of the thirsty ground like a stubborn little star. I bent down to touch the soft petals, and wondered at the stubborn force of life.

I asked myself: How can this be? How did this one get away?

In the distance, a combine rasped and thrashed, sending up harvest dust. Old Doug ought to be done by the end of today. I should think, dad mumbled.

Flat land, as far as eyes could see. The Kellers, the Huffs, the Dodsons, the Beans, the Lockes, a patchwork quilt of small farms, old roots set down by grandfathers and great grandfathers. As far as I could look back, the days were about seasons of crops and endless labor. Men in the fields, always an eye on the sky and an eye on the crops. Talk of rain and drought and snow storms and pests and spraying and machines and the price of corn and government subsidies and interest rates from the Tri-State Bank, and yeah, last Sunday's game when there was one. Still, my 4-H was good. The County Fairs were a treat. So were the Shriners' parades.

Winter. I would look out the window at the frozen fields. It was then the sky would fall upon me, when my days inside the house were long and dark and as jumpy as mom's incessant strokes on the piano keys.

Surely, the world out there's not flat, not flat at all! I'd told myself.

We drove on. I could see Tommy from afar. Where the road forked, my brother sat on the big rock and read, waiting for me. I ran up to him. We hugged.

Take care, he said with a smile.

See ya at Thanksgiving!

He mounted his bike, took one fork to town, to the library. Dad took the other fork, to Ottumwa.

Did you go over to say goodbye to the Huffs? Magda and her twin, say what, uh, what's her name?

No.

Why?

I couldn't get away.

Hmm.

After a while, he said, Josie's gonna to miss you bad. She'd be the only girl home.

He has to tell me?

I looked straight ahead. Guilt was a centipede with too many legs and a slow crawl.

He drove on without another word. He glanced at me sideways once. I turned to face him. A small twitch pulled at the corner of his mouth.

You're sure, Mary Ashley?

I'm sure, dad.

Can't he see?

I was flying the coop. At sixteen, Ottumwa pointed my way out. Still my heart was a bunch of tumbling buckets on pulleys, seven going up, eight coming down, pounding away the first stretch of the road.

Plonk! Ploonk! Ploonk!

I lowered the window to let the rushing air brush against my face. I turned a deaf ear to the plonking, and the fitful buckets went away. I looked up at the aquamarine sky with the gauzy strands of cloud. I looked out at the trees on the plots of farmland where houses and barns and silos huddled. Still green, still full. River birches gathered where a stream flowed. Rows of poplar staked out the boundaries. There was a certain order of things under the sun, pretty picture from afar.

Few cars on the highway. Still they zoomed past dad's old Ford station wagon. Dad seemed unhurried. My hair flew about my face. I felt strangely light and giddy.

My new life was not what I'd thought it would be. Days, at Senior High, there were looks that came my way that made me feel I was different from the other students. Giggles died, gossips hushed when I walked near a crowd. I'd wanted to be on the basketball team. The coach smiled. When the roll call came, the slot went to another girl.

Nights, at the convent, I lay awake trying to figure out what I'd missed most these days. Did I ever think that life would be so cut off as an aspirant? Truly, I'd only thought of getting away from home. Now, I found that I missed being myself!

Then, I strained to listen to the big world outside, by way of the trains arriving and departing down the Amtrak Station in town. I listened out for the rumble of the locomotives, horn blaring and whistle blowing, and the grind of wheels on the rails—freight trains that came through during the night, and the California Zephyr that called during the day.

Now, that was music to my ear!

Eastward, the California Zephyr went on to Chicago and there, one could catch another train onto New York City.

Far enough, New York City!

I looked into my small hand mirror and was taken aback by the face that was gawking out—mouth gaping open, jaw dropped, eyes ridden with the appetite of a caterpillar, eating to sleep to eat to sleep to …

I was stirring to the rhythm of life inside me, wriggling to come out a butterfly.

Still, now and then, I've this tinge of guilt for having flown the coop, and then, for having made good my efforts.

To make amends, I work like there's no tomorrow. At the end of the day, I tell myself, it's in work where I find myself, where I find peace.

30

Back on Speer heading towards LoDo, I turn at the drop of a hat onto 14th. Cruising by Civic Center Park, I pull into the first parking space I come upon, and step out into a totally improbable afternoon—as improbable as the sculpture of a gigantic red chair in front of the Public Library, and, yes, as improbable, too, as the yearling that stands on its seat.

How does it get up there? I stare at this piece of whimsical art, struck by the wonder of what we have in us to make ordinary things extraordinary.

I walk into the park, feel the crunch of the thirsty lawn under my feet. A caged bird set free, I savor my tentative wings. The breeze soft, the air luminous, the grounds sparkle with that deep autumnal palette which colors everything a variegated gold and rust. The tree branches are nearly stripped save for a few diehards clinging on. Dropped gold littered everywhere. Withered mums droop over exposed beds where dead greens rot. Still, the sun's warm glow makes it the golden hour of the day.

Cutting through the amphitheater, I pick up my pace to hurry back to the open space. Someone squats on the stepped seating, elbows propped on raised knees, hands cushioning chin. He reaches over to grab the little bundle by his side as my footsteps come upon him from behind. Listless red eyes look up from nowhere to stare into nowhere. I walk on.

Some mother's son.

Lost to himself. On this splendid afternoon, he has no eye for the nimbus of gilded rays over the Capitol dome. No eye for the

grand classical theater where he finds himself, no eye for the
invitation of open space, no eye for the skyscrapers that rim the
Park, no eye for the weathered sculptures—cowboy and Indian and
broncos—gleaming in the mellow light unbowed to season's
changes.

Cold bronze statues they are, ma. Ain't got no life in em. I
can almost hear the lost son scoffing in the crisp air.

Another lost son cares even less. He curls up on the shadowed
side of the stepped seating. Beyond the sun, beyond reach, he has
his arms cradled over his head, cocooning himself within his
ragged overcoat. A total shut-off, a total oblivion.

I walk briskly on, in this urban oasis that keeps the city at bay.
Still, the Republic Plaza, a looming, gleaming monolith harking
back to the space odyssey eons, silently shrieks for attention.

Jed up in his office?

Why won't I give him a buzz?

Ash, things have changed, he might say.

I know.

Then why?

Why what?

Why now?

Redemption.

What're you talking about, Ash?

A cool breeze stirs like a swath of silk that slips over bare skin.
A warm flush swells up. The feel of my old silk robe, faded and
threadbare at the seams, but ever a treasure, more than just a find at
a rummage sale. Those days when I went hunting for old fabric
remnants. Those days when I was back in the City getting set to
start my own studio. Yet deep inside me I was restless, pining for
cherry blossom days and ancient magnolia nights.

Walk with me, Haruo, I say to myself.

Haruo …

Wear it like a poem, miss, you said, dark watery eyes beaming.

I smiled and draped the silver-gray robe over my sweatshirt.
Over me luxuriated a burst of spidery chrysanthemums, snowy
white and muted gold that shone over lush green leaves. Blushing,

I looked to you, the stranger standing by my side.

You shook your head and corrected yourself, I should've said, miss, you're the poetry in it.

Your dark watery eyes looking at me. Then, you took off your black beret and tipped your head ever so slightly, your head bald without a shadow of a hair. I spotted the serious Nikon in your hand. But it was your wistful smile that had captivated me as we stood alone amid a sea of people that flea market morning in Spring.

I see you in your photography, Haruo, your impassioned eyes in your close-up shots of faces, your studies of people in motion, of people in repose. Your work is everyday living caught in stills. Your passion for life shines on through them even as you have lost your battle to cancer.

Your last poem, a lone evergreen shrouded in mist that caught the first light of day, arrived from Karuizawa not three months after you had gone home to live out your last days with your family. Your shaky hand read: When you see this, you know that I'm gone.

I've been mourning for you ever since.

Walk with me, Haruo.

The park is sparse on a workday. On the broad walk, an elderly couple strolls ahead. The man pauses, pans his camera at the City and County Building with its curved façade and imposing columns. A slim tower shoots up the clear blue sky breaking the postcard vista of the Front Range in the distance. She stands by his side but her eyes are elsewhere. Someone bends over a trash bin nearby. He picks up a couple of aluminum cans, crushes them in his hand and stuffs them into his coat pocket.

A mother's watching. I'm watching.

Caw, caw, caw, a loud black flutter falls at my feet. I step aside. Two flapping crows fight over a dropped peanut, letting out a loud cackle. One quick beak snatches the prize and flies off. The sore loser turns to peck after my heel, clucking noisily. I steady myself and step out of its way as fast as I can. It takes wing and I saunter on.

Silly bird, I chuckle. But his caw reverberates darkly in my head.

A large pond lies ahead where I see the flat gleam of water as quiet as a sheet of glass. Approaching, I see a pair of bronze seal sculptures facing each other in the pond. A child rides on each, playful hands reaching over to catch the spray of water spouting out of the seal's mouth. I stroll around the pond, pausing to glance at the shallow water no deeper than wading depth. The mirror reflection pulls down the blue sky and throws back a dark sheen.

I lower myself to take a closer look. Kneeling down, I rest my hands on the ledge of the pond to peer into the darkly water. Before my eyes, a shimmering eddy punches through the glazed surface with widening rings.

A whisper of a girl's face looks up at me through the glimmering swirls. Longing eyes shining through the shadowy depths, cool like star sapphires. Coppery gold hair flying in the breeze, pale porcelain cheeks, lips as supple as a plump cherry. Her lips move, speaking to me. I lower my head, cock my ear over the water to listen.

Redeem me, oh, redeem me, please, a small voice murmurs.

I raise my head back up, straighten myself to hang onto the water's edge to face her. But when I stare back into the gleaming darkness, the face that looks up is my own! I dip my fingers into the cold water, stirring up dizzying eddies to look for my girl's face.

Come back! Oh, come back!

When the rings die down, it's my own face that blinks up at me. Yet I know that it's the girl in my dream who has come to call. I know it from the same deep soothing feeling as I had in my dream, warm as a sip of bedtime cognac.

"Drop something, miss?"

I turn to look up. A young man with a baffled look stands right behind me, straddling over a bike. He gets off it in a jiffy, pushes up the bill of his baseball cap and looks down into the pond.

"No, no!" I say, getting back up on my feet. "Thanks for asking."

He turns from the pond to observe me.

I see that he has a courier bag cross-strapped over his body.

"Beautiful day, isn't it?" I say.

"Sure is, for November?"

"Have a nice day!"

"You too."

He gets back on his bike and speeds out of the park to cross the street. I turn back to the pond.

My girl!

Caw, caw! A crow perches on the head of the bronze child, then sweeps down to strut on the parched bottom of a drained pond. The seals are dry-mouthed. Not a drop of water in sight!

My heart leaps up my throat, stifling my cry. I stagger, my legs giving way. I slump onto the ledge of the pond. At the bottom, brown heaps of windblown leaves huddle and shiver.

But I've more pressing thoughts.

I call her *my* girl?

But what girl is she who comes in a dream?

Only in a dream, day and night?

She of my dream … not a dream?

The amber sun that had come over me while I slept was no sun. No sun at all but her blazing coppery curls brushing against my face! Same curls that tangled my fingers though I'd made myself see them not coppery bright, not curly. Wanted them honey blond and straight. Wanted them mine. Not Jed's anybody's, but mine.

Her hair then?

Not a dream then, not a dream at all!

A sudden haze films over my eyes, fogging up my vision. I'm seeing red, burning red …

Go away, go away! I shut my eyes.

A red hot vision drops into my head …

No, not that red glow again? I shudder.

It's day now. See!

I open my eyes to a brilliant afternoon in the park. The

mellow sun hangs high, showering gold. Even the breeze sends little warm smooches. But something gnaws at me. It brings to mind what had happened two nights ago when I stayed back late in the studio.

I had spotted it from the corner of my eye. A luminous haze radiating over my floor-to-ceiling silk brushwork, washing my giant blue hydrangeas *red!* I saw it as I was making my way up the spiral stairs. I scampered back down to the gallery floor, shot straight up the glass front to peer into the street for passing taillights.

Dark outside, but for a bright yellow cone shed by the street lamp. The street was quiet on a weeknight.

Inside, the little spotlights over the fan-driven River Indigo punctuated the dark reflective glass. Halogens glared, fan motor hummed, the blue cloth rippled, letting down a quivering puddle of gray shadow.

At the rear of the gallery, my hydrangeas dimly hung.

Red glow gone?

I held my breath. I was about to look back when I caught my own reflection on the glass—eyes glinting like searchlights, mouth agape. I stumbled backward, thrown off by that grimace of fear. My teeth clattered. I let out a cry, gnashing, fighting back a surge of anger dredged out of nowhere. Steeping anger, long been stewing ... boiling over. Within me?

I was gasping for air as I spun around to get away. Away from that seething anger I don't own!

It's not mine!

Not mine!

The whole room spun with me, the wall hangings tossed and flapped soundlessly. I hobbled to lean against the curved stair-wall. My knees gave way and I slid down the floor, panting ...

Then, the reeling stopped as suddenly as it had sprung up. The spell broke. The raging outburst had subsided. I was let go. I picked myself up to tear down the basement, not turning back to see if my hydrangeas were indeed blue. I sprinted out the back door in a flash.

Mrs. Norton's trembling voice rang in my ear: Danger ...
can't you see the danger? Something dark in there ... Sinister ...
Early next morning, I walked into the studio and went straight
to work. The panic of the night before had totally slipped my
mind.
    Until now.
    But I want to think no more of that. I want only to relish this
afternoon's amber moment with my girl.

Lazy shadow elongating at my feet ...
Looking west to where the sun is heading, to where the blue
mountains lie, I'm seized with a longing for the girl whose face I'd
a glimpse of only a moment ago. Much yearning is in her eyes ...
speaking to me on this, my breakaway day.
    What's she telling me?
    Redeem me, oh, redeem me, please ...
    She is as remote as the snow-capped mountains in the distance.
But her starry sapphire eyes, her lustrous coppery hair stay with
me.
    Over the noise of the city, I stretch to gaze at the quiet
mountains ... as if I'd known them from another lifetime.
    Timeless under the sun, and beckoning ...
    When the snow melts, my baby will come, I say aloud to
myself.
    Then, I'll come.
    Back to the mountains ...

31

He drains his chardonnay, jiggles the glass, stares blankly into the bottom.

"What timing, Ash!" Pushing his chair back noisily, he gets up to leave.

That's all? About my expecting, that is.

I look up from the last morsel of the take-out chicken parmesan on my plate. He shies away from my eyes.

"Gotta finish up in the office," he mutters.

He bends down to peck my cheek. Old habit, I suppose. He shrugs and heads out the back door, jacket slung over one shoulder.

Jed walks out, heels not touching floor. Cat out on a night romp.

How late? I don't ask.

He has been mouthing: Hey, gotta make partner at the firm, hon! Gotta rake in high visibility work.

Like the competition for Aspen's performing and visual arts complex. I don't ask. Word around is that the selection committee is headed by the newly widowed Kate Norton who also chairs the board.

Those late nights, those weekend onsite visits to Aspen have given high colors to his cheeks, and a chirp to his voice.

Jiminy Cricket! The day I met him I must have left my eyes locked up in the bottom drawer of my desk. Jed, the architect hired to remodel the art gallery next door. He poked his head into my studio and said, Your place?

Yes, my bank's, and mine.

He went on babbling admiration for what I had done with that old SoHo storefront. It's nothing really, I said. Just had a couple of non-load bearing walls torn down to open up the space.

Hey, you've got an eye for proportion!

Then he went on, Whoa, just love your colors—that fabulous piece over there!

That was how he came into my life. Jed's got a silver tongue. He can coax a bird down a tree. And he's got that affable grin.

It was Spring. And he made that time of the year bearable for me.

What does Haruo mean? I asked.

It means that I come to you in Spring. A tinge of sadness in your voice.

But you were gone before Spring arrived. Burnished in my heart, your wistful smile and that lone evergreen in the mist, first light of day—the last thing you shared with me from afar.

I'd thought that I walked into my marriage with my eyes open. From the start, something about Jed touched me to the core. We each had to swim in a very big pond, professionally speaking. I've been plowing a lonely groove, trying to get established, doing what I love to do. He, prodding along doing small remodeling projects, thinking up big ideas everyday.

Gotta aim for the stars, he'd told me once. If you aim for the treetop, hon, you'll land nowhere. Then he chuckled, Ah, forget about the stars, just give me the Pritzker!

Jed, charming Jed, was just being facetious, I'd thought. But then there is more to Jed than meets the eye, more than just believing in oneself to get ahead.

Though I'm still struggling, now that both of us are on our way to where we think we'd like to be for now, whatever common ground I'd thought we did share seems to have vanished into thin air. Our driven lives have become increasingly separate, and we, increasingly estranged. I wonder when will we split up for good.

But what of love?
Was it love?
Truly, ever?

A long cool gulp of the 2% milk down my throat. I fork in a mouthful of the greens.

I stretch, tilt my head back, hang out my arms as I slouch down the chair. Eyes closed, inhale … exhale … slow and easy.

A tune drifts into my head, *Si-ilver silver serpent … Si-ilver silver serpent …*

What ditty is that?

I open my eyes to a table of soiled plates and empty glasses. The curious ditty croons on in my head, light as a dandelion parachute drifting in the air. I hum along, *Si-ilver silver serpent … Si-ilver silver serpent …*

"Josie, how're you?"
"Fine."
"Hey, I'm expecting!"
"Yeah?"
"I'm so-o very exited!"
"Yeah?"
"Josie, um, is everything alright?"
"Everything's fine."
"How's work?"
"Fine."
"Going home for Thanksgiving?"
"Nope."
"What about Christmas?"
"Yeah, what about Christmas?"
"Going home?"
"I'm staying put here."
"Mom and dad will miss ya."
"Huh?"
"Hmm, will you come visit me? Love to have ya!"
"Why?"
I flinch.

"Come see Denver, Josie."

"Nah, thanks anyway."

"Think about it, please, will ya?" I say, clearing the lump in my throat.

"Gotta go. Bye."

She hangs up. I can feel the Alaskan chill breathing down my neck. Sisters drifting apart as years go by. Josie has been an librarian in Juneau for three years now. Why hadn't I make the effort to visit her? Was it already way too late?

"Hi, Tommy, gotta minute?"

"Hey, Ash, congrat! Wonderful news! Mom had just called. When's the baby due?"

"In May."

"You guys tickled?"

"Oh, yeah ..."

"What's up, Ash?"

"Have you, um, talked to Josie lately?"

"No, why?"

"She sounded glum. Glummer, I should say."

"What do you mean?"

"I mean distant."

"Caught her at a bad moment, maybe. I'll give her a call. Been a while since we last talked."

"Umm."

"Got a call coming in ... hey, it's my boss. Later, Ash."

My brother, an attorney in Des Moines. We're all so proud of you, Tommy.

"How're you doing, Mary Ashley?"

"I'm fine, dad."

"Your mom gotta thinking, uh, we'd like to come see you, uh, around Thanksgiving, if that would suit you." He goes on breathlessly, "She, uh, she's so excited about your expecting, and, uh, it's been so long since we last saw you ... and besides, uh, she says she'd like to see Denver ... never, uh, been out West ... "

"Not this year, dad."

"Well, uh, well, just a thought, Mary Ashley."

I happen to look out the glass front. I can't take my eyes off him. Ben crossing the street, long legs in faded jeans, brisk strides the tempo of my heartbeat. He hops aside to dodge an oncoming car. Blaring horn melts into daylight, into the shadow that flows over the asphalt.

I've yet to thank him for putting up my work tables. Well, he's just next door.

He came in through the back door one day after four. Kara and I were belatedly preparing dyes for the Holiday Edition of the silk cravats and the shawls—rust gold, maroon, and dark green.

We both looked up at the small knock. The door had been left ajar for air. Kara had said she could use the fresh air.

"Hi, Ben!" Kara called out.

"Hi! Sorry to interrupt."

"It's okay, Ben," I said.

There he stood against the late afternoon sun. The canting light drew a sharp profile of his face as he turned to look up at the old brick wall.

"A sash window in your office needs more work," he said.

He showed up at quitting time the next day, his tool belt strapped below his waist. I had thought he came to replace the sashes in one of the double-hung windows in my office. But I heard no steps going up the stairs.

I looked up from stretching out a length of Shandong silk for brush work and saw him standing there, staring at the patch of old brickwork under the stairs.

"I can get that floor resurfaced for you, if you want me to," he said, clearing his throat. Not the first time he had offered.

There was a somber tone in his voice. He held his breath as he looked my way. His eyes gleamed like marbles in the dull light.

"Tha-nks, Ben. I'll thi-nk a-bout it."

My voice quivered. My cords were tight as if I was being stifled.

Go away, you hear?

I heard then a small hollow voice bounding off the deep like an echo in my head. I must have looked flustered for I saw Ben tense up. As if on cue, he reached into his jean pocket to grope at something.

Although he had said that he would be back to finish up some small jobs, I'd a hunch that it was not the sash window or that patch of old floor bricks that had brought him back to the house. When I happened to walk past him, I could feel his eyes burning me. Then, there was that flush that came over his face, the small twitching at the corners of his mouth, and his tipsy grin.

Now, I should be by the sink downstairs doing a dye job, but I loiter by the glass front, looking out to catch a glimpse of him. My head throbs. I shut my eyes to call up the scent that had greeted me early this morning when I walked into the basement.

Outside, there were smudged boot prints on the snow dusted steps. An intruder had come in the night. Yet, I did not jump. Gray light stole into the dim space after me. I flipped on all the lights.

There was this whiff in the stale air, a spike much like an intoxicating night bloom I once knew sweltering in the sultry air. Only this was the scent of a warm body that had come in the night.

I know that scent by day. And by heart.

So, I kept the door ajar to let go of the night scent. There was only this damp patch on the rubber mat by the door. The floor was dry. Ben must have removed his wet boots when he came in and walked in his socked feet.

It did occur to me to have the back door lock changed. But, nothing's been missed, or out of place. I've been thinking of asking him about his night visits. I keep putting it off. For one thing, his coming by reassures me that the house is safe. Some peace of mind to get me through the day. Nights, too, when I need to stay late.

No more red haze over my blue hydrangeas. No more ugly look of fear on my face in the glass reflection.

But why, really, why does Ben come in the night? Once? Twice? More times? I don't know for sure.

I glance at the spots where the bodies fell. The dark cloud hanging still.

"Excuse me," I said as I made my way past him one afternoon on the stairs. He pressed his back flat against the brick wall to make room. His tool belt clunked. *Plunk ... plunk!* A small scraper slipped out and dropped down the wood tread. He kicked it out of my way. A warm moist breath fell on my nape. A brush of his body heat sent charges inside me. His scent suffused with gender and sweat hung over the narrow passage.

My cheeks were on fire, my body sluggish. The moment held still and held on long afterwards, for I had walked away carrying his scent with me. A scent that lingered, to be called upon to relish a wakeful night when my eyes grew bleary with desire.

Then, I dreamed. A dream so tender, so tantalizing that I wept. I wept over a night bouquet which had come to seduce. It was no other than that intoxicating ancient magnolia in the faraway place of my heart.

I'm beside myself seeing him walking down the street! Head bowed, hair ruffled, Ben, more than a little reserved, more than a little improbable.

Ben, you a night lizard scouting up my wall looking for a meal?

How was the harvest of your night, Ben?

You, a day lizard, Ash?

Be quiet!

*   *   *

"How's your Thanksgiving?" Kara asks.

She sees the bags under my eyes.

"Uh?" I bow over the swatches of silk chiffon, organza, charmeuse, and dupioni that had just arrived.

"Your Thanksgiving, Ashley."

"Fine. We'd last minute company."

"Cool. Who came?" Her voice has a ring of mock glee.

"Jed's parents and sister flew in from New York."

A Thanksgiving to forget.

It starts up all over again. Ceaseless cicadas shrieking inside my head. Careless chatters and more ...

"Really?"

"Is this planned?"

"I'd thought you would rather not rush into family till you make partner or something. Didn't you say, Jed?"

Jed left for Vail the day after Thanksgiving and we did not see him till late afternoon Sunday, in time to see his folks off.

"To make a presentation on that Vail complex," he'd said. "Gotta get that commission!" Jed winked, thrusting a thumbs-up in the air.

"Of course you will, Jed," his mom said, smiling broadly, her high pitch voice too young for her age, too thin for her bulk.

"She'll see to it, won't she?" His dad leaned over him, whispered conspiratorially while shooting a knowing glance at his old lady.

She shifted in her chair, pursed her lips, stole a look at me but said nothing. I turned to stare at the flickering candle flame on the dining table.

Early Friday, Jed on his way out rushed back to snatch his laptop. An afterthought, for appearance. At the door, he flashed a big smile and said, "Hey, Ash will show you her charming studio, won't you, hon? Guys, you'll get to see how I'd transformed that old dump!"

"Jed's *so* good in what he does. *Always*," his mom said when she stepped into the gallery, her eyes on the curve stair-wall so obviously his signature touch.

"Business good?" Jed's dad, a dentist in practice with partners, wanted to know.

His mom who had been keeping accounts in his office to keep an eye on him shrugged and wandered off with Jan.

They hovered over my gift corner. I offered them shawls and a cravat for the dad. Jan could not decide on the brushwork maroon dupioni or the tie-dyed gold silk chiffon, so she took both.

"Okay with you, Ash? See, I'm in for a total makeover."

Jed's kid sister, her dad's hygienist, was newly divorced and wore a peevish look that kept everybody at arm's length.

Cicadas that got no season, got no reason ... got to drown them out.

Drown out all the chatter that streams through my head. Drown out the wrangling thoughts in the night when I lie waxing to let go, mulling over the new life ahead.

"Kara, you know how the Chinese unwind a silk cocoon?"

"Huh?"

Across the work table, she looks at me with big eyes.

"I saw girls in a Suzhou silk factory, gosh, such nimble fingers picking out the end of a filament from a wet cocoon." I gesture to show and tell. "Pull it out, twist together the filaments from seven or eight other cocoons and wind the twisted thread onto a coiled bobbin of the reeling mill. Just amazing how they *ever* know where the end is!"

"Cool! How much silk is there in one little cocoon?"

"More than 1000 yards!"

"Gee-whiz!"

The end is the beginning ... is the end.

Huh?

I wipe that dippy smile off my face, and start to hum, "*Si-ilver silver serpent ... Si-ilver silver serpent ... "*

"What song's tha-at, Ashley?   So-o we-ird."
"Uh, what?"

I walk past the glass front. Across the street, the Mile High crew is eating their lunch. Joey is there, but Ben is nowhere to be seen.

"Jed, I want a divorce."
He glances at me as if I was about to trick him. Or, trap him.
Baby's on the way, what's the catch, huh?
Jed does not know me at all.
"Can we talk about it another time?"   He hisses under his breath.
Talk? When had we last talked, Jed?
He looks distracted. Something's on his mind. Something's holding him back.
What are we waiting for, Jed?
He paces the floor, goes right back into the bathroom where he has been blow-drying his hair after a seemingly interminable shower.
He comes back out, puts his cell down on the bedside table, and yawns.
I bolt up in bed. "You know it hasn't been working out, you and I ..."
"Come on, Ash!" he cuts me off. He switches off his bedside lamp, slumps into bed.
He does not ask, is this about Kate?
In the past, where there were others he had sworn denial. This time around, he keeps mum.
"You need to hear this, Jed. I'll not ask for child support. I'll keep the house because I'd paid the down payment, and have been paying the mortgage."
I know he's listening even though he has his back towards me.
"Not the right time," he slurs.

"Excuse me, Jed, when's the right time for you?"

He pulls the comforter over his ears, the way he puts on blinders as he skims over his huge credit card debt. Soon he starts to snore.

I'll go to a lawyer to have the papers drawn up, I tell myself. It's over. Eight years' a blip. A blur.

Getting out of bed, I pick up my robe and head for the guest room. Eyes glaring at my back. I spin around to look down the moonlit hallway. Outside the window, bare branches of the linden quivering, throwing shaky shadow down the floor. I let out a sigh.

The guest room is cold. I turn up the thermostat. Shivering under the comforter, I draw my knees up my chest. My bosoms are full and sore. I'm taut as a wound-up coil. I yawn and stretch, easing the strain, letting go of the darkness ...

A cramp in my leg wakes me. I grit my teeth to straighten my legs and point my toes towards my head. The cramp eases. There I lie, flat on my back. I set myself to visualize that I'm floating on water. Letting go ...

A small voice drones from somewhere deep, *I'm with you ... with you. You're not alone... not alone.*

My girl? I whisper back, my eyes shut, drifting away.

Sleep comes like a newborn lamb cuddling up to its nursing mama in an old barn I once knew.

Blushing pink peonies on beige, fluffy white peonies on silvery gray, blooming lilacs on muted green, shades of coral on coral, foam-crested waves of aquamarine, all done in billowy silk chiffon to call up many a summer dream, to be draped on willowy bodies with masks for faces, long legs strutting down the catwalk ...

Think that's what D'Souza wants?

More whims and fancies: Pale new moon on a slinky body swaying against a cobalt sky, hand-wrinkled silk to add texture; an immense jaundiced eye spying across black-and-white prison stripes; a pair of glossy hot lips wrapping around a sheath of black silk.

Think I've got it? Well, in my head, at least. Ah, only in my head!

A taste of flat beer in my mouth, my tongue like sandpaper. I putter around the work island. My body is as stiff as my dad's cranky old Ford wagon.

Bolts of silk sitting idle on the wall rack, bottles of dye gathering dust on the shelves.

I have unopened e-mails and unheard phone messages.

Lately, Jed's home after nine or so. If he has not eaten out already, he would grab a microwave dinner, sit down with his laptop, or put his feet up in front of the TV. Then, he would get into the shower and call it a day.

I call it one more day of holding out.

Jed does not talk about the Vail project or his prospect of making partner at Mullen Spiegel & Associates, Architects. Neither does he ask how I am doing, work or otherwise. It's as if we've crossed a divide, and there's no turning back. No pretending either.

Yet I've been putting off seeing an attorney. My days are a grind, my nights a torpor. I just can't seem to pick myself up to handle even the daily chores. Funds are low. There're overdue bills and few receipts coming in. I'm hopelessly mired in inertia.

Sitting up in bed staring at the blank page, my eyelids grow heavy, my drawing hand flaccid. The pencil slips off, sketch book crashes down the floor …

It's midnight when I open my eyes. I've slumped over to my side in bed. The house is dark. Nothing stirs. I get up to go down to get a glass of milk in the kitchen. I look into the garage, Jed's BMW is gone. Has he come in at all this evening? I don't recall.

Back to bed, I lie awake. My eyes grow misty, swimming over the dark ceiling. My mind wanders. Like a homing pigeon, always back to him.

Haruo, I'm with child.

He beams, twinkles in his eyes. I unclench my fists held against my thighs, and reach up to touch his rueful smile. My lips quiver. I rest my hands over my belly, feel the small roundness, and tune in to the rhythm of my breathing.

Hmmmm! A wisp of a sigh warbling into my ear. I'm drowsy all over again.

When my morning alarm rings, I'm surprised to find Jed curl up in sleep next to me. Jed, the stranger, father of my unborn child.

I grab my robe before getting out of bed.

What was it like before ... before I'm shy of being naked when he's in bed with me, before I'm loath to touch, be touched ... before love sours like a wine gone stale?

What's it with you, Jed?

You and Kate? You and whoever?

"Ashley, is that you?" Kara calls from the top of the stairs as I walk in the back door. She stays up in the gallery whenever she is by herself.

"Hey, thanks for opening up, Kara!"

She comes down the stairs and watches me as I slip off my coat and hang it up on the wall peg.

"I, uh, was going to call you," she says.

"I'd forgotten to set the alarm."

It's almost noon.

"Sleeping well?"

"Nah," I shrug, my back towards her.

"How's your checkup?"

I'd told her I was going for my ob/gyn appointment when I left yesterday morning.

"Doing great. Thanks."

"Did you come back to work after I left yesterday?" She lingers over my bleary eyes.

"No, should have, though," I sigh.

"So you didn't stop by after I left?"

"No, why?"

"I, uh, I found this by the back door when I came in this morning."

She comes up to me and hands me a soiled binder, its torn envelope hanging loose.

"This envelope came yesterday after you were gone. I'd left it unopened and in good condition on your desk upstairs."

I look at this tattered thing in my hand, a faux leather binder embossed with the logo of Norton Development on its cover. Ripped pages with color prints of nearby properties slip out and crash onto the floor.

The whole sorry sight looks as if somebody had exploded over it and trashed it in a tantrum. Neither of us bother to bend down to pick up the strewn pages.

"What's that?" Kara asks, her unblinking eyes shift back to me.

"Could be some promotion material." I shrug.

"Ash, it was hand delivered by a courier! I signed for it."

"U-uh!"

"Who junk it, Ash? If you haven't even seen it, then, who? Who-o co-ould've?" Her voice trails off in a tremble.

My cell phone rings. I turn to take the call although I've half a mind not to.

Hello, hello … Above the statics and mumbling, I hear Kara rustling into her parka, then shutting the door behind her.

32

I'm being watched. Unseen eyes at my back, darkly watching. A wisp of chill air brushes past. The hair on my nape tingles. Dark ears listening … Lowering my voice, cradling the phone close to my lips, "See you in a bit, " I whisper and hang up.

I grab my purse, slip out of the office. All's quiet in the gallery. The front door has not chimed the past hour. No one has come in.

Kara gone? Didn't she tell me she's taking the afternoon off? An appointment has come up, didn't she say?

She tells me what she has been hearing from the floor: Norton died here? Grandfather too, way back when the place was, hmm, a brothel. Dropped dead, both of them, in the basement. Creepy, eh?

Kara, I say, curiosity will die down. In time.

In time? She looks away.

I lock the glass entry door and put up the CLOSE sign. The world can wait. I hurry down the basement, throw on my coat and tiptoe out.

Whew, a breath of fresh air!

Walking briskly out the alley, I cross over to the sunny side of the street.

Ah, the sunny side of the street!

The sun's glare is a rush of pinpricks into my eyes. I panic, stumbling to lean against the nearest lamppost.

The sun, the sun, give me the sun!

Someone's clamoring for the sun. I shut my eyes only to swim in a bright red pool of tears. I fumble for my sunglasses.

"Honey, are you alright? Is something the matter?" An elderly woman stops to ask.

"Oh, no. The sun's ju-ust too bright."

I turn to her and manage a smile. Straightening up, I move away from the lamppost.

"O-oh? Sure you're alright?"

"I'm okay. Thanks!"

Through my tears, I see that she's with an elderly gentleman, her arm resting on his. He lowers his head, says to me softly, "Do take care, miss."

"Thank you," I nod. I tuck in my coat, thrust my hands inside my pockets and walk on.

Feeling jagged, I pick up my pace, eyes on the ground. Not looking back though I can see them still in my head—two ruffled old birds wing-locked on the ground, buzzing heads. I envy them for their being old birds together, for journeying together.

I walk on.

The blood red film in my eyes dissipates as quickly as it has come. Even through my sunglasses, I can tell that the pavement is no longer washed in red. The sky is blue without trepidation. The Honda that zips past is metallic silver. Behind it, a white Jeep, then a blue Toyota.

All's well ... baby's okay, yes, my baby's okay! I'm just being hypersensitive to the sudden bright light, that's all. It comes to mind mom's fluctuating moods the times she was pregnant. There were the frequent blues, the constant complaints about being cold or being warm in short spurts.

So, I've got the jitters of the moment. No upsetting of the applecart. I've been working long hours on end. Getting out for a bit is a good break.

The Corner Bistro is three short blocks away, but I arrive panting, and my brow is damp with perspiration under the cool sun. I unbutton my coat, fling it open to catch a draft as I walk across the street.

A breath ... ah, a breath of air, for heaven's sake!

What catches the eye about this corner building is the bold new look of glass and steel against a façade of weathered red bricks newly sandblasted. There's a lot of buzz about this award-winning renovation, though I heard not a word from Jed. No surprise there!

I walk up to the stainless steel portal where a curve of wraparound glass gives a view of the sparkling foyer. At the glass entry door, I stop short. I am blindsided by a sudden vision. Before me is an open door of heavy dark wood leading into a dim interior. A gray sandstone lintel arches over the door. Above it, white letters on a big black sign: *Hobb's Apothecary, Drugs, Minerals, Perfumes and Oils.*

In a flash, the vision disappears.

Déjà vu?

Might have seen this somewhere, in a historic photo, maybe. It's so surreal. Only a moment ago I'd thought I was actually standing in front of this historic building as it once was way back in time.

The double glass doors swing open. With a flourish, two gentlemen in business suits on their way out stand aside to let me through. I steady myself, smile in return.

Inside the foyer, I find myself standing under a wash of reflected light that has spilled in from the adjoining hall. I look up. A shining sea overhead! A high ceiling of beveled mirrors set in grids refracts cool sharp rays, dazzling and exacting. Discreet cove lighting lines the wood paneled perimeter walls. The dining area hums and stirs sedately.

I feel as if I've just drifted in from somewhere dark and crammed … and find myself awakened in this light filled space.

A scent of rose water … a whiff of lavender … and that heady aromatic orange oil spiced with cloves! Fragrances that lace the air seep into my head.

Ah, sachets and poultices, and all things nice!

Huh?

Past a lush of fern on a high marble pedestal, through a blur of dark mahogany booths brightened with stark white table linen, a medley of scarlet and orange and aubergine upholstery and shifting bodies, I look for her.

Looking for you, light of my life!

My girl?

A small, dark-suited figure is ensconced in one of the booths in the far corner, luminous and dark all at once. I nod to the maitre d' and he shows me to her booth. Under the soft light of the milk-white sconce, her hair a silvery sheen, her eyes a deep gray green. A sunny smile lights up her face as she looks up at me.

"Mrs. Norton!"

Who-o?

I give her my hand. She holds onto it, pulls me gently down to her and brushes both my cheeks.

"How have you been?"

"I'm fine, thanks, and you?"

"Good."

She glances up at me. Her eyes clear. No ripples. I'm relieved.

Across the table, I get a fleeting glimpse of her face as it once might have been, fresh and striking as the single stem of spider chrysanthemum on the table, untouched by shadow.

"I want to thank you for your kind thoughts, and for the lovely orchid," she says.

The day before Thanksgiving I'd sent her an Oncidium. A Sharry Baby as a diversion from her prize roses.

"Wonderful chocolate-scented blooms!" She gushes, beaming from across the table. Eyes of a mother, indulgent of every small favor which comes her way. I have always longed for such eyes. I want such eyes for myself. For my baby.

"I've been thinking of you."

She smiles. Yet her smile is wistful. It reminds me of a most glorious bloom that has sadly past its prime. It'll always be so, I'm afraid.

She, my Michael's mother?

"Would you care to have something to eat?" she asks.

"Oh, yes!" I'm famished.

She asks the waiter to bring us appetizers for a light meal, something the kitchen recommends.

"Would you care to have a drink? Some wine?"

"Mineral water, please."

"Beaujolais please, your wine steward's choice," she says to the waiter.

"What brought you to town, Mrs. Norton?"

"I stopped by Michael's office," she sighs. "I've decided to keep it as it is, for myself."

Ah, Michael!

"Huh?"

"I want to get out of the house more often," she fidgets with her napkin. "The business people and my attorneys have been bringing me papers to sign. I thought I'd like to come down to do it in his office."

"Hmm."

"And to see you."

"I'm glad you've asked me to come."

Here, an unhurried place. Except for a handful of executive types having late lunches, cupping their last fill of coffee, the place is quiet at three in the afternoon. I have a feeling I know what is on her mind. I glance out the window.

She waits till she has my eyes. Then she asks, "What have you decided?"

"About what?"

"Moving out of your place."

"Uh …" I lower my eyes.

"Have you taken a look at the portfolio my manager sent you? About the properties near here."

"Sorry, I haven't." I cringe at my words.

You're not leaving me, Ash!

Uh?

"Yes?" She knits her brow.

The waiter comes by with his serving tray. He pauses for our attention. "Shredded crab meat over asparagus spears; goat cheese spinach puffs; smoked salmon canapés with crème fraîche; seared sea scallops with pear purée and arugula; avocado, fennel and citrus salad," he announces in a low voice as he places the dainty servings before us.

The wine steward presents Mrs. Norton a couple of selections, offering her a tasting. She declines, nodding a hasty approval to one. The waiter uncaps a small bottle of Perrier and pours into my chilled stemmed glass with a twist of lime on the rim.

"Enjoy," he grins, gesturing towards the dishes.

I sit still, my eyes on the glistening green and crispy golden fare in front of me. The seared scallop alone is enough to make my mouth water.

"Please help yourself."

"Bon appétit," I raise my glass to her.

"Bon appétit."

A hint of a smile passes her lips as she sips her wine.

"Are you sure you won't care for wine?"

Her eyes are full on my face, but she dwells in some faraway thoughts.

"No, thanks."

"Delicious," I look down as I help myself to more crab meat and asparagus.

She asks the waiter to bring us another order of the same.

"Have you been working hard?"

"I've, uh, some catching up to do. I work, uh, only when my assistant is with me."

Huh?

"Please leave your building at once. Seriously." Her voice, suddenly staccato.

"Not right now. I, eh, I ..."

No, please don't!

"If I may ask, Ashley, are you expecting?"

Why didn't I break the good news to her from the start? Why was I not eager to share?

"I'm, yes, I'm, umm ... "

Butterflies breaking loose. A flutter of bright yellow specks dancing over my head.

"Sweet dear," she bursts out, "oh, sweet dear."

She springs up from her seat to come over to me. I quickly

rise to be taken into her arms. I feel her small-bone fragility.

"Congratulations! I'm *so-o* happy for you," she whispers into my ear as I bow to catch her words.

There is something exquisite about her exuberant good mood, tremulous like a gazillion stars on a clear night.

Stars over the Mosquito Range!

Where?

"When is the baby due?"

She sits back down, perching on the edge of her seat.

"In May."

There is a glimmer in her eyes. She lets out a slow breath, inhales deeply as if she is gathering air to fan the seed of fire that has just sprung up.

"Michael's birthday is in May. *You* know?"

"Oh?"

"May 24," she tells me.

"Mrs. Norton, um, my baby, Jed and I ..."

Darn, what am I trying to say?

"Call me Evelyn, dear," she interrupts, leaning forward. "Now, now, when will you stop work?"

"Um, not for a while yet."

"Then, we must move you out of the building, my dear. Right away!"

We?

Don't leave me, ple-ease!

"This, um, is not a good time."

"For the baby's sake, please. I'm so-o afraid. There's, uh, danger ... "

Danger? Wha-at danger?

I see her swallow her words, her neck muscles tighten.

"I, uh, I can't move. Not just now, please ..."

She clenches her jaws. My heart skips a beat.

"I know you care for me, Mrs. Nor-, Evelyn."

I reach across the table for her hand. She grasps mine. Small dainty hands, her gold wedding band stays on her ring finger.

"Please, dear, I want no harm to come to you."

There is a tremor in her voice, barely audible. But her eyes glint like sparked flint.

You're safe, Ash! We're safe.

Yes, my girl.

The chrysanthemum sends out a scent cool as morning dew. She follows my eyes to gaze at the many spider-legged petals.

"How's Kate?" I decide to change the subject.

What is it with Kate, and Jed, anyway?

"Fine, I suppose."

She shrugs but does not seem surprised by my question.

"Last time I saw her was at the reading of Michael's will," she says in an even tone though the corners of her mouth sag ever so slightly.

"Hmm."

"I know she's seeing someone."

She steals a disquieting look at me.

I begin to regret to have asked. I don't want to invite her to look into my failed marriage. I'm over it now. I want to look ahead and move on. I take a long sip of the Perrier, glance up at the ornately framed pencil-and-charcoal drawing of the historic Union Station on the wall of our booth.

"I expect that she'll re-marry, eventually. His two former wives did," she continues impassively. "Kate's got the penthouse in town, the house in Vail. They are hers to keep. Then, there's a handsome allowance for as long as she remains a Norton. For now, that premium's plenty attractive. It'll wear off, I dare say. Knowing Kate, she will play the field awhile, and do her calculations. It's, um, not easy to be a young widow, especially one without entitlement."

Her voice trails off. She was a young widow once. But then she had a son. Now, she's a matriarch without a family, the Norton estate without an heir. The irony of her plight does not escape her.

What Michael had said comes to mind—"My old lady, she's a dedicated Norton, keeps the home hearth burning."

For whom? She might have asked herself that after Michael was gone.

The seed of fire has burst into flame. She sees herself a flame tender once again.

She sips her Darjeeling, her eyes radiating a new light.

"Norton Development will take care of all your remodeling and relocating expenses. And, your lost income, of course. Now, please take a break till after the baby has come," she says in a matter-of-fact way.

Huh?

But, why? Why is she doing this?

As an afterthought, she goes on, "Please accept this offer in remembrance of Michael. I know he'd want you to."

I lift my eyes from my kiwi and strawberry tart, put down my fork and look at her. I'm momentarily lost for words.

"Michael had been most generous, as a friend. We were not, um ... "

"Say no more, I know," she cuts in.

"I appreciate your kind offer, Evelyn. But, I really can't ... "

"Think nothing of it, dear."

Then a new found voice in me says, "I need a little more time, please?"

Just a little more time.

A force within me has erupted, a surge of energy spikes up. A tenuous young shoot is rearing its head relentlessly to light.

"Promise me then, *never* be alone in that house."

I look helplessly at her. As if from afar, I see her eyes swim towards me, urgent and tender, gleaming with resolve.

"Christmas's around the corner. First thing after the New Year then?" she says.

Ye-es!

I nod. A smile blossoms over her face. She reaches across the table for my hands.

"Oh, dear, you're cold. Here, have some hot tea!"

"Let me, please." I refill my cup, cradling it in my hands.

She sees that I'm studying her pearl drop earrings with the diamond studs. She turns her head sideways ever so slightly. In the blink of an eye, the diamond catches fire from a sunlit sparkle glittering from behind. I know what it is without looking.

Shimmy, shimmy, shim, shim ...
A glimmer of a sunburst strikes atop a Chantilly apothecary jar, shimmying away. The aromatic oil, a liquid gold, undulating in a blur.

I open the door and walk into a long dark tunnel. My bedroom, a long dark tunnel? A pin of a light beckoning at the far end. I grope along. But I touch no tunnel walls. Nothing. Empty and dark and nothing ...

Out, out, I want to get out!

I hear the echo bounce out of nowhere, reverberating: Ou-out, ou-out ...

All of a sudden, the booming stops. The hurtling stops. I look around. The pin of light gone. The tunnel gone. I roll over ...

I stand now inside my bedroom in the dusk. I strain to see through a shroud of ground fog. All's hushed. The bed is made, the comforter neatly spread out.

I hold my breath for I see someone standing by the dresser facing the blank wall where the mirror ought to be. She is letting loose her honey blond hair tied up in the back. Like mine. In the hazy dim light, her silky straight hair a shiny waterfall. She picks up my hair brush and brushes her hair in long even strokes the way I do. She is draped in a red mist.

I walk up gingerly from behind. My heart pounding, gasping for air.

Who-o is she?

Let me see her face.

I plant myself on the floor, but I'm shaking like a wind swept tree ...

Shaking … I shake myself awake, bolt upright in bed. Eyes wide open to pry into the dark.

Just a dream. A strange dream!

I'm shivering … Drenched in sweat, my face, neck and chest moist to the touch. And I'm co-old! So-o co-old … I snuggle up under my comforter to keep warm, to keep the jitters down.

I turn on the bedside lamp, shoot a quick glance at my dresser. The wall mirror is there, a slippery, silvery sheen at three in the morning. An edgy calm hangs in the air. I close my eyes.

What comes to mind this very moment is that lone bur oak out in the back field at home. Wind-whipped, hammered and pummeled through countless storms, it grapples on, hoary and twisted but standing tall, majestic in winter, heady in summer, and full of poetry spring and fall. I'm suddenly homesick for that tree!

Now, I wish I can rush the night and hurry up the sun!

Um, I'll sit up and wait for morning to come. Meanwhile, I keep watch over me. Over my baby.

And I'll be by your side, Ash!

Sweet, sweet girl!

I yawn. My eyelids droop, letting go …

"A gift? From whom?" Jed asks.

He's in tonight. He who sleeps in the guest room is waiting for my next move.

Kate's move? I get cynical these days. I'm ill-disposed to be in limbo, but I just don't seem to have the energy to pursue the divorce at this time. Also, can't pay the lawyer's fees right now.

He sees me pull the lush cashmere throw out of the gift box as he comes through my bedroom to get to his closet. The guest room closet is way too small for his wardrobe.

"Evelyn, um, Mrs. Norton," I say without looking up.

"You seeing her?"

I hear him scuff out of the room. Then I flip open the gift card: Keep warm, my dear Ashley. Take good care, love, Evelyn.

33

Her coppery gold hair aglow under the sun, her flimsy gown sails the breeze. She dashes forth, about to take wing. Behind her, I'm flapping to catch up.

She twitters like a lark. A peel of laughter rippling the air. Blue and dappling green, sky and earth whirling. Wild flower confetti over her, over me. I sprint after this giggly child who has made off with my heart.

Wa-it! Wait for me!

She hears me? She hears me not?

Panting, I fall behind, head over heels with laughter. Just then, a glimpse of her bare feet in the air.

Oh, dear! Poor, poor feet, scratched and scarred, her soles so very chapped!

Shoes, my girl, haven't you got shoes?

She pauses, turns around. I see the gathering cloud in her eyes, threatening rain.

Don't cry, oh, please don't!

I reach out for her ... so near and yet so far. My arms flailing, waking me. I open my eyes to a pale morning filtering in through the window blinds.

Must you come to me only in a dream, my girl? I sigh.

*   *   *

"Who-o are you talk ... talking to, Ash-ley?"

She stands by the door, goggling my way, her mouth open, her backpack against her feet on the floor. She is clutching her parka, stopping short of hanging it up on the wall peg.

How long has she been standing there?

"Hi, Kara!"

"Ashley, you were talking to yourself!"

She sidesteps the spot at the foot of the stairs and walks gingerly up to me, her eyes keen on my face. She does not spare a look at the pot of pomegranate dye simmering on the work table.

"Just, um, thinking aloud," I say lamely.

She gives me this wilting look that says, oh, yeah?

Bloody tiresome, you, Kara! My eyes shoot back.

I'm flushed but she can't tell for my face is steamed up by the sweet vapor of the bubbly, bursting pomegranate seeds bled to a brilliant crimson infusion. I turn to stare into a brew more radiant than cochineal red, lustier than vermillion, but I can almost see the deep burgundy when it's applied on silk. On cotton, it will be a ripe plum, or a shade of fuchsia, or ... I reach over to pick up my bottle of vinegar.

Splash! The pot topples over. The pomegranate brew spills like fresh blood. Over the hotplate, over the stainless steel work surface, splattering, sizzling ... Mindlessly, I grab the pot handle with my bare hand.

Ka-plunk!

Ouch! I dash over to the wash basin to run water over my hand. I turn back to look. The orange glow coil of the hot plate is hissing loudly. Viscous fluid singeing down the side of the hotplate, congealing. Brown like coagulated blood. Smoke curls up with a burnt fume.

"Ice! Let me get ice!" Kara cries.

She pulls out an ice tray from the under-counter fridge, dumps out the cubes. I take the hastily wrapped ice pack from her.

"Thanks!"

"Bad?"

A red hot handle has been scorched onto my palm. Numb and sore at the same time. Kara bends over to look.

"O-oh, that hurts!"

"So-o very stu-pid of me!"

She unplugs the hot plate. The electric coils darken, fizzling still. Bottom of the pot, the pomegranate brew is a gummy brown mess, sickly sweet.

"Ashley, won't you take some time off?"

Wipe off that smug look, Kara!

"Not right now!"

"Hey, how about taking a break before the baby comes? Think sea and sand, think white powder slope, ahem ..."

Whoa, not a good suggestion? She pauses, steals a look at me frowning, and says, "Just to get away from here a bit, okay?"

"Huh?"

"Ple-ase, Ashley. You're not yourself lately."

"Stuffs on my mind."

"It's, uh, something else."

"What else?"

"Like talking to yourself. To someone you think you see, perhaps?"

I shiver.

"You okay?"

"Just a chill. It'll pass."

She knits her brow, takes a step back.

"Ashley, there's something I, uh, I want to talk to you about," she says, lowering her eyes.

"Yes?"

"I'm gonna, uh, to quit Fine Arts. My dad thinks that I, uh, I gotta go into something that can find me a job."

"Um."

"Like, get a teacher's certificate or something."

The girl's turning red in the face.

I see that certain smile on my dad's face when he heard that I had chosen the convent. What safer path in life can there be?

"Kara, that doesn't mean that you give up what you truly like to do."

"Ashley, I didn't mean to leave you like, uh, like this," she sputters, "I'd have wanted to wait till after the holidays. It's just not gonna work, exams and all. And, there's this, uh, this other thing, you know ..."

She shakes her head as if to ward off whatever that's bugging her.

I no longer wish to know. An errant bee's buzzing inside my head, but I manage to say, "It's alright, Kara."

She looks relieved, but stares uneasily at her unfinished batik piece at one end of the work island next to my *tjanting* and the jar of wax.

"Oh, yes, I'll send in your studio grade. You've done well."

"Ashley, I do so enjoy working with you! Thanks for everything," she says sheepishly.

She throws her arms around me. Then, she whispers into my ear, "Take care, Ashley. Ple-ase, take care."

I hear the tremor in her voice. I want to hear no more of that. I turn to write her a check for her month's pay though she is quitting early.

"Thanks so very much!" She sounds as if she has a lump in her throat.

I perch on the edge of the stool, place my scalded palm on my lap, spreading the hurt. A cold chuckle rumbles up my throat. I tense up.

At the door, she turns back, "B-bye now, Ashley! T-take care."

Go now! Go!

As if I've just come to, I'm struck by the lingering quiver in Kara's voice. But what rouses me more is the chill that is creeping upon me. I shiver. A hollow gurgling seizes my throat. Choking, coughing, I stumble backward, wrap my arms around my body to stop my shakes. A searing pain shoots clear through. I open up my burnt palm. Red and blistered and ugly. Tears stream down my cheeks.

Don't cry, Ashley!

I'm here with you, always.

I shudder for there's a bite in the undertone as if she knows that she's all I've got. Then, soft kisses blowing in my ear ...

M-my girl?

*   *   *

I'm as parched as a heap of crackling leaves. Pacing the floor, I pause to stare at the wall hanging over the brick wall where there was once a window. The day's still young …

Wait till it's mellow, I tell myself.

Ah, mellow it is when the sun blazes its way beyond the jagged white peaks, etching a silhouette of tangerine glow against the closing dusk.

He'll come, then. I can almost hear the jangling of his tool belt.

As I'd gone to him at high noon … to our canopy bed draped in red velvet.

So he comes, his silhouette at the door …

Then what?

I'd gaze into his eyes where I see the endless blue mountains jutting up against a flaming sky. I'd hear him whisper: When night falls, you'll hear every dark stirring in the woods—the slightest flapping of wings, a hooting, a coyote's call, and you know you're not alone.

Is this your only fondling of the night?

Take in a deep breath, the scent of the ponderosa would lull you to sleep.

So, here we are, lone travellers crossing paths on our separate journeys. Shall we tarry a bit?

What about me?

Where're you going, my girl?

To where the sun shines.

She reaches out for my hand, but I feel no touch. Just a waft of chill air.

Come, now!

I close my eyes, take in a deep breath. Full of trepidation, I exhale slowly, then opening my eyes …

*   *   *

There she stands, in the dim surround of what looks like the underside of a staircase lit by a kerosene lamp hung on a haphazard nail. She has her back against the brick wall where a grid of sunlight punches in through a paned window. It cuts a bright swath over the crimson damask drapes flanking the opening. It slips over the lazy settee below and glides down onto the dusty-rose rug.

I squint to take her in against the backlight. Her face is as fresh as morning dew kissed by the first light of day. Her hair a dazzling coppery glow, her jeweled eyes a lambent blue. Same mesmerizing face I saw in my dream, and in the pool reflection of that Fall day in the park.

Standing before me, my girl, a softly radiant bloom! She is unaware that I'm not three feet away from her. I'm nowhere in the picture!

She looks around, startled by what she sees around her. A heap of dirt piled high on the floor at the back of the stairs, loose bricks stacked against the wall, a dirt-filled bucket nearby. The rug on which the billiard table stands in the middle of the room has been rolled up against the table legs. Dirt scattered over the wood plank floor underneath. A damp earthy smell fills the air.

"Whoa! What's happening here?"

She lowers her head, peering down into the dingy hollow under the stairs. Someone's crouching down there, spading up the soil. Dirt over his hair, over his sweaty undershirt, his rolled-up baggy pants on suspenders are smudged with dirt.

"What're you doo-ing, Big Roy?"

"Yoh, miss, mind yar skirt! All dirt here," he huffs, cocking his big head to look up at her. His voice is gruff, but his eyes are those of a puppy's.

Lifting up her skirt, she looks down at her slippers—a low-heeled satin pair, same fawn color as the pinafore dress she has on over a scallop-collared white blouse. Porcelain skin, tapering fingers, she looks more a daughter from a genteel household than a, um, ...

She, the girl in red?

Red, as in damask? I turn to the sunlit damask drapes framing the back window—folds of scarlet floral swirls against a deep crimson background. Like freshly spilled blood. I turn away.

Gathering up her skirt around her lithesome body, the girl steps back but does not leave.

"You going to the festival tomorrow?"

"Sure din, miss."

"Uh ... " She turns away.

He hops up from the hollow, squats down on the edge. He takes care not to lean against the stack of loose bricks he had dug up. He wipes his brow with the back of his hand, smearing dirt, then runs it over his bristled crew cut.

"Me coz Gopher, Goff, we call him, tells me he put em lamps all over da city," he says, chortling.

She turns to face him. She runs her fingers nonchalantly down her hair, but her rapt eyes betray her.

"Color ones like ya ever seen. He strings em up on da grandstand, and along em streets, all em one-hundred-feefty incandes ones, in each a em cars for da nite a da Music Trolley. Ten a em Tramway's biggest, says he. Whoa, big enough for em 22-piece, 25-piece bands, to ride up and down em streets nite a da concert ... " He lifts his eyes, staring at those bright lamps in his head.

She sees them, too, for her eyes sparkle.

"Ahem, and all em lamps in da Brown Palace Hotel, too," he goes on. "Dat ball room, Goff tells me, em chando-leers clink better dan icicos, and em lil globe lamps big like em ripe melons from Rocky Ford. Goff says he and em City Electric guys go in der to put up even more a em lamps for da fancy ball. Says em gents and ladies gonna dance after da big parade come last nite a da festival ..."

She butts in. "It's the Pa-rade of the Sla-ves of the Sil-ver Ser-pent! And, um, the Silver Serpent Ball's what they call it." Her voice turns flinty. Her words come out in little hard lumps. She swallows hard, clearing her throat.

Then she raises her eyes to that mystical creature only she can see, and breaks into soft strains, "Si-ilver silver serpent, King of the si-ilver serpent, light, oh light m-my heart, guide, oh guide m-my mind ... slave to you, si-ilver silver serpent ..."

Si-ilver silver serpent ... I hum along. The refrain comes so naturally.

She whirls around, throwing herself to her song. Her eyes glistening.

My heart misses a beat.

"Watch out, miss," Big Roy shoves the bucket of dirt out of her way.

"Si-ilver silver serpent ... slaves of the sil-ver serpent ..." She twirls right up to the billiard table nearly tripping over the rolled up rug. She steps on the roll, reaches up to turn on the three-lamp brass pendant light that hangs over the table. A green glow shines through the glass shades.

"Gloom be gone!" She commands as she throws her arms up with a flourish. Never mind the afternoon sun is slanting in brightly through the back window.

"Si-il-ver silver ser-r-pent ..."

She twirls around to the other side of the billiard table where stands an enormous mahogany sideboard against the wall. A run of her coppery gold hair flashes across the sideboard mirror. She throws a passing glance at the mirror, catches her own glittery eyes in the dizzying reflection. She twirls on ...

Those misty, lustrous blue eyes! I see in them a yearning like a whirling eddy you know not how deep, how dark.

"Sil-sil ..." She bursts out laughing as she twirls back to where Big Roy squats.

Her eyes watering so ...

He joins her, yelping like a puppy.

"Tell me, what did Goff say about lighting the floats? Fourteen of them, eh?" she asks abruptly. She dabs the corners of her eyes with her index fingers.

"Nah, Goff says nodin about em floats. Ya mean, da floats a da nite parade?"

"Um,"

"No electric lites on em floats, miss," Big Roy shakes his head. "Dey be carryin torches, candles. Same for em wheelmen da nite a da bicycles. Dey be carryin lanterns. Big, red, and round. I seen em Chinamen makin em lanterns out a paper down da street, whole big bunches a em."

He gets on his feet, holds his arms out in a circle to show her the size of the lantern. "Yay big, ever one a em."

"Errr ..." She turns her back to him.

"Ya gotta see for yarself, miss."

"No electric lights? Surely there gotta be electric lights on the floats. Gosh, I'd love to see the gold chariot float, the silver one, too, and the costumes of the King, the Queen, the Princes and the Princesses!" She purses her lips, then prattles on. "And the many Slaves they've got! Um, Sla-aves of the Sil-ilver Ser-r-pent ... I hear they got all their costumes made in France."

"Yoh, don't know nodin about dat, miss."

Footsteps shuffling down the stairs. Both of them stop short.

"What the ... what the racket's going on down there?" A woman's voice floats down.

"Hannah! Come here! Listen to Big Roy!"

A plump woman with a ruddy complexion and peppery gray hair tied in a bun shows up at the foot of the stairs.

"What's this? *Gott im Himmel*, what's happening here?" She cries out.

"Yoh, yoh, wa-watch yar steps!" Big Roy hollers.

Hannah skids on the scattered dirt as if on cue. She throws her arms up in the air. Fleshy arms, her flour-dusted brown sleeves are rolled up to her elbows. Flustered, she glares at the guy. He catches her scowl, quickly retreats under the stairs.

"What you think you're doing, Big Roy? Digging up the house, *ja?*" Hannah huffs. She tugs back her brown skirt as she bends down to look. Her starched white apron puckers up over her ample bosom.

"Open her up, she says," he mutters into the hole.

"What?"

"Dat's what ma'am says." He looks up, grinning.

"*Ja?* Turning everything upside down?"

The girl starts to giggle. Hannah turns around.

"Miss Lena! I thought you'd gone out this afternoon. What for, you down here? Got nothing better to do than to listen to his Goff stories? You see for yourself parade and all tomorrow, *ja?*"

Lena your name?

Lena, my girl!

Lena bites her lips, looks dispiritedly at her slippers. Hannah pauses, wipes her hand on her dish cloth draped over her left shoulder. She comes up to peer into the girl's face.

"You okay, Miss Lena?"

The girl nods, looking glum.

"Guests having drinks now with the girls in the parlor, Miss Lena, you know that, *ja?*" Hannah shoots her eyes up the ceiling.

"Hey, look!" Big Roy yells. He's sweeping dirt off a half-buried plank of timber with his bare hands.

"Hush! They can hear you upstairs," Hannah says raising a chubby finger over her mouth.

"A trap door!"

He twists and yanks loose the bent nails holding down the plank.

Ka-plunk! He pulls the plank up and leans it against the brick wall, sprinkling dirt.

The women step back, then edge up gingerly.

I can't take my eyes off Lena. Her face is flushed, her eyes listless. The flurry of good spirits that had lit up the basement moments ago has all but vanished.

"Here's what ma'am says gotta be ..." he mumbles as he looks down at what he has uncovered.

"What's that?"

"Let me see!" Lena peers over Hannah's shoulder.

Big Roy leaps upon his feet, grabs the hanging kerosene lamp from the nail. He shines it down a small dug trough, about waist high in depth, and not more than two feet by three.

Lena gasps, staggers back. She looks away.

"Dat's it. Jus a hole in da ground. Ma'am says she'd it dug when da house a goin up."

"Whatever for?" Hannah asks.

"Hide dins, I reckon."

"What she wanna hide?"

"Somedin about cases a Californinia liquor comin in on da train tomorro. Gotta store em some place good, she says."

"Tomorrow? *Nein, nein!* The train's not going to haul no freight tomorrow! All the cars are going to carry people. Heard they're expecting thousands to come from all over to the festival. Some are already here. I see new faces upstairs," Hannah says.

"Anyway, we just gotta some cases in last week," she goes on. "You brought them down yourself, Big Roy! You gotta them stored away in that cupboard back there, *ja?*"

She points to a tall cupboard with a big red ribbon bow over a padlock tucked at one rear corner of the basement.

"Ma'am says liquor comin tomorro for da yello costume party. Dat's what she a told me," he protests, sweat and dirt over his brow.

"*Ja, ja,* I know all about the party Saturday after the festival. Jam tarts and custard tarts and mincemeat tarts and whatever more ... " Hannah rattles on. She stares dubiously into the hole. "Liquor down there? Sure she said so, *ja?*"

"Dat's what she says."

He spanks his hands over his pants, slapping dirt off.

Hannah shakes her head at the mess of a place.

"Ugh, you best clean up good right away, Big Roy. Gentlemen may fancy a game of billiard down here, *ja?*"

"Nah, ma'am says no guest down here til we get liquor. Maybe after da festival, cause I gotta go and have me some fun. Hee, hee!"

"Three days of festival. When're you gonna clean up?"

"Later, ma'am says she gonna tell me. Jus sweep off loose dirt rite now. Dat's what she says."

"Yellow costume party!" Lena cries. "Ah, I've got the most beau-ti-ful gown for the party! A gorgeous sunflower gown, bright as the noon sun!"

She hums, breaks into a little waltz. Lifting the skirt of her dream gown, she twirls around in the tight space.

Shubert, Lena?

Big Roy's grinning ear to ear, watching her. Hannah glowering at him.

"Mind your step, Miss Lena! Come, we go now."

She reaches out to nudge the girl's elbow as she whirls dreamily by.

A swan! She glides like a swan, serene in her movement.

She slips past me. I see that her eyes are shut. She folds up her waltzing after a final twirl and walks stiltedly up the stairs. My heart trails after her, after the wake of excitement she has left behind.

Hannah follows her. As she's about to shuffle up the stairs, she turns around.

"By the by, Big Roy, you seen my bottle of Rough-on-Rats, *ja*?"

"Nope, Hannah!"

"Been what I came down here for. Looking for it all over. Don't seem to find it nowhere ..."

Darkness falls before my eyes ... The stage lights have dimmed, the curtains dropped in a hurry. A period scene has shut down. I feel unfinished, abandoned.

Natural light spills mutely down the stairs into the basement. I turn to look for the paned window where the sun had slid in. A brick wall is in its place. No sun-swank crimson drapes in sight, just my wall hanging covering up the brick-in window. Darkly menacing, that imprint of a big rusty nail in the path of an approaching tire tread.

Florescent tubes shed a dull light over my cluttered work island. In my mind's eye, the brass pendant lamp is still gleaming, the glass shades radiating a green glow over the green felt billiard table. The spirited chatter of an idle afternoon hums on ...

I've been thrown upon the crest of a wave. Now I've got to chase the tide out to look for a festival that had come to pass a long, long time ago. Riding high ... the pitch is so feverish, so rousing that I must go, right away, go see it for myself.

Go, go see it!

I grab my coat and head out. At the door, I glance back at the forbidding gloom under the stairs.

Why the bother to bury the liquor when it was for a party at week's end? The thought flits through my mind. But I'm in a hurry and rush on out.

Outside, the afternoon sun is showering gold over the asphalt. As I'm about to get into my car, I catch sight of a pair of legs in scruffy jeans walking down the alley. I pause in spite of myself. I study his gait—his tool belt strapped low, swaying gently to the movement of his hips. My heart throbs to the beat of his strides. Sun and breeze trailing him, shining into my eyes.

He sees me. He nods.

I turn quickly to get into my car.

Go now, hurry!

I turn on the ignition. When I pull out the alley, I can't help feeling that I'm about to miss something. I'm to miss the very hour of the day when I'd relish a quiet glimpse into his eyes.

Maybe, not so quiet ...

Hurry! Oh, hurry, please!

34

I walk the narrow corridor along the perimeter of the Denver Public Library. Someone paces about in this tight passageway framed by tall block columns. He's studying the row of shadows on the wall. Chuckling to himself, he digs one hand noisily into the crumpled paper bag he's carrying.

A caged animal without a cage. Somewhere, a mother's heart is in pieces. I look away and walk on.

Hurry!

Yes, Lena!

The front entrance is around the corner.

The Parade. Oh where?

Inside the library, a high ceiling bright with rows of square light fixtures stares down a central hall, a long thoroughfare of sorts. People entering, people leaving, both ends of the hall.

I look back to where I'd come in, where daylight stays out. I walk fast, rushed along by the foot traffic, and by this bottom-of-the-shaft-shut-in feeling that has come over me. The tall volume of space on either side is boxed up into what looks like levels of brightly lit reading halls.

A low hum reverberates in the hallway. I look down at the black grid flooring. Dark clouds swarming, I pine for natural light.

Where to?

"Elevator's end of the hall, to your right," someone says.

I got out the elevator. 5th floor. A sign above the open doors: Western History and Genealogy.

A large oil painting of snow-capped mountains hangs in the foyer. Prints of historic trains line the side wall. On exhibit in glass cases, an antique model train and railroad memorabilia.

Inside the reading room, a sea of soft milk white lamps anchors the ceiling, static light that drowns out the hour of the day. In a heartbeat, I walk up a window. At my feet, the sprawl of the city. I gasp. Towers punctuate the sky, building upon building standing tall, squatting low, clustering side by side, apartment blocks, shoulder to shoulder. Traffic skirts the Civic Center Park, crisscrossing the streets, coursing along, fanning out. Birds skimming over tree tops.

All this, so suddenly new?

I look west, past the city hall's gold eagle clock tower to where the Front Range lies. High clouds, pearl white light, faint blue sky tinged with an orange glow. My eyes linger over the faraway vista—endless blue mountains, peak upon pristine peak. Almost a dream. I'm inexplicably overtaken with nostalgia.

How I pine for the cool tingling air, up where the light sparkles!

Shall we go?

I turn away from the window and head towards the librarian's desk.

"What can I help you with?" he asks with a smile.

"Um, anything about the Festival of Mountain and Plain?" Words tumble out of my mouth.

"We can look up the newspapers. You know the year?"

"1895."

"Let's go to the Post. I don't think, uh, we have them digitalized as yet. They're available on microfilm."

He leads the way to a bank of filing cabinets, scans through the labels and pulls open a drawer. He takes out a box and hands it to me.

"It took place in the Fall," he says helpfully. "That may well be the very first festival back then."

I sit in front of the microfilm reader, load the reel and start to scroll. The reel turns. The newsprint zips across the screen. My heart pounds. It leaps up my throat at the October 16 headline: "THE FESTIVAL OPENED ... DENVER IN HER GLORY. In Every Way an Event for Colorado ... Thousands of Visitors in Town To-day. A BRILLIANT EXHIBITION."

Ah, my Queen City!

Show me! Quick!

Silver and gold ... silver and gold ... Fa-lala-lala ... si-ilver-r and ...

The microfilm scrolls on. The monochromic black newsprint races past, jumbling words and zipping through line drawings. A big blur swarms before my eyes.

All of a sudden, a blue sky punches through the dizzying gray. A blast of festive colors vaults out of the screen—yellow and white, gold and silver. Tinsels and streamers dance in the breeze, shimmering in the autumn sun, casting a holiday spell upon the merry crowd. A patchwork quilt of colors shuttling past, enlivened with sound and motion—women in long gowns, fancy bonnets, woolen shawls over their shoulders, dangling little drawstring purses; checks and stripes and solids, men in suits and hats, some carrying canes. People saunter along, gawking at buildings so shrouded with decorations that they can only be made out by the pedestrians and carriages gathered at their entrances. Even street lamps are gaily adorned, and the shop windows on Sixteenth ...

Ah-h-h, lo-ook! Over there, the mannequin in the Denver Dry Goods window! Isn't she gorgeous? Gosh, her gold crown! Her snow white satin gown, who-oa! She looks so-o alive, like you, like me ...

Oh, yes, Lena!

See that? A shield of silver by her side. Oh, so-o beautiful! That's the State seal emblazoned on it.

She wants me to know.

And the shield of fruits and fresh produce she's carrying ... ah, to show that ours is a state of plenty. Oh, yes!

Let's cross the street. That Ballin and Ransohoff store! Look, all decked out in silver and gold!

Ah, and that Paris Building, over there, on California! Whoa, isn't it just splendid ... all frilly yellow and shiny white? See it?

This girlish voice from the past, babbling with glee, is bent on showing me the gala of her lifetime.

Oh, yes, Lena, I see! I see it all!

Her exuberance is compelling. I hanker for more—more of her that comes shining through from a bygone era, a bygone world.

Yet, might it be, um, that she's seeing through my eyes instead? And for the very first time? That she had, after all, missed the festivities that she so looked forward to. Now, in front of the microfilm reader, she's conjuring up the festivities as seen through others' eyes.

Please, oh, please read on!

The microfilm reader humming ...

Cable cars rattling along the overcrowded streets. A four-horse carriage plods its way around a corner, nearly knocking down a passerby. Horses neigh, hoofs kicking in the air. Scuffling and shuffling, throngs gather along16th and Larimer.

Watch where ya're goin!

Make way, make way!

Out-of-towners pour in from the Union Station onto the 17th, along the parade route. Mountains of people moving. Someone shouts above the din. People jostling on the pavements, heads turn, eagerly awaiting.

At Colfax and Broadway, the State flag and the Old Glory flying high above the grandstand decked out with buntings in festive yellow and white. Waves upon waves of spectators swarm into the neighboring streets. Musicians from the bandstand charge up the air with Stars and Stripes Forever.

Across the grandstand, a sea of children gather like a flock of twittering birds. Dressed in red, white and blue, they sit in formation of ...

A living flag! That's it, a living flag!

Ah, sweet Michael, are you here?

You see what I see?

Oh, The Star Spangled Banner!

Are you in one of the private boxes in front?

All the fine-suited gentlemen ... Mayor McMurray, Governor McIntire. Are you with them, Michael?

You'll Senator Norton be, won't you?
Norton?
Yes, yes, you will. I know you will.
Oh, where, where're you, my sweet Michael?
Michael Norton, Sr.?
Le-ena ... you ... the girl in red?
That evening, at my studio's opening?
Here comes the Parade! The Pageant of Progress!
Sil-ver-rr and go-old ... sil-ver and go-old!

She breaks into this rapturous refrain, warbling to the marching beat of drums and the rhythm of synchronized steps, the trotting of hoofs, the fluttering of flags.

All eyes are on the Marshall, the Grand Marshall, and the mounted police. They ride in formation to the heralding trumpets and drum roll.

Look at em smashing uniforms!

Look at em beautiful harnesses on em horses!

So-o handsome!

Chatter swells, buzzing like bees ...

Hush, hush!

The military band leading the parade strikes the first note. Trumpets blare, cymbals clang, drums go a-rap-tapping, piccolos and flutes and clarinets weave through the rising resonance of horns and trombones and tubas rich and deep. The big brass gleaming under the sun. The big marching tune sparkling the air. The air bubbling with cheers and applause and laughter.

Lena's taking in the magic. She rides the crest of the waves, melting into a feverish pitch. I melt in with her.

A horse neighs.

Look! The float of cliff dwellers!

What!

I see it now. A horse-drawn float comes into view carrying a paper mâché landscape of canyons and mesas. Earthen dwellings nestling under the cliffs.

Em Pueblo settlers! Someone yells from the sidewalk.

Next comes a troupe of Indians in brilliant feathered headgears, red and green jackets and leggings, striped blankets of rainbow colors on their backs. They fall in step with the drumbeats, huge plumes fluttering.

Utes and Pueblos. Big Roy told me they're coming to the parade. Look yonder, what's coming up?

PIKES PEAK OR BUST!—announce the big letters on the covered wagon and the gold fever hitches right on.

Pikes Peak! Pikes Peak! Pikes Peak! The crowd chants in unison. Loud cheers gush out.

Whoa, Cherry Creek Gold!

Trotting into view is a float of glittering gold foil with a wavy blue ribbon that runs through it. Oh my, oh my! A blanket of gold dust carpeting the banks of the Creek. It blinds the eye and gladdens the heart. Right here in the city, folks! Gold rush, right here! The crowd breaks into a thunderous applause.

Hurrah, hurrah for gold!

She claps excitedly.

Big band music starts up from behind. The crowd goes wild, clapping, cheering.

On its heels are pioneers with ox-teams, wagons and stagecoaches. Then come cowboys on horsebacks, branding wagons, and prospectors with pickaxes ... The boom takes off.

Sil-ver and go-old ...

GOLD!

Oh, yes, I've got gold! Pikes Peak gold, double eagles, huh! You twirl a piece, massage its gleaming faces, flick it between your fingers—peak and eagle and peak and eagle and peak ...

A-ah, it's tingling against my burning flesh, my bosoms hot and cold and hot and cold ... I laugh heartily for it tickles so.

Oh, you, teaser you!

You look at me with burning eyes. Am I your dreamiest little blue columbine? My long spurs filled with nectar, just for you ....

Now, I see it in your eyes, that thrilling glint of gold! So, Michael, you, too, must have come quite a ways to appreciate the sweet jingle of gold.

Yeah, it's like catching sight of a festive bonfire, it stays on your mind. Forever, huh?

Ah, sweet Michael, I shine! Just like gold, I shine splendid, don't I?

Hee-eh-eh ...

Huh?

Breathlessly, she coos.

A temptress of the flesh! Coy and tantalizing and cynical all at once. I'm taken aback. This sunbeam girl, yet a child, who lights my way to the parade of a lifetime has suddenly fallen into shadow, leaving me dumbfounded.

This new voice muses on, oblivious of the Cowboy Band striking up a stomping tune. Oblivious of the oohs-and-ahs over the thirty-piece band's huge metal drum mounted on a coach drawn by four small horses costumed in yellow.

Oblivious of me. All of a sudden, I feel I'm eavesdropping. Yet, I listen on.

Gold, my glittering gold, is nothing next to you, my sweet Michael. Nothing, you hear?

You're my greater gold. Always.

What worth to me is my gold? I ask. Ah, these twenty dollar double eagles, they sit, cold and heavy, in my palm, beaming at me! They turn green every prying eye, and jingle as good as the ones in madam's pocket as she goes swishing about in her noisy taffeta skirt.

Still, they pale next to you, sweet Michael ... for, indeed, you're my true gold. My one and only love!

Now, where, sweet Michael, oh, where're you?

Oh, where ...?

Ah, speaking of love ... Lo-ve?

Her voice fades.

Lena, oh, Lena!

Silence.

A chasm opens up, dividing us.

Are you the girl in red, Lena?

You-u-u ... g-gir-rl-rl ... in ... r-r-red-r-red-r-red ... ?

An echo bounces back from afar.

Lena, please, oh, please stay!

The chasm grows, dark and wide, as unbridgeable as life and death.

I sit bolted upright in front of the blank microfilm reader. Empty and alone. A flapping noise of the film strip wakes me. The roll has spun to it's end. Mechanically, I set it to rewind, then to scroll forward. I scan through the pages I had missed earlier, wanting the festivities to resume.

Waiting for her ...

Wednesday, October 17, 1895. City at night. I read: "In glittering letters formed by hundreds of incandescent lamps the words 'Mountain and Plain Welcome' dazzled the eyes of thousands as they stood boldly out on the capitol building last night. ... From the high ground over the viaducts the city looked like a mammoth map of red, green, blue, violet and white light. The dome of the state house twinkled above a very sea of color. Sixteenth Street, from Larimer up, was a brilliant kaleidoscope of checkered blaze. ... "

I pause to listen.

Silence.

I read on: "But, ah, the trolley musicale!"

The trol-ley mu-u-si-cale?

She throws me this silken cord of a voice, so titillating, so tenuous, reverberating from nowhere.

Wake up, Lena!

The trol-ley musi-cale? Trams, all lit up?

Yes, in ropes of electric lights ... Let's go watch!

Go-o wat-ch?

Yes! Come, let's go!

She surely must want to watch a spectacle she had missed in life. After all, she's been clamoring for it.

Hey, Lena, what about the Silver Serpent, the King, the Queen, and their slaves? The Parade of the Silver Serpent?

Silence.

I hold my breath, listening up ... Her mood, like the tide, ebbing, flowing, washing up snippets of memories.

A small giggle rippling through, interspersed with her intoning Big Roy's gruff voice: *Me coz Gopher, Goff, we call him, hmm, says he put all em lamps, all em one-hunred-feefty incandes ones, in each a em cars for da nite a da Music Trolley. Ten a em Tramway's biggest, says he.*

Hee-ee-ah-hee ...

Whoa, big enough for em 22-piece, 25-piece bands, to ride up and down em streets nite a da concert ...

Silence.

Then, in her own subdued voice: *Ah, Big Roy tells me so ... that afternoon before ...*

The silken cord's straining.

Before what?

Be-before ... bee-fore ...

A sigh escapes.

Before what, Lena?

She's picking up some dusty jigsaws of memory.

Wh-ere's m-my go-old? M-my GO-OLD, oh where's ...?

Her shuddering cry reverberates in my head like an echo rumbling through a canyon. It sends chill right through me.

"Miss, are you alright?"

I jolt up. The librarian who has helped me earlier looks at me intently over the microfilm reader. A small twitch at the corner of his mouth.

"Yes, why?"

"You're trembling, miss."

"Uh-huh?"

I turn instead to look for *her*—she who has blazed her way into my heart. Her eyes, sapphire blue, her hair bright like copper under the sun.

But, her face? Her face is as hazy as mist at dawn.

She's no illusion, I know. But ...

The screen glares. The machine is running blank. The film has run to its end.

"You had your eyes closed for a long time,"

"I, uh, I must have dozed off."

"Anything I can do, miss?"

"Oh, no, thanks! I can manage."

The machine clatters as I unwind the reel, dislodge the film roll and put it back in its box. My hands shake the whole time. I clasp them tight over my laps, staring at the blank screen.

"Miss, I can put that away for you, if you wish."

"Thank you."

I avert his eyes, and get up from my seat. Heavy and stiff, I pick up my coat, my purse, in slow motion.

Before heading out the door, I'm drawn to the window to look west, to where the darkening ranges lie silhouetted against an expanse of blood orange luminosity. In that very flaming moment, I hear the mountains calling out, *Come home, mountain child, come home ...*

A tug in my heart ... as if I'm longing for an embrace.

The sundown glow is waning. The city lights are coming on, pale against a dusky sky. Down below, the holiday lights of the City and County Building are calling up a season of good cheer. I cling onto this fringe between light and dark even as it is fading before my eyes.

As I pause, a trepidation comes over me. A fog is creeping into my head. A fog that eats away one's senses, leaving one stranded in the dark, lost and stunned.

I shudder, for on this day I've crossed the bridge of time and space to the other world that I hadn't known existed.

I'm looking for a way back.

35

A train of images streaming past ... bands marching, hoofs trotting ... sunny faces, beaming eyes ...

Three little papooses swaddled in sleep not roused by the brassy trombones, nor the brilliant piccolos. Not even a twitch on their sweet faces amid the stirring *drum-drum-drum* and the guttural war chanting! Colorful plumed headdresses fluttering, thumping a dance with bows and arrows, spinning a turn here, throwing a twist there.

Drum-drum-drum ... bear dancing, waddling along, shuffling past. Coming through ... throngs of school children marching, waving, laughing.

He-eh, eeh ...he-eh!

I roll onto my side, borne by a crescendo of excitement.

The gold dome is ablaze, the city aglow. A lit canvas ... a sea of twinkling red, green, blue and white light lifting the capitol building out of the night. And the night carries on ...

A river of brightly lit red lanterns snaking through the streets—a thousand and more cyclists on their bikes, red lanterns borne over their shoulders. Bands on trolleys lit with rope-lights striking up breezy tunes as they course along the city streets. The crowd applauding ...

Dazzling floats sailing down the streets. Music from heaven drifting in the air—a harpist playing atop a splendid float bedecked with garlands. At her feet, musicians strumming lutes, serenading with flutes.

Under crystal chandeliers, gentlemen in tuxedos clicking polished heels, bowing low, taking to the dance floor sweeping gowns, fancy slippers. Waltzing the perfumed night ...

Fa-lala-lala ... si-ilver-r ... Silver and gold ... si-ilver-r and gold ... fa-lala-lala ...

Oh, more! Please!

Starry eyes ...

I turn to her, eager for her eyes.

Cl-ack! A lightning bolt cleaves down, out of nowhere, wiping away every coy smile, dispelling every charmed moment.

Eeegh-egh-egh! Woe-ooh-woe!

An unearthly cry rips the night, reverberating from some bowels dark and deep ...

I open my eyes stark wide, looking into emptiness. Darkness swirls, my head throbbing ...

Woe-ooh-woe!

My teeth clattering ...

A muffled sob next to my pillow. Then, a groan. I shudder, roll myself up to cocoon under the comforter. Listening to my own ragged breathing ...

Please, no more ... no more throes of the night!

A dead calm follows, heavy as a pall. After an eternal while, the eerie calm loosens its grip. The pall has let drop. A sigh of relief.

Still, I pull the pillow over my head and force my mind to the freight train that rumbled through my Ottumwa nights. I had peeked out the window many a time and saw the long line of coal cars rolling past. Dark loads moving under a pale moon, going places.

Those wakeful hours had dragged on. Tossing and turning on my steel-frame bed, I had listened out to the loud snort of the approaching horn, to the shrill whistle that blistered the night.

A shriek. Some sharp wheels screeching the rail?

The train ... it's only the train, I murmur.

Wheels grinding close ... closer, grating past ...

I, too, am gone. Gone with that rumbling train into a drowsy sleep.

I wake up with a heavy body and a light head. Take in a deep breath. Exhale slowly. Close my eyes. Not letting go, yesterday's fun on the streets.

Hmm ... I had dreamt a very old dream last night, a most sumptuous old dream, full of joy and laughter.

And *she* was with me!

I stir to find my legs, spread my hands to touch the small mound on my belly. A surge of warmth comes over me. I picture a tender young shoot sprouting.

The morning sun washes over my window. A new day to pursue old dreams. I crawl out of bed humming, *Si-ilver and go-old ... fa-lala-lala, fa-lala-lala ...*

Sunlit copper hair, star sapphire eyes. Smiling, a resplendent peony in bloom ... Yet I can't quite put together a picture of her face in my head, just a feeling that there's a dazzling radiance about her.

How ... how can this be?

I've got this yearning for her. She who steeps my nights in festivities and makes restless my days. Yet, I've no picture of her face in my head!

Like a mellow wine, the bouquet of my dream lingers, urging yet another sip.

Lena, you here?

I walk past the guest room without looking in. *Si-ilver and gold ... fa-lala-lala, fa-lala-lala ...* I don't quite remember when was the last time I ran into Jed. I hurry down the kitchen to look for breakfast.

Champagne snow shimmering in the air. It powders my face, my hair. Soft sun smooching ... But I'm in no mood to relish. I so long for her eyes, for her rippling laughter. I walk briskly to the Library.

Straight up to the 5th floor where we were just yesterday. I turn on the microfilm reader. News prints scrolling, running a murky stream of black and white. I perch on the edge of my seat, hold my breath to wait for the burst of color, for the music to start up and cheers to roar.

Come on, Lena!

I shift in my seat. My eyes follow the newsprint listlessly. Words strung into sentences, sentences into paragraphs. Line drawings illustrate the carnival scenes, flat and drab and lifeless. Where's the hilarious fun with the allegorical Silver Serpent and its many Slaves? Where's the exuberance, the palpable pride?

Where're you, Lena?

I read on, nonetheless. Some tidbits. Any tidbits.

J. Carl Mohr suicides by swallowing morphine after quarreling with wife who had left him … J.G. Kilpatrick drops dead of an apparent heart attack … J. H. McLain company of Canton, Ohio files lawsuit against C. A. Creighton and John J. Huddart for $654,07 for failure to pay for building materials used in the construction of the Dolores county court house … Maine Mutual Life Insurance files lawsuit against George Root and others to recover $1,758.40 which they had collected as agents of the company … Jefferson Water and Power Company incorporates with an initial stock holding of $100,000 … a 7-year old boy missing from home, thought to have followed the Indians to the City Park … Bronco Jim has been found drunk and beaten after the Parade of the Slaves of the Silver Serpent … a driver is crushed by stomping horse … complaints against balking horses used in the parade … casualties of broken bones, sprained ankles, a head concussion sustained by a woman cyclist …

News stories with no rhyme nor rhythm, like yesterday, like today. Then, this: Boarder Reported Missing …

I bolt up to read: Galena Saber, 16, who goes by the name of Lena, was reported missing October 18, by Cybil Thiel, madam of a classy parlor on Holladay Street. Miss Saber, a celebrated beauty of the house, is rumored to be the mistress of a prominent local businessman with political ambitions. It is speculated that she had planned her departure as her personal belongings were found missing. Her disappearance was not noted until the last day of the Festival due to the many goings-on in the house.

O-oh, Lena!

I see now your face in the sideboard mirror, the shine of tears, the glimmer of yearning. Twirling, laughing, you filled the basement with a weepy, simmering pitch ... Big Roy was watching, saw and heard none, the day before the festival opened. Hannah, too. She saw only the dirt scattered over the rolled up rug.

Lena, would you have turned around, gone upstairs, packed your bags, and run away from it all?

Where would you have gone?

Not to the Parade. You were at the Parade with me only yesterday and, um, for the very first time.

Not to him. You were looking for him then.

Now, where, sweet Michael, oh, where're you?

Are you in one of those private boxes in front?

All the fine-suited gentlemen ... Mayor McMurray, Governor McIntire. Are you with them, Michael?

You'll Senator Norton be, won't you?

I see now, Lena, you were looking out for yourself ... for a new life.

Where would you have gone when you've every reason to stay? Stay for the Parade. For him.

I scroll on. Scanning the pages. An entry on October 21, 1895 reads:

Famous Madam Fell to Her Death. Cybil Thiel, age 48, famed madam of established Holladay house of "Gents' furnishings," fell to her death down a flight of stairs around midnight of October 19. Earlier that Saturday evening the house was hosting the much publicized Yellow Costume Party held to poke fun at the legislature which had ordered the ladies of pleasure to mark themselves by wearing yellow. The accident occurred after the boarders and guests had retired to their rooms. The police was summoned to the scene when the house was roused by a loud crash and found her at the bottom of the stairs. The death is ruled a misadventure.

Another death? I gasp.

Where, oh, where were you then, Lena?

Scanning ... October 24, 1895.

A small entry reads: Madam Cybil Thiel, Red Light Queen, laid to rest. A small crowd gathered at the Fairmont Cemetery yesterday afternoon to say goodbye to the famous madam. Pastor Arnold Swift recited the scripture at the burial ceremony.

I scroll on, scrutinizing column by column, page after page.

Anything more about Lena?

Scrolling ...

Stop!

October 25, 1895, front page headline: City Mourns Michael Norton.

The City mourns the death of prominent Denver businessman and civic leader Michael Norton. He is lauded for his contribution to city planning, his success in banking and commerce, and his efforts in waging a clean-up campaign against corruption and prostitution. It has been widely speculated that he was to be appointed U.S. Senator before his untimely passing, at age 35. He died of a massive stroke on October 24. He is survived by his wife, Mary Hayes, daughter of Denver business tycoon Robert Hayes. The couple is expecting their first child. A private funeral service is being planned. The family remains in seclusion.

Whoosh!

A spinning top flings loose inside my head: *Whir-rrr ... whir-rrr ... whir-rrr ...*

My eyes glaze over. Cowered on the floor, the wreck of a fetal posture, the wasted face furrowed with fear. I saw that visage in the grainy old photo Mrs. Norton put in front of me. And, again, in the Michael I had found in my basement the night of my studio's opening. It's a look I have been trying to wipe off my mind.

I close my eyes only to hear Mrs. Norton's choked-up murmur: It's not natural, n-not na-tural ... She was adamant in telling me that it was a hundred-year old death that has come back to haunt.

Did you see h-her? She had asked.

Who?

The gi-irl in red.

"Who's this girl in red?" Detective Cohen had asked the day after Michael's passing.

Nobody seemed to know, or could recall what she looked like, except that she was stunning.

"Stunning?"

"Stunningly beautiful."

"And she wore red."

Lena, my girl!

Michael Sr. was found dead in the house, why did he come at all?

Did he come to look for you, Lena?

Whir-rrr ... whir-rrr ... whirr-rrr ... The top spins on.

I lean forward, my eyes burning into the screen, scanning ... page after page. The film keeps on rolling ... days slip by, then months. No more news of Galena Saber. A missing boarder was forgotten.

The screen blurs into a running gray. The humming stops. The film roll has rattled to an end. A blinding glare punches out of the screen. I turn off the machine.

Whir-rrr-rrr ... rrr-rrr...

Lena, could it be that you had not left the house at all?

Were you there with your *sweet Michael* the day he passed away?

My girl, what really happened, huh?

Why the horrified look on his face?

I stop. Ask no more. I rather dream dreams that take my breath away, day into night into day ...

I step outside into a translucent haze—a shroud that is white and bright and mute. And vast. I reach for my sunglasses. Shades over my eyes. Hidden and safe. The air is a cold wet hand over my brow. I wipe off the sweat with a quick sweep of my scarf.

Footsteps behind me? I look back. It's only the breeze that tosses up my scarf. A waft of fine white powder puffs over my face. It quiets my flush. I sigh. Easy now ...

Forget his wretched face. Their wretched faces. Ghastly both.

I only want to hear my girl laugh. Such a happy laugh, like silver bells tinkling.

My coat flies open. I tuck it close to my body, wrap my arms snug around. Trudging on, my legs slow.

Alongside the library, a gray figure huddles in a wedge of the pallid light that has slanted down between the columns of the long corridor. A man strolls past with his dachshund. The sausage dog jumps up, snarls at where the shadow slumps into day. The man tugs at the leash without a word, without looking. The dog hushes, spins around to make out as if he's chasing his tail. But I see that he's looking up at me surreptitiously, growling under his breath.

I look down at my feet and see no shadow. The noon sun is overhead.

The man turns, nods at me with a polite smile. The dog wags his tail. They stroll on.

The traffic at midday crawls along Broadway. I pick up my pace, cross the street to my parked car. A light dusting of snow over its hood. I get in, start the wind shield wiper and pull out. What looks like a parking ticket flies off, but I don't care.

Lena's waiting for me!

My back door is ajar. Fresh foot prints on the steps down. Nothing moves. Not a sound. I look down the alley. A Mile High truck is parked near the dumpster.

I walk down the steps gingerly, listening up. A rasping, gurgling sound grumbles through the door in short spurts. I press close to peep into my lit basement. Someone is standing at the bottom of the stairs, back to the door, shoulders riding up and down, wheezing loudly. He has one hand grasping the stair rail as if he is trying to pull himself up the stairs.

I push the door wide open. The guy jerks around. I stumble backwards. Stiff limbed and loose jointed, he flails like a yanked puppet. I stop short.

"Jed?"

Sweat beads over his brow, face white as a sheet, his eyes dart about furtively.

"You alright?"

He opens his mouth. No word comes.

"Sit down." I take his arm to guide him to my swivel stool by the work table.

"No, no! I, uh, I ..."

He swerves around, grabs my shoulder and lumbers towards the door.

"A-ir, a-ir!"

We stagger out into the open air together. He lets go of me to lean against the door jamb. Eyes shut, he manages one shallow breath, then another.

"Asthma?"

"Ugh, ugh ..."

A twitch at the corner of his mouth.

"Got your Albuterol?"

He shakes his head.

"Som-some-thing, uh, in the-ere ..."

He shudders, his eyes stark wide. In his shadowed irises, a flicker of fear leaps up. He's staring darkly. It's as if he has turned his sight inward and is seeing things inside his head.

Then he winces, as if to shutter off what he's looking at. He turns away to avoid my eyes, but I catch his grimace. Fidgeting, he edges away from the open door. From me.

"You'd left the door unlocked, " he says after a bit.

Did I?

I'm taken aback by his steely tone. He throws a glance at me.

An edgy look crosses his face. He turns away, puffing loudly, then squints at his watch.

"Gotta go!"

"Sure you're okay?"

He steals a look back into the open door, clambers up the steps as if someone's at his heels. I spot the chill glint in his eyes.

"Why did you come, Jed?"

It is within his earshot, but he walks on. My eyes follow him till he turns out the alley. Then I step back in and look around. I turn to lock the door as I always do when I come in or get out.

Lena, you here?

I can hear a pin drop but I get no drift of her. I pick myself up to climb the stairs.

Up in the gallery, a red glow permeates the floor. My holiday gala piece of giant amaryllis is holding court. Luminously red, spiked with deep yellow stamens, the blooms at their peak proffering joy and the luscious life.

Ah, the luscious life!

I walk up to the glass front. Jed is walking hurriedly towards his blue BMW parked by the curb. He seems none the worse for what had happened. He pauses to survey the parked cars on both sides of the street. Then he gathers his overcoat, and is about to get into what he fondly calls his Z4. He stops short, turns around to glance into my gallery. His downturn mouth gives his face a look of scorn. He sees me looking out at him. Biting his lips, he turns to get into his car.

I step back. Like a burrower, I scurry down my hole. Jed, too. He scoots off, fast as a squirrel on the chase.

One may think that he has seen a ghost.

It's only me, Jed?

Still, I look behind me.

I step up front again and stand awhile looking out. The sky is opening up though it is only a narrow band of blue that I can see above the buildings. I squint at the drenching light.

A bright new light, as soothing as warm tea.

I inhale deeply, taking it in. A buoyant feeling comes over me as if this is how it must feel after a drink of the most luscious light in a long, long while. I feel like laughing out loud. Instead, I chortle under my breath. Cars roll along the shiny wet asphalt making muffled splashing noises.

Holiday shoppers are about, carrying bags and boxes, walking past, looking in, eyes bright with the season's bidding. I step away from the glass front. They peer into my gift corner filled with things to indulge the holiday spirit. They puzzle over the "Close" sign.

I turn to gaze at the enormous pair of red lips I had just put up before ... before I took time off. Kisses being blown from the back wall. Alluring kisses, lush and sensuous. Close-up, three layers of superimposed kissing lips seize you and hold you in a trance. Deep scarlet on gossamer silk chiffon, blooming rose on sheer organza, and peachy coral on georgette crepe. Under the halogens, they are utterly ravishing.

In cool contrast, the display up the mezzanine is somber. Shades of white on white, raw silk and doupioni and noil bleached and ribbed and streaked—aspens in snow. A lone trunk here, a whole grove there, in close-ups and in panoramic views. Coolly lyrical.

I shiver.

Lena?

You here?

Lena, the way Jed looks at me lately, uh, he gives me the creeps.

In the gloom, away from the softly-lit table lamp, his white shirt stands out against the amber glow of the fireplace. Stark white. A tie, neatly worn. I reach out to dim the table lamp by my side. I see now that he sits stiffly on the edge of the armchair, his hands clutching the armrests.

I look at his face, a well-sculpted face set in hard lines. Strong lines, I'd once thought. Nose straight and sharp, thin lips bitten into one penciled line made harsh by his square jaw. A face no smile would've soften. Not in this light. The shadow has a way of bringing out the dark side of every face.

I squirm now as our eyes meet.

His eyes, not the pining gaze indulged in some private thoughts, not the clouded gaze darkened by a simmering ill temper. Those eyes I had encountered lately when we happened to pass each other by.

But, these eyes here ... they show something else, something I hadn't seen before.

Jed, your eyes—a big cat's stalking eyes they're. Vacant, tense, fathomless ... A sudden, dark glint shoots through ... ready to leap.

Steeling myself, I return his stare.

He shifts, looks away, as if I've got X-ray eyes seeing through him.

What is it, Jed?

I half expect him to pounce on me this very instant and blurt out: Hey, Ash, old gal, don't you wish you haven't started the whole thing?

The whole thing refers to my pregnancy, I suppose. Looks nasty on him, eh, to go ahead with the divorce right at this time? As if he cares, really. I myself don't, frankly.

I'd snap back: Jed, believe me, the delay's half killing me, as it does you. I know. So, why wait? But, uh, where's my energy?

Just as well that Jed sleeps in the guest room. Nights he's in, that is. I sleep far better by myself.

Still, that stalker's look of his unnerves me.

He shifts now in his chair as if he's sitting on pins and needles. But I know that he has his stealthy eyes on me, watching me.

Why?

Lena, I tell this to you only. No one else.

Who else?

I hurry downstairs, take off my coat and let it slip down the floor. My cell phone tumbles out of my coat pocket. I had it turned off when I was in the Library. I pick it up, turn it back on, and run the messages.

Jed's voice: Hey, Ash, you around? Coming over this minute. Hmm, to show your, uh, my curved stair-wall to a prospective client. See ya!

Recorded at 11: 42 am.

Next message: Ashley, Diane here calling for Bufoni. Are we to expect your samples soon? By the way, do you read your e-mails? Give us a call back, will ya?

I'm about to stop listening, then her voice comes on, soft and calm: Ashley, this is Evelyn. How're you doing? I'd very much like to see you.

I can picture her, a small woman in a hilltop mansion looking out into the horizon, the setting sun in her eyes.

My old lady, she keeps the hearth and her old flame burning, Michael had said of her. For whom? She must have asked herself that question over and over again now that her son is gone.

The spark in her eyes. I saw it light up when she turned to me that day at the Corner Bistro. Soft and soliciting. She, a mother. I, a mother to be.

A flutter tickles my throat, then a little twitter.

Time to eat.

I walk over to the fridge under the work island and take out my one leftover pomegranate, the only edible thing around. Splitting it into quarters, I tear off the rind and start suckling the jam-packed little glistening red eyes. Ruby garnet juice trickles down my chin, dribbling over the stainless steel countertop. I spit out the seeds and go for more, savoring every mouthful.

Slurp!

I look across the room at the mirror above the heavily carved mahogany sideboard. There, in the reflection I see my drooling mouth, gleaming red.

I'm eating for two now!

Slurp, slurp ...

I hold still and stare at myself in the mirror for a long, long while.

Then I make my way over to the sink, slosh water over my mouth and scrub soap over my stained hands. Then I go back to wipe clean the work island countertop and discard the bloody mess left behind.

A shaft of the ripe sun has slid in through the paned window at the back. This is the golden hour when he would come. Didn't he say he would? I walk up to the back window. I blink at the glare and turn away.

I turn to the old brick wall. The tall span radiating the ocher warmth of earthen bricks. I'd called it a historical footnote of the house. That it's here, still standing, gives me a strange comfort. I would touch it fondly as I walk up or down the stairs. Something grips me about it. As if a long forgotten cache is dimly flickering. What can that be?

Another déjà vu feeling?

My heart misses a beat at the slightest noise outside the backdoor. I think only of the curvature of his back as he bends down, hunching his broad shoulders. I savor my every racy impulse as we brush past each other, carrying off a whiff of his workday sweat, his body scent.

That day the sash window was done, he said he would be back another day to repair the loose grout on the exposed brick wall. He scrutinized the wall as we walked down the stairs. "No, not the expansion joints, but these here, and here." He pointed to quite a few along the span. He squatted down to where the old stringer met the wall. "See how the mortar crumbles. The sand blasting did it no good." He rubbed his fingers over the disintegrating grout, then he looked up at me.

I caught the high color on his cheeks. I blushed. He seemed not to have noticed. He turned back to the wall, frowning over a spot of loose grout.

My eyes were on the soft curl of his tousled hair. I quite forgot what I'd said about the worn look of the old brick wall giving character to my gallery. Or, anything else.

A warm flutter comes over me this very minute. I sit on the swivel stool to rest my feet. I stare at the single damask drape on one side of the window, keeping my eyes level so I don't have to look down the floor by the settee. Nor do I turn to look at the patch of old brickwork under the stairs where Big Roy did his digging.

The sun has receded some, and the room bathes in a saffron hue. I take in a deep breath, let it out slowly, and look to the door.

36

He stands at the door, a dark figure against a luminous backlight. This, the improbable moment, the improbable hour of the day I so long for. My heart leaps up my throat. I say not a word but stare at his shadow on the floor.

Steady now, steady.

He freezes momentarily. A still shot of someone who looks suddenly vulnerable, as if he's about to take a step into uncharted territory.

I sit, holding my breath.

"Ashley?"

"Yes, Ben?"

He steps inside, removes his tool belt and drops it gently down the floor. He doesn't take his eyes off me. He moves about stiffly, as if he is pulled taut. He listens, and not just with his ears.

I hold still, very still.

"Ashley, are you done for the day?" He asks hesitantly, though he can see that there is nothing laid out on the work island, or in the wash basins.

"I'm done, why?"

"Like to go for a walk?" He speaks quietly but his tone is earnest.

"I like that." I smile as if I've been expecting him to ask me that all along.

All the while he has this watchful look on his face, one hand in his jeans pocket. Then he lets himself go, quickly picks up my coat from the floor and helps me into it. At the door, I catch him frowning at the patch of old brickwork under the stairs.

We walk out into an amber light—yellow and gold and ocher fused into one big brilliant floodlight that imbues the air. A slippery sort of light. It makes you think you see things clearly, then, maybe, not clearly at all.

The sun on our faces, our long shadows behind us, an improbable pair walking side by side. People get thrown together, like fallen leaves that are wind-swept into puddles. Another waft of breeze comes along, the leaves get scattered every which way.

We walk on without a word. Yet, I'm at ease, strolling with Ben. Ben of striding long limbs and smoldering body heat.

To the light ... ah, the light!

There are eyes along the way, looking us over.

Blink. A lady and a dog?

Blink. She in a camel-colored overcoat covering her slightly thickened waist. Her honey blond hair soft over her shoulders, her black-and-cinnamon silk scarf streaming behind her. She's a breeze, not made for walking. Look at the skimmers on her feet! He? He's got work boots on, encrusted with plaster dirt and whatnot. Well, those can walk miles. Done with his day? Where's he taking her? That scruffy look of his, hair rumpled, jacket frayed at the cuffs and, uh, those well worn jeans!

Blink, blink, blink ...

We exchange an amused look and keep on walking. Traffic passes us by, but we are on a peaceable island, basking in silence.

My body is warming up, my face flushed.

Down the street, canyon wall of buildings on either side, the far sun is blowtorching the sky. The hot white orb skims over the snow-capped mountains and sets them afire. The paling blue sky is burnished with a pinkish coppery sheen, a tinge of violet, and so many shades of gold. Under this softly glowing canopy, I walk on air.

Hold the light, please!

Oh, make it last!

For it's a light that hushes the noise within and douses the yearning. A light that folds you in and lifts you up, making you feel you've got wings.

Ah, light of my life!

This light is new. This light is old. As old as the mountains.

As old as me ...

I see it now. It takes my breath away. Peaks and canyons and meadowlands. Light and shadow and light. It scales the craggy slopes, glides across swales, slips down gulches, rolls over meadows where the only shadows I see are from the clouds. And I'm upon the clouds!

But I'm from the flat lands, flat as a table top and dull as reciting the multiplication table.

"Where I'm from, the sun goes down flat. Land's flat. Everything's flat."

I sigh. Ben has this oddly pensive look as if he sees what I see, from way back.

But what does he see?

The cornfields, or the mountains?

Dark clouds are gathering in his eyes. Something's at the tip of his tongue, but he's holding back. He takes in a gulp of air, swallows it down.

"Let's turn here, shall we?" I say, looking down 17th towards the Union Station.

We walk in the shade along 17th. We pass by this red brick and sandstone building with a big Christmas wreath on its arched transom. I pause. The plaque is gleaming still. It says: The Oxford. I peer through the glass into the lobby. Ben, too, looks in.

Does he see what I see?

The Oxford of old when it was new. The vintage pendant lamps on the high ceiling, they stay aglow, today as days bygone.

"Historic hotels are so nostalgic," I say.

He peers inside for another look. He turns around, registers a double take. He searches my face for a clue as to what is puzzling him.

"Have you been inside?" he asks.

"Might have." I shrug. I can't think of when, though. Just a déjà vu feeling.

As I turn to walk away, I brush against the pyramidal evergreen in a planter urn by the door. Its decorative mini lights shiver and blink. Ben reaches over to steady me. His grip is firm. I hang on for a bit.

"I'm fine," I say haltingly, looking up at him.

He must have seen the flutter in my eyes. He lets go of my arm. The butterflies flit out of my head in a hurry.

"You okay?"

I nod, smiling wanly.

We continue on our impromptu stroll towards the historic gray stone building that faces the T-junction of the street. The orange sign, Union Station, straddles the clock on top in an arc. Staid and imposing, the building squats squarely, an anchor of time past and time present. At this hour, a mellow light softens the relief of the sculptural façade. It glazes over the tall arched windows, highlighting the green patina on the metal grid frames. It brings out the details in the expanse of the metal awning over the entrances.

"Considering the times I've driven past, I seem to be seeing the building for the first time!" I say.

"Yeah?"

We pause before crossing Wynkoop. I gaze dreamily at the clock above. A very old timepiece, vaguely familiar.

"I got here on the California Zephyr some years back," Ben says as he holds open the door for me.

"The Sou- South Pa-rk! " I blurt out.

Have we finally broken the ice?

"What?"

"Yes?"

"You said something?"

"No, I didn't."

He looks troubled, his eyes wary. I turn quickly to look around the great hall. A cavernous place, empty of people, but full of itself, full of its past grandeur now a distant memory. I can almost hear the echo of the hustle-bustle from the time when the trains were rolling in. What I'm hearing right now is a small rumble at one corner of the floor. A janitor is pushing his cleaning cart. A door slams shut somewhere. The bang of wood reverberating. Keys jangling. Footsteps clomping along a corridor.

Ben tells me, "The California Zephyr gets in around seven. The place will come alive."

So, we are the errant callers at this hour, as unhurried as the rows of high-back benches that sit empty in the hall. He seems to have read my mind. A hint of a smile lights up his face.

Ah, yes, I came with the golden light!

She croons, her voice sparkling. A flash leaps up before my eyes. I squint. The hall is suddenly flooded in a golden light! A golden light that pulses in with the arriving passengers—women in long sleeve blouses and long skirts, shawls over their shoulders, bonnets on their heads, baskets in hand; men in long sleeve shirts and hats, some with neckerchiefs, some with jackets on their arms, carrying carpet bags, duffle bags, small suitcases. Their faces are flushed, their eyes red. It's a summer light that lingers and stretches the day.

I look for her in the golden light. Ben tenses up, looks where I look.

Let stay the light, please, oh, ple-ease!

I hear the tremor in her voice. A sudden flush comes over me. My heart beats wildly. My eyes dart to the front door.

Gotta get out, quick!

"You alright?" Ben's voice booms from somewhere far away.

The light burns out in the blink of an eye. I glare at him. I'd so wanted the light to stay. For a glimpse of her, she who is eager to get away.

He looks at me darkly. I shy away from his eyes.

The great hall turns sullen in an instant. A gloom has descended which no floodlights can dispel. I walk listlessly up to one of the rear doors leading out to the empty platforms. On the far side of the platform, a RTD light rail train courses along its own track, heading for the city center.

The western sky is pulling up a gray pallor over the fading streaks of gold and purple. A trace of pink washes over a fish belly white. Just ahead, a needle rears up over the surrounding buildings to jab into the sky. It's the naked tip of the Millennium Bridge's hoisting post.

The lights are coming on around the Central Platte Valley. Dusk is closing in. The scene takes on an impressionistic blur. My eyes grow dim.

"A-Ashley, please leave your place right away. I fear for your safety."

At last, at last! Ben blurts out what he must. His voice is strained, but his words are loud and clear. He holds his breath, waiting to hear from me.

I look up at him with glazed eyes.

"It's been a long day, Ben. Shall we go, huh?"

"Yes. But what do you say about moving out?"

"I, uh, I'll think about it."

"Ashley, I fear for you. Get out of your place right away!" He gets hold of my arm. His eyes are fiery, his breath short.

"Let go, please!"

He lets go. "Ashley, you're not yourself. Something's already happening to you. "

"What are you talking about?"

All gibberish!

I turn to walk away. He's right at my heels. He goes on, "A young girl died in that house before her time. She can't rest. She wears red. You *have* seen her!" He steps into my path, facing me. "The deaths that followed were all suspicious and unnatural: a madam, Michael Norton Sr., the Michael you know, and Hank."

"What's happening to me, you think?" I counter, in a tone so defiant, so unfeeling, that I'm taken aback.

"Being possessed, by *her!*"

Po-oss-essed?

"She takes over your consciousness. You see things, hear things, through her. You'll end up losing yourself altogether, Ashley. Or, worse. Get out quick, please!"

"How do you know?"

"I can sense things. You're under her influence, Ashley."

His voice is strident. It jangles above the drone that is gathering in the hall. I keep on walking, past people looking at the schedule board, past people shifting on the wood benches, past people wheeling their bags. An uniformed guard has come to stand by one of the doors leading to the platform.

The buzz grows louder. Ben screams—his eyes, his mouth spewing words, but I hear only the echoes of flapping wings and loud squawks. A magpie jamboree is swirling over my head—One for sorrow. Two for joy. Three for a girl. Four for a boy. Five for silver. Six for gold. Seven for a secret never told.

Gold, my gold?

"Gold?" I let slip.

"Yes, Hank lost his life for stealing old gold coins from your basement. I saw the imprint on his palm. The girl had them hidden in the crevices of the old brick wall as she was about to ..."

No, no! Say no more!

Just go ... go get me my gold!

Squeak-squawk ... Chatter-clatter-chatter-clat ... Swoop! I open my eyes wide. Wide with doubt? Wide with fear?

"Ashley, I'll retrieve the coins to show you. Will you get out of there soonest you can?"

Tell no secret, you hear, Ashley?

Ben strains to listen. He balks at the divide that is separating us. But he is undeterred. He is resolute. He is steeling up ... There are prying eyes around us, gawking at a squabbling couple. We head for the door.

We step out into a calm evening, the sky a cobalt blue. The cold air jolts me. It wakes me as if I've been dozing off even as the hall was jostling with people. I look up at Ben, at his tousled hair, his quivering lips. He has this grave, brooding look in his eyes, studying me with a tinge of sadness. The unwavering gleam touches me to the core, sending me into a flutter.

A gust sweeps past, whips open my coat. My scarf takes off. Ben leaps up after it. He catches it and turns to drape it over my shoulders as if it is something he is wont to do.

His eyes sparkle like falling water. I fall in with the flow, but he retreats, as gently as he would let go of an alighting butterfly on his finger tip. But I see him clenching his jaws.

Silently, we stand in front of the Station looking at the Holiday Tree, the stem hoisted tall with cascading strands of lighted bulbs. A waft of wind weaves through, the lights sway and bobble. I shut my eyes and drift with the swishing and the strumming as the tree of lights dances away in my head.

We linger awhile longer. The city buzzes around us, drumming a beat to move on. The pavement is no place to tarry. As we turn to leave, a yellow cab passes us by.

"Shall we?" Ben asks.

"No, let's walk."

I want to stay our evening together. He nods, smiling faintly. We're of the same mind. We walk towards the 16th. At the street corner, we glance down at the Millennium Bridge beyond the rails. Hardly a footbridge that it is, but a stranded ghost ship, its towering white mast spiking eerily into the sky. Stark bright with floodlights, the whole specter is surreal. It looks weirdly out of place rising amid the clutter of buildings where it has found itself grounded.

We walk in silence. Under the quiet glow of street lamps, we trudge over our slow shadows. A mall shuttle rolls past, cars roll past, spacing out the gloom with bursts of headlights and taillights. The blocks are long. A damp cold is in the air. I slip my hands into my coat pockets. A sudden gloom creeps upon me. It gnaws like a swarm of biting gnats. I'm seized with a longing so huge and deep that I shudder.

I look around me, feeling lost.

"Ashley!" Ben calls out as if he senses my mood change.

He knows!

Surely.

"It's the cold." I say, lowering my head so he won't catch my eyes.

We are about to turn into the alley when a blue Z4 pulls out.
Jed's astonished face looks out the windshield, but he does not
stop. He guns his motor and is gone.

Why's Jed here? Ben and I look at each other. I shrug.
Neither of us care to guess. Ben walks me to my car parked in the
alley. He holds open the car door for me.

"Goodnight, Ashley. Please take care. Think about what I'd
said."

"You've far to go?"

"Not far."

"Mountain roads can be treacherous at night," I say out of the
blue.

Ben bends over to peer into my eyes. I shift in my seat and
stare back mutely. If I were astonished at what I've just said, I do
not show it. He reaches over for my hand and holds it firmly.
Eyes so very sad. Then he lets go, a staunch smile steals over his
face, subtle and stoic. But it stirs me not.

For I do know sadness.

As I drive off, I look into my rearview mirror. Ben, a stark
figure standing tall in the empty alley. The light at my backdoor
casting a weak glow ...

The picture congeals in my mind, dim and blurry. But I'm as
unmoved as a studded rock that has set down roots.

37

I walk in from the garage. A recording of Mrs. Norton's voice comes through the phone's answering machine, "... I'd like to see you, dear, see how you're..."

Click. Silence. A mother's cut off.

A shadow shifts away from the console table where the phone sits under a table lamp. A squirrel scuttles up a tree, its bushy tail bobbing after him.

I plunk myself down at the kitchen table. My stomach growls. I fumble to open a can of King Oscar. With my fingers, I fish out the brisling sardines into my mouth. I pick pimento-stuffed olives right out of the jar, and crunch down the rice crackers. One big gulp of the 2% milk straight out of the carton, then another, and another.

After I've had my fill, I push myself away from the sloppy meal and slump down on the chair. My head's swimming under the pool of light from the pendant lamp.

Dead tired, I crawl into bed right after my shower. A deep breath in, blow it out slowly. I stretch my legs, wiggle my toes. My hands over my belly. Gently, baby's swimming inside! A mouthful of toffee soused in sherry—I call up the taste, roll over drooling.

Cold, dark and dank all around. She takes my hand but keeps me at arm's length. Like ice, her hand, but I hang on. We grope our way, trudging towards a beckoning pin of light.

How much farther?

Not far!
Her voice like nectar, Lena my girl!
I can't see her, but I feel this shuffling as if she's swaddled in a large cloak and is lumbering along. I'm shivering but she does not take me in.
Take me in, p-please, Lena?

You saw Jed, the other day?
Jed-ed-ed ...
That day I found him in my basement.
Ah, Jed!

A charred crow hurtles out of an angry sky. It hits ground right at my feet. I hop back. Whoa, the sky's on fire! Tongues of flame crackling, hotly lashing the mountainside, spitting ambers, spewing fumes ... Cicadas in my ear, coyotes in my ear, but the mute cries blast the loudest. I take to my feet, running blindly through the thick smoke.
I toss and turn, roiled in sweat. I jerk myself awake to a wall of pitch darkness closing in ...

Pick me up some singin stones, Ma!
Child, says a woman as she lays down her hoe to wipe her brow with her sleeve. We ain't got no stone that sing. Lucky if we can coax some weeny spuds out of the thin soil here.
Mother and child stand, heads bowed, on a hardscrabble plot hewed out of a slope heavy with rocks.
Ma, there ain't no such thing as a stone that sings, is there?
Like you ain't gonna squeeze water out of it, child.

Come with me, my girl, I say, holding out my hand.
We walk along the shore, she and I, hand in hand, looking for singing stones.
Listen, I say.
We open our hearts to the breaking waves as they hit shore. She picks up a smooth stone, puts it to her ear.
It sings! She jumps up, laughing. And I'm filled with song.

The sun lifts my bed, rocking it, fluffing it with a downy warmth. A small noise at my door. A pair of shifty squirrel eyes peeking in. A flick of its tail, the little sly thing scurries back out.

Go away! I roll over on my side.

Lena, my girl ...

But she's gone. Emptiness rattles like a broken drum, giving no beat.

Turquoise waves crowned with white foam crest, roll over, swell again, swaying ever so gently, lulling me ... I close my eyes as I drift upon the shining sea. *Swish-swash ... swi-ish-swa-ash ...* Like a songbird, a piccolo pulses the air ... the air ripples with children's laughter as they waddle on the beach ...

Swish-swash ... swi-ish-swa-ash ...

I squint at the distant horizon where a razor sharp line cleaves the blue sky from a glittering sea ... Glittering *red!* A glittering *red* sea! Billowing towards me are waves upon waves of curvy lines and smooth, thick folds. The red tide surges over me without break, scarlet tendrils chasing florid swirls chasing tendrils ... pushing to no shore. No shore at all!

I thrash about, thrusting my head up for air ... choking, heaving ... Then I see, the drowning sea is a spread of crimson damask! Dark and heavy and stifling ...

Time to go ... she whispers into my ear.

Lena?

Let's go, now!

She wakes me as if she has been watching over me. I open my eyes. My room is bathed in groggy dusk. She leaves my bedside. I'm about to turn on my bedside lamp when I spot a radiant glow. I hold my breath, stunned by what I see.

There, in the far corner, a lustrous night bloom, the splendor of the hour! Shrouded in a crimson light lush with scarlet swirls, a halo of coppery shine over her head, this wisp of a girl is coming through ... quietly setting my heart afire!

Smothered with tenderness, I'm transfixed by this sighting of her, the girl in red. She is not of this world but she's my girl Lena!

Her lambent blue eyes beckon. I hop out of bed and run towards her. I'm stopped short. The aura about her holds me at bay. She's showing me the gulf between us.

Where's the girl who had taken me to the Parade? So full of glee and babble was she. How I long to put my arms around her this very moment, to snuggle up against her soft gold curls!

There she stands, small and delicate, dwarfed by the big bold floral of her gown. It flows in a stylized damask pattern—a scarlet silk satin weave of sweeping curves set against a rich crimson background.

The drowning red sea of my dream!

Come, Ashley!

I follow her without pause.

She, the girl of my dream ... my life!

I throw on some clothes and rush down the stairs. The console table lamp sheds a tipsy cone of light. I dash down the hallway into the kitchen. A whiff of a fishy smell pricks my nose. On the table, an empty sardine can slick with oil, a sprinkling of cracker crumbs, an open jar of olives. They serve up a vague memory of a sloppy meal way back ... when?

I pick up my overcoat draped on the back of a kitchen chair and slip into it. My scarf slips down the floor. I have no mind to pick it up.

Let's go!

A blast of the super bright headlamps hits my rearview mirror as I back out the garage. The white glare is blinding. I squint, step on my brake, my eyes tearing up. A car swerves, pulls up by the curb across the street and cuts its beams. Wide awake, I pause to take in a deep breath, then roll out the driveway into the night.

A powdery snow is drifting down. Under a hazy moon, the night is swathed in a luminous mist. A breeze stirs, twirling silvery dust, sending a silvery puff over the lilac shrubs in my yard.

When the lilacs bloom, my baby will come ...

Yet, I shiver as I take one last look at my pallid house and the hushed yard. I should like a welcome wreath on my front door. The thought drops breezily into my head. Crystals fly onto my windshield, thaw, trickle down, one small streak merges into another, then another, till a brilliant patchwork of shuddering streams covers my vision. My house melts away in a blur.

I must go to him now.

Him?

Yes, he's got what's mine ...

The rhythmic swipe of my wiper blades keeps beat, keeping me awake. Christmas lights glow on dark evergreens, string lights cling on bare branches, icicle lights glimmer down eaves, the neighborhood sparkles with the season.

I turn into traffic on Speer. Cars crunch along the asphalt, headlights chasing taillights, splashing wetness. I glance at the rearview mirror. A pair of bright white beams glares from behind. But my eyes are on the shimmering flurries under the street lamps, on the tremulous tree lights along Cherry Creek.

My eyes grow heavy ... Lights zip past, smooth as a high speed train in a blur.

Wake up!

I blink ... my heart pounding wildly. I grip the steering wheel and stare ahead. Snowflake confetti gleaming. My hands are cold, my cheeks flushed. As I turn into Market, the pair of bright white beams behind me slows down as I slow down. The tailing car takes its time turning, keeping a safe distance.

Market is droopy on this white night. Few cars are about. The bars and restaurants are lit but empty. The scene is surreal, but not unfamiliar, for I had walked through many such desolate dreams, some snowy, some not, looking for shelter. Always looking for shelter ...

I turn into my dark alley lit only with an errant flame in my heart. It has sent me flying into this speckled night, this night of all nights when I know not what is dream and what is not, when

time does not tick, when everything cries out in silence …
And I … I burn for I know not what.

My heart leaps up when I fling open the door. My basement is
awash in fluorescent light, but none so bright as what he is holding
in his hands. I rush up to him.
"Ben!"
I almost snatch them out of his hands, the fistfuls of found
gold.
"Ashley!" He gives me this stunned look.
Mine, all mine!
*Here, Ma, gold! Galena brings ya gold … Pa, bless his soul,
died before he even got to see a smidgen of silver.*
*Here, Ma! Sorry to tell ya, Ma, my gold didn't come out of a
mine. It came out of someone's pocket.*
Don't call it soiled, Ma. Gold's gold.
And, I'd thought it came with love …
Lo-ove, Ma!
My eyes are feverish. He steps back, nearly tripping over the
halogen work lamp set up to shine on that old brick wall with the
chiseled-out grout.
My double eagles!
He lets out a cry, his mouth agape, his eyes wide open. A hurt
animal fallen in fear, same as the ones I had come upon down the
gulch.
He shudders, backing away. I edge up close, stretch out my
hands. His glazed eyes are upon my face as he lets the coins slip
through his fingers into my cupped hands.
Ah, sweet tinkling!
I stare at the bright coins that weigh on my trembling hands.
They glitter good. So-o good! Through dust and dirt, they glitter:
PIKES PEAK GOLD TWENTY D. Hard, cold pieces that dazzle
the eyes and make greedy the heart.
All of a sudden, I clamp shut my jaws, biting my tongue.
Blood, sweet, sweet taste of blood!
What use is my gold without life?
I glare at him. He looks bewildered.

Baffled, eh, Ben?

I wince, tasting blood. Tasting fear, a throbbing fear … I struggle to break away, to listen to a different pulse, one that flushes me with a tremulous desire. I look for Ben. Ben of long legs striding down the street, the rhythm of my heartbeat …

"Ben!"

"Ashley!"

So close, yet so far. That tantalizing scent of his comes over me like a caressing hand. I linger over his muscled arms with sleeves rolled up, his disheveled hair peppered with grout dust. I look into his eyes. Clouded with anguish. Beaming through, yet a fiery spark, holding still …

"Ben, uh … "

Something has slipped my mind. My head's light … I'm fading out of the picture.

"Ash-ley!"

He's receding. Long arms reaching across a divide to get hold of my shoulders.

"Wake up, Ashley!"

I'm wallowing in a stupor …

He holds onto me, shaking me gently.

"Ashley! Say I'm Ashley! I'm Ashley!"

I open my eyes, loll around and droop.

"Say something, Ashley, ple-ease!"

Now, I lean upon his scent, his moist breath upon my face.

"Ashley, look, look around. Say, this is where I work. I'm an artist. I dye cloth. Say it!"

I peep through one dazed eye and mumble … Ash-ley, say, uh, say… I'm an …

Ye-es, I wax and dye …

Blue sky and cinnamon earth, emerald leaves and magenta blooms. Every blade, every petal under the sun, washed with equatorial scents … Troupes of *Kuda Lumping* dancing … the batik horses coming through my head, now trotting, now galloping, little brass ankle bells tinkling, casting me a spell, putting me in a trance …

Whoa, *kuda lumping* is me-e! I, uh, I'm galloping away …

Whe-ere to?

Frenzied eyes peering through …

Twinkling stars on a clear night over the Mosquito Range.

Ben?

A saber of cold light slits in through the rear window. I turn to look out at the falling snow.

"No, no! No window there! Look at me, Ashley!"

Strong arms swoop me up, fold me in.

Ple-ase, get me out of the quicksand!

"Whe-re am … I?"

"We're getting out of your basement."

A blast of chill air hits my face. Numbness burns. I look up. Little white cabbage butterflies swarming the ink black sky!

Ben's carrying me up the steps … into the white whirl. I hang onto him, my head resting on his shoulder. Shining through, in my mind, this brass engraving on a paved footpath I'd come across: "When you see only one set of footprints, it was then that I carried you." Trailing alongside, there's this one set of little brass paw prints …

"Let go of my wife!"

A shout rings out from behind. Jed steps out of the shadow from his furtive watch at the door. His stalker's face is blotchy red from the cold.

"Let go of her!"

Stealthy eyes peer into my basement, then turn darkly upon us.

Ben puts me down when we touch ground up in the alley. He has his arm over my shoulders as I slump against him.

"Come with me," he burbles into my ear.

"Leave her," Jed growls. "Come home, Ash."

I press closer to Ben.

The stalker lunges at us. He takes a swipe at Ben, then a direct blow.

Flumph!

Ben stumbles backwards. Mean kicks fly in hot pursuit. Shadows scuffle and snarl. I flounder, keeling over on the snowy ground, desperately peering through the flakes.

A loud groan. A shadow lurches forward, staggering before he doubles over.

"Ben!"

I clamber up on my feet. Jed leaps over to me, grabs my arm.

He drags me headlong with bruising force, away from Ben. I tussle to get away.

"Let go, Jed!"

My coat flaps open. Heavy metal tumbles out of my pockets, punching holes into the snowy ground.

Jed pauses, drops to his knees, pulling me down with him. He brushes away the fluffy snow with his gloved hand, picking up the wet gold coins. In spite of himself, he loosens his grip on me to fumble for his coat pocket, to sweep for more dropped coins.

I bolt up, tottering towards Ben.

"Ben, you thief!" Jed scoffs. "You'll have to answer for breaking in!"

Ah, Jed, you, too, you'll have me to answer to!

"Ben, you hurt bad?"

I kneel beside him. He lifts his head, a trickle of blood drips down the corner of his mouth. His brow is furrowed with pain, but his eyes are ablaze.

"Ashley?"

"Yes, Ben?"

He struggles to get on his feet. He falters, slumps onto his side, his hands over his groin.

"I'll be okay," he says.

Flurries twirl. Glimmering flakes streaking over our faces. I bend down and kiss him, lingering over his soft lips. I cradle his head with my hands, not letting go. Through a sheen of wetness, I see that his eyes glisten with a palpable sadness.

"Ashley!"

"Hang on, I'll call for the ambulance."

My cell phone's gone.

"Ben, your phone?"

Fumbling for his phone and scrambling to get back up, he looks at me. Fire in his eyes. "You are Ashley. Always," he says resolutely. But I hear the pleading in his voice.

Footsteps shuffling up from behind.

"Ashley, be safe," Ben cries out.

Jed grapples my arms from behind to pull me up on my feet. I spin around to scream in his face, "Get the ambulance! I'm not leaving him here."

"We go, now!"

"No! No! No!"

He's hauling me away from Ben. I wriggle, thrashing about, my feet scuffing snow.

"Jed, let go!"

I break free, scrabbling to get away. In spite of myself, I reel around to look at Ben through the thickening whiteness, through my tears. All's a glittery blur ...

Jed is fury. Jed is vengeance. He pounces upon me. His grip is crushing. I flinch at the twisting, stabbing pain on my shoulder.

"What do you want, Jed?"

Jed, Jed, Jed!

Ben's hobbling after us.

"Get around the corner ... " Jed huffs.

Shoving and scuffling, he lugs me out ... out on the street where a lone car sits by the curb covered with snow. His Z-4.

"Call the ambulance, Jed, ple-ease!"

The icy glint in his eyes sends daggers. A bone-chilling fear hits me. All I can think of is my baby.

My baby, Jed! I want my baby!

Rhooooom-oooom-oom ...

A big truck rumbles out of the fuzzy darkness, zooming down a wobbly overpass. Tires grind and churn, packing snow as they roll, shrieking the night with a harrowing roar. Headlamps blind with a piercing white glare.

I squint at the rush of silvery flakes skittering over my face. In a split second, I am teetering at the edge of a dark abyss. A clap of thunder explodes on the side of my head.

Lightning lashing down, splintering my eyes, lacerating my heart ...

A hard push from behind, I am flung out into a screeching wilderness. A little red bird swooping down, snatching me up …
   The white night's no more.

End of tunnel!
   Light's smiling on me. All's a blur, but I know I've arrived.
   Hot tears streaming down my cheeks …
   Real tears, eh?
   Sweet, swe-eet tears!
   I hurl away that mantle of agony—my crimson damask! In my death throes I covet life. I cling piteously to the sight of one blighted China woman, cloaked in flaming red, walking the craggy high cliff.
   Holding on, my one crimson hope to return to light …
   So, I walk. I walk in my crimson scourge, searing with rage, wrecked by my bitter end …
   I'm that homing pigeon with wings clipped, goaded by instinct and a gnawing memory.
   That … that eternal damnation is me!
   Eyes wide open, I've traded eternal peace for a promise to return to light!
   So, in the murky-nowhere-gloom, I point myself to this pin of light and trudge on.
   On and on, until …

   Woe, oh, woe! You be damned, you heartless monk!
   Cursed prayer beads and prayer robe over where I lay to hold me down. You be damned!
   With your endless chanting of Amitabha … Amitabha … your wooden fish croaking bok-bok-bok … you cast me a spell. A spell that spins me a pall to shut out the light.
   That one pin of light, gone!
   Gone!

Damn your Amitabha!

Damn your bok-bok-bok!

Damn you who believe in infinite wisdom and mercy! So pious are you that you didn't see fit to grant me salvation.

Ah, wouldn't you give the say and have me dug out? Wouldn't you have the crimson damask lifted from my worm-eaten body and cast it to the wind?

Ah, no! No peace for a ravaged soul! You'd rather doom a young girl to the fate of her wanton doing?

But, could it be ... you didn't know that I'm burning in red?

You couldn't have known, could you?

Of this loony China woman in her red yoke, stumping in my head ... It's all in my head then, isn't it?

And you, you only thought of granting me eternal peace? In your infinite mercy, you did all you could to give me peace?

Then, it's I, I be damned!

Woe! Will that threadbare damask ever rot away and give me release?

WILL IT?

Like a rusty saw, the rancor of my wretched end grates on me, yeah, telling me I've yet a life to redeem!

Time stands still. Darkness blinds.

I grit my teeth and stump on ...

One day, your scribbled incantation is ripped off the bolted door, your prayer beads scattered, your prayer robe lifted off me.

All of a sudden, the chanting stops, the bok-bok-bok stops.

The pin of light pokes through the dark once again ...

I stir.

Dazed, I point to the pin of beckoning light, my crimson scourge on my back, plodding on and on ...

Until this night when light's smiling on me.

AT LONG LAST!

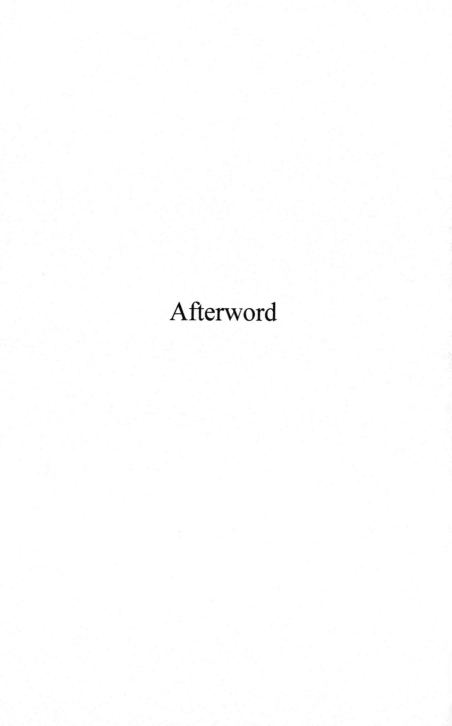

Afterword

38

Rest in peace, Ashley.

I smile into the mirror, Ashley smiling back.

"I'm Ashley," I whisper. My new found voice is sedate and soft. I laugh. The sound of a spring brook murmuring. I laugh again. It's the sound of a self-possessed woman laughing because it pleases her. Not the laugh I was wont to, a laugh to please others.

Gray green eyes staring out of the mirror, filmy all of a sudden. Pining for my sapphire eyes? Ah, sapphire eyes! A distant memory now, a spent dream left behind on a flowered meadow long, long ago.

I run a hand over my face. Like petal. I run my fingers through my hair. Like water, it falls over my shoulders. Breathlessly blond, like honey. The sense of touch is exquisite. So new, *so* old.

At least I've been merciful, I say, looking straight into the mirrored face. Yes, merciful. You were blanked out in a flash. I wished you none of the wretched death throes I'd gone through, and, none of the crimson curse which I'd brought upon myself, that damask fate which I'd snatched with my dying breath. There will be no stumping blind for you, Ashley. Like I did, like she did, that loony China woman doomed to hell.

Rest in peace, Ashley!

I look down my thickened waist, smooth my hands over my small round abdomen. I laugh most heartily, standing inside the small bathroom in my hospital suite.

"Ouch!" A sharp pain jabs at my right shoulder. It shoots down my elbow held up by an arm sling. I take little shallow breaths to ease the pain.

They said I'd dislocated my shoulder when I hit ground two nights ago. I rather think that Jed had twisted it.

They said it's a miracle that I'm alive, and my baby's safe. Why, their eyes queried, would a woman four month pregnant find herself in the path of a truck on a snowy night? What on earth happened on that deserted street?

They said that the semi swerved off only inches from where I fell. It blew me away, blanketing me with the white stuff and landed me on a snow drift. How very lucky!

They said that the semi plowed into a brick building, busted open the pub that was inside. It was plain luck that the owner decided to close early that empty weeknight.

They said the driver cracked a few ribs, gashed his face, and lost his mind. He won't hear that no one was hurt. He kept hollering, I hit her, I hit her! The girl in red, she flew out of nowhere into my Mack! It's like, like a bright red flash that punched through a blast of snow and smashed into my windshield. I skidded, spun into a big roar. I sure as hell hit her! Hit her good! Blood all over ...

They said I can go home any time.

Home?

I smile into the mirror. I'm startled to find the reflection of Jed's face showing up next to mine. He is standing behind me by the bathroom door. He's frowning, and he's got nails for eyes. I stare at the purple bruise on one side of my face. I feel for Ashley, the shock of the blow hit her almost harder than the impact.

I turn around, go past him and walk back into the room. Cradling my slung arm, I sit on the edge of my bed where I can reach the call button to the nursing station.

He comes up to me. "How're you, hon?"

I can almost hear him gnashing his teeth. No, it's just me seething away.

"Better."

"You're nuts, Ash! You'd reported that I threw you in front of the truck? You'd accused me of attempted murder and assault? For Christ's sake!" Jed explodes, sputtering in rapid fire. Veins pop up on his neck like earthworms out of the soggy earth after a rainfall.

I sit with my head down, admiring my unscathed feet. I take my time to look up at him. He reads me: Yell all you want, you know what you did!

He casts a sheepish look at the door, listening out for footsteps.

"Withdraw your statements, Ash!" he tells me now in a squeezed voice. "You know you've made all those things up. You were distraught by what had happened that night."

"What happened that night?"

"What happened was that Ben had broken into your basement, vandalized and stole from you. The guy's a thief, a no-good bum. I fought to protect you, to keep him from hurting you." He spins on in an impassioned tone though he avoids my eyes. "I saw you leave the house. I couldn't have let you drive out alone in the night, hon. You, in your condition, and it was a lousy night out. I followed you to bring you home. I wanted you home safe, our baby safe, Ash."

He pulls up a chair. Sitting down, he levels his stare at me. I turn to feast my eyes at the rose bouquets Mrs. Norton had brought from her greenhouse. Her prized scented roses, pink and cream and yellow and white, on my bedside table, on the small dresser against the wall, their fragrance fills the whole room.

I smile to myself.

Jed reaches out for my free hand. I slip it behind my back.

"Ash, listen!"

Listen? I give him a hard look.

Jed does not tell me that he has filed charges against Ben for burglary, vandalism, and assault. He has forgotten that I'm the owner of my studio and the building's tenant.

Jed does not tell me that Ben had staggered back into my basement that very night and dug up the skeletal remains of a young girl from under the stairs.

"You saw the girl in my basement?"

"Huh?" He squirms in his chair.

I look at him: Remember my harrowed face, Jed? The wreck of me stumping, stumping away … that day you dropped in her basement while she was out. How you gasped! You thought you were going to have a heart attack, didn't you?

He turns white as a sheet.

"That day I found you in my basement with what I'd thought was your asthma attack. Was it then that you hatched your deadly scheme? Or, was it the other evening when I saw you driving away after you had come to spy and to strike up a pack with *her*? You thought you had help, Jed. Something evil in her basement, eh? You would say, Ashley wasn't herself lately. She was erratic, impulsive. She had no call whatsoever to drive out that snowy night. Accident can happen."

"This is utterly preposterous, Ash."

"You wanted Ashley out of your way, so you premeditated her murder. But I live to tell on you. I needed a little blackout moment to take possession of my new life. For that, thanks, Jed!"

"What're you ta-talking about? This is absurd, Ash!"

He jumps out of the chair and starts to pace. He clasps his hands to steady his shakes.

"Jed?"

He pauses. He can barely lay eyes on me.

"Please return me my gold."

"What gold?"

I glare at him.

"Ash, alright. I'm just holding them in safekeeping for you."

"Please bring them to me in the next hour, will you?"

I laugh heartily. Ah, a rippling creek singing after my heart!

A ripple of a different sort intrudes. It brings back a scene long past, etched deep.

*   *   *

Run, run!   Down the gulch ... my feet scuffing bare along the ragged bank by the stream where the water runs dark and deep ... Needles and cones, twigs and stones, scrapes and scratches ...

Blood dripping down my legs ... spotting the ground I ran over on.

Back here, gir-rl!   A coyote howls from the ledge above, he who ain't my pa, howling, wanting ...

I look up the tall ledge in the late afternoon sun, then down at the rushing water below.

There I pause, on the craggy bank.   My eyes following the fast stream till it's no more.

39

Jeez, bag of old bones! Hundred-plus years old, I'd say. Girl of sixteen? Seventeen? Got coppery gold hair to die for. A mouth of stained teeth, like peat, like moss. Gee whiz ... So gabs a loose mouth from the coroner's office.

Stained teeth? Stained by the bile I retched up?

That Rough on Rats burned through my guts, ate me alive.

Mercy, oh, mercy! Ma'am, couldn't you have used your cyanide, the fine white salts in a pouch that you procured from the gold miners who passed through. Couldn't you have shot me in the head, like that hurt horse in your stable?

So, I died a poisoned rat, a most piteous sight.

Old bones tell no tales, eh?

Who cares to know anyway?

My word to the mortuary: A decent funeral for the abandoned bones. Best casket. No pauper's burial. Clean her up. Get rid of any remnant clothing. No fiber of any kind to be interred with the bones.

Damn the damask!

I wear black on this day, a cold January day that I come to lay my old bones to rest. The noon sun is bright, the sky cloudless. But

I'm as hoary as that bare branched sycamore bracing the chill wind. It stands alone among the evergreens on the drive into Fairmount Cemetery.

I, too, stand alone, redeemed into a world I don't belong. All that was lush and green had long shriveled up, the cicada song had dropped off many a summer ago. For I'm one who has molted into another's body more than a century late. So hell-bent was I for a new lease on life I let nothing stand in my way. Yet old grudges, like bad dreams, refuse to give up the ghost. I'm left rankling to break loose, to live anew. But the life I'm to lead is not mine, and the world out there is frightfully new ...

Mrs. Norton touches my hand gently. "It's good of you to bury her, poor lost soul," she says. There is a tremble in her voice.

I nod and turn away. I do not want to see that watery glint in her eyes, that underneath it all is a morass of pain. What mother can let go the trauma of her son's passing? But she is more than willing to let her dark fears be buried with the old bones unearthed in that cursed basement. She is quite sure that they belonged to the girl in red whom her son was last seen with. Her eyes are tearing up, but she looks stoic enough.

Out the window, a chapel stands among the evergreens. A lone doe loiters among the headstones. I keep mum, aching over my old bones, needing to let go of bad memories.

"We'll have peace afterwards, " she says, sounding hopeful.

The day Evelyn took me home from the hospital, we were both a little lost. She was in high spirits, bent on believing she had recovered something she had lost, something that would give meaning to her remaining days.

Know how I felt then? I felt so worn out that I was glad to have a place to lay down my head. All the tomorrows can wait.

"Welcome home, Ashley." She beamed as she led me into this imposing mansion which she called home. I paused at the arched entrance to look back at the curved drive up the slope. I seemed to recall blazing red maples splashing over blue spruces one Fall day not long ago.

Home at last, my Michael's estate built by his heir! But deep down, a twinge of irony gnawed, made poignant by the stroke of fate that had brought me to his doorstep, late only by a century and then some.

But, how ever could she have known? That was way before her time. I was that ancient lone spruce on the spine of the ridge that had already been standing when the mesa was just a plain mesa.

Evelyn put me in the suite next to hers.

"It's Michael's room. It's just for the time being. I hope you don't mind. You'll move into your own suite after it's been refurbished to your liking."

She showed me his quarters, a mahogany paneled suite lit with onyx wall sconces and recessed lighting, a huge bed with mahogany carved headboard, and a sitting area by the windows with charcoal-gray velvet draperies.

"Michael kept his room as he had it before his marriages. He did it for me, I know. He and his wives always had their own places in town."

She smiled wistfully as she stole a look at me. Once again, she wanted to decipher my feelings for her son. She could never have known that my heart was still festering over the betrayal of his grandfather. He, whom I had foolishly called 'my sweet Michael' once upon a time. He who without so many words bartered to have my life snuffed out.

I bit my lips as tears came. She seemed reassured. She hugged me gently and said, "We'll have a bright new beginning, my dear."

"Oh, yes, and we'll have to think of the nursery, won't we, dear? This is so-o exciting," she gushed.

That first night, I heard her soft footfall outside my door. I had on all the lights to dispel the dark tunnel that was yet burrowing in my head. I heard her slip into my room.

"Oh, dear, you'll catch cold!"

She found me standing in front of the full length mirror in the brightly lit dressing room. Except for my arm sling, I had not a stitch on. I was entranced by my gleaming new body. She stood dazed, awed by my well-sculpted body of palpable grace, a pulsed song you could touch. She came up behind me, put her hand tenderly over my small bulging belly, seduced by the promise of the new life within.

We stood transfixed. I heard her sobbing quietly. Gently, she rested her silvery gray head against my shoulder. Then she took the silk robe from the wall hook and draped it over me.

In my head, there was this silvery crescent moon that hung over the Mosquito Range. Dark mountains met up with the ink blue sky. Sky studded with stars. Brilliant twinkles pulsating the night. Night air thin as dandelion hairs clogging up your breathing, faint as a dragonfly skittering over water.

Shivering, I faltered. She held onto me, eased me back on my feet. Frail as she looked, she held on steadily.

"To bed, my dear!"

I looked up at her and murmured, "I haven't slept for over a hundred years, you know?"

"I know, dear, I know."

She helped me to bed and tugged me in.

"Goodnight, Ashley!"

She kissed me on my forehead. Her eyes glittered. They glittered through my sleep. They kept me from going back to the dark place.

I woke up to find her hovering over me. A smile lit up her face. She told me that I had slept night into day into night into day. She walked over to the windows to throw open the drapes. The morning sun was glorious.

A bright new day, indeed! I felt I was truly home then.

*   *   *

"John will walk you there," she says solicitously as she looks out at the grave yard.

"There's no need, Evelyn."

"Thanks, John, I want to be by myself," I say to the chauffeur who is holding open the limo door.

I leave her to wait inside the limo and walk alone among the tombstones. The air is nippy, the sky a blue vault. I walk slowly. My heart is laden with years. It weighs me down as I stand at the foot of the dug grave. The smell of damp earth is suffocating even in the open air. I cuddle my slung arm and turn to the bouquet of stargazer lilies sitting on top of the casket. A bold drama of life, big and lush and pink, sending out fragrance beyond compare. I take in a deep breath.

To keep my mind from wandering, I listen intently as the pastor intones:

"I am the resurrection and the life, says the Lord: She who believes in me, though she were dead, yet shall she live: and whosoever lives and believes in me shall never die ...

Rest eternal grant unto her, O Lord. And let light perpetual shine upon her. Amen."

"Amen," I say.

"Lena!"

I hold still, not turning to the voice from behind.

Ben steps up to stand by my side. His eyes are stark and gloomy.

I'm Ashley, Ben!

"I'm here to bury Galena Saber."

A cold wind stirs. I turn to look at the threesome of tall spruces shuddering at the ground's edge.

A soundless croak blistering his throat: NO! O-oh no!

I hear yet the withering cry he had let out that night he floundered about the snow-covered ground, trying in vain to reach Ashley.

That night, Ben, you were blinded by the drifting snow, and there was too much noise in your head.

It's over, Ben.

I bend down to scoop up dirt with my free hand, cast it over the casket as it is being lowered into the ground.

Bye, now, old bones sapped of marrow and spirit!

Ben takes out some loose things from his jeans pocket and flings them thudding onto the casket. All at once, I recognize what they are! The old prayer beads and that chipped block of wood fish.

The chanting of *amitabha* ... *bok-bok-bok* ... leaps out of the dark to echo in my head. I chortle. Ah, those old bones won't hurt any, you hear, you dodo monk? I laugh through the tears that are welling up my eyes.

It comes to me now that you might yet have another reason not to have me dug up. A worldly reason for a ho-hum mind stewed in scriptures. You opted to leave the house with no questions asked and no messy business to attend to, eh? Haven't I given her peace? You might have said.

Peace? Ah, hell knows no fury!

It was you, Ben, who had unshackled me from the godforsaken chanting and the wakeful beating of the wood fish. You knew not what you did, but you had brought me back the pin of light at the end of the tunnel.

I hear John coming up from behind.

I turn to Ben and say, "You know that I've dismissed all the charges Jed had brought against you. I told the investigators that I'd hired you to excavate under the stairs, and that you had protected me against my husband's irrational behavior. I'm sorry, Ben, for the pain caused you."

He lowers his head and says not a word. He does not look up when I turn to walk away.

"Who's he?" Evelyn asks as we drive off.

"Ben, the workman. He was there that night." I look out the window and see him standing by the grave site still.

She follows my view out the window.

"He dug up the girl?"

"Yes."

"He's my witness when Jed goes on trial," I say without emotion.

"Now, dear, try not to think of what had happened that night."

I nod and turn to look back out the window at the receding trees.

I see Ben standing on the patch of brickwork over where my bones lay. Then, I see him come tirelessly looking for me in that house of old where I stayed eternally young.

"Miss, miss," you'd called out to me, night after night. And I'd thought you a bumpkin. So, I kept watch over you. You came and you learned at last that what met the eye was not what you had made it out to be.

Ah, how your eyes can deceive you, and your heart can lead you astray! I know, for I'd learned it the hard way.

But then, you spoke most tenderly, and your eyes shone with good will.

"How can I bring you peace, miss?"

Life, the lush rhythm of life!

But you heard me not, Ben. You heard me not!

CPSIA information can be obtained
at www.ICGtesting.com
Printed in the USA
BVOW06s1840090417
480763BV00011B/166/P